All Summer Long

BOOKS BY BOB GREENE

All Summer Long (1993)
To Our Children's Children (with D. G. Fulford) (1993)
Hang Time (1992)
He Was a Midwestern Boy on His Own (1991)
Homecoming (1989)
Be True to Your School (1987)
Cheeseburgers (1985)
Good Morning, Merry Sunshine (1984)
American Beat (1983)
Bagtime (with Paul Galloway) (1977)
Johnny Deadline, Reporter (1976)
Billion Dollar Baby (1974)
Running: A Nixon-McGovern Campaign Journal (1973)
We Didn't Have None of Them Fat Funky Angels on
    the Wall of Heartbreak Hotel, and Other Reports
    From America (1971)

BOB GREENE

DOUBLEDAY
New York
London
Toronto
Sydney
Auckland

A Novel

All Summer

Long

PUBLISHED BY DOUBLEDAY
a division of Bantam Doubleday Dell Publishing Group, Inc.
1540 Broadway, New York, New York 10036

DOUBLEDAY and the portrayal of an anchor with a dolphin are trademarks of Doubleday, a division of Bantam Doubleday Dell Publishing Group, Inc.

All of the characters in this book are fictitious, and any resemblance to actual persons, living or dead, is purely coincidental.

Grateful acknowledgment is made for permission to reprint lyrics from the following songs:
"All Summer Long," lyrics and music by Brian Wilson, © 1964, renewed 1992, Irving Music, Inc. (BMI). All rights reserved. International copyright secured. Used by permission.
"I'm Gonna Be Strong," by Barry Mann and Cynthia Weil, © 1963, 1977, renewed 1991, Screen Gems-EMI Music, Inc. All rights reserved. International copyright secured. Used by permission.
"Things We Said Today," words and music by John Lennon and Paul McCartney, © 1964 Northern Songs Limited. All rights controlled and administered by MCA Music Publishing, a division of MCA Inc., New York, New York 10019, under license from ATV Music. All rights reserved. Used by permission.

Library of Congress Cataloging-in-Publication Data

Greene, Bob.
All summer long / Bob Greene.—1st ed.
    p.   cm.
1. Men—Travel—United States—Fiction. I. Title.
PS3557.R37963A79   1993
813'.54—dc20   93-20143
CIP

10   9   8   7   6   5   4   3   2   1

For Herman Gollob

All Summer Long

One

IT'S LATE SEPTEMBER NOW. This afternoon feels like the kind of early-autumn day when I'd come home from school and throw my books on the counter in the breakfast room and go upstairs to listen to the last Columbus Jets baseball games of the season on the radio. The kind of afternoon that still has more than a touch of summer in it. At this time of day, four or five o'clock, the sun would shine brightly on the front lawns in the neighborhood, and for a minute or two I would half believe that it was still July. In September, though, the sun always went away quickly, and with it the warmth. September nights are not summer nights.

I look out the window today, and I think about the months just past, the months since May, and I can't help smiling. I smile, and shake my head. I can't believe we did it.

A couple of minutes ago I got up and went into the kitchen and pulled a beer out of the refrigerator. I took a knife and sliced some of that hard yellow cheese and put it on a plate, and then I went over to pick out a CD, but I decided I didn't need to hear any music. Music always helps me to think about the places I was when I first heard the songs—the places I was, and the people I was with. Right now I don't require music to remember the summer just past. The summer was one long song all by itself.

We had said that it was going to be the best thing we had ever done. That's usually a jinx—if you talk out loud about how good something is going to be, that's usually a guarantee that things won't be so good at all. I think all of us understood that. We needed to say how good it was going to be just so that we would get started. Saying that was like a push away from the dock, like the push that gets you out into the water, and once you're there it's just as easy to keep going as to turn back.

A second or two ago there was a sound outside; for some reason it reminded me again of those late September afternoons when I was a kid. The sound back then was the evening paper hitting the front stoop. My dad would just be getting home from work, and the first thing he would do was go out and look for the paper. He would still be in his business suit; he would bend down and pick up the paper, rolled up with a rubber band around it, and he would take the paper into the living room and sit back in his special chair with the news of the day. He would take off his suit jacket, to celebrate evening, but the tie would stay on. He wouldn't even loosen it until after dinner.

The sound I just heard couldn't have been the evening paper. There is no evening paper anymore; there hasn't been an evening paper in this town for years. I'm as old as my dad was on those afternoons when he'd come driving home from his office. My feet are propped up on the windowsill, and I look out at the neighborhood. In a couple of hours it will be dark. It's supposed to be chilly tonight.

There are days now when the summer just past seems like a dream. It seems like a dream, and I have to ask myself whether it really happened. But it happened, all right. Maybe the time will come when I can think about it without smiling.

I hope not. I don't care how cold the temperature gets tonight. I sit and I look out the window and I think, and I feel the warmth of the sun.

Two

ALL OF THIS STARTED last Memorial Day. I had been looking forward to the trip back to Bristol. I could not, of course, have known what it would lead to.

We had all received the fliers in the mail: "Bristol High School Class of '65—Twenty-five Years and Counting!" Connie Twyford, the girl in our class who used to draw the covers for the yearbooks, had drawn a caricature of a tiger with a receding hairline and a potbelly. The middle-aged cartoon tiger dominated the reunion invitation.

I knew as soon as I got the flier that I would be going to the reunion. I hadn't gone to the tenth reunion or the fifteenth, but I had gone to the twentieth, five years ago, and it had been one of the nicest weekends I could remember.

I'd been a little uneasy before the twentieth reunion. I suppose just about everyone is nervous on an occasion like that. It's ridiculous but it's inevitable. We all go through our adult lives being judged by strangers, and we do our best to earn their approval. The people we went to high school with, though, made their judgments about us long ago—and maybe those are the judgments that stick. At least that's what, on some level, we're afraid of.

Five minutes into the twentieth reunion, I knew it was going to be okay. I saw people who had never spoken to each other in high school sitting down and sharing stories; the star athletes and the kids who hadn't been big enough to try out for the teams were suddenly all on the same playing field. Twenty years level things out; twenty years out of high school, most people have had their triumphs and their disappointments, and the world is just too fickle for anyone to worry about what mean and offhanded thing some guy might have said half a lifetime ago.

The twentieth reunion had been three days of unspoken reassurance—reassurance for all of us that whatever grudges anyone might have had, all of that was done with. Some of us had stayed in town after high school, and some of us had gone out to see what lay beyond Bristol. But at that twentieth reunion, a lot of nerves were calmed, a lot of unseen wounds soothed. Whatever we had become, all of us, for better or for worse, were forever a part of the Bristol High School Class of '65.

The good feelings of that weekend must have had some lingering impact. Because five years had passed, and when I got the flier last spring about the twenty-fifth reunion on Memorial Day, I didn't have to check any calendar to see whether or not I could go. I knew that I'd be heading for Ohio.

Bristol is about fifteen miles southeast of Columbus. It's a town of twenty thousand people; if people in New York were to locate it on a map, they'd probably assume it was rural. Farm country. But that's not quite true.

Bristol has always been quiet. It feels more like an established suburb than an old-time small town. When we were growing up most of our fathers commuted to Columbus to go to work. People didn't have to do that—there were shops and restaurants and businesses in Bristol itself, enough so that a person could make a living. But the money and success were in Columbus, and our fathers knew it. Today a lot of the mothers know it, too; the traffic out of Bristol toward downtown Columbus each weekday morning is still heavy, as is the travel back to Bristol at the close of office hours. The only difference is that now there are almost as many moms commuting to work in Columbus as there are dads. Or so I hear.

It's a short commute. Bristol is close enough to Columbus that most of our cultural reference points—although I'm sure we never used that phrase—were always Columbus reference points. We watched Columbus TV stations and our parents read Columbus newspapers and we followed Ohio State football. Even now, when I try to envision 100,000 of anything, my automatic visual image is of a packed Ohio Stadium on a Saturday afternoon. CNN reports that 100,000 people are rioting in the streets in some revolution-torn country halfway across the world? Let me think . . . Ohio Stadium holds about 80,000 when it's sold out, which is always, so that would be the entire game-day population of Ohio Stadium, plus another 25 percent, rioting in the streets. That's the picture I get in my mind—although it's a pretty unlikely scene: 100,000 angry rioters wearing scarlet-and-gray tam-o'-shanters and waving scarlet-and-gray seat cushions as they charge down some dusty foreign street to the strains of "The Buckeye Battle Cry" as played by the Ohio State University Marching Band.

Anyway . . . even though we went to school in Bristol and had our best friends in Bristol and fell in love for the first time in Bristol and slept in our beds in our parents' houses in Bristol, to us the capital of the outside world was Columbus. New York and Chicago and Los Angeles might have been more majestic cities, but we couldn't drive there for cheeseburgers on a Friday after school and still be home in time for dinner.

If Columbus was the capital of the outside world, it was also the gateway to the outside world. There's no airport in Bristol. So it was Port Columbus where my plane landed last May, on the Friday before Memorial Day, carrying me toward the twenty-fifth reunion of my graduating class at Bristol High School.

I got a cab right away at the taxi stand on the lower level of the airport, and asked the driver to take me to Bristol. "Caroline, No," that great, relatively obscure Beach Boys song, was on the radio. Not many stations play "Caroline, No"; most stations play the Beach Boys' big hits— "Surfin' U.S.A." and "Little Deuce Coupe" and stuff like that. I was pleasantly surprised.

"What station is that?" I said to the driver.

He was a young guy, around twenty-six or twenty-seven. "WCOL," he said.

"WCOL?" I said. "Playing that?"

"Yeah, why wouldn't they?" the driver said.

"I thought WCOL was all-talk," I said.

"I think it used to be," the driver said. "But now it's oldies. One of those music-you-grew-up-with stations."

"Weird world," I said.

When we were in high school, WCOL was the big AM rock station in Columbus. Bristol had no radio station of its own. WCOL was the only station that we ever listened to—this was in the days before every city had five or six rock stations. Hard as it is to believe now, no other station in Columbus played the Beatles.

Whenever I would come back to Ohio for a visit, WCOL seemed to have changed formats. For a while, if I recall, it was all-news. Then it was all-talk. There was a period when it featured a lot of play-by-play sports broadcasts. I think it was even big-band for a while. And now, according to the cabdriver, it had gone all-oldies. The cycle was complete. "Caroline, No" ended, and the Zombies' "She's Not There" began, and as we headed toward Bristol on a Friday afternoon the songs coming out of WCOL's spot on the dial were the same songs that had come out of that same spot twenty-five springs before.

"Do you remember Dr. Bop?" I said to the driver.

"I'm sorry?" he said, looking in the rearview mirror. The sound from the radio, mixed with the wind coming through his open window, had blocked out what I was saying. He lowered the volume.

"Dr. Bop," I said. "He was one of the WCOL disc jockeys."

"I'm afraid not," the driver said.

"You wouldn't have figured it," I said. "Most disc jockeys back then, they were young white guys with Top 40 voices. Dr. Bop was this middle-aged black guy who wore surgical scrubs to all his personal appearances. He was a big star in central Ohio, at least for a few years."

"That's a new one on me," the driver said.

" 'This is Dr. Bop, on the scene, with a stack of shellac and his record machine,' " I said.

The driver didn't respond.

"That's what Dr. Bop used to say on the air about three times every hour," I said. "I guess there's no way you'd remember. You might not even have been born when Dr. Bop was on WCOL."

"I'm new here," the driver said. "I just moved to Columbus two years ago."

He pulled his cab into the parking lot of the Holiday Inn a mile or so outside of Bristol. I paid him and grabbed my bags and walked into the lobby.

I know plenty of people in Bristol, and I could have stayed in a guest bedroom of someone's home—in fact, I knew that Michael and his wife had thought I was being kind of rude when I told them I had reservations at the motel. At least his wife had. She had said that it was foolish for me to pay for a room.

"It's okay," I had told her when I called to tell them where I would be staying and when I would be arriving. "I get phone calls at all times of the day and night, and it's just better for me to stay at the Holiday Inn."

"You probably don't get phone calls any later at night than our kids do," Ellen had said. "And if the phone rings for you and it wakes us up, we can go right back to sleep." It's strange—Michael is the one who was my best friend when we were growing up in Bristol, but Ellen has always talked to me as if she and I have known each other all our lives. I've probably seen Ellen on fewer than twenty occasions in all the years that she and Michael have been married. He met her at college, and by the time she moved to Bristol I was long gone. But she can talk to me like she's some affectionate but ultimately judgmental sister.

"I just don't want to get underfoot," I had told Ellen.

"Underfoot?" she'd said over the long-distance line. "Michael's your best friend, and you're coming home for the reunion and you're afraid you're going to get underfoot? I think this phone-calls-at-night thing is just an excuse. I think you don't like us."

She had been kidding, but I felt I had to explain, so I had begun to go into a long justification when Michael picked up the other line. He was sort of chuckling, a chuckle I've been hearing from him ever since kindergarten, and I knew right away from the tone of his voice that he got it.

"It's all right," he had said. "Call us from the motel when you get in, and we'll pick you up."

He knew that it wasn't the phone calls. It's just that at this point in my life, at the end of the day I want some time to be by myself. It's force of habit by now. I've spent so many nights in so many hotel rooms that they feel more like home to me than a home. Especially during the reunion weekend, I didn't think I'd be able to sleep in a strange house. Even if it was Michael's house.

And now I was in the lobby of the Holiday Inn, handing my credit card to the desk clerk and asking if he was holding any phone messages for me.

As the clerk typed my name into the computer, I noticed a stack of the weekly Bristol *News* on the counter. I reached over to pick one up and saw my picture on the front page. It was a publicity shot that was about five years old.

The headline read: "Ben Kroeger to Return to Bristol for Class Reunion." I glanced at the story. The lead paragraph said that more than one hundred members of the Class of '65, including me, were expected to be in town over the weekend.

I put fifty cents next to the stack of papers and took one. The clerk handed me my key.

"I was just reading about you, Mr. Kroeger," he said. "Welcome home."

"Thanks," I said. "Nice to be home."

I am one of those people who, if you were sitting next to me on an airplane, you would have a vague feeling that you had seen me someplace before, but you probably wouldn't be able to figure out exactly where.

If you were curious enough to keep wondering, and polite enough not to wake me up (I spend about 95 percent of my time on planes sleeping), you might get out of your seat and ask the flight attendant whether she knew who I was. She would probably say that I seemed familiar to her, too, but that she couldn't quite say from where.

If both you and the flight attendant were really curious, she would check the flight manifest and match my seat number to my name. That's when one of you would realize where you knew me from.

"Oh, that's right," one of you would say. "I've seen him on TV." Then you might name the network you recalled seeing me on. Chances are you would have the wrong network. It wouldn't be your fault. I'm not like one of those anchormen whose faces have become the living logos of their networks. These days I'm just the guy you see standing in front of some building somewhere in the rain, summing up some story into a hand-held microphone. The generic network correspondent out in the field—the kind of guy you zap through as you're searching the channels for something to watch.

I never set out to be an electronically generated image on a TV screen. I wanted to be a newspaper reporter, and that's what I'd been, starting with the Bristol High School *Beacon*. I loved looking for ideas and interviewing people and sitting down alone at a typewriter and putting stories together. That's what I did at the *Beacon*, and that's what I did on my college paper, and that's what I did for the old Washington *Star* right out of school. My editors at the *Star*, sensing that I had very little interest in political news, encouraged me to go out and find stories that might not be covered otherwise. "Talk to people who've never talked to a reporter before," as one of my editors advised me. "Talk to people who'll never hold a press conference."

Which I did, for five very good years. The *Star* was a distant second to the *Post* in Washington, but because every news organization in the country has bureaus in D.C., and because each of those bureaus checked both Washington papers daily, my work was being seen by all the bureau chiefs in town. The potential newspaper readers in suburban Arlington and Alexandria and Silver Spring might have been choosing to skip reading the *Star*—"I love your paper, but I'm so busy, and it takes so long to read the *Post* as it is"—but the assignment editors at all the news bureaus had to read us. It was part of their job. Lucky for them, too. We were an awfully good newspaper.

So they read us, which meant that, among other parts of the *Star*, they read me, and one day I got a call from the network that would become my employer, asking me if I would be willing to do a TV version of a story I had done in the paper, a story about a World War I naval veteran trying to find his surviving shipmates. I checked with my editors, who made sure that the paper would be mentioned when the anchorman introduced me on national television. The *Star* had a very limited promotional budget, and the free on-air plug for the paper was something that might translate into a few new readers. Or so my editors hoped.

That first story worked out all right, and the network kept asking me back for more, and one day I was invited to fly to New York, where the man who was then president of the news division offered me a full-time job. My assignment would be open-ended, he explained. "The whole world will be your beat," is what he said. Not the world of politics and government and diplomacy—the network already had enough correspondents to cover those disciplines. I would do the same kind of stories I had been writing for the paper, only I would have camera crews and producers with me.

When you grow up in the world of newspapers, that phrase "the whole world will be your beat" is as seductive as any perfume that has ever wafted your way. Newspaper reporters are accustomed to debating with assistant city editors over why a cab was necessary to get to a story when perfectly good buses travel along the same route. At least newspaper reporters were accustomed to engaging in such debates when I broke in. For a network to offer better . . . well, the *Star* was in financial trouble, and all of us on the paper suspected that we'd be looking for work sooner or later, so I said yes to the network and moved my stuff into their Washington bureau.

It was great. I'm not going to pretend it wasn't. I've heard too many former newspaper guys who've gone into TV complain about how TV is so shallow and unsatisfying next to life in the city room. I find that they say this mostly to their old newspaper colleagues. The fact is, no one made me do it—no one ever held a gun to a newspaperman's head and forced him to step before the cameras—and it was a kick. Seeing places I never thought I'd see, having people be eager to talk to me because of the network I represented, flipping on a TV set in some hotel somewhere at the end of the day and watching the piece I'd completed an hour earlier bounce off a satellite out in space and right down into my room—it was hard to beat.

For those first couple of years, I was constantly doing the sort of stories I'd been hired to do. They seemed to make a pretty good impression. I was mentioned favorably in a *Newsweek* piece about promising newcomers in television news, which made my network bosses think they ought to use me more. That kind of thing is so bizarre; had the *Newsweek* writer left me out of his story, or had his editors had to trim the reference to me from the story because of space constraints, my TV work would have been exactly the same. But because of the mention in *Newsweek*, my bosses looked at me with new appreciation. For a while there you couldn't turn on the TV without seeing me.

Two things happened. First, network news was becoming increasingly anchor-driven, and I was never cut out to be an anchor. That's not any kind of false modesty on my part; it's just a fact. I could do a pretty good field piece, but there was no way I could ever sit behind a desk in the studio and authoritatively read the news of the day into a camera. I lacked the physical presence, the look, the ability to read copy with conviction and confidence. Those things are a gift, and I didn't have them. It's not like I tried and failed. Everyone, starting with me, always knew that whatever qualities I brought to the network, anchor potential was not one of them.

Which left me doing my field pieces. Which was fine; that's what I was there for. But the second thing to happen was that, with the advent of cable television and the expansion of local newscasts, network news stopped meaning as much as it once did to American viewers. When there were just the three major networks, network correspondents were virtually all household names. Back then, it didn't matter if they were doing basic nuts-and-bolts wire-service stuff—the fact was, they were doing it on CBS or NBC or ABC, and every television viewer in the country was paying attention. Network TV was exotic; I remember once in the mid-sixties, when I was away at college, there was a civil disturbance on the streets of Columbus. I called home to Bristol to ask my parents how everything was. My mom said, "Murray Fromson is in town!" Fromson was a CBS correspondent, and had been flown in to put together a story about the troubles in the streets. The presence of a CBS correspondent in central Ohio was so momentous that, in my parents' house, it outweighed the news value of the story that Fromson had come to cover.

Today in central Ohio, a family would react that way if one of the three network evening news anchors—or Phil Donahue or Oprah Winfrey—came into town. But with a few exceptions, the days of the network correspondent as celebrity are over. And I'm not one of those exceptions. I still get on the air regularly, and I try my best to do a good job, and I'm proud of my efforts more often than I'm not. But I don't fool myself. To the public, I'm one of a thousand television reporters, network and cable and local, who pass through their consciousness. They've seen me somewhere, and if they run into me out in the real world and manage to match my face with my name they will probably figure out that the somewhere they've seen me is TV news. I'm the vaguely familiar guy who's asleep in the next seat on the airplane—the guy who, depending on whether or not they remember to mention it at the dinner table when the trip is over, they'll tell their spouses they saw on the flight.

Home is home, though, and network news, while changed dramatically from what it once was, is still network news. I may have my built-in career limitations, but in Bristol when I come across the TV screens, holding a microphone while standing in front of a building, I am not just another correspondent in the rain. I am a person who used to be the editor of the Bristol High School *Beacon*.

Which is why, on this Friday afternoon in May, I found myself walking down the long first-floor corridor of the Holiday Inn to my room clutching a copy of the weekly Bristol *News* in my hand, a copy of the Bristol *News* that featured on its front page the slightly outdated photograph of me and the headline that said I would be in town over the weekend to attend a twenty-fifth high school reunion—a reunion that, only if you read past the headline and into the story itself, you would learn was to be attended by the other members of that graduating class, too.

I slipped my key into the door of the room and walked inside. I hoped my former classmates wouldn't hold that headline against me, although I wouldn't blame them if they did. If I were them and I read the headline, I'd certainly hold it against me.

There were two beds in the room. I tossed my carry-on bag onto the one closer to the window, sat down on the other one, and reached for the phone to call Michael and tell him I had arrived safely in Bristol.

Three

MICHAEL AND I were standing in Jeff Erdmann's driveway. The sun had just gone all the way down, and the Christmas-tree lights that had been strung between the roof of the house and the basketball hoop were coloring the night. Up against a row of neatly trimmed bushes was a big gray plastic garbage can filled with ice; Ellen had walked over to pull cans of beer out of the ice, and now she was coming back with one for each of us.

She looked up at the lights. "Christmas in May?" she said.

"Ah, it's nice," Michael said. "It looks like an open house."

"I never saw Christmas lights at an open house," Ellen said.

"Come on," Michael said. "They always had lights."

People had been arriving at the first event of the reunion for the past hour. Michael had picked me up at the motel, and I'd had dinner at his house before heading over here. Jeff Erdmann was a guy who, like Michael, still lived in Bristol; he had been sort of silent and unsocial back in school, but now he was a successful pediatrician and he took care of the children of half the families in town. He and his wife had volunteered to be the hosts of the Friday-night party—an outdoor open house with a disc jockey and dancing.

"I never even heard of open houses until I moved to Bristol," Ellen said. I like Ellen, but she can make the simplest statement sound like a challenge.

"You must have had them in Boston," Michael said.

"We didn't call them open houses," she said.

"Then what did you call them?" Michael said.

"I don't know," she said. "Parties. I guess we called them parties."

"Nah, you probably just forget," Michael said.

"I'm telling you, I never heard a party called an open house," she said. "An open house was when someone was trying to sell their house and people could come look."

I leaned against the garage door and looked around. During the summers in Bristol, there must have been open houses three or four times every week. There was no great mystery to them. A kid would talk his or her parents into having an open house, and the word would go out, and every high school student in Bristol would show up. It didn't cost anything to get in and there was no guest list; it was just a driveway party with music on a summer night, and anyone could come. The only rule was the one imposed by the mayor of Bristol: Anyone who held an open house had to hire an off-duty cop to be on hand, just in case there was trouble. As far as I knew, there never was.

So tonight was our reunion open house. An off-duty Bristol cop, a good fifteen years younger than any of us, stood by the end of the driveway in uniform, calling the men "sir" and the women "ma'am" as they arrived.

"Is he here for nostalgic effect, or is it still the rule?" I said to Michael.

"It's definitely still the rule," Michael said. "New mayor, same rule. You can't have these things without a cop."

"Like we're going to go on a crime spree, right?" I said.

"Like we were going to go on one back then, right?" Michael said.

It was good seeing the men and women from our class show up at the open house, but it was a vaguely different feeling from the one at the twentieth reunion. At the twentieth, most of us hadn't seen one another since high school graduation. So everyone who showed up was a potential surprise. At the twentieth, when each new person walked into the reunion, it was like that scene in *The Twilight Zone* when the person who had undergone plastic surgery was going to get the bandages unwrapped from his face. There had been this undeniable sense of voyeuristic anticipation—it was all very friendly and low-key, but everyone was waiting to see what had happened to everyone else over the years. Everyone had been polite, but if you looked closely into their eyes you could almost hear the shrieks that were bouncing around inside their heads.

Not tonight. We had all seen each other five years ago. Tonight wasn't the same thing as seeing a person you last had seen at eighteen and now he was thirty-eight; tonight you were seeing forty-three-year-olds you had seen five years before, and it was more like saying hello again to adult neighbors who had been on a long trip. There weren't many surprises.

I sensed something else that was different, too, but I wasn't quite sure what it was. I was trying to figure it out when Terry Lucas came walking up.

He was singing along with a record that was playing: "Don't you know that I danced, I danced, till a quarter to three . . ."

When you're a kid you assume that everyone gets bigger as they get older. In Terry's case, and in the cases of a lot of the people at the open house, they seemed to have grown smaller. It's almost like what happens to an imposing rock that sits by an ocean and is worn away by the relentless years of waves hitting it. Terry was a great big kid in high school. For some reason, even though I went through all four years of Bristol with him, my specific memory of him is of one scene, like a snapshot.

We're in the locker room, ready to go out and play basketball in gym. Terry is a tall, fat, hairy guy who's good on the basketball court more because of his bulk than because of his athletic ability. He's sitting on the bench in front of his locker pulling elastic pads over both of his knees. I can see the pads: They're brand-new, like they've never been worn, and in the front, the parts that cover the kneecaps, the pads are bright blue. I look at Terry and I wonder what it is about such a big guy that makes him go out and buy kneepads. None of the rest of us wear them; we just play the game. You're not required to wear them. But here's huge, hairy Terry Lucas, carefully pulling on those kneepads. Did his mother make him buy them? Does he nurse some fear of injury that has not occurred to the rest of us? In my mind I can smell the chlorine in the locker room, and I can almost smell the fresh elastic from the kneepads in the warm, close quarters.

Here was Terry Lucas tonight, and he seemed to be only about 60 percent as large as I remembered him in the locker room. He was gray now; as rambunctious and overbearing as he had been on the basketball court, he had never been very confident with girls, but tonight his wife of twenty years was on his arm. One thing that hadn't changed was the voice. Terry was always a distractingly loud person.

"The line forms behind me!" he yelled as he noticed Jeff Erdmann, his wife, and their two teenaged sons carrying out eight big pizzas from the kitchen. They placed the pizzas on a picnic table that had been covered with a plastic cloth.

Jeff Erdmann—Dr. Erdmann—announced to the men and women standing around the driveway, "I hope this is enough to start with."

Terry spread his arms out as if he wanted to embrace all eight pizzas.

"Oh, it's enough," he said. "But what about all the other people?"

It was the same joke he had made a hundred times at high school open houses and athletic banquets, and tonight he laughed at his own words, and the other men and women, up for the weekend and a quarter of a century removed from enforced daily study-hall contact with Terry, laughed along with him.

Emboldened by their response, he turned to me and said, "What I want to know is, how'd a guy as ugly as you ever get on television?"

He had said the same thing at the twentieth reunion, and I knew that for whatever reason he was just showing off and looking for more laughs. But then he turned to Michael and said, "Your best friend's on national TV and you're still going to Bristol High School every morning," and the joke didn't work and nobody laughed. It would have been a better moment if they had; if everyone had laughed, the moment would have passed and Terry would have moved on to his next joke.

But the silence hung in the air. I was still leaning against the garage door. Michael was next to me, like on so many Bristol nights before, and he didn't say anything. After a second or two the guy running the portable stereo system put on "Glad All Over" by the Dave Clark Five, and the sounds of the drums covered the brief discomfort. Men and women lined up to take slices of the pizza. Ellen draped her arm over Michael's shoulder, and the three of us stood there.

It's a pretty good indication that you know someone well when you can honestly say that you can't remember a time before you were friends. With Michael and me, that's how it is. We were playing together before we even started school, and on the first day of kindergarten, when everyone is so scared of the new world they have just entered, we had each other to depend on.

That first year in school—I don't know why this still embarrasses me—I was very shy and afraid to speak up. Five years old, I guess you're allowed. One day the teacher had the whole class sit in a semicircle around her while she read to us. As she was reading the story, I got a nosebleed.

I'd never had a nosebleed before. I didn't know what to do about it. I held my hand up to my face to try to stop the bleeding. It didn't work. My hand was covered with blood, and I used the sleeve of my shirt, but that didn't help much either. Pretty soon most of the shirt was bloody, and I was still bleeding. I was sitting near the back of the group, and I must have been keeping so quiet that the teacher didn't notice what was happening. The worse the bleeding got, the more reluctant I was to say anything. I suppose I thought it was my fault.

I remember wondering, in a panic, how much more time was left before the bell rang and the school day ended. I knew that my mom would be waiting outside the front door of the school and that she would take care of everything. But our kindergarten session was only about half finished, and I realized that I'd have to go on bleeding for a long time before the afternoon was over.

Then Michael saw me—he was sitting on the other end of the semicircle. I remember him standing up and walking right over to me. That doesn't sound like much now, but when you're that age and it has been impressed upon you never to walk around without asking for permission when the teacher is talking, standing up and going over to your friend is not something that you do lightly.

Michael came over to me and took one close look and then said to the teacher: "Ben's hurt." He said it right in the middle of one of her sentences, and she looked up from the book, an expression of alarm on her face, and she stopped everything and took me down to the nurse's office, where she stayed with me until the nurse had controlled the bleeding. Michael had tried to walk to the nurse's office with us, but the teacher had told him to remain in the classroom with the substitute she had hurriedly recruited from the room next door. When I returned to the classroom—my face and hands had been cleaned up, but my clothes were still bloody—he was waiting in the doorway.

I'm not sure that we've ever talked about that. It is said that people change during their lives, but Michael hasn't. I can quite truthfully say that I have never seen or heard of him doing a mean or dishonest thing. During high school he was very active in student government, and he was one of the three or four guys in our class who were always the leaders in everything. He easily could have lorded it over some of the people who were awkward or unattractive or unsure of themselves in social situations—any kid who is on top of the closed world of an American high school probably could be excused for going through at least a transitory period of being uncaring toward others—but Michael never did. There was an essential sweetness to Michael. When we were younger I wouldn't have chosen to use that particular word, but it's the right word. There is a sweetness to Michael that I have found in very few people.

And it probably worked against him. We went away to different colleges. Michael studied English, and when he graduated he got a job teaching at a private school near Boston, where Ellen's family lived. He liked teaching. Those first few years out of college, when no one was making much money, the job didn't separate him from the rest of the people he had grown up with; everyone was making the salaries that twenty-two-year-olds make, and Michael happened to be making his salary as a teacher. I don't think it ever occurred to him then that unless he looked elsewhere for a career, a gap might develop between his life and the lives of some of his more asset-driven contemporaries.

When his dad got sick he came back to Bristol to stay with him and help out. That was supposed to be temporary, but when it became apparent that his dad wasn't going to get better anytime soon, Michael and Ellen left Boston so that they could be close by. Michael got a job with the Bristol School System. There were no openings in the high school, so Michael taught third grade for two years before there was a vacancy teaching eleventh-grade English. That's what he still does. He teaches English to juniors at Bristol High School; his classroom is the same one in which we studied *Silas Marner* and *The Red Badge of Courage*.

I hear he's great at it. I hear the students love him. In every high school there's a teacher the students like so much that they want to call him by his first name. That's how it is with Michael. They call him "Mr. Wolff" until they feel comfortable enough to try calling him "Mike." When he doesn't stop them—when they realize that it's okay with him—it's as if they're in heaven. I remember that feeling. When a teacher you respect and admire lets you call him by his first name, you feel like a grownup. When he allows you to do that you feel somehow worthy.

At the party, when Terry Lucas made the remark about Michael still going to Bristol High School every morning, I suppose that Terry, in his limited way, genuinely did believe that because of the facts of adult life, Michael was somehow a little beneath Terry and so many of the others. Terry is one of those guys who makes more than $100,000 a year by doing something that he would be hard pressed to define. From what I understand, it's something corporate in the area of marketing; I'm sure he has a business card that would help explain it. He can say something like what he said to Michael and not conceive that Michael might resent it or, on some level, be wounded by it. Especially when it is said in front of Michael's wife, in the company of Michael's old classmates.

I didn't need to say anything to Michael about the moment that had just passed. We know each other too well for that to be necessary. The people at the party in the driveway worked on the pizza, and from the speakers Dave Clark's voice boomed out: "I'm feeling glad all over . . ." I looked next to me at Michael, with Ellen resting her head against him. Five years old in that classroom, and he sensed that I needed his help. I can still hear his voice as he said the words to our teacher, instinctively knowing that it didn't matter that he was interrupting her. Two words, clear and calm and urgent: "Ben's hurt." Tonight I looked over at him, and for the first time, in the red-and-green glow of Christmas-tree lights on a late-spring evening, I noticed the deep, weary lines that had begun to form at the corners of his eyes.

I'm not much of a dancer, but around ten o'clock the disc jockey put on "Don't Let the Sun Catch You Crying," and Susan Bayme, whom I used to work with on the school paper, came up with her hand extended and asked me if I would join her. Her husband, who graduated from Bristol a few years before we did, was over at the front edge of the lawn, by the sidewalk, talking to some other men who weren't a part of the class and who, like him, had been dragged along.

"I don't know, Susan," I said. "I'm not very good at this."

"It's a slow song," she said. "No one's going to laugh at you."

So we joined the others on the driveway. We talked a little bit—I'd always liked her in school, and we'd had a pleasant conversation at the twentieth reunion—and she said, "So . . . Nancy didn't come?"

"No," I said. "She's not here."

"She was here last time, right?"

"Yes," I said.

"I remember talking to her," Susan said. "I thought she was nice."

"I hadn't realized that this was Jeff Erdmann's house," I said, changing the subject. "I think the Gerners used to live in it when we were kids."

Taking the hint, Susan started talking about Bristol things and we danced until the record ended.

Late in the evening I began to figure out what had been nagging me about the reunion—what had been feeling different than the reunion five years ago.

I think it happened when Garry Richmond walked up. Garry used to imagine himself as a tough kid, almost a juvenile delinquent. That should have been laughable; not that Garry should envision himself as tough—kids have always fantasized that they are tough—but that there should be any potential space, even emotional space, for a would-be juvenile delinquent in Bristol. As elementary school pupils in the late fifties, we read newspaper dispatches with New York datelines about bands of youth gang members—"juvenile delinquents"—who were roaming Manhattan, Brooklyn, and the Bronx, causing clergymen and civic leaders to warn about the upcoming lost generation.

Garry Richmond, in fifth grade, had decided that he, too, was a juvenile delinquent. Which was certainly his right—as we were being taught in school, in this country you can be anything you want to be. The problem was that Bristol didn't look anything like the South Bronx. Bristol, if the truth be told, looked like the neighborhood in *Leave It to Beaver*, and still does. There were no gangs. Lots of Pony League baseball teams, but no gangs.

But Garry, all of eleven years old, took to wearing a wool jacket with leather sleeves, on the back of which, in shiny electrical tape that he had appropriated from his father's basement workshop, he wrote the word: "Dukes." That was the gang that Garry had envisioned: the Dukes.

He was a forlorn sight, walking up and down Maple Avenue after school with his hair greased back (he used that pink stuff that clogged up by the bottom of the comb), a sneer on his face, and that Dukes jacket hunched up around his neck. Never mind that he, like all the rest of us, had to be home for dinner by the time his dad pulled in the driveway from work. Garry tried to make us feel that he was a little bit dangerous—he cussed openly and showed us rubbers in the drawer of his big brother's nightstand—and when he told us that he wanted us to wear Dukes jackets, we complied out of a combination of intimidation and a flighty, tingling feeling that if we wore Dukes jackets, the streets of Bristol might suddenly seem more daunting and perilous.

Our dalliance with membership in the imaginary Dukes didn't last long; I think my own membership set the record for brevity. I borrowed some electrical tape from Garry (my dad didn't have a workshop) and wrote the word on the back of a sweatshirt. I wore the sweatshirt home to dinner, trying to stay face-forward at all times when in the presence of my father. After dinner, though, when I left the table, he glanced up and saw my back.

"All right," he said. "Hold it right there. What's that?"

"What's what?" I said.

"The Dukes," my father said.

Scrambling for a logical explanation, I was able to come up with: "Huh?"

My father personally removed the tape from the back of my shirt—the expression on his face as he peeled it off made it seem as if the task was as distasteful to him as, say, boning a rotten and moldering mackerel with his bare hands—and as he dropped the tape into the kitchen wastebasket, splaying his fingers several times to get across the point that he despised even touching electrical tape that had once spelled out the word "Dukes," he let it be known that never again was that particular word ever to be spoken, never mind worn, in his house.

Garry Richmond soon came to the realization that there was no room for the Dukes in Bristol. Still, he did his best to maintain his surly attitude. One day he was over at my house, and my dad said to him, "Hello, Garry. How are you?" And Garry—he was about four foot eight at the time, wearing new saddle shoes that his mother had bought him for school—sneered up at my dad and said in his best James Dean imitation: "Livin'."

Livin'. Tonight Garry was walking with a cane—one of his legs had been smashed in a car accident out on the Three-C Highway when he was in his early twenties, and he has had to use the cane ever since—and he was almost too polite. Five years ago—I remember this because I had laughed out loud when he said it—he had walked up to me after not having seen me in twenty years, had leaned on the cane, and had snarled: "Want to rumble?"

Tonight Garry told us that his dad's transmission repair business, which he had taken over when his dad retired, had come upon difficult times. "The chain operations are killing us," he said. "They advertise on national TV, and the customers all go to them because they seem like they're big-time. Our company's been in the family for sixty years, and been in Bristol for sixty years. But people would rather drive up the freeway to one of the chains, because the chains have professional football players as their spokesmen on TV. I had to lay three people off last week, including a guy who my dad had break me into the business."

"Not Luke," Michael said.

"You remember Luke?" Garry said.

"Sure," Michael said. "He worked on my first car when we were seniors. I still see him around town."

Luke had seemed a rather dashing figure, sort of a cowboy, back in the bay area of the transmission shop. He was a rangy guy who wore a patch bearing his name over the left pocket of his shirt. He must have been in his late twenties when we were growing up. It's not like we knew him well—we'd see him when we had car problems. His life was different than our dads' lives—in a way it seemed better than our dads' lives. We didn't think about how much money Luke did or didn't make, or whether he would have preferred not to have a job that required him to post his name above his shirt pocket. He spent his days climbing over and under cars, which looked like more fun than doing whatever it was that men did in offices. And he genuinely was great with engines.

"You really laid Luke off?" Michael said.

"It killed me," Garry said. "I didn't have any choice. Some days we have two customers total."

Garry began to provide us with the details of just how lousy business had been, and as I listened his tone didn't sound all that different from what I had been hearing all evening. Not that everyone was having business troubles; some people were doing fine financially. What struck me about the tone was not the specific monetary complaints, but the subtle difference in attitude from the reunion five years ago.

At the twentieth, the unspoken feeling was that life had leveled everything out, and that we had all become pretty much what we were going to be. The lack of competitiveness had been comforting; I had felt that whatever there was that used to make people instinctively try to outdo one another, that was gone. This was who we were, for the long haul. It was almost as if we were taking a deep breath at the end of a steep climb up a mountain.

Yet there's a double edge to the theory about everyone finally becoming what they were destined to become. Yes, it allows you to take the deep breath and survey what you have done with your years on earth. But it's kind of scary, too. If you've become what you were meant to become, then what happens next? That's what I was sensing tonight: People were looking at one another and wondering whether we were still on the incline of some mountain, or whether we had reached the top and were now heading back down—whether the climb was over and this was the beginning of the long, slow slide.

I was thinking about all of this as Garry Richmond laid out his business problems to Michael and Ellen and me, but all I said to Garry was, "That's too bad about Luke. How old is he now?"

"I asked him that when we were talking in my office," Garry said. "He told me he was fifty-eight."

We didn't say a word, but Garry jumped right back in, as if he were reading our minds, as if he had to defend himself.

"I had no choice at all," he said. "I'm telling you—two customers some days. Two customers. All day long. How do you pay your people when you have two customers walking in the door between the time you open and the time you close?"

Sometime after midnight the crowd in the driveway began to thin out. Michael and Ellen gave me a lift to the motel.

"You need a ride tomorrow night, right?" Michael said.

"I do," I said. "Are you going to have room? What about Ronnie?"

"He'll have his own car," Michael said.

"Ronnie and Marilyn are going to stay with us," Ellen said. "You don't see them checking into a motel. And Ronnie could probably buy the motel."

"Cut it out," Michael said.

"Even for Ronnie, that wouldn't be very cost-efficient," I said to Ellen. "Buying a motel just so he could stay there for one night."

"With his luck, he'd turn around and sell it for twice as much the next morning," Ellen said.

We arrived at the front door of the Holiday Inn. "What time does Ronnie get to town tomorrow?" I said to Michael.

"He wasn't sure," Michael said. "It depends on when his meetings end. But he said he'll be here in plenty of time for the dinner."

"Coat and tie tomorrow night, right?" I said.

"Coat and tie," Michael said, our voices an echo of hundreds of conversations we'd had in preparation for hundreds of Bristol Saturday nights.

Four

AT ROLLING CREEK COUNTRY CLUB, just outside of Bristol, the photographer said, "Three more on this roll, and then you can go back to the party."

Michael and Ronnie and I had our arms slung over each other's shoulders. We were standing in the back row on a set of risers that had been erected for the official reunion picture. The photograph was just for class members; the spouses who had come to the reunion stood off to the side, out of camera range. I glanced around at the other men and women from the class. By happenstance or by design, the people who had been the closest friends in high school had ended up standing next to each other for this photo.

"All right," the photographer said. "Look at me, please."

There was a flash.

"That's good," the photographer said. "Two more."

"Will you look at Karen Glaser?" Ronnie said.

"Be quiet," Michael said, smiling toward the camera. "That's her husband standing next to the risers. He can hear you."

"Am I wrong, or is she looking much better than she did in high school?" Ronnie said.

Another flash. "Very good," the photographer said. "Everyone try to smile for this last one."

"All those evenings she and I spent down in her parents' basement," Ronnie said.

"Not interested, Ronnie," I said, maintaining eye contact with the camera.

"She never looked like that," Ronnie said.

"If she had, she wouldn't have been spending her evenings with you," Michael said.

There was a final flash. "Thank you all," the photographer called out. "We're going to have these developed and have copies ready for you by the end of the party. We'll see you in a few hours."

"Do you think she remembers those nights?" Ronnie said.

"I think we can safely assume that you've crossed people's minds over the years," I said.

Ronnie had pulled into town around three that afternoon. He and Marilyn had driven down from Cleveland in Ronnie's Jeep—I had a feeling that they had left Marilyn's Mercedes at home on purpose, to avoid people making the predictable comments. Although there was really no way that people weren't going to say anything. Not after what had happened to Ronnie.

If, twenty-five years ago, some scientist had been assigned by an ultrasecret government agency to go into an underground laboratory and build from scratch an absolutely average high school male, Ronnie Hepps is what the scientist would have come up with. Ronnie wasn't stupid and he wasn't smart. He wasn't uncoordinated and he wasn't a varsity letterman. He wasn't smooth with girls and he wasn't bashful. He was just a Bristol guy who seemed fairly contented most of the time, and he and Michael and I were each other's best friends. We hung out together all through school. On weekend nights, it wasn't a question of who we would spend time with—the only question was whose car we would take. I can still tell you Ronnie's parents' phone number, even though I probably haven't dialed it in twenty years. Dial a number twenty thousand or thirty thousand times when you're a kid, it tends to stick somewhere in the recesses of your mind.

If Ronnie ever had a worry in the world, he didn't mention it to us. He was a guy who seemed happy to skip across the surface of life; even when the three of us were getting ready to go off to three different colleges, Ronnie was the one whom the prospect of leaving Bristol and leaving each other didn't seem to faze. Inside, I was more than a little frightened by the thought of what might lie ahead, and I knew that Michael was reflective and even melancholy. For Ronnie, though, going away from everything you grew up with was just something that was expected. To him, it was like when teams in gym class chose sides for football. You had no control over what team was going to pick you, so why worry about it?

In college Ronnie met Marilyn Steele at a fraternity-sorority mixer, and by the time they were seniors they were engaged. We got to know her during summer vacations, when she would come to visit him in Bristol. They seemed to get along with each other well enough, but it was like everything that Ronnie did: He had met her and he had liked her pretty much, so he would marry her without looking around for anyone else or even questioning whether she was the one woman in the world who was meant for him. It was just easier that way.

Of our three weddings, Ronnie and Marilyn's was the first. They moved up to Cleveland—if it bothered Ronnie at all to pull up roots in Bristol, he sure didn't show it—and he went to work for Marilyn's father. Sidney Steele ran a hugely successful import-export business in Cleveland, and there was no problem creating a job for his new son-in-law.

This was a good thing; I have had some of the best times of my life in the company of Ronnie Hepps, but he was not a guy who would necessarily shine in a job interview. He was a guy who would be one of twenty who talked to the personnel director, and he would not be among the five who would be called back for the final round. He wouldn't be the worst of the twenty. But there would be no way that the personnel man would single him out and think that here was a fellow who could really help the firm.

So luckily for Ronnie, he went to work for Sidney Steele's company, where no job interview was necessary. Ronnie made a good salary— Sidney Steele's daughter was not going to live poorly, not in Cleveland, with all of Sidney's friends paying attention—and as far as any of us could tell Ronnie was, as usual, pleased with his life, in a passive kind of way.

Then two occurrences transpired. First, Sidney Steele's company, which had been privately held ever since Sidney Steele founded it, went public. After the stock offering, Ronnie, as the husband of Marilyn Steele, became the beneficiary, with her, of approximately six million dollars. This was news that made it back to Bristol rather quickly. Ronnie Hepps was a multimillionaire. It was not lost on people that Ronnie was a person who, at Bristol High School, had on several occasions come within one final exam of being held back a grade. Human nature being what it is, Ronnie's newfound financial status, while the subject of much gossip, did not result in parades of jubilation down Main Street.

The second occurrence was that Sidney Steele died suddenly in 1986. Marilyn was his only child. When the company had gone public, a management contract had guaranteed continuing day-to-day control of the firm to Sidney Steele. A clause in the contract also guaranteed that a member of the Steele family, to be designated by Sidney, would retain the title of chairman for at least ten years following Sidney's death. The stockholders would be free to put a new chief operating officer in place, but Sidney Steele's designated relative would sit in the chairman's office.

Millions of women, during the seventies and eighties, had embraced the idea of seeking influence in the traditionally male-dominated world of business. Marilyn Steele Hepps was not one of them.

So it was that Ronnie Hepps became chairman of the board of Steele International. Sidney Steele had left Ronnie and Marilyn an inheritance-plus-stock package that was reliably reported to be worth seventy million dollars. Ronnie Hepps was suddenly one of the wealthiest men in the state of Ohio.

He served on the boards of numerous charities in Cleveland; he was offered, and had accepted, a seat on the Board of Regents of the university at which he had sporadically attended classes. When he and Michael and I got together, Ronnie always made it clear that at some level he realized the essential cosmic absurdity of what had taken place. It amused him and interested him—probably on an only slightly higher level than, say, a Three Stooges movie.

So tonight Ronnie was oblivious to the looks that were being shot in his direction by his former classmates—classmates who had to deal with the idea that Ronnie Hepps now had more money in his possession than any twenty of them would compile in their entire lifetimes of work.

Possibly another man would be cognizant of those looks from his classmates, and would feel slightly uncomfortable at being the object of both the looks and the thoughts behind them.

"Are we having dinner soon?" Ronnie said.

A buffet supper was being served in the main dining room at Rolling Creek. Michael and Ronnie and I lined up with our classmates and waited our turns in front of the tables that bore steaming containers of chicken, roast beef, and vegetables.

A man I didn't recognize was standing behind us with two plates in his hands. He introduced himself as Leon Bergman; he said that he was the husband of Sally Carruthers, who had been a Bristol cheerleader in our class.

"Sally and I met at Ohio State," he said to us. "I went to high school at Eastmoor, in Columbus. I think we played you guys in football one year."

His voice was a growl. It was the kind of growl that some men seem to develop as they get older and more prosperous. I've never heard a poor man speak with that particular kind of growl. I guess it's a growl that comes with power. You hear it in a lot of country-club locker rooms. Sally Carruthers, if I recall, had been the Bristol student responsible for launching the petition drive that got an apple machine installed in our student lounge. The girl behind the apple-machine movement grew up to marry a man who growled.

"I had to drive down to Cincinnati this morning to play golf," Leon Bergman growled. "I'd promised some clients that I'd play in this pro-am thing with them, and then I looked on the calendar and saw that Sally's reunion was this weekend. So we went to that outdoor party last night, and I got up at four o'clock this morning and was on the golf course in Cincinnati by eight. I drove straight back so we could be here."

Sally was across the dining room. Her husband raised both plates so that she could see them, indicating that he would bring her dinner over.

"Sally's looking great," Michael said to Leon Bergman.

"I bought her a Cadillac last week," he said.

He didn't have a cigar in his mouth as he said it, but it was a cigar-in-the-mouth kind of thing. Yeah, Sally's a good girl. I bought her a Cadillac last week.

After Sally's husband had filled the two plates and had walked away, Ronnie said, "I know some people who do business with him. He's supposed to be a pretty good guy."

But I found myself thinking that it was one more sign of what had been striking me about the weekend. I was all excited to be back in Bristol for the reunion. Maybe it's because I didn't live here anymore, but what I wanted was what I remembered from Bristol. I didn't want to meet some guy who bragged that he just bought Sally Carruthers a Cadillac. I knew that wasn't fair—Leon Bergman had no obligation to be anything other than what he really was—but it bothered me nonetheless.

It was like something else that had happened earlier in the evening. There was a guy named Phil Garvin in our class; he hadn't been one of my best friends, like Michael and Ronnie, but I had liked him and he knew a lot about music and we talked whenever we ran into each other. One summer he had a copy of Bob Dylan's *Blonde on Blonde* album, which had just come out. I remember sitting on a corner with him one warm and starlit Bristol night talking about all the songs on *Blonde on Blonde*, trying to come up with theories about what Dylan had meant by the lyrics. What did it signify—to be stuck inside of Mobile with those Memphis blues again? Maybe that was just a rhythmic sentence that Dylan had composed; maybe there was a secret inside it. But in the middle of Ohio, two kids were fascinated by the possibilities that song bespoke, and we talked about it long into a summer night. I remember the streetlights being on and no cars at all driving up Phil Garvin's street, and I remember us trying to figure out why an album would be called *Blonde on Blonde*. Bob Dylan had no idea that we even existed, yet it was as if he had sent us smoke signals and had expected us to try to decode them.

Tonight at the country club I had seen Phil Garvin, now hefty and florid-faced, sitting with his wife. I had joined them at their table, and immediately Phil had told me three detailed stories in a row about relatives or friends' parents who had died. I got to hear every bit of hospital procedure, every interpretation of laboratory results, every pronouncement attributed to every physician who had known when it was "too late to try anything else." That was a phrase that Phil used more than once: "The doctor said that it was too late to try anything else," just before saying, "If you had seen Donny's dad in those last days, you'd have known it was a blessing."

Phil's a good-hearted guy. It was apparent that he had gone to visit the relatives, and the parents of his friends, when they were ill and in the hospital, which was more than a lot of people do. But I found myself looking at him and thinking of that summer night when nothing seemed more pressing or important than deciphering *Blonde on Blonde* track by track. Phil talked compassionately tonight about sickness and death, and I looked in his face and tried to find the kid who wanted to know why the Memphis blues were stuck inside of Mobile.

A band had been playing at the reunion, but they were on break, and they had put on a tape that would run until they returned in fifteen minutes. It was a summer tape—all the songs were songs associated with summer. "Summer Means Fun" by Bruce and Terry came on, and then "Wonderful Summer" by Robin Ward, and then "A Summer Song" by Chad and Jeremy. The Beach Boys' "All Summer Long" came out of the speakers in the country club's dining room:

> Sitting in my car outside your house,
> 'member when you spilled Coke all over your blouse?

Michael and Ronnie and I were carrying our plates back to our table. I looked at them as the song continued:

> T-shirts, cutoffs, and a pair of thongs,
> We've been having fun all summer long.

And that's when I understood; that's when I understood everything that had been going on inside my head for the last two days.

"Put your food down," I said.

"Why?" Ronnie said.

"We can eat dinner later," I said. "Let's go outside for a while. I have to talk to you guys about something."

———

We sat on the wooden bench that overlooked the first of Rolling Creek's six tennis courts. Across the parking lot behind us, the band had started up again in the country club's main building. In front of us, all the way across the six courts, I could see the highway leading into Bristol.

"Were your parents members here?" Ronnie said.

"Not mine," Michael said.

"Mine were for a few years when I was a kid," I said. "They quit, though."

"Rolling Creek dropouts," Michael said.

"Sort of, I guess," I said. "I think they just didn't like spending the money."

Rolling Creek had been a kind of summer hangout for all of us. Bristol was a small enough town so that it didn't really matter if your parents were members of the club; sooner or later, if you were a kid, you'd be invited swimming here by one of your friends, or you'd be invited to a party. Being a member was more important to the adults. If you were a member, you had a regular golf game; if you were a member, you could tell yourself that you had risen to a certain echelon of Bristol society. Ronnie's parents had been members forever, and he used to bring us out here all the time.

On so many summer afternoons we'd climb out of the Rolling Creek pool, our hair wet, and we'd slip our jeans and shirts over our bathing suits and let the sun dry us out. Then we'd pile into someone's car for the short drive into Bristol. That's how our summer days ended—the three of us together, heading home.

Now here we were. The tennis-court lights weren't on, so the only illumination was from the tall vapor lamps in the parking lot.

"What's up, Ben?" Ronnie said to me.

"I don't know," I said. "This weekend is just making me think."

"That's what reunions are for," Michael said.

"I know," I said. "But it's not just that. It's the idea that summer is about to start."

"Yeah, it does have that feeling, doesn't it?" Michael said.

"It doesn't," I said. "That's the problem."

"It doesn't feel like summer to you?" Ronnie said.

"No," I said. "It doesn't anymore."

And that was the truth. It used to be, when the three of us spent all of our time together, that summer was the greatest gift in the world. At this precise time of the year, summer was the gift that lay directly ahead. Summer was everything—it was freedom, it was joy, it was the promise of adventure and maybe of romance. The beginning of summer was the time when, for some reason, you felt that things just might change for the better.

I tried to explain that to Michael and Ronnie.

"So basically you're saying that there was no school in the morning," Ronnie said.

"No, I'm serious," I said. "I don't know what it was about summer. But it used to be the best part of our lives, and now it's not."

"You don't like summer anymore?" Ronnie said.

"That's not it," I said. "It just doesn't mean anything anymore."

My foot bumped against something under the bench. It was a tennis ball that someone had forgotten to put back in the can at the end of the day. I kicked at it and it rolled out in front of us. Ronnie picked it up and began to bounce it off the chain-link fence surrounding the courts.

I told them what was going through my head. I was rambling, but I did my best to try to make them understand. Summer, I said, was always the time of the best friendships, the most intense loves, the fewest rules, the strongest memories. The three of us had known each other all our lives—but when we thought of each other, about 90 percent of our best memories were summer memories. It's no coincidence that there are about a million summer songs that used to come out of the radio, and only a handful of songs about winter or autumn or spring. For some reason, for everyone in the world the three months of summer are the months that are the most precious. At least they used to be.

Because today, as grownups, we all walk through the summer as if it's just one more part of the year. It's hotter, yes, and in August it's hard to get business associates on the phone. But the summer of our memories—the summer that meant everything, the three months that made the very word "summer" cause an almost physiological reaction in us every time we heard it—that summer is gone. Summer doesn't mean much, and nothing proves that more definitively than the fact that most of us no longer even stop to realize that it doesn't mean much.

"But the reunion's good," Michael said.

"That's the thing," I said. "The reunion has been fine, but the understanding is that it's transitory. It's here and it's gone. A reunion is supposed to be a reminder of better times. It's not supposed to be a promise of anything. It's like a taunt. 'This is what you used to have.' "

"And?" Ronnie said.

"I was standing in there, and I was thinking about what's going to happen tomorrow," I said. "Everyone's going to say goodbye to each other, and then we'll all go back to our homes, and the three of us will promise to keep in touch more than we usually do. And we won't. And pretty soon it will be fall.

"But when I was in there, I made myself think about what would happen if we could do it the old way."

"We can't," Michael said. "We're not seventeen."

"No, and we never will be again," I said. "But it's summer. Summer's starting. And I was wondering what would happen if somehow all of our obligations and all of the constrictions of our daily lives were removed. If the three of us now—the middle-aged three of us . . ."

"Middle-aged," Ronnie said.

"It's true," Michael said. "We are."

". . . what would happen if the three of us the way we are now could give ourselves one more summer together."

A Rolling Creek security guard walked by, nodded hello to us, and continued his rounds.

"A summer together to do what?" Michael said.

"I don't know," I said. "That's the whole point. Every day now, I basically know what I have to do. But what would happen if the three of us just took off? If we just set out together?"

"People don't do that," Ronnie said.

"I can just see telling Ellen that I'm leaving," Michael said.

"You'd come back," I said. "This would just be for the summer."

Ronnie kept throwing the tennis ball against the fence. He had found a spot on the chain link that he knew would return the ball to him in the same arc every time.

"There's such a thing as work," he said.

"You'll go to work this summer, and you'll go to work next summer, and you'll go to work every summer for the rest of your life," I said. "And we'll never do this, and maybe once in a while we'll talk about what it would have been like if we'd done it, and we'll never again have a summer as good as the summer when we were seventeen. And maybe when we get real old, we'll get together and wonder what would have happened if we'd done it."

Michael looked at me. Part of him seemed ready to laugh, but another part of him didn't. "What would we tell people we were doing?" he said.

"Giving ourselves a gift," I said.

"And what would we tell them the gift was?" Michael said.

"That's easy," I said. "One more summer in the sun."

We must have talked about it for another half hour. Then we walked back toward the party.

"Do you remember that old TV show, *The Millionaire*?" Michael said.

"Sure," I said.

"When that guy would show up at strangers' houses and knock on their doors and hand them a cashier's check for a million dollars, to do anything with that they wanted?" he said.

"The millionaire's name was John Beresford Tipton," I said. "You never saw his face on the show. You just saw the guy he sent out to give away the money."

"Kind of like *Charlie's Angels*," Ronnie said.

"Kind of," I said. We were almost at the door of the main building. I turned to Michael. "Why are you thinking about *The Millionaire?*"

"I'm thinking that I wish that guy would show up and tell us we could do this," Michael said. "Show up and tell us that we could hit the road for the summer."

"Maybe they should make a TV show about a guy who does that," Ronnie said. "A guy who snaps his fingers and lets old best friends take off together for the summer."

"It'd get better ratings than the original show," Michael said.

"You think so?" I said.

"Sure," Michael said. "The payoff's better. The guy on *The Millionaire* only offered money."

He had a bounce in his step as he said it. And that was the moment, for the first time since we'd started talking, when I knew that we might have a chance of actually doing it.

Five

I FLEW BACK to Washington the next morning. As soon as my plane landed at National Airport I went to a pay phone and called Nancy.

"So you enjoyed it," she said after I had told her about the weekend.

"I wish you would have come," I said.

"It wouldn't have been worth it, having to answer all the questions," she said.

Nancy and I were divorced two years ago. Both of us would have had to be blind not to see it coming. All those years of traveling for the network had finally kicked in.

When we met I was already working as a correspondent, and she said that she knew what she was getting into. Most men, their wives expect them to be late for dinner once in a while. With me, the phone would ring in the middle of the night and she'd know without asking that she wouldn't see me for the next week.

At first that routine was vaguely glamorous, in a tenuous kind of way. I felt like a doctor on call, except that I wasn't helping anybody. No matter where I was in the world, I would call Nancy two or three times a day to tell her how my story was coming. If I was in the Pacific time zone, I would call her during the East Coast feed of the evening news and we'd watch my piece together. Well, she'd watch; that was the whole idea. I wouldn't be seeing the piece until the West Coast feed of the show came into whatever city I was in two or three hours later, so she'd turn the volume up and hold the receiver near the TV set, and she'd offer her critique of the story. There's a certain seductiveness to that kind of life—the correspondent out in the field, his wife watching him bounce down into their living room and evaluating the story shot by shot with him—but it's the most fragile kind of seductiveness. Once a woman has seen her husband's electronic visage shoot down from the satellite thirty or forty times, it becomes a pretty poor substitute for having him at home. After that fortieth time she'll continue to watch, but it's unfair to expect her to marvel at the technology and the hectic serendipity of modern life that allows them to experience this.

So it wasn't all that surprising that, after a couple of years, I would call from some hotel room in Utah and listen to the phone ring and ring. I suppose some marriages can readily handle the exigencies of one partner being constantly gone—there certainly have been enough magazine articles about deliriously happy commuter marriages. For Nancy and me, though, what worked in theory collapsed to tatters in practice. Her friends got to sit down at their dinner tables with their husbands every night; Nancy got to watch me on a color screen. You can set a VCR for that, which she learned to do.

We thought the birth of Hannah might help make things better. In a way, it did; Hannah, at the age of eight, is a better person than either Nancy or I—I say that only because Nancy would tell you the same thing, without hesitation—but if a life on the road tends to make you less than perfect as a husband, it makes you even more lacking as a father. Try telling your child, virtually on a weekly basis, why you have to go away again. Go through enough of those goodbye scenes at the front door, and when you think of those scenes, think of her growing taller with each succeeding trip. You know the way a lot of families measure their children's growth with a pencil and a yardstick held against the kitchen wall? With me it might as well have been on the wall of the hallway next to the front door. Gotta go, Hannah, and boy, aren't you getting big. It seems that last time I said goodbye you were still crawling.

If I sound dispassionate in relating that, don't believe it. There are some things that hurt so deeply that it's best to avoid describing them. When Nancy said that she and Hannah were leaving, it was totally foreseeable and totally paralyzing. Sort of like a firing squad. Except a firing squad wouldn't be so painful, and you wouldn't have to wake up the next morning and wonder if it was all a terrible dream.

We're four blocks away from each other in Bethesda. I'm welcome to come to dinner at their house anytime. Anytime I'm in town. Of course, Nancy's seeing somebody now—what a phrase, "seeing somebody," as if it's a matter of vision—so it's best if I call in advance. Hannah shows me stories that she's written in school. Her teacher says that she exhibits real promise. In April, Hannah told me that she and her mother—I've actually started referring to Nancy as "her mother"—were going to the Delaware shore for the summer. Nancy had found a cottage to rent. I got the distinct feeling that it was better if I didn't know too many details of Nancy's social arrangements.

So maybe the lure of a summer with Michael and Ronnie, a summer of constant motion and ready laughter and continuous good company, was not altogether unexplainable. Sorry if, in recounting all that, I'm sounding a little down. I only get that way when I stop to think. I try to avoid such moments as much as possible.

It must have been about three days after the reunion that I called Ronnie.

His secretary put me right through to him, but his voice sounded funny, as if he were inside a cave.

"You don't have me on a speakerphone," I said.

"It's been a very bad day for me." As weird as the tinny speakerphone voice was, I could tell immediately that his very bad day had nothing to do with any significant problem in his personal life and everything to do with some business deal that hadn't gone his way. I've been hearing Ronnie talk about "very bad days" for thirty years, and the timbre of his voice was approximately the same as when he would report to us that he had flunked a physics quiz.

"Come on, Ronnie," I said. "I can't deal with you putting me on a speakerphone."

"I can't deal with picking up the telephone today," he said.

So we had our discussion—a discussion that had the potential of disrupting a number of lives—with me talking into the mouthpiece of a real telephone while I heard Ronnie's voice echo back to me from his office in Cleveland. I could almost see him with his feet up on the desk, his hands clasped behind his head, and his eyes closed. Come to think of it, maybe his very bad day wasn't the result of a business deal, after all. Maybe it was just a hangover.

In any case, by the time we hung up he had told me that he was willing to be convinced. That was enough for me. I told him I'd be flying to Cleveland the next day.

I had already laid the groundwork with my bosses. I'd seen the schedule for the weeks ahead—the network's plans for me included a swing through the Northeast to "gauge the mood of the electorate" as the fall House and Senate campaigns approached—and I could envision the scenario: Walking into coffee shops in Vermont and New Hampshire, waiting for a producer and camera crew to select the right angles and set up their lights and check their batteries and test the audio levels and make sure the color balance was correct for the video—all so that I could ask some fellow munching on a doughnut what he thought of the various candidates and issues. The fellow with the doughnut would be cooperative beyond all reason—that network logo on the camera is more charming and persuasive than any salesman's hearty smile—and when we finished the taping the fellow would ask me what night this interview would be on TV.

And I wouldn't have the heart to tell him that the chances were very dim that the interview would ever be on TV. The fellow with the doughnut would be one of perhaps forty people we did quick interviews with in the course of the week—videotape is cheap—and maybe another sixty people would be interviewed by producers around the region, for the purpose of being "folded into" the piece. Of those one hundred people, three or four would make it into the story. Assuming, of course, that the story even made the air. Plenty don't. All of us have spent days, even weeks, on certain pieces, only to find that the executive producers in New York have lost interest during the time between sending us out and seeing the result of our work. The operative phrase for this is: "Your story went away."

So as I was thinking about this particular interview, and all the similar interviews that we would be conducting for the same piece, it occurred to me that I did not want to go. I did not want to do this story. Depending on the whims of the executive producers, the story might or might not "go away"; I, though, most certainly wanted to go away, at least for the summer.

When I presented the proposal to the Washington bureau chief, it was all he could do to keep from breaking into a jack-o'-lantern grin. He, like every executive of every network, had been ordered to drastically trim costs, to cut his budget until he heard screams. I was suggesting taking the summer off? Was it a leave of absence I wanted? Well, of course. This would be unsalaried, naturally. If it turned out that I needed the three months, I could have them—but I would be temporarily off the payroll. The bureau chief assumed I had sufficient savings stashed away to get me through until September.

Yes, I did. I had come to the network before the days of budget tightening. I have never been a fiscally profligate person. I had enough to get me through the summer.

I almost had to physically grab and restrain the bureau chief to prevent him from phoning this glorious news to cost control central. I reminded him that this summer leave of absence was contingent upon several factors. He asked me when I could let him know for sure. Hoping he could contain his enthusiasm, I told him I should have the answer within the week.

An hour later I called Ronnie and made my reservations to fly to Cleveland. The fellow with the doughnut in the New England coffee shop would have to wait for some other correspondent to show up. It wouldn't be a long wait. There are plenty of us out there, and we're all assigned to the same stories.

Cleveland is nothing like Bristol; it's not even anything like Columbus. At the extreme northern end of the state, on Lake Erie, Cleveland has long had the image of a gritty industrial city. For those of us who grew up in central Ohio, Cleveland represented a very different world. All of the Cleveland jokes that still get told by lazy comedians may be based on one national stereotype of the city—a gray and dismal place where bodies of water tend to catch fire. People in Cleveland will tell you that reputation is outmoded, if indeed it ever was accurate; for those of us in central Ohio, though, Cleveland was never a joke. We were rather intimidated by it.

Cleveland was much more big-time than we were. To us, Cleveland had more in common with New York than it did with Bristol, or Columbus. A trip to Cleveland made Bristol people at least think about putting on a suit and tie. Now central Ohio is having better economic times than Cleveland, but for a lot of us the image remains. The impulse to laugh at Cleveland just never occurs. For generations, one of the places where people from central Ohio moved to a higher rung was Cleveland. When we heard that someone's father was being transferred to Cleveland, the signal was that he was on the ascent.

So when Ronnie married Marilyn Steele and they said that they were going to live in Cleveland, we didn't regard it as him being just up the road in Ohio. He was in a separate universe. At Ronnie's wedding, when the ceremony was over and Michael and I went back to our hotel rooms, we felt that something had changed. Cleveland was a smoke-stack city, where big and important things happened, and now Ronnie was a part of it. His life was going to be a little savvier than ours. I remember the wedding reception—Michael and I looking around at Sidney Steele's friends, Cleveland manufacturing guys with money. We might as well have been invisible.

On this afternoon I got a United flight from Washington into Cleveland. Ronnie had told me to come to dinner at his house; I had said I'd meet him at his office if he wanted, but he said it was going to be a "crazy day." At home he'd be able to talk without interruptions.

My cab from Hopkins Airport got me there just before he arrived from work. Marilyn said that he'd be home any minute; he had called from the car to say he was on his way.

"You know," she said, "you've got him talking about this trip of yours."

The house was what you'd expect: carpeting you could comfortably sleep on and wake up without a sore back, furniture that looked as if it was lifted from some Scottish castle, a huge pool out in back. Marilyn manifestly belonged here; you could look into her face and, somewhere in there, find a girl who must have once resembled all the girls we went to school with. Now, though, you knew that she could walk into a store and have the clerks calling her "ma'am" and pronouncing it with conviction. Her house seemed like somebody's mother's house to me—where do you buy furniture like that?—but it wasn't somebody's mother's house. It was Marilyn's house.

"Would you have a problem with him going?" I said.

"Ronnie works hard," Marilyn said. "Ronnie deserves to relax." I got the distinct impression that if we did it, Marilyn would make it through the summer just fine. I didn't envision her sitting at the front window, lighting candles for her husband.

I heard Ronnie's car pull into the driveway. He came in through the kitchen. If I could look at Marilyn and sense that she fit in perfectly here, I looked at Ronnie and would have believed it if someone had told me that he was the handyman, except for some reason the handyman was wearing a $1,200 suit. He opened the refrigerator door and pulled out a beer, but he could have been someone who was just passing through.

"How was your flight?" he said. A guy shows up at your house to make a case for your leaving for three months, you'd think there might be some tension. But with Ronnie, it was "How was your flight?" And he meant it. There was no hidden subtext. Oh—you've come to tell me to leave my family for the summer. How was your flight?

The cook served us chicken salad in the dining room; Ronnie and Marilyn's son and daughter, who looked more like Ronnie than like Marilyn, ate silently, as if dinner with us was a task to be completed as quickly as possible, and they left the table after no more than twelve minutes. As expensive and elegant as the house was, Ronnie at the head of the table seemed as if he could be munching a pizza in some freeway-exit dive. It was as if he couldn't see what was around him here, or just didn't choose to.

"So tell him your idea, Ronnie," Marilyn said after the kids had left.

Ronnie stood up, went to the kitchen, and got himself another beer. As he returned, he said, "Here's what I've been thinking. A couple of years ago we went down to Florida and chartered a yacht. I mean, not just a yacht—this boat was big."

"It slept twelve," Marilyn said.

"It had a captain, a crew, a cook—everything," Ronnie said. "You charter through this ship brokerage, and everything is included. So I'm thinking, we charter it for the summer. Just for the three of us. We live out on the water."

"The whole summer on the boat?" I said.

"We fish, we get tan . . ." Ronnie said.

Somehow it instantly felt wrong. It took me a moment to figure out why.

"What do you think?" Marilyn said. "The three of you on the boat."

"I don't know, Ronnie," I said.

"Now you don't want to go?" he said. "I've got Marilyn talked into it."

"I want to go," I said. "But the boat . . ."

"The boat is beautiful," Marilyn said. "It's like a hotel."

"Do you remember the overnight at Lake Hope?" I said to Ronnie.

He started to laugh. "That was nuts," he said.

When we were sophomores at Bristol, this sort of high school fraternity we belonged to had a camping trip in a wooded park near Lake Hope, about an hour away from where we lived. All four classes of the fraternity were there—freshmen, sophomores, juniors, and seniors—and it was one of the first occasions we had been together at night with guys in the classes ahead of us. We were a little in awe of them; all during the years we were growing up, they had experienced everything just before we did—first beers, first driver's licenses, first chemistry labs. It was as if Bristol was a giant baseball team, and we were always in the on-deck circle right behind them.

So we all went on the overnight at Lake Hope. Ronnie and Michael and I and some other guys from our class were in a tent, and in the middle of the night it started raining, hard. Here we were, surrounded by forest, and the rain was pounding against the top of the tent and mud was seeping up through the bottom, and it was entirely dark and we were alone. And then we heard this chanting start.

The chanting was coming from up the hill. We stuck our heads outside in the storm. We could hear the voices:

"Raise a little hell, raise a little hell, fuck, fuck, fuck, fuck, raise a little hell . . ."

Coming down the hill were some of the juniors. Mark Vigoda, the Graham twins . . . guys who, before that night, we had never imagined spending time with. They were the guys who had already done everything that we'd be doing the next year; they were destined to have that leg up on us forever. Now they were coming down the hill, in their underwear, covered with mud from the downpour.

"Raise a little hell, raise a little hell, fuck, fuck, fuck, fuck, raise a little hell . . ."

They burst into our tent, knocking it over. They were carrying some supplies from the cookout we'd had at dinner—mostly bottles of ketchup and mustard. They opened the bottles and started flinging the stuff at us. It was pitch-black except for the moon, and the ketchup and mustard were flying through the air, and Ronnie grabbed one of the bottles and began to heave mustard at the Graham twins, and we were laughing so hard we couldn't stand up, the mud and the mustard and the ketchup coating us. Our tent had collapsed, we didn't know who else might be in the woods, but for some reason we felt safe. No one was responsible for us here, but we were together, and we felt older because Mark Vigoda and the Graham twins were here and laughing, too. If our parents had known we were out in the storm they would have been frantic, but the rain suddenly got more fierce and we thought that was even funnier. It was anarchy but it was easy and innocent anarchy; we were all together, self-contained, in charge of our own night. Vigoda and the Grahams motioned for us to join them as they ran toward the tents where the freshmen were—the freshmen who probably never thought they would be able to spend time with us, because we had always been a year more advanced than they. Filthy and wet, we ran through the woods: "Raise a little hell, raise a little hell . . ."

"I don't want to have a boat with a captain and a chef," I said to Ronnie at the dinner table. "We've got to be our own captains."

Ronnie was nodding. It was possible that he understood.

"But where will you go?" Marilyn said.

"I don't know," I said. "That's part of it. I just don't know."

"With the boat you wouldn't even have to plan what you were going to do all day," she said.

"Believe me, it's not going to be so complicated that we have to do much planning," I said.

"I've already told some of my friends about your idea," she said. "You know what they all say? They say that it sounds like the three of you are running away from something."

"They're wrong," I said. "We're not going to be running away from anything. We're going to be running to something."

"Running to what?" she said.

"I'm not sure," I said. "I guess that's what we're going to find out."

"I was going to pay for the boat," Ronnie said.

"That would have been very nice of you," I said.

"Really," he said. "I was. The summer was going to be on me."

"It still can be," I said.

"You want me to pay for everything?" he said.

"Not for me," I said. "But there's no way Michael is going to be able to afford three months of this."

"Michael has told you yes?" Marilyn said.

"Not yet," I said. That was going to come next. I was sure of one thing: It was going to be easier to persuade Michael to go off for the summer than to persuade him to let Ronnie pay for it. Michael is a lot of things, and one of those things is that he is a very proud man.

Michael and I walked up Main Street toward the Bristol Grille. This was just after dusk the next night; I had told Ronnie that I was going to Bristol, and that I'd let him know when I had some news.

"Do you know what your daughter said when I called to tell you I was coming?" I said.

"What?" Michael said.

"I asked for you, and she said, 'He's not home now. He's at the Pontiac dealer.'"

Michael's chuckle confirmed he understood. When we were kids, Michael's dad had driven a Pontiac—a big blue Bonneville. White seat covers. Michael's dad was never a very racy guy, but the white upholstery in the blue Bonneville was pretty cool. For some reason, that car was always in the shop. Michael's dad ran a grocery, and he never had time to take the car in during the day, so after the store would close for the evening he would take the car to the dealership. He was constantly finding something wrong with it. I'd have dinner with my family at home, and I'd call Michael and ask if he wanted to go somewhere, and he'd say, "I don't have a car. My dad's got the car down at the Pontiac dealership."

And now Michael's daughter was telling me that he had his own Pontiac down at the dealership.

"Did Leslie understand why you thought that was funny?" Michael said.

"Of course not," I said. "She's your daughter. She's not going to think its ironic that you're at the Pontiac dealer. That's what dads do. Go to Pontiac dealers."

When I had arrived in Bristol that afternoon, I'd told Michael that Ronnie was willing to do it—to take the summer off and hit the road with us. I had also said that Ronnie had offered to pay for the summer. I left out that I was going to be paying my own way; I tried to give the impression that Ronnie was going to take care of everything for all of us. I had tried to be offhanded about it; I think the phrase I'd used was "Ronnie's going to put the whole thing on his American Express card."

So we walked along Main Street. Getting the summer months off wasn't going to be a problem for Michael—as a teacher at Bristol High School, he had the summer off anyway. But I knew that the idea of him taking Ronnie's charity—and that's how Michael would see it, as charity—was another matter entirely. Michael wasn't buying my implication that Ronnie would be paying my way too; he knew the truth, and he also knew that, Bristol being Bristol, everyone else would know it by the time we were past the city limits.

"What's the big deal?" I said. "At dinner at Ronnie's house last night, he was talking about Robert Gunderson. Do you remember Gunderson?"

"He went to Whiteside?" Michael said. "Basketball player?"

"Right," I said. "Now he's up in Cleveland. He's a friend of Ronnie's. Gunderson is expanding his business. He told Ronnie he was 'short of capital.' And Ronnie wrote him a check for fifty thousand dollars."

"So he invested in Gunderson's company," Michael said.

"He wrote a check," I said. "Ronnie's Ronnie. You can call it an investment if you want to. What he did was write a check for fifty thousand. And it's no different from when he would lend one of us five dollars for dinner when we were all in Bristol. The only difference is, the five bucks came from his dad, and the fifty thousand came from Marilyn's dad."

"What's the point?" Michael said.

"If he can spend fifty thousand dollars on Robert Gunderson's new building, he can buy some plane tickets and rent some hotel rooms for you," I said. "He wants to do it. You don't feel bad about the fifty thousand for Gunderson. You shouldn't feel bad about letting him do the summer for you."

"The investment with Gunderson may pay off for Ronnie," Michael said.

"So may the summer," I said.

We got to the Bristol Grille. When we were growing up, Bristol had been dry—no liquor sales were allowed anywhere within the city limits—but at some point in the last five years the city council had approved a variation that allowed the Bristol Grille to open. It's the kind of place that features grilled fish, charbroiled sandwiches, "gourmet pizzas"—a white-tablecloth place that wants to be casual yet offer fancy dining at the same time. You see restaurants like this in most cities, but Bristol never had one before, because without a liquor license it didn't make economic sense.

Next to the main dining room was a separate area with a big wooden U-shaped bar. Michael and I found two adjacent stools and each ordered a beer. The place was already beginning to fill up for the evening.

"You wonder what Bristol would have been like when we were growing up if our parents and their friends had been able to drink in town," Michael said.

"They did," I said. "They drank at home. Or at each other's houses."

"Or they'd go over to Millview," he said. "Or to Rockton." Millview and Rockton were two nearby towns, somewhat more blue-collar than Bristol; from what I remembered, the bars along the main drags in Millview and Rockton were pretty scuzzy-looking places, at least from the outside.

"You think some of our parents' friends were hanging out in those joints?" I said.

"I guarantee it," Michael said.

"But don't you think they'd be embarrassed if anyone saw them there?" I said.

"That's probably one of the reasons that Bristol was always dry," he said. "The only Bristol people who would see a person drinking at one of those Millview or Rockton places were other Bristol people who'd driven over. And they weren't going to say anything."

"Well, at least at this place, no one has to drive home on the highway drunk," I said.

"Yeah, but if someone gets drunk and embarrasses himself here, there's no buffer zone," Michael said. "You make a fool of yourself here, it's like doing it on your front lawn, with all your neighbors watching. The word spreads pretty fast."

"I don't know," I said. "This seems like a nice place to me. It makes Bristol feel a little different. I mean, look at that."

I nodded toward a piano where a woman was playing a jazz tune; two men with horns—one a saxophone, one a clarinet—were accompanying her. Seven or eight people were gathered around, watching and listening. The woman at the piano was a professional entertainer—a picture of her was mounted inside a glass case near the front door along with a sign saying that she appeared here four nights a week—but the two men clearly were amateurs. They were playing with her for the fun of it, and they weren't bad.

"Who would have guessed that Bristol had jazz musicians living in town?" I said. "Pretty exotic. It wasn't like this when we were kids."

"Look closely at those guys," Michael said.

"What?" I said, looking.

"You don't recognize them?" he said.

I couldn't place them.

"They were two classes behind us," Michael said. "They played in the Bristol High School marching band. They come here almost every night. I think those are the same instruments they used to play on the field at halftime of the football games."

"Well, it's still sort of nice," I said. "So what if they went to Bristol with us? That's what's so great about Bristol. How many places do you have guys from the marching band still playing music for people in town twenty-five years later? I'm telling you, Michael . . . I was walking around this afternoon, past Gebhardt's Drugstore and the public library and the Memorial Circle, and I was thinking that the one reason you might not go with Ronnie and me this summer is that things are too good here."

"Right," he said.

"I'm serious," I said. "It was just so peaceful on the streets this afternoon. I could have wandered around all night."

"Ben, Bristol isn't a theme park," he said.

"I didn't say that it was a theme park."

"But you think it is," he said. "You blow in here once or twice a year, and you stroll around and think how nice and safe it feels, and you think it's some sort of theme park. But it isn't. It may be a theme park to you, but I live here. You walk past the elementary school and have all these nostalgic thoughts about walking down the hallways when we were kids. But it's not nostalgic to me. I drop my own children off at that school every day. I go to PTA meetings in that school. I go to meetings with my kids' teachers in that school when their report cards come out and their grades aren't so good. And a few of the teachers who taught us are still there, and when our eyes meet there are all kinds of unspoken things going on. Because now I'm one of them. I may teach next door at the high school, but on payday all of us get the same light blue checks in the same light blue envelopes from the Bristol Board of Education. Me and Miss Tybor and Ralph Watson. They taught us, and now I'm one of them and I know exactly how little they make, because I'm making the same thing. Bristol isn't some hazy dream for me to walk around in, Ben. I pay my bank loan here. I go to the doctor here."

"So you wouldn't mind getting out of here for the summer," I said.

"I would die to get out of here for the summer," he said.

"And you wouldn't feel bad about Ronnie helping to pay the freight," I said.

He didn't say anything for a moment. The two guys from the marching band were playing "Satin Doll" along with the pianist.

"I figure I can feel bad about it later," he said.

"You're not worried that people will think that it's odd for you to take off?" I said.

"Hey, I'm starting to act crazy anyway," he said, laughing. "Ellen asked me to pick up a jar of peanut butter at Fleer's Foods this afternoon. We always eat regular peanut butter. But today I rolled the dice and lived life in the fast lane. I bought a jar of chunky."

We walked back to his house; now the streetlights were on. Ellen and the two girls were sitting out on the front stoop, waiting for us.

The kids ran out, each of them grabbing one of Michael's hands. "We got some ice cream at Swendell's," Laura, the younger one, said. "Mint chocolate chip."

"Where is it?" Michael said.

"The kitchen," she said. Bristol families have been going to Swendell's during the summer for more than fifty years. It used to be just a small white shack with screen windows; you'd stand out in the heat of the day, and you could smell the cold sweetness coming out of those screens. The high school kids who worked scooping cones at Swendell's always had homemade ice cream coating their forearms all the way up to their elbows. There was never a second when there wasn't at least one customer outside placing an order. In recent years the place had been expanded; now there's an inside section, where you can order at a counter and sit at a table. But habits die hard in Bristol. In the summer, even when there's no one waiting to order at the counter inside, people line up outside in front of the screen windows. Some people swear that the ice cream tastes better when they order it outside.

"Come on," Michael said to the girls. They walked into the house, toward the kitchen.

I sat on the front stoop next to Ellen.

"You mad at me?" I said.

"For what?" she said.

"You know," I said.

Some boys on bikes rode by and Ellen waved to them. "I think that one in front has a crush on Leslie," she said. "They come by here around twenty times a night."

"Ellen?" I said.

She let out a breath.

"Michael and I have never been apart for more than a week since we got married," she said.

"And you don't want him to go," I said.

"For me, I don't want him to go," she said. "For him, I want him to go more than anything in the world."

That second part surprised me.

"Ben, you don't know how hard it can get for Michael in this town," she said.

"If you told him that you wanted him to stay here this summer, he'd stay," I said.

"I know," she said. "That's why I'm not going to."

One of the girls called from the kitchen: "We're scooping some ice cream for you guys, too."

"We'll be right in," Ellen called.

She reached over and held my hand, as if to signal that we were compatriots. "Some couples in Bristol give each other BMWs and diamond bracelets," she said. "Anytime there's a special occasion, they buy something big. Michael and I are never going to be in a position to do that. But this is something I can give him. I think it's important that he gets out for a while and sees some things other than Bristol things. I want him to have this summer. But, Ben, it's going to be lonely for me here."

"He'll be back," I said. I hoped it didn't sound flippant. It wasn't supposed to be.

Ellen kept holding my hand, and then she let go and we got up and walked inside toward the ice cream.

Later, after the girls were in bed, Michael and Ellen and I were sitting on the front stoop again. I was telling them the same Lake Hope story I had mentioned to Ronnie; somehow the memory of that night in the rain and the mud, charging up and down the hills between the trees, symbolized to me the essential fantasy of kids being on their own, with no rules, the beneficiaries of total if temporary freedom.

"But there are consequences, too," Michael said. "Remember Greg Grayson?"

"What about him?" I said.

"The eclipse," Michael said.

"The eclipse was that same trip?" I said. "That's right, it was."

"Yep," Michael said.

The day we went to Lake Hope was the day that there was supposed to be an eclipse of the sun. There had been stories in the newspaper about it for weeks—tips on ways to make cardboard-and-paper devices so you could see the shadow of the eclipse without looking directly into it, safety warnings about the damage you could do to your eyes by staring at the sun, advice from scientists and doctors about the most cautious methods for experiencing the eclipse without putting your eyesight at risk.

Greg Grayson's father had given him repeated lectures about the dangers of the eclipse. Mr. Grayson made it sound as if even looking momentarily at the eclipse was akin to riding to earth straddled atop a hydrogen bomb. Before we left for the overnight, Mr. Grayson made Greg promise that under no circumstances would he look at the eclipse.

When we were at Lake Hope, though, we were so wrapped up in swimming and fishing that we almost forgot about the eclipse. We were out in rowboats on the lake when someone noticed that something weird was happening with the sun. Someone was wearing a watch, and checked. Yep. It was the right time for the eclipse to be visible in Ohio.

So we stopped our fishing and looked up at the sun. It was no big deal. For the next few minutes we would look up for a couple of seconds, then look away, then look up again. It just felt like a cloudy afternoon. Soon enough we were swimming in Lake Hope again. The eclipse wasn't all that thrilling, really.

Especially compared to what happened that night—the juniors charging down the hill at us, and the tent collapsing, and the mud and the ketchup and the mustard. Now, *that* was history. That was memorable. So when the school bus that had taken us to Lake Hope pulled back into Bristol the next day, we were so happy and so excited and so full of our frenzied independence that the eclipse already seemed as if it had happened a thousand years ago. Some of our parents were waiting in the school parking lot, where the bus dropped us off, and we ran down the steps, still caked with mud, and we were yelling and laughing, and Mr. Grayson was peering past the rest of us, looking for Greg, and when he spotted him he called:

"How was it?"

And Greg, who had loved the overnight, yelled out to his dad: "Great!"

And Mr. Grayson, his voice full of an enthusiasm that I now realize was a trap, called: "Did you see the eclipse?"

And Greg, still so happy, called: "Yeah!"

And Mr. Grayson grounded him. Just like that. To this day I think it was a setup; I think Mr. Grayson acted excited to see his son just so he could trick Greg into admitting he had looked at the eclipse.

Greg Grayson was grounded for two weeks—two entire weeks during the summer—because he had looked at the eclipse. As far as I know he was the only person to suffer from that eclipse. His eyesight was fine. He just couldn't leave his house at night for two weeks.

We sat on Michael's front stoop now, and we related the story of Greg Grayson and the eclipse to Ellen, and she said, "He never should have told the truth."

"He didn't know," Michael said. "He didn't know his dad was setting him up."

She looked at him, teasing. "That's the difference between you and Ben," she said to Michael. "Ben thinks of the overnight and the image he gets is of freedom and you guys chasing each other through the mud. You think of the same trip and you think of some kid getting punished for looking at the eclipse."

"I remember both things," Michael said.

I went for a walk after they had gone upstairs. Bristol is one of the only places I know where people still have no qualms about going out for a walk after midnight. Tonight, though, I was alone on the streets.

I went past Swendell's. It was closed for the night; the screen windows were locked until tomorrow, when the lines for ice cream would start forming just after nine o'clock. Mostly little kids and their moms, so early in the day. By that time I'd be on a plane for Washington. I had a lot of arrangements to take care of at the office, and goodbyes to make.

Six

"YOU HUNGRY YET?" Ronnie said.

"Not really," Michael said.

"I am," I said from the back seat.

Ronnie was behind the wheel. Michael was next to him. In back, I was reading a copy of *USA Today* I had picked up when we'd stopped for gas an hour before. The deal we had made was that we would take shifts. Driver, shotgun, back-seat rider—a continuing summer-long rotation. It was a routine we had developed many years ago, and we had agreed to go with it again. Although I knew that, within a few days, another part of the old routine would set in. Ronnie would end up driving more than his fair share, because he liked it; I would end up driving the least, because I've never been all that good at it—not only do I not enjoy it, but the other two would just as soon not have me in control of the car.

"Well, do we wait for dinner, or do we stop somewhere?" Ronnie said. His left arm was sticking out the driver's-side window; this was our first day on the road, but his arm was already getting red. He was wearing a short-sleeved tennis shirt. It wouldn't be long before he had one of those farmer's tans that we all used to sport during the long summers of cruising.

"Let's just get a Coke or something," Michael said.

We were not on the interstate; we had decided to veer off and drive through some towns. Up ahead we could see a swimming pool. We slowed down; a sign said that it was the Harborville Community Pool. We were still in Ohio, heading west.

Ronnie pulled into the gravel parking lot. None of us had ever been in Harborville.

"Do you think you have to be a member to get in this place?" Michael said.

"We're not going swimming," Ronnie said. "We're just going to buy Cokes."

"Yeah, but if it's like Bristol, you can't get into the community swimming pool unless you have a summer membership," Michael said.

"Am I going to have to go through this the whole summer?" Ronnie said, rolling his eyes. "We'll get in, all right?"

The three of us climbed out of the car. We'd been riding for two hours. It ached a little bit to unbend in the afternoon sun. Somehow this was an aspect I didn't recall from our summers as kids—stiff joints caused by sitting in the same position too long inside the car. I could see Ronnie and Michael slowly flexing their arms and legs, too.

Little children with their parents, and teenagers in groups, were walking across the parking lot to the entrance gate. At the gate a kid in shorts and a Harborville Recreation Department T-shirt was checking membership cards.

"I told you," Michael said.

"Relax," Ronnie said. "We're not trying to break into Fort Knox."

We had left Bristol around 8 A.M. Ronnie's original idea had been to bring one of his own cars for the summer, but at the last minute we decided to do rentals; that way, if there were times we wanted to get on an airplane, we wouldn't have to worry about leaving the car behind. We'd just chuck the rental and get another one in the next city. Ronnie had rented a Ford (we had talked him out of a Lincoln Town Car; Michael had said, "This is supposed to be a vacation, not a motorcade").

I had packed my bags in Washington and flown back to Bristol via Columbus; Ronnie had driven down from Cleveland. We had picked Michael up at his house. Ellen and the girls had helped him carry his bags to the car, and had helped lift them into the trunk. When Ellen reached into the trunk, to carefully arrange Michael's bags so that they wouldn't get crushed, he and she looked at each other and for a moment I thought he was going to pull the bags out and walk right back into the house. But he didn't; he hugged her and the kids, and we climbed in and drove off.

"Stop it," Ronnie had said as we drove away from the house and Michael leaned out the window and kept waving goodbye. Michael was twisted completely around in the front seat.

When he had finally pulled himself back into the car, Ronnie said, "You're not going off to war, you know. You can go home anytime you want."

"Just drive," Michael had said.

We walked up to the gate at the Harborville Community Pool, and Ronnie approached the kid checking membership cards.

"We're just going in to get something to eat," Ronnie said.

"Are you members or guests?" the kid said.

"We're just hungry," Ronnie said.

"None of you have cards?" the kid said. He must have been fifteen or sixteen.

"Look," Ronnie said, not unfriendly but clearly not ready to walk away. "How much does it cost for a member to bring a guest?"

"It's a dollar a guest," the kid said.

"Are you a member?" Ronnie said.

"Yes, sir," the kid said. "Our family is."

"Here, then," Ronnie said, digging into his pocket. He came out with a five-dollar bill, and handed it to the kid. "Take this. We'll be your guests."

"I don't know . . . ," the kid said.

"Go ahead," Ronnie said.

"I don't believe this," Michael said to me. "Ronnie's negotiating with this poor kid."

The kid was clearly confused. Ronnie patted him on the shoulder and we walked in.

"You want me to call *Business Week* and give them the exclusive on how you hardballed that deal?" I said.

"You would rather have gotten back in the car and looked for another place?" Ronnie said.

Inside the fence, we saw maybe two hundred people, almost all in bathing suits, more than half of them children and teenagers. The snack bar was at the far end of the pool. As we walked toward it I looked around, and what I got was the sense of a curtain going up.

Girls and boys, in groups of two and three, were staking out their territory for the summer. At a pool like this there is a certain feeling in early June—it's almost as though a famous and long-running summer-stock stage play is beginning, and the play is guaranteed to be a hit, except that the script is going to be written during the course of the play itself. The play was a hit last summer, and for scores of summers before. Some of these kids who were pulling chairs tightly together—and thus making the unspoken point that they were best friends, and would be in their own specific subsections of the pool deck every sunny day until September—had undoubtedly been here last year, and the year before. For some of the younger ones, this might be the first summer—at least the first summer without their parents watching them from their own chairs and lounges several rows back.

You could tell who the first-timers were; they were a little tentative in picking out their chairs. They were the youngest of the kids who were on their own; they sneaked glances at the older teenagers, the ones who presumably were part of recent legend here at this pool. Last summer these youngest ones were brought to the pool by their moms and dads; now they were entering this town's summer pipeline. They would have four or five or six summers here at the pool, creating little legends of their own, and then they would leave town, either never to come back or to come back as adults—adults who might as well be invisible to the pool teenagers.

As we were—three invisible men heading toward the snack bar. "Look at that," Michael said, nodding toward some chairs just over to the left.

Three guys—they were little guys, they might as well have been Michael and Ronnie and me when we were twelve or thirteen—had put their towels down on some wood-slatted lounges. Three older guys, with the look of a high school football backfield, had pulled themselves out of the pool and sauntered over to the same lounges. We couldn't hear what was being said—the air was filled with that dense summer pool sound of screaming kids and splashing water and background music and announcements over the PA system—but the scenario was clear. The older guys were motioning to the younger guys, telling them that the lounges were theirs. The younger guys—skinny, fresh-faced kids—were just looking up. It was easy to tell that they weren't going to make a fuss. And sure enough, they picked up their towels and moved on.

"They don't even feel bad about it," Michael said. Indeed, rather than seeming put down, the younger kids were laughing and whispering to each other.

"Why should they?" I said. "This was their first brush with the famous." The fact that the older guys had made them move was almost irrelevant. What was important was the older guys—the football backfield, if that's who they were—had initiated contact with these kids. Never mind that it was latently hostile contact. Last year these young kids were sitting with their moms. Today, at the beginning of the summer, they had officially, if somewhat sheepishly, joined a different world.

"They'll be talking about it tonight," Michael said. "They'll be telling their friends."

And they would be. The friends of the young kids would be hanging on every word of their description of what had just transpired—and the kids would inevitably heighten the particulars of the interchange until it sounded like a heavyweight championship fight.

"Talk about confidence," I said, gesturing to the lounges where this had just taken place. The older guys, having reclaimed the lounges, had left them unadorned and had returned to the water. The unspoken message was that they didn't have to worry about reserving the lounges by putting towels or shirts on top of them. They could reserve them merely by saying the lounges were theirs. It wasn't that they were bullies; it was just that, without question, they were high school seniors-to-be. This was their year to rule. By July no one would even think to sit on their lounges; by July every kid in town would know who those lounges belonged to.

"It never changes," Michael said.

He was right in more than one way. Not only does this kind of thing never change; it never really goes away. Only the setting progresses. When I was a young newspaper reporter, I was sent out on my first presidential campaign—the Nixon-McGovern campaign. I was quite charged up to be sent on this particular assignment, although it would not have done to display my excitement. On a trip west with President Nixon we were to leave from Andrews Air Force Base. The press, except for a handful of reporters, would not fly on Air Force One, but would travel on an accompanying press plane, a 727 that had been chartered from United. We had been instructed to be at Andrews at 9 A.M., but I had arrived at 8, just so I would be sure not to be left behind.

The Secret Service guys checked my credentials, searched my luggage, and cleared me to get onto the plane. It was configured like any other commercial jet—a small first-class cabin, with coach behind. There was no assigned seating. Only a handful of other reporters were on board when I got on, and first class was empty.

I should have known something was up—the other reporters who were on the plane had chosen seats back in coach. But, congratulating myself for having the foresight to arrive so early, I grabbed an aisle seat in first class and waited for everyone else to get to the airport.

When the others did show up, they filed past me and filled up the coach section. The seats around me in first class remained unclaimed. By this time I was more than a little confused, but I knew no one to ask. And then, just before the doors closed, a contingent of men, some of them carrying camera equipment, came onto the plane.

"Hi," one of them said, not at all unpleasantly. "I'm afraid these are reserved."

The men were from CBS News; they were the network's traveling White House crew. Cameraman, sound man, lighting man, producer, radio correspondent, radio producer, backup technicians . . . it was clear that these men were accustomed to flying all over the world with the President. The network's chief White House correspondent—it was Dan Rather at the time, Walter Cronkite was still anchoring—was flying on Air Force One with President Nixon as part of the rotating press pool. But these men, Rather's colleagues on the CBS varsity, were on the press plane, and had laid claim on the seats.

The one who had spoken to me didn't need to say anything more. He knew from looking at me that I wasn't going to put up a commotion, and he wasn't being combative about it, anyway. Someday maybe I'd get my turn.

So I got up—what was I going to do, argue with them?—and went to the rear of the plane. Almost every seat had been taken. I found a middle seat near the galley in the back, which was where I sat for the four-hour flight.

I wasn't particularly unhappy about it (although I sensed that the older reporters sitting next to me were—right up until the moments before takeoff, when I had come trudging down the aisle, they had thought that they had lucked out and had an empty middle seat to stretch into during the long flight). I was a little embarrassed not to have known, but I figured it came with the territory. Next time I wouldn't make the same mistake.

It wasn't all that different from what we had just seen happen to the three kids at the community pool. They wouldn't be making the same mistake again, either. Of course the football backfield hadn't felt any need to mark the lounges as reserved. The lounges were reserved because they said they were reserved. Case closed, no hard feelings, and meet you at the deep end.

The snack bar was one of the old kinds—when you ordered a hamburger, the guy in the paper hat behind the counter actually threw a piece of meat onto the hot grill just for you, instead of popping something into a microwave. He slid his scraper under my burger, wrapped it in a piece of flimsy white paper, handed it to me, and took my money. Michael and Ronnie were just drinking Cokes. We sat at a white metal picnic table with a view of the pool.

"I sort of like this place," Michael said, looking around.

"We can stay here all summer if you want," Ronnie said.

"I do like it," Michael said.

There was a lifeguard tower about halfway down the length of the pool, right where the shallow end dipped suddenly deeper. Some girls were flirting with the lifeguard; he had some of that zinc stuff on his nose, and the girls put water on their hands and flung it at him, playing. He looked like a college student on vacation—maybe a guy who had grown up in this town, and had hung out at this pool, now adapting to a new role.

And he was playing the role pretty well. If he were still a high school kid at the pool—if, for example, he were one of the members of the football backfield—he would probably have responded to the girls flinging the water. Now, though, it wouldn't have been cool for him to participate in the game the girls were initiating, or even to acknowledge that he was aware of their presence. For this summer, he had been elevated—literally, the lifeguard tower was about five feet high—so he toyed with the whistle that hung from a lanyard around his neck and allowed only the slightest smile to show on his face. Just as a signal that he did, indeed, know that the girls were down there below him.

"Which one do you think?" Ronnie said. He was talking about the girls.

"Which one he'll end up with?" Michael said.

"Yeah," Ronnie said.

One of the girls had a startlingly grownup figure; she was wearing a tiny white bikini, hanging out of it, really.

"I think definitely that one," Ronnie said, meaning her.

"I don't know," Michael said.

The other girls looked more their ages—looked more like girls who were halfway through high school. Through the luck of genetics, and the conscious selection of that white bathing suit, the one girl, although she was clearly their classmate, appeared to live in a separate cosmos.

"It won't be her," I said, already trying to envision the plot of this swimming pool's summer stage play.

"How do you know?" Ronnie said.

"It won't be her because it's supposed to be her," I said. "It would come too easy for her. She won't stay awake at night thinking about the lifeguard. By the end of the day she'll have had fifteen or twenty other guys at the pool act nice to her. I'd say it will be her friend in the yellow."

One of the girls in the group was tall and skinny, in a yellow one-piece suit. She stayed toward the back; she wasn't talking to the lifeguard or actively splashing him. But she wasn't taking her eyes off him, either. She seemed to be too shy to say anything.

"She'll be the one," I said.

I didn't know, of course, and we wouldn't be around to find out. But it was certain that the fellow with the zinc on his nose would develop at least one romance at this pool before the summer ended. Some things in the stage play were not subject to change. He'd be here every day— or at least six days a week, the recreation department gave him one day off—and after a while, after the initial joking parries were over and that beginning-of-summer tingle had died down and settled into a sun-soaked routine, one of the girls would decide she was sick of the kids her own age who were always showing off and being too loud.

I had a feeling the skinny girl in the yellow had already, perhaps without even knowing it, begun to make that decision. Every day she would look for the guy with the zinc on his nose, and she would get a sad feeling in her stomach on the mornings when she showed up and realized it was his day off. Her friends would ask her what was wrong, and she would say nothing, nothing was wrong. And the next day, when she would see him, she would be happy, and maybe after she had gone through this enough times she would work up the nerve to tell him that she'd noticed he wasn't there the day before.

And he would say that, yeah, he'd had the day off—he was at the juncture in his life when talking about a day off carried a lot of weight, implicit was that he was working here and getting paid for it, unlike the boys her age, who were here because they wanted to be here; they had nothing better to do, but he was a man and he had a job and he came here every day because it was his obligation and because the town, through its recreation department, considered him vital to the running of the pool and gave him a salary to come here—and the girl would repeat that she'd noticed he hadn't been around.

And if this summer stage play followed anywhere close to the scripts of all the other summer stage plays before it, the guy with the zinc on his nose, upon hearing that the girl in the yellow bathing suit had taken note of his absence, would offer her some seemingly flippant yet beseechingly genuine variation of the phrase: "Miss me?" And the girl in the yellow bathing suit would redden and then say either "Yes" or "No"—which word didn't matter, they both already knew that she had missed him—and that would be the start of it. Probably the time when they first really spent hours together would be a rainy day at the pool— that's how it always works, on rainy days no one comes to the pool, except the lifeguards have to come just in case the weather clears up, and the girl, knowing this, would come, too, and they would talk all day. And once this started it would develop into something that all of her friends at the pool, and all the boys her own age, would whisper about all summer, and that one day twenty or thirty years later would be a memory that both the girl in the yellow bathing suit and the guy with the zinc on his nose would identify with this summer, each of them wondering what had become of the other.

Or maybe twenty or thirty years from now she and the lifeguard wouldn't be wondering what had become of each other—they would know, because they would be married to each other and living here in this town, maybe a little bit bored with each other, spending the afternoon at the community pool watching their own children do cannonballs into the deep end and not even thinking about the day when they first laid eyes on each other, he too cool to notice her, she too shy to speak.

She wasn't speaking now; she was standing at the back of the group while her friend in the too-small white bikini stood beneath the lifeguard tower with her arms raised, flinging the water upward and saying something that we couldn't hear above the high-pitched ambient wash of pool noise.

"What makes you think she'll be the one?" Ronnie said.

"I don't know," I said. "I may be wrong."

The three young kids—the ones who had been evicted from their lounges by the members of the football backfield—were waiting to order hamburgers from the fellow behind the counter with the paper hat. They hadn't even known that we had observed their fleeting poolside drama; they were jabbering to themselves trying to catch the attention of the burger cook. Next summer they wouldn't be on the low rung; next summer they'd have a year of tenure at the pool, and maybe in a few more years they'd be the football backfield, chasing younger kids from their lounges. And perhaps some year in the future they'd be Michael and Ronnie and me—three men in their forties who might as well be invisible at a community pool filled with kids too busy beginning their summer to think about what residual warmth the summer might someday provide them.

"You done?" Ronnie said.

"I'm done," I said, tossing the piece of paper that had been wrapped around my burger into a nearby trash can.

We walked out the gate toward Ronnie's rental car. We heard a voice: "Sir?"

It was the kid in charge of checking membership cards.

"Sir," the kid said to Ronnie, "you gave me too much. There are only three of you, right?"

He was holding out two one-dollar bills for Ronnie to take.

"You gave me a five," the kid said. "Here's your change."

"That's very honest of you," Ronnie said. "You go ahead and keep it."

"Really?" the kid said, brightening. He hadn't anticipated running into a high roller at the gatehouse of the pool.

"Have a good summer," Ronnie said to him.

"You, too," the kid said, staring at us as we crossed the gravel lot.

Seven

JUST BEFORE SUNDOWN Ronnie spotted a billboard for an expensive-sounding Italian restaurant. After leaving the swimming pool we had gotten back onto the freeway, where most of the billboards were advertising fast-food places or budget motels. This place, though, looked like it was serious dining.

"You really want to eat somewhere nice?" Michael said.

"This is our first night," Ronnie said. "We won't make a habit of it."

So we pulled off, and the maître d' led us to a table with four place settings. The afternoon, in the hours since departing the pool, had not been quite what I'd anticipated.

I suppose it was inevitable—the idea of the three of us setting out for the summer, as enticing as it had sounded, was a bit different from the reality of being in some car pointed up a freeway with no certain destination. I'm accustomed to having a specific place where I'm due at a specific time. Most people, once they work for a living, are like that; those are the rules of the game. Regardless of the details of your job, a timetable is always part of it. With my job, the timetable has centered on broadcast deadlines to make, and planes to catch. With Ronnie it has always been meetings and appointments, arranged by a secretary and kept on a calendar. With Michael the timetable is delineated by bells—the bells at Bristol High School that end one period and begin the next, the same bells he, and we, used to wait so restlessly for.

So in the car, I silently wondered what we were getting into. Here we were, on the first day of the journey—and I found myself sneaking glances at my watch. Force of habit—I had nowhere I had to be. But as the miles passed, every lull in the conversation, every song that played on the radio, hung in the air like a question mark. I kept waiting for one of the others to say it: What are we doing here?

But no one did. Michael came the closest. When Ronnie stopped for gas and the figure on the pump passed twenty dollars, Michael said, "It's hard to believe the Bristol bus was only a nickel."

On summer afternoons like this, when we were in elementary school, the Bristol bus was our main vehicle—both literally and metaphorically—for vagabondlike adventure. The Bristol bus was an anomaly, in that it didn't really go anywhere. Real buses took you into neighboring towns and suburbs, even all the way into Columbus. The Bristol bus merely made little uneven circles around Bristol. Since almost everyone in town had cars, the Bristol bus was just about always empty. There was no pressing need for it—it must have been the product of some contractual arrangement between the city of Bristol and the local transit authority. It was a nickel ride to nowhere, and Michael and I loved it.

On a summer day we'd go to the bus stop on Main Street, pull our nickels from our pants pockets, and get on. The Bristol bus was a full-sized bus, but if there were two or three other people on board, that was a lot. We'd drop our nickels into the contraption by the driver—he knew us by name—and we'd watch the coins tumble past the glass sides and clunk against the metal bottom, bouncing slightly. Then we'd pick our seats—always sitting next to each other, even when there was no one else on board, we were ten years old—and we'd see the sights.

Those sights never changed, but we savored them. The Shell gas station, the high school football stadium, Fleer's Foods, the police station—it didn't matter that we'd seen them all a thousand times. On the Bristol bus we could pretend that we were grownups. We had decided to go; we had paid the nickels. Our parents had no idea where we were—well, they did know, of course, they knew that we were on the Bristol bus, but we were out of their sight, they did not know precisely where the Bristol bus was along its route—and for us the Bristol bus might as well have been an ocean liner crossing the Atlantic. Had we thought to analyze why we liked that bus so much, the answer would have been simple—the Bristol bus, with its tightly circumscribed local route and its liberty from the four walls of our homes and the watchful gaze of our parents, was the perfect union of security and wanderlust. We were on our own, but we knew that in twelve minutes we'd be back where we started.

And if we decided we wanted to go around again, the driver would usually manage to forget to charge us another nickel.

Now, on this first leg of our summer, we knew that we wouldn't be circling around in twelve minutes. Rather than letting that knowledge calm us—the whole idea, after all, had been to give ourselves a summer without time constraints or geographic objectives—we were a little agitated by it. I'm used to trying to put a whole lifetime into thirty-seven hours or so, and then moving on to another assignment, another story. In their own lives, Ronnie and Michael were used to the same kind of regimen. It was going to take some adjusting, this concept of throwing all of that away. As we were escorted to our table in the Italian restaurant, I sensed that it was going to be more difficult than any of us had foreseen.

"I'm going to call home before we order," Michael said.

"We're going to go through this every night, right?" Ronnie said.

"Better get used to it," Michael said. He had promised Ellen and the girls that he would phone them once a day. Ellen had protested that it was too expensive, but the matter wasn't open to debate. "I'm not doing it for you," Michael had told her. "I'm doing it for me."

So while Ronnie and I waited at the table, Michael went off in search of a pay phone. After a few seconds had passed, Ronnie said, "I guess I should, too." And he got up to make his own call home.

Leaving me to accept the three menus from the waiter.

Before leaving Bethesda, I had gone over to see Nancy and Hannah. I'm still not used to the routine of having to make a reservation to see my own wife—ex-wife, although I can't get used to that phrase—and daughter. But the ground rules are that neither of us is expected to show up unannounced—if Nancy wants to come to my house or I want to go to hers, we have to phone first. So I had told her that I wanted to stop by before taking off for the summer.

Nancy was packing when I got there; she and Hannah were about to begin their summer at the shore.

I half wanted Nancy to chide me that I ought to take a film crew with me to make an anthropological documentary about arrested development. At least that would have been a reminder of the way things used to be between us. Nancy is a very smart woman, always has been, and if she'd jabbed me a little about the questionable wisdom of the trip, I would have understood, and even approved. When I first met Nancy it was as if she could read every self-doubt I had, and translate each into a one-liner that would make me smile.

That was a long time ago, though. When I got to her place she merely said that she hoped my summer would be a good one. She might as well have been thanking the house painters for touching up the window boxes and telling them that she'd see them next time something started peeling.

I went into Hannah's room. Out of her radio, something by Motley Crue was playing. She was straightening her dolls on top of her chest of drawers. They were the same dolls she'd been collecting since she was three or four; I knew those dolls by name: Jessica, Heather, Lauren, Samantha. I didn't want to startle her, so I made a noise before I walked through the door.

She looked around and smiled. The juxtaposition of what was going on in the room—the sound from the radio of the heavy-metal band singing of boisterous living on the rock-and-roll road, and the sight of Hannah making sure her dolls were in place—just about dissolved my heart. She's right on the cusp—at eight years old, she is just beginning to be intrigued by the world the music represents, yet is still enough of a child to care about her dolls. I looked at her and bit down hard on the inside of my mouth.

"Hi!" she said.

"I just wanted to say goodbye before you and Mom start your trip," I said. "I'm going away, too."

"Oh, yeah," she said, stepping back to examine the line of dolls from a properly panoramic focal point. "Mom told me."

She's so used to me being gone; to her, the summer with Michael and Ronnie was going to be no different from all my hurried trips for the network. Why should it be? To her, all it meant was that I wasn't going to be home.

I told her that I'd be talking to her during the summer, and writing her postcards.

"Will you send me some with shells on them?" she said. That was one of her new hobbies: collecting objects featuring likenesses of shells.

I said I would, and then the phone rang and she answered it. It has only been in the last couple of years that she has worked up the nerve to answer the telephone herself; she always preferred that Nancy or I do it.

"Hi!" she said into the receiver. She paused. "You're kidding!" she said. It was one of her friends; she sat down on her bed and started talking animatedly and excitedly, as if I weren't there. I wonder where she ever got that idea.

Sitting in the restaurant, I didn't know what was taking Michael and Ronnie so long. I should have been content to wait quietly for them at the table and enjoy the placid hours at the end of the day.

But placid hours have not had a prominent place in my life, at least not lately. So I told the waiter I'd be back, and I went to look for them. I don't know what I expected to accomplish; this was just another variation of punching the elevator button again when the car doesn't arrive quickly enough, or feeling the blood pressure shoot up when a cab doesn't start moving a millisecond after the traffic light turns back to green. On some level I hoped that at some point during the summer

I would get over this; it didn't promise to be a very relaxing expedition if I treated every momentary inconvenience and every pause in the day's activity as reason to launch inquiries and devise solutions. That didn't stop me from getting up to look for Ronnie and Michael, though.

Michael was coming back toward the table. I met him at the bar.

"Ellen and the girls were just on their way to Swendell's," he said, sounding as if he wished he was going with them.

"Ronnie's still talking to Marilyn?" I said.

"No, he already talked to her," Michael said. "She had a list of phone messages for him. He wrote them down and he's back there punching his credit card number into the phone."

"I thought he said he wasn't going to do that," I said.

"I know," Michael said. "But apparently there's some deal he's just wrapping up."

Just then Ronnie came around the corner of the bar, making some notes on a little leather-bound pad.

"Fucking scumballs," he said, apparently referring to one of the parties with whom he had just conversed.

"We don't want to hear it," I said to him.

"You wouldn't believe what these guys are trying to pull," he said.

"You're not supposed to be thinking about that stuff," I said.

At that moment I was wondering whether the whole trip was going to be a mistake. Here I was, wound up so tight after years of running on professional overdrive that even the prospect of waiting briefly for the two of them to finish their phone calls and return to the table was too much for me to countenance; here Michael was, his face and his voice betraying his doubts about spending so much time away from his family; here Ronnie was, a deal-doer on a pay phone. At a moment like that it seemed we were so different from the three people who had been best friends more than half a lifetime ago, that we had veered so far and swayed so dramatically from the parallel paths that we had begun together as children—at a moment like that it seemed we were really three strangers now, with nothing in common and nothing to find.

But then there was another moment. We resumed our places at the table, and the waiter announced his list of specials for the evening.

"Tonight we have an excellent four-cheese pasta with spinach leaves and basil," he said. "I'm also recommending the risotto with bay scallops, and the polenta capped with melted goat cheese."

I skimmed the menu. It was very elegant, and I didn't see anything I wanted. "Do you have anything like ravioli?" I said. "Just some ravioli with some meat in it?"

Ronnie looked up at the waiter. "Could you check in the kitchen to see if there's a can of Chef Boyardee you can heat up for this guy?'' he said.

He wasn't making fun. He knows me. The waiter was laughing, and he said, "Unfortunately I've seen our chef at work, and he's no Chef Boyardee. But I'll ask him to come as close as he can."

I was exactly where I wanted to be.

"What did you say came with the four-cheese pasta?" Ronnie said.

"Spinach leaves and basil," the waiter said.

"That's what I'll have," Ronnie said.

"Even as a kid, he could never get enough of spinach leaves and basil," I said to the waiter.

"When he wasn't scarfing down those polentas," Michael said.

"You know what we ought to do tonight?" Ronnie said a couple of hours later, as we were finishing the meal.

Neither Michael nor I replied, so Ronnie answered his own question.

"A marathon," he said.

"Oh, God," Michael said.

"I mean it," Ronnie said. "When's the last time you went on a marathon?"

It used to be a rite of the season. At least two or three times each summer, we would decide to go on marathons. We would get up one morning, stay up all that night, make it all the way through the next day and then not go to bed until late on the second evening. It was disorienting and exhausting and exhilarating; by the end of the marathon we'd be babbling to each other as if we were on laughing gas. The day after a marathon was over, we'd feel as if we'd been pounded on by mallets.

"Why don't we try the marathon in a couple of weeks," I said.

"No, let's do it tonight," Ronnie said. "We'll just drive all night. We can sleep tomorrow."

"I'm pretty tired," Michael said.

"That's the best time to do a marathon, if you don't remember," Ronnie said. "A marathon makes you blast right through your tiredness."

The waiter reappeared with a rolling dessert cart. He pointed out the puff pastries, the various cheesecakes, the mocha tortes.

"Great," Michael said. "I had all that meat sauce for dinner, and all that sweet butter on my bread. And now I'm going to shovel more cholesterol in me for dessert."

Too tired to do the marathon; too judicious to dive into the fat-laden dessert without speculating about the probable upshot.

"The way I figure it," I said, "we're all doomed anyway. We're fooling ourselves to think that eating right or getting enough rest and exercise is going to matter. Our doom was sealed many years ago."

"What are you talking about?" Michael said.

"The DDT trucks," I said.

Every time I saw references in the newspapers to the horrible effects of DDT—the effects that, in the 1970s, had resulted in DDT being banned from use as an insecticide in the United States—I could hardly believe that, as children, we regarded DDT as a joyful symbol of fun. I'm not sure which had a happier image—DDT or cotton candy.

As soon as summer arrived, and with it the return of warm-weather insects, every quiet neighborhood in America knew the sounds that indicated the DDT truck was coming. The sound started as a quiet rumbling several blocks away. It would get increasingly louder—the kids in the neighborhood would have sprinted off in search of it, just in case the DDT truck driver thought he could deprive us by turning away before he reached our street—and then when it was upon us all of our senses would be sated by the thick fog pouring out the back of the truck, and the overwhelming din of the truck's engine and the mechanical fogger, and the sweet, pungent smell of the DDT itself.

We would suck it in. Literally; we would run behind the truck, making sure that we were directly in the path of the fog, and we would swallow just as much of the DDT as we could. The fog was so dense that we couldn't even see each other; we might be just a foot or two away, but it was like being buried in a cloud. We'd use both arms to try to sweep away the DDT, knowing that this tactic wouldn't work, and we truthfully didn't want it to. We'd be laughing and jumping, eating that DDT for minutes on end; the DDT truck driver was like an ice-cream man. If our parents were concerned about anything, it was that we would run too close to the back of the truck and risk getting caught in the wheels. Every mother and father cautioned their children about staying clear of the wheels. None of them, that I recall, mentioned the perils of the DDT itself. And why should they have? They didn't know. The smell of DDT was the smell of summer. A happy summer cloud.

"Can you believe that?" Ronnie said.

"I've got one for you," Michael said. "Fluoroscope machines."

"The bone things?" Ronnie said.

"Green bones," Michael said.

Those have been banned now, too. Every shoe store featured fluoroscope machines that were designed to make sure children's shoes fit correctly. You would go to the shoe store with one of your parents, and there would be this big machine you were supposed to step onto—it was usually marked "X-Ray Fittings," a proud slogan for the modern age. The salesman would slip a pair of shoes on your feet, and then you would step onto a platform and slide your feet into a slot, and then you and the salesman and your mom and dad would peer down into a lens—and you would see the bones of your feet. Outlined in a neon green. You would be able to tell how snugly the shoes fit you.

A lovely device, except that it was predicated on the technology of zapping children's feet with radiation. Which is why it, along with the friendly neighborhood DDT truck, is now a thing of the past.

"Between all the DDT I swallowed as a kid, and all the times I zapped my feet with those green rays, I can't always work up the enthusiasm to read the lists of ingredients on cereal boxes and make sure that everything inside is good for me," I said. "Something tells me it's futile."

Michael decided on a piece of caramel cheesecake for dessert.

And we decided to set off on our marathon as soon as we left the restaurant.

Ronnie was driving along the interstate. We'd been talking and listening to the radio for about an hour.

"Did it always seem this small to you?" Michael said.

The Ford did feel cramped. Of all my memories of cruising Bristol, the sensation of confinement never figured in. Sometimes there used to be five or six of us in a car; a lot of times there were three in the front. Yet I never recall those cars seeming crowded.

Tonight, though, with Ronnie and Michael in front and me in back, we definitely were in close quarters.

"Cars are smaller now," Ronnie said.

"Or we're bigger," I said.

"Not that much bigger," Michael said.

So at least for that first night, being inside the car accentuated the notion that we were back together again—and closer together than we probably would have chosen. In our adult lives, we really didn't spend much time in cars full of other grown people. This feeling—three grown men in a 1990s-scale automobile—was new.

"You see this a lot around Washington," I said. "Whenever the President or some foreign big shot is moving around town, the Secret Service follows in unmarked station wagons. Six or eight big guys crammed into a car. From the outside it looks like they have to duck their heads to avoid bumping against the ceiling."

"Like the twenty clowns who used to come out of the Volkswagen at the circus," Michael said.

"Except in this case the clowns are carrying machine guns," I said.

"I always wondered how they did that," Ronnie said.

"The Secret Service?" I said.

"No," he said. "The clowns in the Volkswagen."

If, during the afternoon, I had been concerned about the prognosis for this trip, tonight, with the three of us filling up the car more completely than I would have imagined, it was beginning to seem all right. Granted, I was ready to tell Ronnie that he had been correct—a Lincoln Town Car, with its roomy interior, would be just fine for future rentals—but as the freeway exit signs flashed past us, I was beginning to get over my disquietude about not having a timetable or an absolute destination. I knew I wouldn't be able to shake my daily ways quite so easily—habits built up over so many years don't just vanish by being wished away—but tonight in the car made me believe that it wouldn't be impossible. Zipping up the highway, accompanied by the sound of our voices and the music from the radio, I felt, for the first time since morning, free of tension.

Ronnie was moving the radio through the stations—I had forgotten how addicted he had always been to the buttons on car radios; watching him now, I knew without even asking what he must be like with a TV zapper in his hand—and some rap song came on that featured the word "chauvinism."

"What did he rhyme with that?" I said.

"I wasn't paying attention," Ronnie said.

"I don't think there are any words that rhyme with 'chauvinism,' " I said.

"Songs don't have to rhyme anymore," Michael said.

"They have to come close," I said. "There's no word that is even remotely near to rhyming with 'chauvinism.' "

"Tell it to this guy who's singing," Ronnie said. "He's probably paying for a Palm Beach estate with the royalties he's getting for not knowing how to rhyme."

"I remember the first time I heard that word," I said. "I was in college, and I asked this girl out on a date. It must have been at the very beginning of the women's movement, because I didn't have a clue. I took her back to her dorm after the date, and I automatically walked in front of her so that I could open the door of the building for her. So I held the door open, and she gave me this really snide look, and she said, 'Well, I see chauvinism is not dead.' And I said, 'Thank you.' "

" 'Thank you'?" Michael said.

"Yeah," I said. "I thought she was complimenting me. I thought chauvinism meant chivalry. Like Sir Walter Raleigh throwing his cape across a mud puddle so a lady could avoid getting her shoes dirty."

"Did you feel stupid?" Ronnie said.

"Not at the time," I said. "I felt very flattered."

"You felt very flattered," Ronnie said, moving into the passing lane.

I didn't know about the others, but for me the words we spoke in the car that first night seemed to be the words of three people who had broken off a conversation in mid-sentence years earlier, and who now had suddenly picked up the same conversation right where it left off. I don't think we said one important thing all evening.

Yet in the close quarters of that car, with the highway stretching out ahead, I felt that these were anything but unimportant moments. In my business I had gotten used to the idea that if time spent with people was not easily converted into professional gain, then I had somehow cheated myself. The time invested didn't necessarily have to be for a story I would prepare for broadcast within twenty-four hours. But the person I talked to at least had to qualify as a "contact"; I had to store that person, like string, for possible use further down the line. I don't know when that happened to me. It just did. Maybe it happens to all of us.

On our first night on the road my only purpose for being in that car was to be in that car. The matters we talked about were not globally consequential; the topics would never merit discussion on a Sunday-morning interview show. But I found myself cherishing the minutes.

We never did make it through the marathon. Late at night the song "Yesterday" came on the radio, and I called forward to Michael to remind him about the day we heard the song for the first time. He didn't answer, and I could see that he was asleep, his head resting against the top of the seat.

"He's been out for a couple of minutes," Ronnie said.

So Paul McCartney's voice filled the car, and only two of us heard it. On the summer night in 1965 when "Yesterday" was first released, Michael and I had been cruising around Bristol in his father's car. We would be heading off to college within the month; we knew we were nearing the end of something, although we did our best not to discuss it.

That summer night in Bristol it was very late, and the disc jockey on WCOL over in Columbus said that the new Beatles record was just in, and then he played "Yesterday." For a few moments we didn't think it was really a Beatles song. It didn't sound like the Beatles. The song was so beautiful, and so adult, that it had to be by someone else. At the same time, though, we could tell that the voice was McCartney's. We were about to embark on a new chapter in our lives; the song coming out of the radio told us that the Beatles might be starting on a new chapter in theirs, too.

The whole next day we listened for the song. It didn't come onto the radio. We thought that the song was called "Tomorrow." That's how we had remembered it; we had only heard it once, and we'd had a couple of beers that night, and we thought there was an almost unexplainably moving new Beatles song called "Tomorrow." We told people about it; they had not heard the new song. For most of the day we listened for "Tomorrow"—we didn't drop everything else to listen for it, we just made a point of keeping the radio on all the time so that we would hear it if WCOL decided to play it—and at some point midway through that next evening the disc jockey did play the song. It was just as beautiful as we had remembered, and of course it was not called "Tomorrow."

That's what I was going to remind Michael about; I was going to see if he recalled the time when we thought "Yesterday" was "Tomorrow." But he was asleep; Paul McCartney sang to us, and Michael slept, and there was going to be no marathon, at least not on this night. Soon enough Ronnie spotted a Quality Inn sign and we pulled off the highway.

Eight

"ARE YOU SURE this is all taken care of?" Michael said as we walked along Addison Street in Chicago, toward the press gate of Wrigley Field.

"Don't worry," I said. "I talked to the guy again right before we came over."

"But you don't have the tickets with you?" he said.

"They'll be waiting for us at the gate, with our field passes," I said.

Ronnie stopped on the sidewalk and looked up at the stadium.

"Where's the ivy?" he said.

"Inside," I said. "The ivy is inside."

The first week had been marked by two essential elements: a lot of time spent lying in the sun next to motel swimming pools, talking and drinking cans of soda pop and, at least for Ronnie and me, fighting the vestigial urge to go to a pay telephone every fifteen minutes to check in at the office; and the decision, made very early on, that it was going to have to be three rooms each night, not two.

The initial two-room plan had been part of our strategy to cut down costs and thus keep Michael from feeling overly bad about Ronnie paying. I would pay for one room, Ronnie would pay for the other. We would always make sure that one of the rooms had twin beds; we would alternate having a roommate, and every third night a different one of us would get a room of his own.

It didn't work. Best friends or not, it had been a long time since any of us had shared a room with a male. That first night at the Quality Inn after our aborted marathon, I lay awake listening to Michael snore. Michael and I used to sleep over at each other's houses all the time when we were kids. But kids don't snore; kids don't leave whiskers all over the bathroom counter; kids don't make waking-up noises that would seem more appropriate for a hospital ward than a summer-vacation motel.

"What's the chances of you cleaning up in the bathroom when you're done?" I said to Michael the next morning, and before the last word was even out of my mouth I knew that these living arrangements were fated to fail. There was no way we were all going to make it through the summer together if we didn't have our own rooms.

"We're like little old ladies, set in our ways," Michael said the second afternoon, as we lay in the sun by the pool beside a Ramada Inn just over the Indiana line. The night before, he and Ronnie had shared a room; around 1 A.M. Ronnie had called a business associate on the West Coast (Ronnie had been unable to wean himself from the phone, making probably twenty calls a day; his rationale to us was that he wasn't really conducting business, he was just checking up on things). It was 11 P.M. in California, and Ronnie wanted to catch this fellow before the guy went to bed. The conversation apparently had been detailed and a little heated, and a half hour into it Michael had asked Ronnie how much longer he planned to be on, which Ronnie took as a request to get off.

So it was pretty clear: If we were going to make it through to September, we would have to have our own rooms. "I like you guys fine," Ronnie said at the Ramada pool. "I just never want to see either of you in your pajamas again."

A woman in her early twenties walked by in her swimsuit just as Ronnie was saying that, and gave us a quizzical look.

"It's not what you think, honey," Ronnie said to her, drawing on his cigar. Ronnie had been smoking a lot of cigars this trip.

She raised her eyebrows and walked on.

"Don't call women 'honey,' " Michael said to him.

"Right," Ronnie said. "And don't smoke cigars."

"Could we try not to make this *The Odd Couple?*" I said. And that night, at the next place, we got three rooms. It made every difference. The next morning, at breakfast, we were genuinely pleased to see each other and to start the day.

Michael didn't put up any argument about the added cost to Ronnie; Michael's smart enough to know that if the point of all this was to enjoy the summer, the benefits of any kind of false pride would be far outweighed by the indignities of a summer with roommates. "Why don't we just admit it," Ronnie said at the next pool. "We're too old to share rooms with each other."

"Like I told you," Michael said. "Old biddies, set in our ways."

"It must be a bitch to be in prison," Ronnie said.

"What are you talking about?" Michael said.

"Think about it," Ronnie said. "I bet you every guy in prison has to have a roommate."

I started laughing. "That's what you always read about in the investigative reports of the horrors that go on behind bars," I said. "The roommate problem."

"Well, I wouldn't like it," Ronnie said.

" 'Warden, could I please switch roommates?' " I said to Ronnie. " 'We just haven't been getting along as well as I'd hoped.' "

"All right, all right," Ronnie said.

" 'We just don't seem to have anything in common, Warden,' " I said.

"You want to get some ribs tonight?" Ronnie said.

"I just need to know one thing," Michael said to Ronnie. "How did you go from being a kid who was afraid to ask a girl to dance to being a person who calls perfect strangers 'honey'?"

Ronnie did this "heh-heh-heh" thing through his cigar and closed his eyes as he angled his head backward so that the sun would strike his face directly.

With the rooming problem taken care of, we spent that first week soaking up sun and checking out small towns and—in the case of Michael and me—making a daily bet on how many times Ronnie would have to indulge his phone-call habit. In a pizza place early one evening, with the TV tuned to WGN out of Chicago on cable, we sat looking at a Cubs game and I said, "You want to go there?"

"Chicago?" Michael said.

"Wrigley Field," I said.

During a strike by the major league baseball players in the early 1980s, the network had sent me with a crew to Chicago. We were to cover the first game after the end of the strike, and Wrigley Field was where we were supposed to do the story. The public relations director of the Cubs had set us up with passes and access to the field and the locker rooms; it had been enjoyable, both as a story and as a way to spend the day, and the man from the Cubs had told me to feel free to give him a call anytime I was passing through town. Over the years I had been in Chicago a couple of times, and I had called him and he had got me into the ballpark. I figured that now I'd do it again.

"I heard that place is sold out all the time," Ronnie said.

"I don't think it should be a problem," I said.

"Do you think we can use our old Jet Badges to get in?" Michael said.

I felt myself grinning. Jet Badges were sold by the Columbus Jets baseball team as a promotional gimmick designed to get kids to go to the ballpark. In the middle of the 1950s, the Columbus Jets were worried that they might be in trouble. Because games played by the Cleveland Indians and the Cincinnati Redlegs were telecast, it was tough for a minor league team in Ohio to draw fans. It was easier for people to stay home and watch the Indians or the Reds on TV—why drive all the way out to West Mound Street in Columbus to see minor leaguers when you could see the big leagues without leaving your house?

So each spring, at schools in central Ohio, Jet Badges were offered for sale. I think they cost fifty cents. The badges were made of blue metal, and they featured the Jets' logo—a cartoon baseball player riding atop a bat that was streaking through the sky like a jet—and if you wore your Jet Badge to Jet Stadium while accompanied by a paying adult, you could get in by paying another fifty cents. Plus, there were certain special Jet Badge Nights during the season, and on those nights your Jet Badge got you in for free. Just about every boy in central Ohio owned a Jet Badge; they were a fashion statement. You wore them even if you weren't going to the game.

"Howie Goss," Michael said.

"John Powers," I said.

Goss and Powers were two Columbus Jets stars of that era. Living in Bristol, we were never going to get to see Mickey Mantle or Whitey Ford in person. But on nights when we could persuade our fathers to drive from Bristol to Columbus and take us to Jets games, we were happy to watch the exploits of Howie Goss and John Powers and to make those two minor league journeymen, at least temporarily, our heroes. I had a box turtle once, and I named the turtle HowPow. "How" for Howie Goss; "Pow" for John Powers. I suppose maybe there were once boys growing up in New York who named their turtles DiMaggio.

On nights when our dads would take us, it would feel special. Jet Stadium was a rickety old structure in a down-at-the-heels neighborhood. Beyond the left-field wall was a cemetery.

But sitting in Jet Stadium with our fathers, we felt like we were doing something important. We didn't even consider the possibility that the players down on the field might be bitter that they were stuck in the minors; they were on that field, and they were wearing clean white uniforms, and they were getting paid to play baseball at night. That was more than good enough for us. And our dads—at Jet Stadium they were a little looser than they were at the dinner table at home. At home, after work, they would be stiff and nervous and still wound up from their day at the office; they would be men in suits. At Jet Stadium, for a few hours, they would be tieless and at ease; their eyes would be alertly focused on the players on the field, and so would our eyes. We would be watching the Jets together.

Once I remember getting my feelings hurt at a Jets game. It was one of the first times I went to a game; I was eight or nine years old. My dad and I were sitting up near the top of the stands on the first-base side, and in front of us were two kids named Earl Wieberg and Danny Cox. They were my age, but I didn't know them that well. They were with their own fathers; they knew much more about baseball than I did.

The count must have been three balls, two strikes on a batter, because all of a sudden Earl and Danny began to chant: "Three and two, what'll he do? Three and two, what'll he do?" Caught up in the excitement of the moment, I started to chant with them: "Three and two, what'll he do?"

They turned around.

"Do you even know what 'three and two' means?" Earl said.

I had no idea. But I said, "Yes."

"What does it mean?" Danny said.

I sat there in silence. I didn't know.

They laughed. Then they turned back toward the field and began again: "Three and two, what'll he do? . . ."

My dad and I sat together and watched the diamond. I don't recall whether the batter walked or got a hit or struck out.

The usher opened the metal gate and let us onto the field. We were wearing our passes around our necks; my acquaintance on the Cubs' staff had been as good as his word. I stepped down onto the grass first; Michael and Ronnie seemed hesitant.

"Go ahead, sir," the usher said to Michael.

They joined me. They seemed a little tentative, as if the players were going to come over and tell them to get off and go up into the stands where they belonged. But the players paid us no notice at all. The Cubs were taking batting practice, and the Los Angeles Dodgers were lounging around their dugout along the first-base line.

Shawon Dunston, inside the batting cage, took a wicked swing at a pitch and sent the ball screaming into left field. "Come on," I said to Michael and Ronnie. Their feet might as well have been stuck to the ground. I motioned with my head, and they walked with me to the batting cage, where we could watch from close range.

I must admit, I was enjoying this. This was a part of my life I wanted them to see. Going places the rest of the world can't go, talking with people the rest of the world can't talk with, crossing lines that are meant to keep the public away . . . it's something you get used to rather quickly in my business, and if you've got any sense of perspective you figure out early on that it's sort of a juvenile thing to feel proud of. The people on the "Press Only" side of the barricades are no better, and often a lot worse, than the people being held at bay. But this was new to Michael and Ronnie, and I guess I was showing off for them a little bit, bringing them here.

Dunston hit another ball hard down the third-base line. The stands were beginning to fill up—we had purposely arrived early, precisely so we could do this: stand and watch the pre-game drills. It was a beautiful, warm June evening in Chicago; off in the distance we could see the office towers of the Loop. On an evening like this you would be hard pressed to find someone to complain about Wrigley having finally switched to night baseball.

The Cub infielders trotted into position to limber up. A coach hit a bouncer to the third baseman, who scooped it up apparently without thinking about it, and rifled it perfectly to the first baseman.

"Do you know how hard it is just to throw the ball that far and get it to the right place?" Ronnie said.

Yep. We're all so used to watching sports on TV that the basics behind what we see can get obscured. On the TV screen, professional athletes seem not all that much different from figures in an extremely realistic video game. Here, though, we watched that third baseman do it again—the ball traveled in an instantaneous unwavering line to the first baseman—and it reminded me of something that a famous sportscaster had once told me.

This particular man was sometimes derided as a "homer"—as an apologist for the team whose games he broadcast, as a person reluctant to criticize or mock. On the air his style was courtly and almost elegant; after the game, with a few drinks in him, he became more earthy. One night I asked him why he was so unfailingly mannerly and uncensorious when calling the games on television, even when the team was performing atrociously.

"Listen," he said to me. "The way I see it, any ballplayer I see on a major league field is one of the six hundred goddamn greatest players in a world of two billion goddamn people. Every one of those six hundred who are playing in the major leagues is entitled to my respect."

And it's hard to dispute that. There probably aren't too many American boys who don't at one time or another play baseball. On school playgrounds and empty lots all across the country, you see it every warm day of the year. I did it and Michael did it and Ronnie did it; we stepped onto diamonds at one point in our lives, and we tried to see if we were any good. Almost all of us, discovering that we are not so very good, walk away from it. But for six hundred or so boys—

including these men working out a few feet from us—the realization settled in that, for some unfathomable reason, they might be the best at this in the whole world. For some reason they might be the ones to do this on a big league field while all the rest of us, who had tried and had come up lacking, sit back and watch.

I looked over at the third baseman one more time. If I were asked to step into his place and throw the ball to the first baseman, I didn't think I could do it. I don't mean that I couldn't do it well—at this point in my life I probably couldn't do it at all. Either it wouldn't get there on the fly, or it would swerve off to one side, or it would go skidding into the dirt. That's a long way, from third to first.

"We watch these guys on TV, and if their throw is a tenth of a second late we call them jerks," Ronnie said.

The Cubs had, indeed, been on TV the night before. They had played a night game against Houston in the Astrodome—which we had watched at our hotel in Chicago; we had gotten into town late yesterday afternoon—and early this morning the team had flown here, and now they were on the field. They may be professional athletes, but they're people, too, and over the last twenty-four hours they had played a game in Texas, had eaten their late dinners, slept in their hotel rooms, gotten up, shaved, showered, eaten breakfast, been driven to the airport, flown here, come to Wrigley Field, dressed in their uniforms again, come up through the dugout to the field where they were now warming up—all so that tonight, somewhere in America, someone would be able to sit back, look at images on a television screen, and say: "Hit the ball, will you, butthead?"

The Cubs finished with batting practice, and the Dodgers headed toward the batting cage, walking past us. There were probably twenty or thirty sportswriters and broadcasters on the field; to the ballplayers they might as well have been unused pieces of equipment. The players merely stepped around them—and us.

"These are the Los Angeles Dodgers?" Michael said.

He didn't have to explain the question mark in his voice. Up close, some of these men looked to be just a few years out of high school. The oldest of them were significantly younger than we were. The cliché is: You know that you're getting old when baseball players are younger than you. But as we stood with these major leaguers, the thought crystallized: These kids could call us "sir" and not be joking.

And the uniforms didn't help. Well tailored, form-fitting, made out of some body-hugging material, the uniforms made the players look like instructors in a college-town health club, while we, standing by the batting cages . . . well, perhaps we could have passed as the health club's accountants, come to do a field audit.

"The Los Angeles Dodgers are supposed to be Duke Snider with his big old arms sticking out of baggy sleeves," Michael said.

As if sent from the compassionate heavens to make us feel better, Don Zimmer—he was still the manager of the Cubs at that point—climbed out of the dugout to talk to a member of the umpiring crew. Zimmer, like all major league managers, was wearing the same kind of uniform as his team. He was in his mid-fifties; he had, in fact, been a teammate of Duke Snider's on the Dodgers. Here he was in this tight, soft uniform, and he was portly and lumpy and round . . . and it wasn't his fault at all, really. Put any man in his fifties in a glorified ballet costume, and he's going to look like this. It's the way men in their fifties look.

"Is that a rule?" Ronnie said. "That the managers have to wear those things."

"I don't know," I said. "It must be." I looked around us; all of the Cubs' coaching staff, and all of the Dodgers' coaching staff, were in uniforms.

"You'd think it would take away from their advantage over the players," Michael said.

A manager is supposed to be a smart baseball strategist, a shrewd judge of his troops, a man whose experience gives his team a leg up. Put him in the same uniform as his players, though, and you rob him of his edge. The players are the ones who are supposed to be in Superman shape; that's part of their job description. When you send a manager out wearing spandex clothes, you reduce him to the same level as his players. And on that level, the players are going to have the advantage. They're twenty-six years old and they lift weights before breakfast.

"Couldn't they wear business suits, like basketball coaches?" Ronnie said.

"I don't think it's allowed," I said. "If they could, you'd think they would."

"What about Connie Mack?" Michael said.

Come to think of it, Connie Mack, the legendary old-time manager, always was photographed in a business suit and a straw hat. He looked like the boss—you just knew his players addressed him as "Mr. Mack." I tried to envision Connie Mack—white-haired, dour, angular—in a modern baseball uniform.

Ronnie was looking up into the stands. The people in the seats were watching the field; some of them had managed to work their way down to the brick restraining walls along the first-base and third-base lines, and were regarding the players and the rest of us on the grass as if we resided in an exalted world.

"I feel like a seal in the zoo," Ronnie said, not unpleased.

"It's that old psychological distance between the stage and the audience," I said. "The real distance can be three feet, but it always feels like a million miles."

"See that woman in the tank top?" Ronnie said, tipping his head toward an aisle halfway down the first-base side. "She's looking at me."

"If you were up in the stands, she wouldn't be," I said.

"Look," he said. "She is."

"I'm not doubting you," I said.

"I think I'm going to go up there and talk to her," he said.

"I wouldn't," I said. "Cross back over into the audience and she'll figure out that you're no different than she is."

He flashed her a toothy smile. She ducked her head and then waved back.

"See?" he said.

"You could get used to this, couldn't you?" I said.

In the outfield, the Cubs were doing wind sprints. They were different from all the joggers you see in every city every morning and evening; the running Cubs had nothing to do with any health or fitness craze. Half a second slower in those wind sprints and they hazarded the risk of being one of us again—spectators.

An assistant coach motioned to the Cubs, and they trotted back to their dugout and into a tunnel.

"Let's go," I said to Michael and Ronnie.

"Go where?" Michael said.

"To the locker room," I said.

"Us?" he said.

"Come on," I said.

"These passes can get us in there?" Ronnie said.

"These passes can get us anywhere," I said, still showing off.

So we walked down into the Cubs' dugout, moved with a group of writers and broadcasters past a silent security guard who eyed the press passes around our necks, and headed up a long, dim tunnel toward the team locker room. I tried to seem casual about it, but I was hoping that Michael and Ronnie were loving this. If they weren't, it was a wasted effort.

"Look at this," Ronnie said.

We were in the locker room; the Cubs were sitting in front of their cubicles reading mail and adjusting the tape on their shoes and talking quietly with each other. Ronnie was standing next to a bulletin board.

He was silently reading a newspaper clipping that was pinned to the board. It was an interview with a former player who now counseled major leaguers about the pitfalls of life on the road. The former player was quoted as saying that one of his duties was to give professional athletes advice about groupies. His quote was: "I explain to the players that these girls are emotionally ill."

"Can you believe that?" Ronnie said.

The young athletes may have grown up believing that if they became stars one of the side benefits would be that they could have all the women they wanted. But then society's attitude did a quick and total shift—and now they are counseled that any woman who wants them for their stardom must be considered a person who is potentially mentally unbalanced, and thus to be avoided.

"I bet when the guy who's doing the counseling was playing, he didn't follow his own advice," Ronnie said.

Michael was reading the story. "He talks about that," Michael said.

In the story the reporter had asked the counselor how he had dealt with the groupie situation when he was in the big leagues. The counselor had responded with a joke: "I didn't have to worry about groupies coming around. I played for the Indians."

"Good line," Ronnie said, "but it ducks the question."

The locker room had faded striped carpeting, like the living room in the house of a family who couldn't afford the expensive deep-pile stuff. The players' cubicles were made of blond wood. Most of the players sat on plastic-and-canvas director's chairs right in front of their cubicles and faced straight in. The message from their body language was pretty clear: The league might require them to allow reporters in here, but they didn't have to like it. It would have been just as easy for them to face the center of the room. This way any sportswriter who approached them would have to make a special effort to get their attention.

A number of sportswriters and broadcasters had made that effort, and were talking to members of the Cubs. The three of us stood against the wall, watching this routinized pre-game dance. I think Michael and Ronnie had the feeling that, even though we had been given the same passes as the sportswriters, everyone in the room instinctively knew that we weren't sportswriters and didn't belong. I know I felt that way.

Near us a writer was talking to Rick Sutcliffe about a game Sutcliffe had pitched the night before. Apparently the writer was referring to a specific pitch. His question—and it wasn't a question—was: "It looked like a change-up."

In any other segment of journalism the newsmaker would hear that, and wait patiently for the reporter to continue and ask what he wanted to know. In sports, though, "It looked like a change-up" is considered a query, and Sutcliffe, knowing the rules of the game, immediately responded with an answer.

"This is cool," Ronnie said quietly.

In the middle of the room was a long table, on top of which were stacks of letters to the team, and three clear canisters, each containing a different kind of Bazooka bubble gum: regular Bazooka, sugarless Bazooka, and soft Bazooka.

"I haven't chewed Bazooka since I was a kid," Michael said.

"You figure the league has to have a trade-off deal with Bazooka," Ronnie said.

"A trade-off?" Michael said.

"They supply gum in the locker rooms for being the official bubble gum of major league baseball or something," Ronnie said. "I have a friend who does deals like that."

Michael looked a little crestfallen at the thought. I think he was hoping that the players merely liked to chew Bazooka.

Two players came out of the room where the toilets were located. They were in mid-sentence, but even the fragment we overheard was a little epiphany about life as a constant traveler, as real a piece of information in its truncated way as any batting average:

". . . Sudafed, I think. If that makes you tired, try Actifed."

Another pair of players emerged. One was saying to the other:

". . . so he has to decide: Does he give her fifty thousand dollars a year for the rest of his life? I think the answer has to be yeah."

The man who said this moved past Michael and gave him a knowing look. It was artificial; Michael had no idea of the specifics of what the player was talking about, and the player had to realize this. But it's such a strange life the ballplayers must live. For all the stories that have been written about the etiquette of locker-room comportment, the fact remains that there are very few jobs that require men to get dressed in front of strangers who are looking and taking notes. You make a lot of money and you get very famous and you get your picture on baseball cards that children keep in the drawers of their night tables—and you are required to put your clothes on in the presence of people you may not ask to leave, even if on the off chance you are shy. Since privacy is effectively forbidden, some players apparently decide not even to pretend that it is possible. "Does he give her fifty thousand dollars a year for the rest of his life? I think the answer is yeah." The compatriotic glance at Michael was merely an acknowledgment that as long as the art of eavesdropping has been institutionalized in here, this particular man held no illusions of keeping any thought confidential.

Ronnie had wandered over to a chalkboard. Someone in charge had written the day's schedule on the board: "Pitchers: Stretch, 4:05, Hit 4:15. Starters: Stretch 4:40, Hit 4:55. Extra Men: Stretch 4:15, Hit 4:35." Apparently it was a calisthenics-and-batting-practice timetable that was designed to prevent overloading certain parts of the field.

"How do you think the 'extra men' feel?" Michael said.

"What do you mean?" Ronnie said.

"Think about it," Michael said. " 'Extra men' means the scrubs."

"Maybe not," Ronnie said. "Maybe it's like 'designated hitter.' "

"The National League doesn't have designated hitters," Michael said. "Look at the board. There's pitchers, there's starters, and there's 'extra men.' "

"I bet you they're used to it," Ronnie said.

"I don't know," Michael said. "No one wants to be thought of as an 'extra man.' "

Ryne Sandberg walked past us. Sandberg was by far the biggest star on the Cubs—the one member of the team who would be instantly recognizable anywhere in America. Dark-haired and wholesomely handsome, he went to his cubicle, sat on his director's chair, and proceeded to relace his shoes.

We did our best not to stare. Sandberg was considerably younger than we were, yet he seemed destined to be at the same time forever older than we. Baseball stars, by the nature of their loftiness, were always older than the boys who idolized them. Now we were no longer boys, and Sandberg was much our junior, but his calendar age did not really matter. He had made it to the major leagues, and then had risen to the very top of that exclusive stratum; by that fact alone he was older than we were.

He was cordial in his silence. I had read that Sandberg was a quiet, bashful man; as we stood a few feet from his cubicle, it was hard to conceive of what his life must be like. He did not look at us and he did not look at any of the sportswriters in the room, and this was not an act of discourtesy but of necessity; to look would be to invite company. It wasn't exactly that he considered all of us not present. It was just that we were not a part of his world.

"I feel rude being here," Michael said.

"That stuff actually comes in a package," Ronnie said. He was looking across the room, where a third baseman was rubbing black gooey stuff under his eyes. The ballplayer dipped his fingers into a shallow jar, came out with the black gunk, and drew little half-moons on his cheeks, next to his nose.

"What, you thought they mixed it up themselves?" Michael said.

"I just don't know where you'd buy that stuff," Ronnie said. "I don't know what you'd ask for."

The jar had evidently yielded its last treasures, because the third baseman peered down into it, decided there was nothing left, and tossed it, basketball-style, into a trash bucket twenty feet away.

Michael walked back to the bulletin board. A letter from the president of the National League was posted.

"This may explain everything," Michael said.

The letter concerned itself with a small detail of life in the major leagues. It seems that a regulation baseball glove must not exceed a certain number of inches "from the outside edge of the little finger to the inside seam at the base of the index finger," in the words of the league president. The purpose of his letter, he wrote, was to reiterate this policy, and remind all players that to use gloves with wider spans was illegal.

"What does that explain?" I said.

"Not the text of the letter," Michael said. "Look at the top of it. Right underneath the letterhead."

Typed directly under the National League logo were the words:

"Please Post in Clubhouse."

"That's it," Michael said. "We keep calling this place the locker room. But that's not what the players call it. It's not their locker room. It's their clubhouse."

There was, indeed, a distinction. Clubhouse means two things. It's an adult term, meaning for members only; you can walk in here if you want, but unless you're a member of the club, you don't really belong. And it's a little-boy term, too; little boys go to their clubhouses. Forever in the summer little boys have built clubhouses and hidden away there with their friends.

The clubhouse equipment man circulated through the room, nodding at the sportswriters and pointing to the clock. By league policy, it was time for us to get out. The players were given a certain number of minutes before each game to be by themselves.

On our way to the door, Michael stopped in front of the table with the Bazooka canisters on top. The three canisters—regular, sugarless, soft—somehow represented something. Those transparent Bazooka bins, regardless of licensing fees or promotional trade-offs, were a blunt representation of the difference between this world and our world. How many men, on their way to work each day, are lucky enough to be able to stop off at a Bazooka bin?

"I'd love to send some of this to the girls," Michael said.

"I don't know," I said. The gum wasn't ours.

"You can buy some at the store," Ronnie said.

"It wouldn't be the same," Michael said. "I want to tell the girls that this is real baseball players' gum."

There might be many mundane aspects to the daily lives of these players, but at the core there still was magic. If the magic were not present, we would not be down here in this room so many years after standing on the makeshift baseball diamonds of Bristol.

"Go," the clubhouse man said with mock brusqueness. "Take the gum and go."

"I can have some?" Michael said.

"Take it and go," the clubhouse man said.

So Michael reached into the canisters and took three pieces—one of each variety—and dropped the gum carefully into his shirt pocket.

"Thank you, sir," he said to the clubhouse man.

"You're welcome and go," the clubhouse man said.

"They're making the batter's box," Ronnie said.

We were back on the field; the grounds crew was laying white lines around home plate.

"I've got to go see this," Ronnie said. He approached the men who were making the box; he said something to them, which we couldn't hear, and apparently they told him it was okay to observe them from up close. He stood right next to them and watched every move.

"If you told him Michelangelo was doing the Sistine Chapel all over again, he'd have no interest in seeing it," Michael said.

But this was nice. Looking at Ronnie with the groundsmen, I was reminded of what he had been like when we hadn't seen anything in life, when everything was new. He was asking one of the crew members questions; they would point down to the white lines and explain what they were doing.

"At least the grounds crew has a reason to be here," Michael said.

"What are you talking about?" I said.

"I feel funny being down here on the field," he said. "We don't belong here."

"Just relax and enjoy it," I said. "You don't have to have a reason to be everywhere." It was important to me that he like this evening at the park. It wasn't enough for me to know that I had arranged it; it had to be good.

The Dodgers emerged from their dugout. "Eddie!" some people in the stands yelled at their initial sighting of Eddie Murray, the first baseman. "Eddie!" It was loud enough for Murray to hear, but he did not turn his head. Had it been any one of us, we would automatically have swiveled around; someone yells your name, you turn to see who it is. Not these men. They have heard their names hollered so many times by strangers that they have learned how to ignore the sound.

Ronnie said he had to call one of his associates back in Cleveland to check on some things; he said that he was going to find a pay phone,

and would be back in a few minutes. Michael and I located our seats—
my contact in the Cubs' front office had left three tickets for us in
addition to the field passes—and we watched the Dodgers' half of the
first inning and then Ronnie reappeared in the aisle, grinning.

"I have something I want you to see," he said.

"Later," I said. "We're watching the game."

"Trust me," he said.

We excused ourselves as we edged past the other people in our row,
and we followed Ronnie as he hurried to a cement ramp leading up to
the next level of Wrigley Field.

"What are you doing?" Michael said.

"When I was on the phone, I ran into a guy I do some business
with," Ronnie said. "He's a vice president of Commerce Bank. Their
main office is here in Chicago, and they've got a skybox. It's not full
tonight, and he said we were welcome to watch from up there."

At the top of the ramp there was a uniformed attendant. The bank
man had left Ronnie's name; the attendant directed us down a clean,
brightly lighted catwalk, and soon enough we came to a door with a
brass plaque engraved: "Commerce National Bank."

Ronnie knocked. His friend opened the door. We walked into a
carpeted living room. About a dozen men and women in business suits
and office dresses were there; they had come straight from work. On a
side table were chafing dishes filled with roast beef and hot dogs; there
were platters of deli sandwiches. A bartender in a tuxedo poured wine,
beer, and soft drinks.

"Welcome!" Ronnie's friend said. "I think you'll enjoy the game a
little better from up here."

Inside the air-conditioned room, a color television was tuned to the
game in progress. A plate-glass window overlooked the field; through a
door was an outdoor terrace, with three descending tiers, each featuring
five leather seats. There was a TV set outside, too, bolted to the top of
the outdoor terrace and angled so that everyone in the bank's skybox
could watch the game on television at the same time they were watching
it on the field.

"You're sure you have room for us?" Ronnie said.

"I wouldn't have asked you if I didn't," the bank man said. "I don't
want you watching from down there. There's no comparison."

We walked out onto the terrace and took three seats together. Most
of the bank's guests were still inside, as if they were at a cocktail party.

It was weird. We sat in the leather seats; we had brought sandwiches
and drinks out with us. Beyond the right-field wall was that downtown
skyline, like an artist's backdrop. It was still early in the evening; the
sun had not set yet and the lights had not been turned on. The

sensation of leaning back in the soft chairs up here, with the fans in the stands below us and the players performing below them, had a sort of Roman emperor feel that I was not sure I was totally enjoying.

There was the sound of a bat connecting solidly with a pitch, and a Dodger runner moved swiftly from first to second.

"From up here, it's almost more of a spectacle than a game," Michael said. The game on the field did seem curiously disconnected from us. Down in the stands, the customers might have been following each play as a key to the eventual outcome of the contest. Up here, with the cocktail party still going on through the glass behind us, the players might as well have been dancers, or mimes.

"It's not a spectacle to them," I said, nodding toward the players. "In the morning the box score is going to be in every newspaper in America."

On the terrace TV, just above our heads, there were close-ups of players and computer-generated numerical representations of their performances during the season to date. For some reason, the game on the TV seemed more real than the game on the field.

Darkness arrived, and now the park was fully illuminated. I went back inside to get another sandwich. There was a phone in the skybox; one of the guests of the bank, a doctor, was using it. His beeper had gone off, and he was calling in.

"Is he in pain?" the doctor said into the phone. He covered his non-telephone ear with his hand. "Did he say anything about having taken his medication?"

Somehow, if I was a patient calling my doctor at night, I wouldn't want to envision him dealing with my emergency from a skybox at the ballpark. Rationally it didn't make much difference, of course; a doctor can call in from anywhere. Still . . .

"Patch me through to him, then," the doctor said, raising the level of his voice so he could be heard above a sudden upsurge of crowd noise.

I went back outside with my sandwich. Mark Grace came to the plate. He waited out two pitches, then leaned into an inside curve and sent it soaring toward the fence. On the TV and down on the field you could see it hit the brick wall and bounce back onto the outfield grass; on the TV and down on the field you could see the outfielders chase it while Grace sped toward third base. The crowd below us was up and screaming, and Grace dived into third, beating the throw and getting his triple.

With the crowd still chanting in praise of Grace, the door from the inner skybox opened one more time and the hostess from the bank said, "I don't mean to interrupt, but the dessert cart is here."

"The dessert cart?" someone in front of us said.

"If you don't come get it now, it will be gone," the hostess said, her voice teasing.

I looked back through the plate glass. A waitress was at the outer door of the skybox—on the catwalk, where we had knocked. She did, indeed, have a fully loaded dessert cart of the kind that is rolled to your table after dinner at fancy restaurants. So most of us on the terrace stood up to go get our desserts.

"I hope nothing important happens out here," one of the other guests on the terrace said, heading inside.

"You know," Ronnie said, "I almost feel like I should point a zapper at the field and hit the 'pause' button until we get back."

We stood in line at the dessert cart. The waitress on the catwalk—the dessert cart was too large to push inside the skybox—said, "We have carrot cake, cheesecake, caramel-and-pecan turtles, Black Forest cake . . ."

There was an immense scream from the stands below. Startled, we all turned around; through the window we could see Ryne Sandberg rounding first and a Cub runner crossing the plate.

"If you would like," the waitress with the dessert cart said, "we have shots of Bailey's served in chocolate cups."

We were leaving Wrigley. The Cubs had lost the game when the Dodgers mounted a four-run drive in the ninth inning. The ramp from the skyboxes would have taken us right out onto the street, but Ronnie led us back into the stadium itself. The place empties quickly; five minutes after the last out we were almost alone, except for the cleanup crew.

"What are you looking for?" Michael said.

Ronnie seemed to be seeking something in the seats. His eyes were like a searchlight, quite thorough.

"Come on, let's get out of here," Michael said.

But Ronnie still looked.

"You're not looking for that woman, are you?" I said.

He was. He was looking for the woman in the tank top—the woman in the stands with whom he had made eye contact when we were on the field before the game.

"Ronnie, she's gone," I said.

He didn't say anything, but he walked with us toward the exit. He seemed to have been seduced by the idea that the woman in the stands had picked him out. I didn't want to bring up to him again the performer/audience distance theory; I didn't think he needed to hear that were she to see him now, he would be just another fan leaving the ballpark. He had liked the feeling of her eyes on him. Maybe it made him feel like a major leaguer.

Out on Clark Street, I said, "The skybox was something, wasn't it?"

"I don't know," Michael said.

"What do you mean?" Ronnie said. "It's like being a king, sitting out on that terrace. You didn't like that?"

"I did like it," Michael said. "I liked it a lot. But I don't know."

"What?" Ronnie said.

"Look," Michael said to Ronnie. "Ben calls his friend on the phone and gets us the field passes, and we go into the clubhouse. Which was great. And then you run into that friend of yours and get us into the skybox. Which was interesting."

"To say the least," Ronnie said.

"It was very interesting," Michael said. "But to me, that's not what a baseball game is about. You're not supposed to be down on the field with the players. You're not supposed to be up in the sky with the dessert cart."

"You are if you're lucky," Ronnie said.

"Maybe," Michael said. "But to me, none of that is as good as sitting in the stands at Jet Stadium with my dad. He wasn't worrying about work, and he wasn't thinking about any problems he might be having in his life. The baseball game didn't count for anything—it was just the Columbus Jets, no one anywhere else in the world would even be aware the game was being played. I don't think my dad and I even said all that much to each other. We didn't have to talk. We just sat together about halfway up the first-base side, watching the Jets."

I didn't know how much of what Michael was saying was about his dad—the only one of our fathers who was dead—and how much was about the grownup-world logistics of what had just taken place. Major league baseball used to be a distant universe reachable only via the sports sections and the NBC "Game of the Week." It was a universe we were not intended to actually touch. Now, in the last few hours, because of a couple of business contacts, we had been right inside of it. I suspected part of what Michael was feeling had to do with that—with how the world conspires to remove all the mysteries of life.

We moved with the crowd along Addison Street toward the stairs that led up to the elevated train platform.

Ronnie put his arm over Michael's shoulders.

"Tell you what," Ronnie said. "If you really didn't like the evening, there's nothing that says you have to keep the bubble gum."

Michael smiled. He reached into his shirt pocket to make sure the Bazooka he had taken for his daughters was still there.

"I'm definitely keeping the bubble gum," he said. Behind us the lights in the empty ballpark were still blazing brightly in the night.

Nine

THE WAY WE ENDED UP in Omaha was that I had told Michael and Ronnie about playing Airport Roulette, and they didn't believe that I'd ever done it, and the next thing we knew we were in the air.

On the morning after the Cubs game we woke up at the Hyatt just off Michigan Avenue in downtown Chicago. At breakfast I mentioned Airport Roulette again—I guess I had talked about it two or three times during the trip—and we hadn't really thought about where we would head next, anyway, so Michael said, "All right. That's it. We're doing it."

Airport Roulette was a game I had devised when I was first doing stories for the network, back in the days when travel budgets were not a problem, and when I was so new that I was allowed, even encouraged, to go wherever I chose in search of stories. My experience had been that some of the best stories were those that I came upon just by wandering around and seeing what turned up.

Airport Roulette consisted of going to an airport, pointing up at a flight board, and then buying a ticket for whatever city my finger was aimed at. The truth of it was, the Airport Roulette story had grown all out of proportion with my repeated telling of it. As romantic as it sounded, I hadn't done it all that often; maybe two or three times. The network might have been understanding, but my bosses weren't stupid; too many random trips to too many illogical places would not have been tolerated. But Airport Roulette was such a handy allegory for the whimsical nature of life—I had turned those two or three Airport Roulette trips into an ongoing symbol of what I wanted to believe, at the time, was the difference between my job and deskbound jobs.

"Get packed and let's meet in twenty minutes at the checkout desk," Ronnie said.

From my room I called the number of the beach house where Nancy and Hannah were going to be staying for the summer.

On the third ring the phone was answered. It was Hannah's voice, on an answering machine.

"Hi!" she said, that one syllable piercing my heart. "Mom and me are swimming! Call back!"

Then, on the tape, I heard her talking to Nancy. If her voice had been bright and full of confident enthusiasm—almost the voice of a teenager—during the first part of the message, now it seemed, if anything, younger than her eight years. It was softer, unsure; she was looking for direction.

"Do I stop now?" Hannah's voice on the tape said.

"Yes, you can stop," Nancy's taped voice said in the background.

"But what do I do?" Hannah's voice said, nervous.

"Here," Nancy's voice said, then Nancy hit the "stop recording" button.

The next thing I heard was the sound of two beeps, indicating that I should leave my message.

I hung up without saying anything.

At O'Hare International Airport we stood in the United terminal.

"Who's going to do it?" Ronnie said.

"I will," Michael said.

"You can't look in advance," I said.

Michael, his eyes closed, aimed his finger at the airline's bank of video screens.

"Omaha," I said.

"Omaha?" Michael said, opening his eyes. The people around us were shooting quizzical glances in our direction.

"It's definitely Omaha," I said.

Michael looked at the flight schedule on the screen.

"I think it's Honolulu," he said.

"I'm paying for this, and it's Omaha," Ronnie said.

High over Iowa heading west toward Nebraska, I looked down at the geometric patterns of the farmland. We were above the clouds, but it was a relatively clear day, so the few formations below us hardly blocked the view.

"You know what this reminds me of?" Michael, in the next seat, said. "What this summer reminds me of?"

I lowered the window shade to cut down on the glare from the midday sun.

"That time they opened I-71," Michael said.

"You mean that time they didn't open it," I said. "That was the whole point."

Interstate 71 was one of the first superhighways in central Ohio; the initial major link of it connected the middle of the state with Cleveland. A little later construction was begun on the phase of I-71 that would descend to Cincinnati.

An entrance to the Cincinnati link was planned for a point about five miles outside of Bristol. During construction, big metal barrels were put at the head of the entrance ramp, which at that time was just dirt. Highway workers were laying the concrete that would eventually be I-71 South; when they were finished, people from the Bristol area could steer their cars onto that road and drive all the way to Cincinnati without stopping at a single traffic light.

We were itchy, though; we couldn't wait. Not that we necessarily had any reason to want to be in Cincinnati. But the sight of those barrels was a lure, an indication that soon enough there would be one more quick way to get out of Bristol.

So one winter night, with Michael taking lookout duty, Ronnie and I moved the barrels aside. Ronnie got back into his car, and pulled it onto the entrance ramp, and we replaced the barrels right where they had been, and by the light of the moon we drove onto the uncompleted section of I-71. It was a stupid thing to have done; the highway was not ready for traffic, and there were no electric lights. We drove that highway, though; we must have driven for at least twenty miles in the darkness before we realized we had no idea where we were heading or what lay ahead. So we turned the car around and returned to the ramp near Bristol and moved the barrels once more. As far as we knew, we had been the first people, other than the road crews who were building it, to go for a drive on I-71 South.

Apparently that instinct was inside us early—the instinct to get out. "I don't suppose you remember the candy machine at the Rivoli Theater," I said to Michael.

"Not really," he said.

Right outside the auditorium of the Rivoli was a coin-operated candy machine. There were six or eight slots, running horizontally across the front of the machine, each of them containing a sample candy bar, and from somewhere inside the apparatus the kind of bar you selected would drop into the tray at the bottom.

One of the slots never had a candy bar in it. Instead there was a piece of cardboard upon which someone had hand-lettered: MYSTERY. There were big hand-drawn question marks around the word.

If you pulled the knob under the MYSTERY slot, you didn't know what you were going to get. And that's the knob I always pulled.

Generally I was disappointed. The candy bars that dropped out of the well behind the MYSTERY slot were seldom as good as the brand names on display in the neighboring slots; the MYSTERY bars were always off-brands that would not have sold well when displayed in head-to-head competition with the Milky Ways and the Tootsie Rolls.

But I did it every time; I took the chance every time. I didn't envision some bored vending company employee stocking the machine and loading his least popular bars into the MYSTERY well; I was always hoping that something great, maybe something I had never even heard of, would drop out of that slot. Every time I would pull on that knob I would be looking for something better. I took it on faith; something better might be out there.

"You know, I used to love going with Robert Finn on his 7-Up route," I said to Michael.

Robert Finn's father was an executive with the 7-Up bottling licensee in central Ohio; every summer Robert would get hired to do fill-in deliveries. The regular delivery drivers would have vacations during the summer months, and Robert would be the swing guy. Some days I would ride along with him, just for fun; we would pull up at grocery stores and filling stations, and Robert and I would carry wooden crates of 7-Up in and take away the empties from the week just ended. There was no dreariness to it; maybe—probably—it was dreary for the regular route men, but for me, the idea of driving around on a summer day and walking into a place where I'd never been . . . that was great, and what made it even better was that I had a purpose for doing it. I wasn't just hanging around; I was the 7-Up man, or at least the 7-Up man's friend. The first time you do something is always the best; once you've gotten used to the routine you begin to just walk through your days. But that first time through . . . Robert Finn and I would open the front doors of those grocery stores and step inside, and in every store I would look around, checking out the people, checking out the place.

There was an old movie called *Two Weeks in Another Town*. I always liked the sound of those words. I don't think I ever saw it; my sense is that Kirk Douglas was in the movie, but what I liked about it was that title. Two weeks in another town. That sounded just about perfect. Go somewhere you've never been before, spend a couple of weeks, soak it all up, and then get out.

"Did you ever see that movie?" I said to Michael.

"No," he said. "I think it was an Irwin Shaw novel before it was a movie."

"Did you read it?" I said.

"No," he said. "That title really appeals to you? It seems awfully lonely to me."

"I never thought that," I said. The voice of the pilot said that we were beginning our descent into Omaha.

That night, at a Wayfarer's Inn near the Omaha Airport, we stopped in at a bar/restaurant that was attached to the lobby. The place was called the Poodle Skirt, and it had a fifties motif. On the walls were caricatures of Elvis Presley, Fats Domino, Frankie Avalon. Little cards on the tables informed us that this evening free dance lessons were being offered. Men and women our age were doing the Stroll out on the floor.

"I love this kind of place," Ronnie said. "It reminds me of when we went to dances when these songs were new."

But he was wrong. The songs that were playing over the speaker system—"Ebb Tide" by the Platters, "Chances Are" by Johnny Mathis, "You Send Me" by Sam Cooke—all were popular before we were old enough to be going out with girls. We had no real experiences to be recalled by the sounds of these songs; they have been played so much on oldies radio over the years that we have been trained to believe they were a part of our memories, but they weren't. The fifties came and went before we were old enough to shave.

Around the room, just in case any of the customers were bored with the fifties theme, half a dozen television sets were all tuned to ESPN. It seemed to be a can't-miss proposition; if someone wandered into this place and didn't like the music, odds were the person would like the nonstop sports on TV. Indeed, had you walked into this bar and not known what was being shown on the TVs, you might have guessed that a political assassination was being covered live, so intently were most of the men in the room staring up at the various sets. In fact, what they were seeing on the screens was a tractor pull.

"Do you think our dads hung out in places like this when they traveled on business?" Michael said.

"New Orleans jazz bars," I said.

"What?" Michael said.

"That was their generation's version of fifties bars," I said. "Even if they never got to New Orleans, they could find New Orleans jazz bars in every city. Guys playing clarinets and stuff. That was the hook. 'Old New Orleans jazz.' "

"I hate that stuff," Ronnie said.

"It was no different than this," I said. "It was a way to separate traveling businessmen from their money. They could go home at the end of their trips and say, 'I hung out at this old New Orleans-style jazz place in Pittsburgh.' Or Boston. Or Philadelphia. Didn't matter where. It made them feel they had been somewhere."

As we talked, a very good and not very famous song from our era came onto the sound system. It didn't really fit the playlist in this motel bar; it was more Beatles era than fifties, and it had never been popular enough to be instantly recognizable and thus be appropriate for a place like this one. It was a song I had once had my heart broken to, back in the days when I seemed to get my heart broken about every six weeks or so. The song was called "I'm Gonna Be Strong," and it had been sung—was being sung, on the tape in this room—by Gene Pitney.

I tried to listen. But the waitress standing next to me—she was waiting for the bartender to put a load of drinks on her tray—was talking animatedly to one of her colleagues. Both were in their forties, and both were dressed in the required uniform of the room: pink felt skirts with black cutout felt poodles attached to them.

". . . so I was driving along, and I swear, I thought it was a tornado behind my car," she said. Her voice seemed overly loud, or maybe my day had just been too long.

Gene Pitney, across the years, sang: "I can see, you're slipping away from me . . ."

I really wanted to hear the words. A cheer came up from the men in the room, over something that had just happened on ESPN.

Gene Pitney: ". . . but your pity now, would be too much to bear . . ."

"It was a real weird color," the waitress said. "Like a big gray cloud. My son is sitting next to me, and I'm driving as fast as I can. I don't want my son to be scared, so I'm flooring the pedal and he's asking me why I'm driving so fast and I'm going, 'Don't turn around.' . . ."

I looked at the waitress. It wasn't her fault; she was just putting in her eight hours, and she heard this tape repeat itself on the PA system every night of her working life. Still, I wished that the bartender would bring her the drinks she was waiting for.

Gene Pitney: ". . . but I'm gonna be strong, and pretend I don't care."

Sometimes a song makes you recall exactly where you were when you first heard it. I was in my room at my parents' house in Bristol, trying to work up the nerve to call a girl who had told me she didn't want to see me anymore. I thought that, somehow, by dint of logic and willful persuasion, I could change her mind. It seemed very important to me at the time. That song came on WCOL, and I thought Gene Pitney was somehow reading my mind and speaking directly to me.

"All of a sudden," the waitress said to her colleague, "it gets real still . . ."

"You guys about ready to turn in?" Michael said.

"Let me finish my beer," Ronnie said.

"I mean so still you wouldn't believe it," the waitress said.

I looked around the room. Apparently something of overwhelming interest was happening on ESPN; people had walked closer to the TV sets so that they wouldn't miss a moment.

Gene Pitney sang the last words of the song:

". . . and I break down and cry."

A couple of afternoons later, out by the pool (the weather had been good, so we had decided to stay), we were getting some sun and talking when two mothers with young children came out of their rooms and selected lounges right across the way from us. The mothers put their kids' toys and plastic buckets by the edge of the pool. The mothers were wearing baggy shorts and oversized T-shirts.

They took them off to reveal bathing suits that, thirty-five years ago, strippers would have been arrested for wearing onstage. Tiny pieces of cloth that didn't even pretend to try to cover them; these moms were all tan belly and tan leg.

"Honey, you be careful in there," one of them said to her daughter.

The girl, about twelve, said, "The sign says it's only three feet."

"Don't believe the sign until you test how deep it is yourself," the mother said, rubbing oil onto her stomach.

"Am I mistaken," Michael said, "or when we were kids, didn't mothers wear nice one-piece bathing suits with ruffled skirts attached to the waists?"

"I know," I said. "I'm not sure when this happened."

Indeed, the mothers across the pool were not at all unusual; this is how moms at swimming pools dress now. At least a lot of them. They show up in their perfectly normal shorts and perfectly normal shirts, and then they remove them and they're something out of *Penthouse*.

"You're still not over your cold yet, Jason," the second mother said, adjusting the pieces of yarn that formed the top of her bikini. She was talking to her son. "I don't want you to overdo it today."

"I won't, Mom," the child yelled from the pool.

There was never a striptease theater in Bristol, but in Columbus there was one called the Gayety Burlesque. I know this because the Gayety used to take out a small advertisement in the morning newspaper every day. With each ad was a little picture of the stripper who was the current headliner. My favorite—judging only from the newspaper photo, of course, I was eight years old at the time and would never dare to nurture the hope of going anywhere near the Gayety Burlesque; by the time I was a teenager the Gayety was gone—my favorite was a woman named Rose La Rose. In the newspaper ads she was dressed in a black negligee; she had dark hair and a sultry expression, or at least as sultry as an expression can get in a three-inch-by-one-column advertisement. Rose La Rose, to me, was the ultimate promise of unreachable eroticism and forbidden titillation; Rose La Rose, in her newsprint negligee, was everything that I would never in my life get to see.

Rose La Rose was dressed to go slalom skiing in comparison with these two moms across the pool. Rose La Rose, in comparison with these two moms, was dressed to conduct a chapel service.

The first mom took a plastic bottle from a tote bag she had placed next to her lounge. The plastic bottle was filled with water, and had a mechanical spray attachment on top.

She was on her stomach; she reached behind her and sprayed a fine mist over the part of her that the bottom of her bikini did not even endeavor to cover.

"How do you think Donna Reed would have looked in one of those things?" Michael said.

"Take a good look at Donna Reed on the reruns sometime," I said. "She was really beautiful."

"Jason?" the second mom called out. "You had a big lunch. I don't want you to go out of the shallow end for a while."

When we had checked in at the motel, the manager told me that he knew me from somewhere. Two or three days will go by without that happening, and then I'll hear it five or six times in a row. I have no idea why it happens in spurts like that, but after all these years of doing my job I'm well aware that it does.

"Yeah, I've seen you," the manager said. When you have a job in the field that I do, that's about as close to a genuine compliment as you're likely to get. I've seen you. You learn not to expect people to follow that up by saying that they've liked the work they've seen you do. And they don't mean the omission of the follow-up as an insult. Still, you never know quite what to say after someone has informed you that he has seen you. "Thank you" is certainly not the appropriate response.

"Thank you," I said.

"Harry Reasoner stayed here once," he said. For some reason I am always checking into motels where Harry Reasoner had once been a guest.

Over the next couple of days, the manager was constantly checking with me to see if everything was all right. It's such a curious by-product of appearing on television; by virtue of having your picture sent through the air, people you've never met are eager to go out of their way to please you. Even if—as is often the case with me—the people are not sure of precisely what it is you do on television.

Had the motel manager not recognized me—had he been one of the many, many people who walk right past me without the slightest sense that they have ever set eyes on me—he wouldn't have been offering to be of special assistance. I'd be the same person, but he wouldn't be interested. It's a perplexing phenomenon. If you're known to the person you're talking to at a given moment, there's nothing you can tell the person that will convince him that you're really not all that famous. You and Harry Reasoner are on the same level, in that person's eyes. If, on the other hand, the person has never heard of you, you could be Muhammad Ali and the person still wouldn't be impressed. Beauty may not truly be in the eye of the beholder, but fame is. The beholder is the only one who can grant it.

The motel manager had granted it. And by making himself so available to me—seeing if I needed extra towels for the pool, offering to drive me around town in the motel's airport van—the manager was allowing me to take a look into his own life. He talked quite a bit, and I found myself listening.

"I've got to get back to Texas," he told me one morning. He was in his late forties; he had a ruddy face and a flaming red, bulbous nose that hinted at too many late nights closing his own motel bar. He wore a business suit every day, even though just about all of the guests at this place wore shorts and casual shirts. This was an establishment that featured low-end rates.

"I was general manager of an eight-hundred-room place near the Dallas–Fort Worth Airport," he said. "We ran ninety percent occupancy all the time." Over the course of the next several days he would repeat this statement; he never did volunteer how he went from an eight-hundred-room megahotel in Dallas to a sixty-unit budget place on the outskirts of Omaha. And I didn't ask.

"My wife hates it here," he said. "I don't know if she's allergic or what, but she's sneezing all the time. She's miserable all day, and I can't sleep at night, listening to her. I told her that the first job offer back in Texas that I can find, we're gone."

Yet I was struck by the peculiar level of devotion he evidently had to a job he clearly didn't like. The business suits were the tip-off; there was no one here to check on him if he had decided to dress more casually. But the suits were there, every morning. And he would complain to me about what he perceived to be the motel chain's lack of vision for this property: "They're telling me to run it like a budget motel. I argue with them that we'd do better as a full-service place. But I can't make them move an inch on it. We've got to do something to get more business. Most hotels that are near an airport do eighty-five, ninety percent occupancy, all the time. We're only doing sixty-five percent. We just lost another airline crew to the Ramada down the road, so now we're down to one van. I could justify running two vans before that airline crew switched, but with them gone, there aren't enough regular airport runs to keep both vans busy."

One afternoon I was talking with him when a young woman drove up in a sports car. She opened the trunk and pulled out a water pump.

"You get it all?" he said to her.

"I sure did," she said. "I'll put this back in the maintenance room."

When she had moved out of sight he said to me, "She's my assistant manager. She's got a pool at home, and I don't know, maybe a Jacuzzi, too." The expression on his face indicated he didn't know how she, working for him, was able to afford such things. This plainly made him feel puzzled, and perhaps a little cheated. "She had some pipes overflow, so she took our pump home to clean things up," he said, sounding slightly annoyed.

So it was that I became privy to the daily dramas of his life. He kept his desk out in the small lobby itself, rather than behind the check-in counter, to make himself available to the customers; I realized that it would have been easier for him to hide away in back. As unhappy as he seemed, something about him wanted to run this place right. One morning I went out to the pool, and two teenagers, a brother and sister, were waiting to go in. But the motel's custodian was telling them they had to wait. The custodian was at the deep end, checking the chemical content of the water in a test tube. I had seen him doing this the day before; apparently it was a requirement of his job.

"Are you done yet?" the teenage boy said to the custodian.

"Just a minute," the custodian said, scrutinizing the colors in the test tube.

The teenage girl said to her brother, "Look at this." She pointed to a bruise on her leg. "I must have done this yesterday. I got one last week, too, when we were camping over at Crawford Cave. Big old bruise, about yea big."

The motel manager, in his suit, came out of the lobby and knelt beside the custodian. They discussed what they were seeing in the test tube. It was much too hot a day for a business suit.

Here was this poolside tableau. Three guests—the girl, her brother, and me. Michael and Ronnie were still in their rooms. Two employees— the manager and custodian. For whatever reason, the manager insisted on this daily chemical analysis, and insisted on supervising it himself. Regardless of what the custodian thought about having to do this, he did it without question.

The manager stood up. The custodian motioned the brother and sister to go ahead and jump into the pool.

"Morning, Ben," the manager said to me. "Listen, I know we've got you in a room with two single beds. Would you rather have a queen? I can move you if you want."

I said I was fine where I was; I didn't feel like packing and unpacking again.

"You change your mind, you know where to find me," the manager said, sweating through the fabric of the suit.

That evening we decided that we would move on the next morning. We were in Ronnie's room; on his television set, a woman without her shirt on was kissing another woman. It was a R-rated production available on in-room pay-per-view; Ronnie had punched the button for the movie and was keeping it on just as a background visual. Sort of like a painting on the wall.

"I still can't get used to seeing this stuff on TV," Michael said.

Out by the pool, the motel's satellite dish stood constant sentry, its cone pointing deep into space. This motel might have been low-budget—we couldn't even get room service from the Poodle Skirt, there weren't enough waitresses on duty at any one time to allow for such an amenity, and if we wanted our clothes cleaned we had to go to the laundromat across the street—but the motel had its satellite dish up and working; lately it seemed that most of the American landscape was dotted with satellite dishes. At this motel if a guest wanted some eggs brought to his room for breakfast it could not be arranged, but there was that science-fiction machine sitting next to the swimming pool, aimed at the stars, ready to suck dirty movies out of the ionosphere and put them in the guest rooms twenty-four hours a day.

"I'm sure John Glenn must be very proud," Michael said.

In school we had sat in geography class with the blinds pulled down, watching on a big TV set that had been rolled on casters to our classroom from the audiovisual closet down the hall. We had looked at the live black-and-white picture on the screen as our fellow Ohioan—and it's hard to even describe now how thrilling it was to think about that fact—was catapulted into the sky in a desperate effort by the United States to catch up with the Russians in the race for space. Our hearts were rushing as the fire beneath the rocket ignited, and slowly the white ship lifted off the pad, and the absolute danger was palpable and the voice of the capsule communicator inside the control building at Cape Canaveral said: "Godspeed, John Glenn."

In Ronnie's room the woman without a shirt on, delivered to us from a satellite circling the globe, said to the other woman: "Wouldn't you be more comfortable without the sweater?"

And the other woman, her mouth moist from having been kissed by the first woman, pulled her sweater over her head.

We left early. Sometimes I wonder what Michael would have said had he known what lay in store for him. It doesn't really matter, though; he didn't know, of course, and we couldn't very well stay in Omaha all summer. Airport Roulette is fine as far as it goes, but you can't let it take over your whole life.

So that next morning, just after seven o'clock, we met in the lobby. The manager was already there, standing behind the registration desk with a paper cup full of coffee in front of him. He was talking to one of the housekeepers, or rather she was talking to him; she was leaning on the front desk like a customer ready to check in, but she was reading aloud to him from a handwritten list.

I could hear her talking: "112, 116, 118, 124 . . ."

The manager was making check marks on his own piece of paper as she read the numbers aloud.

She kept it up: "206, 210 . . ."

I walked over. I told the manager that we were taking off, and that I wanted to say goodbye. We shook hands, and then I asked him what the numbers were all about.

"Oh, it's just a little system that I have," he said. "Every night I have the housekeepers check what rooms are empty, and then first thing in the morning I match the empty rooms against my occupancy list. I want to make sure they match up."

"To see if anyone has skipped out on you without paying?" I said.

"That's one thing," he said. "Also, you don't want someone to find a key and move into a room he's not paying for. It's a good idea in case of emergencies, too. I like the housekeepers to check every night just in case."

"In case of what?" I said.

"Some sort of accidental incident," he said.

"You mean like a dead person?" I said.

"I just feel better checking," he said.

"Has that ever happened to you?" I said. "A body in a room?"

"Not so to speak," he said. "Not a body that the housekeepers have found. Down in Dallas I had some deaths, but in those cases I always found out there was a problem from friends or family of the deceased guests. The housekeepers didn't discover it during spot checks. That's not to say it couldn't happen, though. We'll do this again after lunch, after all the rooms have been cleaned for the day."

Seven o'clock in the morning; the forecast was for 95 degrees by midday. Today his suit was dark gray. I told him that I hoped he'd find a job he liked in Texas before too many more months passed by.

"Thank you for saying that," he said. "Right now I'm just trying to do a job running this place."

Michael and Ronnie and I departed through the front door, leaving only the housekeeper and the manager in the lobby.

Her voice started up again: "228, 232, 240 . . ." The manager's head was down, his hand making check marks on the list next to his coffee cup.

Ten

THERE IS A SUMMER FEELING I had almost forgotten about. It's the feeling that comes when you soak up so much sun that it seems to fill you up inside. It's almost as if you have chosen to allow the sun to punch you around.

"My mom used to joke about it," Michael said one afternoon. "She would see me out playing in the sun for five and six hours at a time, and she'd say, 'If you were a bottle and the sun were soda pop, you'd be overflowing by now.' "

I told him I remembered her saying that. Actually, Michael's mom would include both of us in her joke; we'd be running back and forth through the sprinkler in his backyard, as if that sprinkler were the most imaginative and innovative amusement park ever devised by man, and Mrs. Wolff would stick her head out the back door: "If you boys were bottles . . ."

That all changed; for one thing, spending time in the summer sun became one more activity to be ruled by a wristwatch. After we grew up we allowed ourselves to relax in the sun, but only to a certain point; if we weren't checking our watches to see if it was time to come out of the sun for an appointment or a scheduled phone call or a family meal, then we were checking our watches to make sure we hadn't overdone our minutes beneath the sun, even in the absence of an overriding reason to go inside. The sun, along with so many other things we had never questioned—sugar, salt, cheeseburgers, french-fried onion rings—had become a potential enemy. The fact that we didn't have enough time for it was seen almost as a hidden blessing. The sun had changed from being the best and most vivid symbol of summer to being an antagonist in the sky, a nemesis to hide from and feel guilty about. We picked up bottles of Coppertone and checked the SPF numbers.

We felt better if the labels on the bottles referred to the contents inside as "sunscreen" rather than "suntan lotion." Sun? Quick—screen us.

So I had just about forgotten what it felt like to let the sun pound away at you. On the road, we stopped wearing our watches. It took us about a week to figure out that there were no regulations governing when a person had to eat lunch or eat dinner; we would hit a town and hang out for a couple of days, swimming and walking the streets and sitting around talking in the afternoon air, getting too much sun, getting so much sun that we stopped paying attention. We were browner than we had been since we were kids, and we paid less mind to it than we had since we were kids. Late one afternoon I looked over at Michael, and I said, "You been putting lemon juice in your hair?"

He laughed. The girls in Bristol had always squirted lemon juice into their hair all summer; the juice was supposed to combine with the sun to make their hair lighter. The girls were always quite open about it. At the Bristol pool they would haul out their lemon juice containers—you could buy them at the grocery, they were made of yellow plastic shaped like lemons and had green twist-off caps, and the girls would soak their hair with lemon juice and comb it through. For a boy to do that would be frowned upon, to put it mildly; if a boy's hair got suspiciously blond during the summer, his friends would accuse him of using lemon juice, and in no way was that accusation ever construed as a compliment. If some guy's hair got too light, he would do everything short of providing family pictures to prove that this was an inherited natural tendency that happened every summer without the assistance of any citrus products. Some guys, in desperation, even invited their friends to smell their hair: "See? You smell lemon? This always happens to my hair." And the variation: "It's the chlorine from the pool that does it."

Michael looked ten years younger than he had on the first night of the reunion. He could have been a golf pro at some municipal course somewhere. "Yeah, right, I have room service bring me a glass of lemon juice with my breakfast every morning," he said to me, his eyes closed, his face turned to the sun.

"If you did, you'd only need a thimbleful," Ronnie said.

"Spare me the hair jokes," Michael said. "You should talk."

But whatever hair that did remain was, indeed, getting bleached out by the sun. He and Ronnie had taken to wearing sunglasses. I have enough trouble adjusting to the change in illumination when I walk from the sun to go inside, and for me sunglasses only make it worse. Some people look rakish and elegantly sophisticated with sunglasses; with sunglasses I tend to walk into walls.

Sometimes in the late afternoon we would go to our rooms to get ready for dinner, and the next thing we'd know it would be nine o'clock and the phone would be ringing. In my room I'd awaken with a start. It would be Michael or Ronnie. The same thing would have happened to each of us. We'd have been so knocked out by the day in the sun and the heat that we'd have lain down on our beds and fallen immediately asleep.

With the sense of disorientation that three abruptly interrupted hours of sun-impelled sleep brings, I would start to wakefulness, momentarily have no idea where I was, then answer the phone to hear one of their voices.

The voice would always be groggy. "I must have conked out," the voice would say. "I don't know what happened. I thought you guys might have gone to dinner without me."

But we hadn't; we had conked out too. More than once the question had been asked: Is ten o'clock too late to have dinner?

It never was. Ten o'clock was proving to be a perfectly fine hour to have dinner. It's not like there was going to be an alarm clock buzzing in the morning.

At lunch one day—we were eating hot dogs in a drive-in parking lot—Ronnie asked me if I had a computer terminal in my office at work.

"Sure," I said. "That's what I write on. Why do you ask?"

"I have one, too," he said. "I can pull up sales figures on it. One day this guy who works for me—I think he's our age, maybe a little older—came into my office and he saw that the screen on my terminal was smudged. He told me he'd be back in a minute. When he came back he said, 'This is the greatest thing going.' He was carrying a bottle of Windex. He said, 'You really ought to keep one of these in your desk. It makes all the difference in the world.' "

"So what's the joke?" I said.

"No joke," Ronnie said. "It's just that he believed that the bottle of Windex was changing his life. I bought one, too. I used it every couple of days. It made my computer screen much clearer. I went home and I told Marilyn what a big improvement it was making in my day."

Michael had gone into the drive-in to get a refill on his Coke, and now he was walking back across the sunbaked parking lot toward us. We were going to decide which direction to head next.

"A bottle of Windex," Ronnie said. "It had come to that. I was actually grateful that a bottle of Windex was making my life better."

On the morning of the Fourth of July we woke up in a small Iowa town called Salena. We hadn't picked it on purpose; we'd been driving, and late the night before we had spotted a motel just off the expressway.

We walked to the center of town at around 9 A.M. The local Fourth of July parade was forming at the elementary school: fife-and-drum corps, cheerleaders, antique cars.

"I want to watch this," Michael said.

"I don't think we're due anywhere, unless you know something I don't," Ronnie said.

This was the kind of town that, in theory, should have been something out of a Grant Wood painting; the kind of town populated by sturdy rural men and women in starched collars and gingham dresses, their children in Buster Brown outfits. That particular America doesn't exist anymore, or at least if it did, I hadn't found it in all my travels. There was probably a time when those archetypes did reside in a village like this. But this morning the woman in charge of making sure the parade formed up correctly was wearing Nike running shoes, track shorts, and a T-shirt featuring the logo of the rock band REO Speedwagon; her hair was freshly permed. Her husband, carrying a clipboard, assisted her; he wore a jogging suit that bore the Puma label on the outside of both the pants and the top, and a St. Louis Cardinals baseball cap. Someday perhaps they, or men and women with American lives similar to theirs, will be featured in oil portraits that recall a vanished time and place. In the middle of the twenty-first century Americans will look at that portrait—she standing in her rock-concert T-shirt, he standing in his sweats—and will pine nostalgically for the era in which the couple lived, when the world was simpler and purer. Except there may be no oil portraits by that time; the husband and wife organizing the parade may be preserved only on videotape, provided that the tape now being used in millions of camcorders in thousands of towns proves resistant to disintegration over the years.

About a dozen of the camcorders were being aimed at the various parade participants at this very moment. The husband and wife appeared to be efficient and conscientious; they tended to the children of the town who were wandering into the street, and made sure that everyone got to the proper spots in the parade line. A fellow who looked to be in his seventies drove his vintage Hudson to the middle of the intersection where the front of the parade was forming. He was confused about where he was supposed to be. Rather than just point, the woman in charge hopped in next to him, navigated for him while he drove around the block, directed him to the position with the other old cars, then, satisfied that he was content and at ease, trotted back to join her husband and to work out the hundred other details that needed to be taken care of before the parade stepped off. Nike shoes and baseball caps notwithstanding, this man and woman, at least upon first reflection, did indeed seem worthy potential models for any portrait artist contemplating a record of people attempting to live honorably and well at this particular time in this particular country.

Along the side streets, the residents of Salena had pulled breakfast-room chairs up to the edges of the lawns. People who didn't have chairs sat on the low curbs, their knees jutting up to mid-chest level. At most of the homes, doughnuts, coffee, and juice were being offered to anyone who asked; everyone seemed to know everyone. We were looking for a spot to view the parade, and a man in madras Bermuda shorts and a golf shirt said, kidding and at the same time friendly and unchallenging: "Lost?"

"Sort of," I said. "Lost on purpose."

"Well, sit down," the man said, motioning to a patch of grass that ran along the curb in front of his house. "Unless you're planning on marching, you might as well watch."

So we did. Michael and Ronnie and I sat on the curb, and within fifteen minutes the parade began. There seemed to be a Fourth of July tradition in Salena—children on every float and in every marching unit tossed wrapped pieces of hard candy to the spectators along the route. It was startling the first time it happened; we were sitting there and this stuff came skipping at us from the solid surface of the street—but after a while it became a nice routine. We would comment on a bugle corps or a Cub Scout pack, and then the candy would come skittering across the blacktop. The children of the neighborhood dashed out to retrieve it; the littler kids weren't having any luck, and some of them cried when they kept getting shut out. Ronnie—he surprises me some-times—noticed this, and assigned himself the job of benefactor for the smallest children. When the candy would bounce toward us he would scoop some up, then search out the boys and girls who had come up empty. He'd call out—"Hey, kid!"—and when he'd catch the eye of the child who'd been left empty-handed, he'd make sure no bigger kids were still around and then he'd roll the candy over to the child. That was a nice touch; it made the kids without candy feel better than if he'd just handed it to them. You could see it in their faces—they liked scooping it up themselves.

I tried to compliment him on it, which clearly annoyed him.

"I thought I recognized these peppermint wheels," he said, holding up a piece of candy with cellophane twisted tightly around it. "I did a deal where we bought about twelve tons of this stuff for like a hundred dollars a ton. It belonged to this cruise line. They used the candy as after-dinner sweets. But the cruise line went out of business and had to liquidate all its inventory. We turned the candy shipment around and sold it to discount stores and made a two thousand percent profit."

"I just meant that what you did for those kids was nice," I said. "You don't have to read me your annual earnings statement."

He looked at me as if I ought to be smart enough to know when he doesn't want to hear something. He held the piece of candy close to my face.

"I swear, this is the same stuff," he said. "Wouldn't that be something, if these people bought the lot that I closed out?"

I shook my head at him and turned back to watch the rest of the parade. It lasted about an hour and a half, and it had the same kind of effect on me as a refreshing shower. It just made me feel great. As the final units marched up the street toward us, I said to Michael, "I could start every morning this way."

"Yeah, but we don't live in the town," he said.

"What's that supposed to mean?" I said.

"I was eavesdropping a little bit," he said. "I was hearing the 'It was better last year' syndrome."

"Well, that's always going to happen," I said.

I had overheard the same comments that Michael had. About ten minutes into the parade, the voice of a man somewhere behind me on the lawn had said, "What do you think?" And the voice of a woman had said, "It's all right, I guess. But it's not as good as last year." More than one person had expressed that sentiment during the course of the parade.

It's unavoidable; wherever you live, whatever the civic touchstones are—Christmas-tree lightings, homecoming bonfires, Labor Day picnics—you're going to hear that. Yeah, it's fine this year. Last year was better. The impulse must lie somewhere near the very nub of human nature.

On this day in Salena, I couldn't take my eyes off the gleaming and freshly polished old-time cars, and I got a lift from the music of the marching barbershop quartet, and I must admit that I even waved back when the mayor of Salena, riding in an open convertible, waved to those of us on the curb.

But to many of the people who lived here, the cars were the same ones they had seen for the last ten or twenty years—except every year one or two of the drivers seem to pass away, and it doesn't seem that they get replaced by new drivers; the younger townspeople don't have an interest in antique cars. The marching barbershop quartet is the same one that sings at every town festivity, and their repertoire is no longer a surprise, even down to the jokes they make between numbers. The mayor is waving, all right; he's up for reelection in November.

So it makes sense that the people in Salena feel that they've seen it before; they have. My guess is that people who had left Salena, and who came back after years of living away from home, probably like the parade better than the people who had stayed.

We stood up after the last unit in the parade—actually it wasn't a unit at all, it was a Salena police car with its siren turned off but its roof light revolving as a harmonious holiday beacon—rolled past us. We walked down the street, and a lady who was trying to figure who we were called, "How'd you enjoy it?"

"It was great," I called back to her. "Much better than last year."

The surprise party at Debby Forbes' house—it's not Debby Forbes anymore, it's Debby Waggoner, but we didn't know that until the man at the rib place in Kansas City told us—was not something we had planned on attending. The news that she was turning forty struck us as implausible. Especially Michael.

"Of course she's turning forty this year," Ronnie said to him. "She's three years younger than we are."

"I can accept myself being forty-three," Michael said. "I cannot accept Debby Forbes being forty."

They went together for only about three months one summer in Bristol. It was the summer right before our senior year; we were going to be seniors, and Debby Forbes' class were going to be freshmen. It hit Michael as hard as I'd ever seen him get hit. I am quite sure that Debby Forbes was the first girl Michael was ever in love with, although he never said it to us in those words.

Debby Forbes was about as beautiful as a high school girl in the middle of Ohio can be, which is very. She had that long butterscotch hair and luminous smile that you expect to see only on the front of shampoo packages. There was nothing exotic or sophisticated about the way Debby Forbes looked. Merely Midwestern perfect. There seems to be one girl like that—and only one—in every high school class, and in Debby's class there was no question but that she was the girl.

That summer before senior year Michael and Ronnie and I would head out together in the evenings. Bristol would be illuminated by streetlights, and the sound track of those nights would be a combination of the music coming out of car radios and the high-pitched chirping of crickets in the fully blossomed trees that lined the streets. Our wandering was aimless, up until Michael met Debby. After that Ronnie and I knew that regardless of whatever else we might do during a given evening, before we all went home we were going to have to find Debby so that Michael could see her.

Debby's parents lived on Rodman Drive, about a mile away from the school. Their house had a screened-in front porch, with couches and chairs on it; Debby's family always kept the lamps inside that porch turned on during the summer months, which made it the easiest house in the neighborhood to spot. That whole porch seemed to glow.

So the three of us—that was the summer when we favored long shorts and moccasins and white T-shirts with dress shirts worn open and untucked in over the T-shirts, it was the uniform for Bristol males that summer—the three of us would come walking up Debby's front lawn, trying not to make any noise in case it was her parents on the porch and not her. From about twenty feet away we could discern who was on the porch; when it was Debby, I could tell that Michael was smiling even when he was walking behind me and I couldn't see him.

All that summer we came as a package deal to Debby's house. We were there only because Michael was so consumed by her, but the etiquette of being consumed by the thought of a girl was such that the presence of Ronnie and me was required, too. It was okay that Michael was in love with Debby, but if he were to begin showing up alone at her house—if she were to be out on her porch with her own friends, which she generally was, and Michael were to come wandering over the grass by himself—that would have thrown the whole Bristol social cosmos out of whack. What would Debby have been expected to do with her friends if Michael were to arrive alone? And, more important, what signal would such an arrival have given about Michael's fundamental priorities? Falling for Debby was one thing; forsaking his best friends for her would have been quite another.

So all that summer the three of us would arrive together. Debby and her friends would be on her parents' porch, and she would come to the screen door and invite us in, and after a few minutes she and Michael would go out for a walk. Ronnie and I would flirt a little with Debby's friends, but it was bloodless flirtation, everyone knew that nothing was going to happen, we were there for one reason and that was to act as Michael's convoy.

I don't know exactly what broke Michael and Debby up. All I remember is that within a few weeks after the end of the summer they were no longer boyfriend and girlfriend, and we didn't see much of her, except in the hallways of school. So my recollections of Debby Forbes are fairly specific: She is sitting on that warmly lighted front porch, and the three of us are heading toward the light with our feet sinking into the thick grass, and my best friend, seventeen years old and in love for the first time in his life, is the happiest I have ever seen him, perhaps not even aware that I notice.

And now, in this new summer of ours, we had driven into St. Louis on a July afternoon and had rented rooms in a hotel that was part of the city's old main train station. We had arrived in St. Louis via a kind of three-cushion shot. After the Fourth of July we had left Salena and headed toward Kansas City. At dinner at a rib place downtown there, the owner of the restaurant, greeting us as he stopped at our table, asked us what we were doing in town and where we were from. His question was just one of professional politeness; apparently he liked to make conversation with his guests when he had the time.

When we told him that we were friends who had all grown up in a place we were sure he had never heard of, he asked us what the name of the place was; in his job he had heard of just about every place. And when we told him, he said that, see, he was right. As a matter of fact, he had heard of Bristol, Ohio; he had a close friend who had a business partner whose wife came from Bristol—they had all gotten together a few months back. Which is how we learned that Debby Forbes, now Debby Waggoner, was living in a suburb of St. Louis, and which is what led Ronnie and me to persuade the restaurant owner to call his friend—Michael wasn't pushing for this, I could tell that he was ambivalent about it—and which in turn was what led to our finding out that Debby was about to turn forty, and that this week her family and friends were having a surprise party for her.

"Let's stop somewhere first," Michael said.

"Like where?" Ronnie said.

"Just somewhere where we can get a drink or something," Michael said.

"It's a party," Ronnie said. "They'll have drinks there."

"Come on," Michael said. "Humor me. Just one."

There are people who spend the rest of their lives dreaming about the first person they ever loved. Michael is not one of them. Debby Forbes did not leave scars on him—he remembered her fondly, but for him she was just something wonderful that once happened to him for three months in a long-ago summer. He had not kept in touch with her, nor ever looked into the possibility of keeping in touch; when he had found out that she was living within driving distance of where we were he was surprised and pleased, but this was not one of those situations where a man finally meets up again with the one woman he has secretly been searching for. At dinner in Kansas City, I think I was more taken with the idea of Debby Forbes being just four hours down I-70 from us than Michael was.

But now, in St. Louis, it was Michael who was asking us if we would stop for a drink first.

"We don't want to be late," I said.

"It doesn't matter if we're late," he said. "She's going to be surprised enough by all the people jumping out at her. We can be a second surprise."

In the bar of a place called the Clayton Inn—Clayton was the suburb where Debby Forbes Waggoner lived—Michael ordered a scotch and soda.

"What are you so nervous about?" Ronnie said.

"I think that's probably obvious," Michael said.

"You worried that she's going to look at you and think you're an old man?" Ronnie said.

Michael just shot him a quick glance.

"She's going to be looking at all of us," Ronnie said. "Relax."

We followed the directions that had been given to us over the phone back in Kansas City. On the phone, the restaurant owner's friend had said that Debby would be thrilled to have us at the party; as far as he knew, we'd be the only people from her hometown who would be there. He said he'd check with his partner—Debby's husband—but he couldn't imagine a reason that we would not be welcome.

So it was, shortly after nightfall, that we found ourselves cruising a side street in Clayton, Missouri, looking for the number 2529 on a house sign.

"I don't see too many cars," Ronnie said. "Are you sure we're on the right street?"

"It's a surprise party, remember?" I said. "The people wouldn't have parked on this street."

We found it by the noise. The party was in progress—apparently Debby had already been delivered to her house and the surprise had been sprung. We pulled the rental car over to the curb, got out, and started up across the lawn.

"I don't know," Michael said.

I didn't either. It had seemed like such a fine idea in Kansas City— the three of us showing up at Debby's house, just like we did all those years ago. To us it fit right into this curious summer; the idea that we would drive all the way across Missouri just so we could drop in at the party didn't strike us as unusual at all. At least it hadn't right up until now. But with the music sounding from the backyard, and the voices wafting through the air, suddenly I was acutely aware that the guests we were about to see had no idea that we were coming, and that they could be excused if they were bewildered about the circumstances of our presence.

We kept walking. There was a swimming pool in back, and two bartenders in tuxedos pouring drinks. We stood off to the side for a moment, just looking in, like we had upon arriving at so many open houses, wondering what lay ahead.

A man was motioning toward us. He hurried over.

"Hi!" he said. "We haven't told her."

He was the friend of the restaurant owner. "You, I recognize, Mr. Kroeger," he said to me. One of these days I fear Ronnie is going to punch somebody for saying that. "And you must be the other friends," he said to Ronnie and Michael.

"That's right," Ronnie said. "We're the other ones."

The man didn't catch the edge, or if he did he chose not to say anything about it. Instead he said, "Jack Waggoner and I have been in business together for almost fifteen years. It's hard for me to think of Debby as anything other than Jack's wife. She's a great gal."

None of us knew how to respond.

"Well, come on," the fellow said. "This ought to get a rise out of her."

We followed him through the crowd. We moved past people who were sipping cocktails and eating hot dogs that were being served from a grill. When we got to a stone patio there were three couples standing together, and one of the women was Debby Forbes. Her hair was blond and cut short, and she was wearing a white blouse and a black skirt that didn't quite reach her knees, and two children, apparently hers, were holding on to her, seemingly a little intimidated by all the people who had materialized in their backyard. She was a very pretty woman out behind her very expensive house; she was Debby Forbes, all right, and tonight she was forty years old.

She looked over at us, smiling but with no decipherable expression on her face. She might have been thinking that we were business associates of her husband, men she had met on previous occasions, and thus she might have been trying to come up with our names so as not to embarrass herself, or him.

This was all happening within the span of a second or two. Debby looked at us, polite and trying to figure out where we had met.

"We've got lots of surprises for you tonight, honey," said the man next to her, who evidently was her husband.

His partner said, "Debby, these gentlemen came all the way from Bristol to wish you a happy birthday. Don't tell me you don't recognize Ben Kroeger from the TV news."

Her eyes focused on me, but only for an instant; I was a catalyst, and through me, in that instant, she figured it all out.

Her husband said, "Did you three have any trouble finding the house?"

She was looking straight at Michael and Michael was looking back.

Debby was showing us around the house. "This is the living room, of course," she was saying, "and . . . honey, do we have to have this out here?"

On a glass coffee table was a videotape with a package that indicated it was something called "*Playboy*'s Sexy Lingerie."

"Hey, you aren't the only one who's getting gifts tonight," her husband said. "Art Branfield brought me this. He said now that I've got a senior citizen for a wife, I'll probably be inclined to watch this kind of stuff."

"I know," Debby said. "I was here when he gave it to you. I just don't think we want to have this lying around the living room. The children know how to use the VCR, you know."

"What do you want me to do, throw it away?" her husband said.

"Just put it somewhere where they can't get at it," Debby said.

So her husband wandered off toward the back of the house with the tape. I had a hunch about what he was going to do with it. When *Playboy* was new—when we were the first generation of children whose fathers had it in the house—many of our dads hid the magazine in their shirt drawers. It was a classic American scene from the fifties and sixties: the copy of *Playboy* stuffed under three or four of a father's freshly laundered white shirts. And now Debby Forbes' husband was taking his *Playboy* video to where he could conceal it from his children. I had a real feeling that the tape was about to be slipped underneath a pile of shirts. Where, if history was any indication, the kids would find it within five minutes of the moment he pulled out of the driveway for work tomorrow morning.

"I have to get this straight again," Debby said to us. "Jack didn't invite you?"

"What, you don't want us to be here?" Ronnie said, grinning.

"No, no, that's not it at all," she said. "I'm just not sure I understand."

"We sort of invited ourselves," I said.

"But what were you doing in town?" Debby said.

"We weren't exactly in town," Ronnie said.

"Then why are you in town?" Debby said.

"For the party," I said.

"You came all the way to St. Louis for my birthday party," Debby said, as if suspecting that this was all a trick and that we were making fun of her.

"We were in Kansas City anyway," Ronnie said.

Michael wasn't saying much. He was looking around the living room as if it were a display in some science-fiction exhibit. He was reading the subscription label on the cover of the July issue of *Vogue*. It was addressed to Ms. Deborah Waggoner. There seemed to be some message in those words that vaguely perplexed him.

Jack Waggoner returned from the back of the house. "Are you folks hungry?" he said to me.

"I might eat one of those hot dogs," Ronnie said.

"We'll get you one," Jack Waggoner said. "Come on, honey," he said to Debby. "Your guests are probably wondering what happened to us."

So Jack and Debby Waggoner, with Ronnie in tow, stepped out of the house and onto the patio. Debby stopped to look at Michael, as if she wanted to say something. But she didn't.

Michael kept picking things up in the living room, as if he were taking inventory. We were alone in there.

"This is all too strange," he said.

"I thought you were going to dust that copy of *Vogue* for fingerprints," I said.

"I don't know," he said. "I just couldn't put that address label together with Debby. She's Ms. Deborah Waggoner in some magazine company's computer somewhere."

"Probably in Boulder, Colorado," I said.

"What are you talking about?" Michael said.

"Didn't you ever notice?" I said. "All those magazine subscription cards seem to be addressed to Boulder, Colorado, for some reason. They're never addressed to the city where the magazine is published."

"That's hardly the point," Michael said.

"Then what is?" I said, although I thought I already knew.

"It's just the stuff around the house here that makes me feel weird," he said. "The magazine label, the Whitney Houston CDs, the golf trophies . . ."

Her husband had a shelfful of golf trophies above the television set. He had been country club champion seven summers ago.

"Look at that," Michael said. He nodded toward a bookshelf. There was a full set of the *World Book Encyclopedia*.

"They have the *World Book* for their kids," he said.

"Why are you surprised by that?" I said. "You've got the same kind of stuff in your house."

"I know," he said. "But I've watched me for the last twenty-five years. When this stuff is happening to you day by day, it kind of sneaks up on you. I haven't seen Debby. She was walking down the hallway at Bristol, and now her husband is country club golf champion."

"Former champion," I said.

"Former champion," Michael said. "That's even worse."

I was just as glad that Ronnie was outside. This was the kind of conversation that drove him crazy. He couldn't see the implications of it—of Debby Forbes now being the digitally coded Ms. Deborah Waggoner in a publishing-house computer in Colorado. One of thousands of Deborahs and Katherines and Judiths in that computer, all of them loyal readers of *Vogue*, all of them bearing decades of history since the hazily recalled days when, somewhere, someone fell in love with them for the first time. That's the way it was supposed to be, of course; the years go by and things change and you become someone you weren't before. That's the way of nature and mortality. It happens to everyone. You don't think about it much, though, until something very minor—a set of encyclopedias in Debby Forbes' living room, for Debby Forbes' children—sparks you and makes you pause. It's happening anew even now; Debby Forbes' children, with the *World Book* and the Whitney Houston CDs in their living room—with the *Playboy* videotape hidden somewhere in their father's furniture—will be parents in a room like this one of these days, proprietors and owners. I thought about Hannah on the beach in Delaware.

Michael was looking at the contents atop an end table. There was a framed citation from Debby's church, commending her for her participation in a literacy volunteer tutoring program.

Ronnie was still outside, which was probably a good thing. He might have laughed at us right now and made some jokes. Maybe we deserved it, but I was just as glad to do without.

A few hours later Jack Waggoner phoned in an order for a dozen pizzas from a favored local place a couple of miles away.

"I'll get it, honey," Debby said to him.

"It's your party," he said. "I'll go."

"It'll just take a few minutes," Debby said. "I'll be back before anyone notices I'm gone."

The three of us volunteered to help her carry the pizzas; we went to her garage and got into her minivan.

"You're driving a van, Debby?" I said to her.

"It's basically a station wagon," she said.

She was seated high above the ground; she might have been a truck driver. Michael was in the front seat next to her; Ronnie and I were in back.

"Damn," Debby said as we pulled into the street. "I need gas."

"You want to take our car?" Ronnie said.

"No," Debby said. "There's a station on the way to the pizza place."

So she pulled into a Mobil station, hopped down from the high seat, detached the hose from a gas pump, and stuck it into the tank of her van.

"Huh," Ronnie said.

"What?" I said.

"That looks pretty sexy, actually," he said.

"You're sick," Michael said.

"How many million times have you seen women pumping gas?" I said.

"Yeah, but never Debby Forbes," Ronnie said. He called out his window to her:

"Hey, Debby! Could you do me a favor?"

"What's that?" she said.

"Could you pump in a few more gallons?" he said.

"He's very sick," Michael said to her.

"You want to take pictures?" Debby said.

That was probably as stupid as any of us got during the evening. The fact was, Debby Forbes was from a time in our lives when you weren't allowed to pump your own gas; when we knew Debby Forbes, the gas station owners most likely would have called the police if anyone had attempted to pump their own gas.

We had picked up the pizza and carried it back to the party, and around midnight we thanked Debby's husband and started back to our hotel. Michael hadn't been able to spend as much time with Debby as he might have wanted; at one point I saw them sitting together on pool chairs, talking quietly, but mostly she'd had to act as a combination of honored guest and hostess. The other people at the party were, as we had expected, a little puzzled—and rightfully so—about what we were doing there; no one seemed willing to accept the explanation that after not seeing Debby for more than twenty years we had come to town just for this night. We were a package deal once again, the three of us, and when we left the party we walked together across Debby Forbes' front lawn, as if recalling by instinct that this was how a summer night was supposed to end.

"So what are you thinking?" I said to Michael on the way to the hotel.

"I don't know," he said. "I don't think I'll know until I wake up in the morning."

"I won't ask you what we used to ask you," Ronnie said to him.

"All right," Michael said. "What is it you used to ask me?"

"We used to ask you how you did," Ronnie said, laughing.

"Don't be a jerk," Michael said.

"We did ask you that," Ronnie said. "You never used to answer, but we asked you."

"I said don't be a jerk," Michael said.

"Isn't that bizarre, Ben?" Ronnie said to me. "That we'd ask that?"

"The bad thing is that we meant it," I said.

Which was true. At the end of the night, if one of us had been out with a girl, the others had this overwhelming need to find out how far he had gotten. It wasn't so much out of prurience as out of jealousy; the idea of being physically close with a female was still so foreign to us—was still, in so many senses, uncharted and thrilling and mysteriously frightening territory—that we almost desperately didn't want our friends to advance too far beyond us. We asked the question quite casually, as if it didn't really matter: "How'd you do?" But it mattered—it mattered in ways that we never would have been able to admit. If one of us had done too well with a girl on a given night—if one of us had progressed into a realm of intimacy that left the others behind—then it meant something. It placed a distance between us. On some level we were very afraid of that. "How'd you do?" we would ask, almost not wanting to hear the answer.

"When's the last time you heard somebody ask that question?" Ronnie said.

"I wish I hadn't heard it just now," Michael said.

"Now I'm saying it as a joke," Ronnie said. "But when's the last time you heard it for real?"

"Is this conversation necessary?" I said.

"You know what I think it is?" Ronnie said. "You know why that question sounds so ridiculous now?"

"I'm not sure I want to know," I said.

"What I think is, when a guy has seen his wife get ready for bed enough times, that guy is a long way removed from being asked, 'How'd you do?' " Ronnie said. "When you're a kid, that sounds like a fantasy—a woman walking naked around your house anytime you want. You'd kill for something like that. But when you get older, and your wife has been walking around naked in front of you for ten or twenty years, and you don't even think to look anymore . . . when that happens, it's hard to believe that you once went crazy wondering about how your friends were doing on dates."

"That's a very nice thought," Michael said. "I'll have to remember to pass it on to Marilyn next time I'm at your house for dinner."

"I wasn't talking about me specifically," Ronnie said. "I was talking about men in general."

"I'll be sure to include that disclaimer when I talk to Marilyn,"

Michael said. "I'm sure she's just overwhelmed with desire every time she sees you get out of the shower, too."

In the middle of the night there was the sound of two people talking outside my door at the hotel. I looked out the peephole.

There was some kind of college convention going on in the hotel; across from my room, a young woman was leaving a young man's room.

"That was nice," I heard her say to him. "I'm really glad I met you."

There was a sudden rushing clunk from the ice machine near the elevator.

"I'll give you a call in the morning," she said to him.

"I think I'm going to sleep in," the young man said, yawning. He was wearing jeans and no shirt.

"I'll give you a call around noon, then," the young woman said. She gave him a quick kiss on the mouth and then walked the few feet to the elevator and punched the button.

The young man had sounded bored and tired. I saw him close his door, and then I heard the sound of him connecting the safety chain inside his room.

I think part of me liked it better when girls weren't supposed to call boys.

Eleven

IN THE MORNING we met in Ronnie's room to decide where we wanted to go next. On the television set—I had begun to notice that Ronnie always kept his TV turned on, all the time, as if he needed it to keep him company—*Good Morning America* had broken for five minutes so that local stations around the country could do news and weather updates.

On Ronnie's TV, the St. Louis weatherman said, "Another muggy day expected along the Mississippi, but storm clouds may be coming our way." He turned to the local anchorman.

"So I'd guess it would be wise to carry an umbrella this morning," the anchorman said.

"You probably should," the weatherman said. "If you don't, that's usually a guarantee that it'll rain on you."

"Isn't that the truth," the anchorman said. "The best way to guarantee rain is to forget your umbrella."

"That is true," Michael said, sitting on a chair next to Ronnie's window.

"How long have you been paying attention to that?" I said.

"To the weather?" Michael said.

"To the weatherman's suggestions about whether or not you should take an umbrella with you," I said.

"I don't know," Michael said. "Why?"

"Because I've been noticing that I've been paying attention to it lately," I said. "I never used to. I mean, who cared if it rained? Now I listen to see if I'm supposed to take an umbrella or not. And I actually obey."

Ronnie joined the conversation. "Is there some sort of message you're trying to draw from this?" he said.

"Yeah," I said. "The message of creeping fuddy-duddiness. We're all becoming fuddy-duddies while we aren't even looking."

Ronnie was staring at the TV set. "Hey, Ben," he said. "You figure if you called that woman she'd talk to you?"

On the screen the local anchorman had finished reading his story, and now his co-anchor was reading hers. She was young and blond, and her lips were bright red, more like an old-time Hollywood starlet than the modern professional ideal of a female broadcast journalist. This did not seem to be bothering Ronnie.

"Why would I want to call her?" I said.

"Just answer," Ronnie said. "If you called the station and said you were you, do you think she'd come to the phone?"

"Probably," I said. "I guess."

"Then call her," he said.

"And say what?" I said.

"Say you have a friend who wants to meet her," Ronnie said.

"Cut it out," I said.

"Look at her," Ronnie said.

"Ten to one you wouldn't be interested if you met her in person," I said.

"Yeah, right," he said. "Look at her. I wouldn't be interested."

"You might not be," I said. "For starters, she probably has an anchor body."

"A what?" he said.

"Anchor body," I said. "It's a very widespread condition in TV news. You have all these anchorwomen with these gorgeous faces and high cheekbones and skinny upper torsos. That's what shows above the desk. But underneath they've got these huge hips and butts, and legs like sequoia trees. They weigh about forty pounds from their waists to the top of their heads, and about two hundred pounds from the waist down."

"Stop it," Ronnie said.

"I'm serious," I said, reeling him in. "Everyone in the television business knows about it. That's the reason you never see some of the most famous woman anchors out on assignment. They can't go because it would shock their fans. You can't photograph women like that full-frame and show it on TV. It's too freakish. Very sad, really."

"Be quiet," he said, fighting the urge to half believe me.

He kept looking at the blond newsreader on the TV set. I could tell that he was wondering about her.

"Anchor bodies," he said.

———

"So you seemed pretty nonchalant last night," I said to Michael.

We were having breakfast in the coffee shop downstairs. Ronnie, apparently having abandoned his fantasies about the newscaster, or at least put them on hold, had told us that he needed to make some business calls and would meet us later. Ronnie appeared to go in spurts; for a day or two it would seem that he had left his office concerns behind, as had been the plan, but then all of a sudden it would be almost as if he had experienced some sort of chemical transformation. He would jolt into a frenzy of telephone calls, as if every call was paramount to the very survival of his company. As far as we could tell, no especially pressing crises were taking place back at the headquarters of Steele International—certainly nothing that would have required Ronnie to abandon his vow to spend the summer away from the pressures of his job. Yet he seemed unable to keep his hands off the phone, unable to remove himself from the negotiating and the entrepreneurial chess games that comprised his life. His participation appeared to be virtually involuntary.

Michael and I waited for him in the coffee shop. I had been mildly puzzled by Michael's interplay with Debby at the party the night before. He had been so transparently nervous before we went there; he had been concerned about what she would be like, and what she would think he was like. Once there, though, his demeanor was like that of an anthropologist on an expedition. He seemed to be observing what was going on, but not really being a part of it.

"That's not quite right," he said.

"Well, if I can ask you, what was going on?" I said.

"It's hard to explain it," he said. "You know what it used to be like when you met a cute girl? And the next day you kept thinking about how cute she was, but you couldn't get a picture of her in your mind?"

"Yep," I said. It was a classic teenage syndrome. The cuter the girl, the less you were able to envision her after she had left.

"It was sort of like that," he said. "It was like I knew that this was Debby Forbes, and I knew that this should be one of those great little life-moments when you get together with someone who used to mean the whole world to you."

"And?" I said.

"As much as I tried, I couldn't shake the feeling that I wasn't there," he said. "It was like everything was going on and I couldn't get a hold on it. I couldn't retain it. And what was really weird was that I was aware of all that. It was like three levels of awareness—I was there, but I felt like I wasn't there, and I knew that later on I was going to know that I had felt like I wasn't there. And there was nothing I could do about it."

"I saw you talking alone by the pool," I said.

"Yeah, just for a few minutes," he said.

"What did you say?" I said.

"I told her I'd call her today," he said.

"You did?" I said.

"Sure," he said. "Why wouldn't I?"

"I don't know," I said. "It just seems . . . I don't know. Her husband and kids and everything."

"They already knew that we'd come all the way to St. Louis for the party," he said.

"But that was different," I said. "That was all three of us."

"Which makes it what?" he said.

"Less . . . something," I said.

"Less dangerous?" he said, almost challenging.

"Yeah, as a matter of fact," I said. "With the three of us, it was probably a little less dangerous."

"Are you telling me you don't think I should call?" he said.

"I'm not saying that," I said.

"Do you want to remind me about Ellen and the girls?" he said.

"I'm not your . . . ," I said, and then caught myself. I had been about to say, "I'm not your mother"—a lamely whimsical line—but that's not a joke I would ever make with Michael. Ever since his mother died when we were sophomores in high school, I have always been careful about even using the word "mother" in his presence. I'm not sure why that is: I have other friends with one or more parents who have died, and I'm not ever conscious of monitoring the references I make when I speak to them. When I meet new people, often at some point in a conversation I will ask, "Are your parents still living?" And I'm sure Michael gets asked that by new acquaintances, too, and I'm sure he has no problem answering them. By this point in his life not only his mother is dead, but his dad, too; it's part of his personal history. Yet the death of Michael's mother was the first experience I had in which someone very close to me lost a parent. It must have hit me harder than I realized at the time, because even now I don't say the word. Not in front of Michael.

"It's none of my business," I said.

"It's just a phone call," he said.

"I know it," I said. "I guess it would be strange for you to show up out of the blue and come to her party and then not call before leaving town."

Michael and I know each other too well.

"Except what?" he said.

"Except nothing," I said. "I'm just a little bit surprised."

"Me, too," he said. "Me, too."

Ronnie came out of the elevator and joined us. He motioned to the waitress and she brought him a menu. When she got to our table, she said to me, "Sir, I'm sorry to bother you. But those people at the table over there were wondering if you were somebody famous?"

Ronnie said, "I knew I should have ordered room service. This meal is already making me nauseous."

Part of me wanted to tell the waitress the truth: that if you have to wonder whether someone is famous, then the person is demonstrably not really famous. But that would have sounded smart-mouthed, and would have satisfied no one. So I turned to the table in question and nodded hello.

And part of me knew that Ronnie, with his only partially kidding flash of resentment, honestly didn't understand. Maybe by this point in our lives, Michael doesn't either. It's been so long, and they can be excused if they forget. Maybe they never really knew.

I spent a good part of the first fourteen years of my life wondering what I'd done wrong. I knew it had to have been something pretty bad; otherwise why would people treat me the way they did?

I was a skinny kid, and I was too bashful to say much, and I had a family who loved me. For a long time I felt that they were the only people who ever would.

In the movies quiet men are often heroes; Gary Cooper is the best example. Gary Cooper had the advantage of looking like Gary Cooper, though, and he always had a camera trained on him, capturing his silence and making it heroic. When you're a quiet little kid, and you're afraid to talk to people, all you want is for the other children your own age to accept you and include you. You hope that they can see and hear what's inside your heart. They can't, of course; they can see only what's in front of them and hear only what is spoken.

My most lasting consistent memory of the years of my childhood is of always standing off to the side, hoping to be spoken to—to be chosen. I know now that if I'd had the courage to be the aggressor—if I had been able to walk up to people and start talking—maybe I could have fooled them into thinking I was one of them. But I never could do that; for some reason it seemed that I always made myself wait for someone to approach me and to invite me into their world. They seldom did. My memory is of waiting for them, and gradually realizing they did not know I was there.

I knew it would have been terrible to be one of the children who were mocked because of things they could not help—the children with physical handicaps or speech impediments or terribly obese bodies. I wasn't one of them; I saw them and I heard what was said to them and sometimes I lay awake at night praying for them. They were cursed by factors they could not control; I was merely invisible. I didn't understand it then, but one of the most confusing things was that there was an obvious reason why those other sad children—the children who had been physically cursed at birth—were treated so meanly. It was awful that people would do that to them, but at least when they went home and closed the doors to their rooms they knew why it was being done. They might hate it and rage against the unfairness of it and weep for it, but they knew.

I didn't know why people didn't want to talk to me; why they didn't want me to be with them. Michael was my friend, and there must have been times when I wondered if he didn't understand that he was getting cheated; why should he get stuck with me? When you're eight or nine years old, and you're convinced that there is something wrong with you that is so bad that people instinctively are aware of it and turn against you because of it, you never express that fear out loud. It's as if you know that, were you to say it aloud, the people who do like you will figure out how bad you are, and you will lose them, too.

One moment in particular, a moment I have never told anyone about:

Around that time, when I was eight or nine, the boys my age formed an after-school football team. I believe it was the first year we played football in any kind of organized way. We showed up on a playground near the school, all of us carrying pads and helmets our parents had bought for us.

Some of the boys seemed to know about football; apparently their fathers had taught them the rules. I didn't know the rules; my dad had bought me the pads and the helmet, but I had not thought to ask him about the rules. I suppose I assumed we would be taught the rules.

So we showed up at the playground, and most of the boys knew what positions they wanted to play: halfback, quarterback, end. I didn't really know the names of the positions. The coach of the team was an eighth-grader, a star of the junior high football team by the name of Chris Jenkins. A boy who lived next door to Chris Jenkins' house was our age, and he had asked Chris Jenkins to coach us, and Chris Jenkins had agreed.

To all of us, Chris Jenkins might have been John Unitas. He was older, he was accomplished, he had seen everything. I had never met Chris Jenkins or even spoken to him, but I knew everything about him. He was everything I was not. We stood there on the playground;

somehow I felt that by being in the middle of this group, I was part of the group.

The boys were yelling to Chris Jenkins, saying what positions they wanted to play. He knew a lot of them; maybe he knew their older brothers or something. He assigned them to their positions, and the leftover boys—I was one of them—got the positions that remained. I was told that I was to be a guard.

It was an inappropriate position for me, because I weighed perhaps the least of anyone on the playground. But I was assigned to the offensive line, and I tried to figure out by looking just what it was a guard was supposed to do. We scrimmaged for about an hour, and then it was time for everyone to go home for dinner.

I hadn't done well, but no one had told me I had done badly, either. So I was feeling kind of happy. I got my stuff together to go home, and as I was walking toward the gate I passed Chris Jenkins, and because I had allowed myself to feel happy, I spoke to him. I felt he probably did not even know my name, and we had not said a word to each other during the practice; our only contact had been when he had called out "Guards," and had motioned to me and to another boy to take that position.

So here was Chris Jenkins, whom I had known about for years, and now he was my coach. And as I walked by him, for one of the first times in my life I took a chance. I took a chance by speaking to him.

I looked up at him and, trying to sound casual, I said, "Hi, Chris." He was talking to some other boys, and he glanced toward me, and he said, "Kroeger, you're a stupid little asshole."

I had no idea what to say. I had no idea what I could say in response to what he had just told me. What I did say, very quietly, was: "I know it."

That's what I said. He called me that name, and I was confused, and that is what I thought to say: "I know it." I was so eager to please him, to be liked, that I must have half believed that if I told him that he was right, that I was every bit as bad as he said, then he might like me anyway.

I walked home, numb, and my parents were waiting. I had never wanted them to know about any of the things that caused me pain—about any of the hurts that were being dealt to me in my life. My parents loved me, and I must have felt that if I were to let them know the pain I was feeling, then that would bring pain to them, too. So I had never told them about any of the things that I was feeling—about being left out, about feeling so alone all the time—and on this particular afternoon I walked into the house and my mother and father asked me how practice had gone. I did not look them in the eyes; I said, "Good," in what must have been a very small voice. My father asked me what position I had played, and I said, "Guard."

In the restaurant in St. Louis, the waitress came back to our table.

"Forgive me for bothering you again, sir," she said. "But now those people at the other table wonder if you would sign an autograph for them. I'm awfully sorry to interrupt you."

Ronnie was fuming. "Look," he said to the waitress. "It's nice that you're starting a fan club for Ben, but do you think I could order some breakfast?"

By the time Ronnie and I became friends—by the time he and Michael and I were hitting the streets of Bristol every night as our package deal—my most awful days were behind me. When I was fifteen things started to change for me. For whatever reason, people were beginning to accept me. I had gone out for the reserve basketball team at Bristol High School and it turned out that I wasn't a bad ball handler or shooter; I played in every reserve game. I had started writing for the school paper and it developed that I had a touch for that; people actually came up to me and wanted to talk about things that I had written. By sophomore year I was no longer afraid to speak to people, and I wasn't convinced that everyone thought I was worthless. Those last three years of high school were good ones. I can't blame Ronnie for forgetting—or never knowing—what my life had been before that. Ronnie, in fact, may have been one of the boys to whom I was invisible; it's not fair to expect him to recall that. How could he? If you're invisible to someone, he has no way of knowing that you were ever there.

And then, with the work I started to do after college, the people I went to school with put me in another category entirely. I was the one guy from Bristol who had done something that made him a little bit well known; I was the one guy in the national eye. Suddenly I was Ben Kroeger, the guy on TV from all over the world. The silent little kid—the kid who was so afraid that he wasn't even good enough to talk to anyone—that kid didn't exist.

But the kid existed for me. He existed inside of me, and although I didn't think about him every day on any conscious level, he was always there ready to tell me not to be so sure about any triumph, not to savor any happiness too fiercely; he was always there to remind me of what things had been like before there was any acclaim or any satisfaction or any applause—what things had been like before there were any good feelings at all. In a way, wherever I went in my adult life, that raw, silent little boy was my closest friend. I didn't choose the friendship; it was there because it had to be.

The waitress was a little flustered. Ronnie was rattling off his breakfast order for her, faster than was necessary, and she was writing it down, and meanwhile the people at the other table were looking, waiting for her to bring the autograph they had requested.

I took a paper napkin and wrote on it: "Good luck and best wishes, Ben Kroeger." I handed it to her.

She told Ronnie that she'd be back with his meal right away. Then she went to the other table and handed the people the napkin.

I could see them looking at it, passing it back and forth. I knew what was happening: They were trying to figure out exactly who I was. That had been the point of sending the waitress over. If I wrote down my name, maybe then they would come up with where it was they had seen me.

I told Michael and Ronnie that I was going up to my room to pack. The truth was, I didn't want to be at the table if it turned out that the people still didn't know me; I didn't want to be there if the waitress had to come back with a request for further assistance in detecting my identity. I didn't want to be there for that to happen in front of Michael and Ronnie.

I made a point of taking the long way out of the restaurant, avoiding the table.

The plan had been for us to spend the day in St. Louis and take off late in the afternoon. I went swimming after breakfast, then took the elevator to Ronnie's room to see what was up. Michael was reading a magazine; Ronnie, once again, was on the phone.

"I'll be with you in a minute," he said to us. "I'm trying to move a little money around."

Ronnie was saying into the phone: "So you think the CDs? I don't know." There was a pause. Then: "I realize that. But if we go into the municipals, I'm not paying any taxes."

Another silence. Then: "I suppose. But check the two rates against each other. I think you can get me almost the same percentage tax-free as you can taxable."

"Trying to move a little money around," Michael said, more than slightly mocking.

Ronnie lifted his hand to request silence.

"What does that bank of yours look like?" Michael called to him, defying his request.

Ronnie, still on the phone, waved his hand with some annoyance.

"Does it have those big white columns in front?" Michael said.

Now Ronnie was grimacing; he was trying to hear what the person on the other end of the line was saying.

"What are that bank's hours?" Michael called out, laughing. "Does it open at ten in the morning and close at two in the afternoon?"

I knew what he was getting at. The first bank we ever went to—the Ohio National Bank branch office on Main Street in Bristol—seemed like something out of Colonial Williamsburg. Big, solid, intimidating, and purely American, it looked as if the United States Treasury had designed it and sent a mammoth government airlift to drop it out of the sky over central Ohio and set it down in Bristol. That Ohio National Bank branch seemed as sturdy and stately as the Supreme Court building.

"Is there talking allowed in your bank?" Michael called out to Ronnie.

When we opened our first savings accounts at the Ohio National Bank we must have been in elementary school; our parents took us. The place was so silent—the way a library is supposed to sound, that's how the Ohio National Bank branch sounded. There was no carpeting—just a hard, cool marble floor. When we walked in with our fifty-cent deposits, we could hear each step as our shoes hit that unyielding marble.

Whatever it was Ronnie was talking to on the phone, it wasn't a bank. He was talking to his account executive at whatever investment house he used, some man who undoubtedly was sitting in front of a computer terminal, punching buttons so that glowing green characters on the screen in front of him could be switched around. I doubt if there was any actual cash in that office, just the figures on the screen hopping and dancing.

Ronnie was smoking another cigar. I had come to understand that the cigar was not the affectation of some would-be hotshot trying to show off and seem older; probably at one point it had been, but now Ronnie truly was what he appeared to be: a tough, middle-aged businessman who knew all the tricks. I wasn't sure that's what I wanted him to be, but that's what he was. At least that is what a part of him was.

At one point on the trip he had been talking to us about a man with whom he had been in negotiations on a deal, and Ronnie had said, "He's a killer." And it definitely wasn't an insult. In Ronnie's world— what had become Ronnie's world—a killer is a winner. A killer is what one strives to be.

I had observed Ronnie on the phone "doing deals," as he invariably called it. He'd sit with the receiver propped between his shoulder and his ear; he would be quite calm—often his eyes would be on the television set—but he would be intractable with the person on the other end. I suppose most successful business people learn to do this, and I suppose if I saw another man doing this I might even be impressed. But when I saw Ronnie do it, part of me was seeing the Ronnie I knew back in Bristol, the bright-eyed, grinning, big-toothed kid who could hardly even add. I thought of that kid, who basically didn't know anything and was always as happy as could be, and I watched Ronnie with us on the road, cutting people dead on the distant ends of phone lines for the crime of trying to take advantage of him. More than once I had heard him say to some unseen voice: "I don't think so. Have a good year. Do you hear me? Have a good year. Call me again a year from now and maybe we'll talk. I'm not going to have time for you until then."

Then he would hang up and immediately shift into lighthearted conversation with Michael and me as if nothing had happened. Clearly it was just part of his repertoire—you make a point with someone by telling him not to bother you for a year, but it's only gamesmanship, it's only business, nothing to really think about. How do you learn how to do that? How does that become a part of your act?

Right now Ronnie was on the phone, moving his money.

"That bank of yours," Michael called to him. "Is your banker writing this all down for you in your passbook?"

Ronnie was shaking his head.

"Do you think your banker would give us each a calendar?" Michael called.

I said to Michael, "You know, I really do think the Ohio National branch on Main Street was the perfect bank. Somehow I trusted it more than I've trusted any bank since."

"Maybe," Michael said. "But I think everything started to go downhill the day they built their drive-through window."

We had agreed to meet in the lobby and check out of the hotel at four-thirty. Ronnie and I were on time, but Michael was nowhere to be seen. That was unusual; he has always been the most punctual of us.

"Maybe he's outside with his bags," Ronnie said.

He wasn't. Ronnie gave the parking attendant his ticket stub, and a few minutes later the rented Lincoln was delivered to us, and Michael still hadn't appeared.

"Should I call his room?" I said.

"I checked his room before I came downstairs," Ronnie said. "He wasn't there."

We got into the car. The day was sweltering; Ronnie put the air conditioner on full blast.

Michael came walking out the front door of the hotel with Debby Forbes.

He did this thing he always used to do when something startled him—he looked at us and jerked his head back in an exaggerated manner, as if he was floored by what he was seeing.

He was pretending to be shocked that we had the car waiting already. But the people who were floored were Ronnie and me. Ronnie seems to pride himself on never being taken by surprise; with him, to show that something is unexpected seems to be a sign of weakness or naïveté. When he saw Michael and Debby, though, he stopped what he was saying in mid-sentence.

Michael knocked on the window on my side, and I opened the door.

"I'm sorry," he said. "I didn't know you were waiting."

"Hi, Debby," I said.

"Hi," she said.

Silence.

"We were having a Coke over in the bar," Michael said.

Behind us, horns were sounding; the car was holding up other traffic coming in and out of the hotel.

Michael turned to Debby. She was wearing pink shorts and a light-blue cotton polo shirt.

"Well . . . ," Michael said.

She leaned up and kissed him on the cheek. Very sweet and friendly.

"I'll call you," he said.

He loaded his stuff into the trunk, got into the back seat, and closed the door.

"Do you want to go, or what?" Ronnie said. He didn't seem to be kidding; he seemed to be waiting for permission from Michael.

"Might as well," Michael said.

Ronnie pulled into traffic. Debby waved to us as we drove away.

I turned around in the front seat and looked back toward Michael.

"I'll tell you later," he said.

Twelve

"I THINK I JUST PISSED next to Conway Twitty," Ronnie said.

We were having dinner at a Mexican restaurant, which I thought was an odd thing to do in Nashville. Ronnie had never been to Nashville, and had said he wanted to see the city. Once we got there he swore that someone had told him that this Mexican restaurant was very good and very popular.

"You think you pissed next to Conway Twitty, or you know you pissed next to Conway Twitty?" Michael said.

"I'm pretty sure," Ronnie said.

He had excused himself from the table to go to the men's room, and now he had returned with this bit of news.

"There was this tall guy with a weird haircut who looked like some kind of a star," Ronnie said. "He was pissing next to me. When I went out of the rest room I heard some women saying that Conway Twitty was in there."

"Was there anyone else in there besides the two of you?" Michael said.

"Not at the urinals," Ronnie said. "I didn't look in the stalls."

"What you are seeing," I said to Michael, "is the true litmus test of celebrity. If people tell their friends that they have pissed next to you in a men's room, then you can safely assume that you have arrived."

"I don't think I've ever looked at who I was pissing next to," Michael said.

"I pissed next to Sonny Randle once," I said.

"That name sounds familiar," Ronnie said.

"He was a pro football player," I said. "St. Louis Cardinals. Wide receiver. I was in college, out on a date, and we were in a restaurant—it was a Howard Johnson's. I went to the men's room, and when I came out this guy I was doubling with . . ."

"There's a phrase I haven't heard in a while," Michael said.

". . . this guy I was doubling with said, 'Do you know who went into the men's room right after you did?' And I asked who, and he said, 'Sonny Randle.' And then this man walks out of the rest room, and the guy I'm doubling with says, 'There he is!' Sonny Randle. And I said, 'I was pissing right next to that guy.' . . ."

"You said 'piss' in front of your date?" Michael said. "At a Howard Johnson's?"

"I don't know what word I used," I said. "The point is, I had been standing next to Sonny Randle. And for about a month, people asked me if I had really pissed next to Sonny Randle."

"I'm trying to remember Sonny Randle," Ronnie said. "Did he ever play quarterback for the Washington Redskins?"

"No," I said. "You're thinking of Sonny Jurgensen. It doesn't really matter, though. What matters is that if a person is important enough that you tell people you pissed next to him, then that person is a star. There can be no question about it."

"I still never looked at anyone I was pissing next to," Michael said.

"Did you ever piss next to anyone else famous?" Ronnie asked me. This topic seemed to interest him. You never know with Ronnie.

"Bill Paley," I said.

"The head of CBS?" Michael said.

"Yep," I said. "In the mid-eighties I was covering this black-tie function at Lincoln Center in New York. And the guest list was like something you see in a society column. And I went into the men's room and I walked up to the urinal, and William S. Paley was at the next one. There we both were, in tuxedos."

"Did you say anything to him?" Ronnie said.

"No," I said. "We may have nodded hello to each other."

"But no real conversation," Ronnie said.

"Nope," I said. "And when I went back to the party, I told everyone I knew that I had pissed next to Bill Paley. And they all couldn't believe it."

"It's hardly unbelievable," Michael said. "Everyone has to piss."

"That's the whole point," I said. "We all know that everyone has to piss. But if you end up pissing next to someone famous, you remember it. Like when I was pissing next to Bill Paley, do you know what I was thinking about?"

"Go ahead," Michael said.

"Sonny Randle," I said. "More than fifteen years had to have gone by since I pissed next to Sonny Randle at the Howard Johnson's, but there I was in Lincoln Center, looking straight ahead at the wall, and I was thinking, 'Once I pissed next to Sonny Randle, and now I am pissing next to Bill Paley.' "

"Is there a moral to this?" Michael said.

"Yes," I said. "The moral is that, no matter how stupid it is to remember that you pissed next to someone famous, you do, indeed, remember it."

"That's hardly a moral," Michael said.

"Still," I said.

Late the next afternoon I walked into Michael's hotel room just as he was getting off the phone with Ellen and the girls. I waited in the doorway until he was finished.

"Ronnie's gone to look at the Grand Ole Opry," I said.

"A frightening concept," Michael said. "Ronnie at the Opry."

"I'm a little surprised he's even interested," I said.

"He told me he has a chance to buy a truckload of country music cassettes at liquidation prices," Michael said. "I think he wants to check out the people at Opryland to see who his customers are going to be."

"Are the cassettes damaged or something?" I said.

"He gave me his standard line," Michael said. "He said they're slightly damaged, but you'd have to examine them with a magnifying glass to figure out what's wrong with them."

"Yeah, the tape inside is probably blank or warped," I said.

"Well, you wouldn't be able to see that with a magnifying glass," Michael said.

His room had a little balcony outside, so we slid the glass doors open and sat out there with our feet propped up on the iron railing.

"So what's the deal?" I said.

"About what?" he said.

I looked at him and he let out a resigned sigh.

"Debby, right?" he said.

"Only if you want to talk about it," I said.

"I don't know," he said after a few moments had passed. "That day after the birthday party I called her to say we were leaving, and she said she wanted to come to the hotel to say goodbye. We just sat downstairs and talked."

"She looked great," I said.

"She looked great," he said.

I have known Michael for too long not to know when something is troubling him. I also know that when he's ready to discuss something, that's when he'll discuss it. We just looked out over Nashville for a while.

"She said she envies us," he said.

"Because of the trip?" I said.

"Yeah, basically," he said. "She said that she'd give anything to take off with her best friends the way that we have. She said that she's never in her life done anything like what we're doing."

"Well, neither have we," I said. "I mean, until now. It's not like we do this every summer."

"She told me that she wished she could come with us," he said.

"What?" I said.

"I thought she was kidding, but she wasn't," he said. "I think she really meant it. She said she had lain awake after her party thinking about how much fun it would be just to pack her bags and take off with us."

"I guess that's the fantasy, isn't it?" I said. "If it wasn't, we wouldn't be here."

"I don't know, Ben," he said. "I don't know what to think."

"Well, she didn't come," I said.

"She told me to call her from the road if I wanted," he said.

"To meet us?"

"She just said to call her," he said.

"Are you thinking about doing it?" I said.

"I'm thinking about her," he said.

The five o'clock sun went behind some high-rise buildings and all of a sudden we were sitting in the shade and the temperature seemed to have dropped about twenty degrees.

"For the first time in the longest time, I didn't feel like someone was looking at me like I was a teacher at Bristol High School," Michael said. "I was talking to Debby and it was like she still thought I was something."

"Don't start that," I said. "I won't listen to that."

"I mean it," he said. "Every person I meet has this little bit of patronization in their voice. In Bristol, I see people our age at the grocery—people younger than us—and if they aren't asking me about how their kids are doing in school, they're full of this false cheer about the football team. It's as if they feel sorry for me and consider me to be their employee at the same time."

"Just stop this," I said.

"It's true," he said. "They do feel that way. And I've been living with it for so long that I've started to half believe they're right. And if anybody would have cause to feel that way, it's Debby. She knew me when I was seventeen years old and I was on top of the world at that high school, and now she knows that I'm just some teacher there, and she'd have every right to think that was funny, or at least sad. And she didn't, Ben. She didn't."

"That doesn't surprise me," I said. "I'm surprised that it would surprise you."

"Why do you think I was so nervous about going to her party?" he said. "It wasn't because of what Ronnie said. I didn't care if she thought I was old. I was just afraid of that moment when she would ask me what I was doing, and I would have to tell her that I was a teacher at Bristol."

"Apparently she didn't mind," I said.

"She told me that she'd always hoped I'd end up doing something like that with my life," he said. "She told me she'd hoped I wouldn't waste it like so many people had."

"Did she say anything about her husband?" I said.

"She said some stuff," Michael said.

"He seems all right," I said.

"I think she's settled in with him for the long haul."

"A lot of times it beats the alternative," I said.

He looked over at me and let it pass.

After a few moments I said, "Are you going to call her again?"

"I really liked seeing her, Ben," he said.

"That was Ellen you were just talking to?" I said.

"Yes, it was," he said. "I call her and the girls every day around this time."

"Did you tell her that we went to Debby's birthday party?"

"Not specifically," he said.

Then:

"It's not like she ever knew Debby."

From inside the room we could hear a hand knocking on Michael's door. I yelled from the balcony, asking who was there. It was Ronnie, back from the Opry. I got up to let him in.

"I don't know what's going on, Ben," Michael said to me.

That evening, after dinner, we went out to the hotel's swimming pool. There was no one in it; the pool was lighted from below, so that the water was bright blue in the black Tennessee night, but we were alone as we sat and talked at a metal table behind the deepest part of the deep end. We weren't going for a swim; the night was quiet and calm, and we didn't feel quite like returning to our rooms yet.

Technically, we weren't absolutely alone at the pool. At another of the metal tables down by the shallow end, near a bug light, a man sat and worked over a set of papers that he had pulled from his briefcase. The bug light provided just enough illumination for him to see what he was doing. We had walked past him on our way to our table. I could tell that he was a salesman, toting up his successes and failures. I've seen these guys enough on the road, and it seems to me that they must be very brave to do what they do.

"What's brave about it?" Ronnie said after I had related this to him and Michael. "It's not like they're cops."

"Yeah, but every day they've got to get on the phone and take a deep breath and tell some voice halfway across the country whether they've struck out or not," I said.

"They're on per diems," he said. "They're taken care of."

"For the moment," I said. "I just think that would be very scary. You get up every morning and you go out to try to sell something to people who would much rather tell you 'no' than 'yes.' And every time you hear a 'no' you must try to convince yourself that it's not personal. But you still have to make that phone call back to your home office and report the 'no.' And I would guess that the people on the other end of the phone are not very interested in the reasons for the 'no's.'"

"You think too much," Ronnie said.

"I balance you out," I said.

As Ronnie and Michael talked about what Ronnie had seen at the Opry in the afternoon—"The main auditorium was like one of those clean, fancy churches the TV evangelists preach in," I heard Ronnie say—I caught myself looking over at the salesman under the bug light.

When I was a kid, there was an advertisement in the back of a comic book for, I believe, some sort of home study course. As I recall, the course was called "The Teaching Machine." I envisioned some sort of big, towering machine with blinking lights—a machine you could put in your room and that would teach you stuff.

With the advertisement was a clip-out coupon. You were supposed to mail it in if you wanted to know more. I filled my name in and put the coupon in an envelope.

One night we were having dinner, and the front doorbell rang. My father got up from his end of the table and went to the screen door. I could hear him talking to someone. After a couple of minutes my dad came back to the table, and through the front window I could see a man in a suit walking to his car, which was parked in our driveway.

"Did you send away for some information in a comic book?" my father said.

It had been six or eight weeks, and I had almost forgotten. Nothing about the Teaching Machine had ever arrived in the mail. I said that I had.

My father had sort of a faraway expression on his face. He wasn't angry at me.

"Before you do that again, talk to your mother or me about it," he said.

He said that the man who had come to the front door had been sent to our house by the Teaching Machine company. The man was a salesman for the company—I know now that he undoubtedly must have been on commission—and every time someone from his territory mailed in a coupon to headquarters, the headquarters sent him the name and address and the man was directed to go to the address in person.

"He told me that he wasn't allowed to do it on the phone," my dad said to my mother. "His company wants all sales calls to be personal."

So the man had driven to our house, and when my dad had heard his purpose for being there he'd had to tell the man that he was sorry, but the person who had sent in the coupon was only eight years old. He told the man that we just weren't in the market for his product.

I had said to my dad, "How does a machine teach you, anyway?"

"It's not really a machine, Ben," my dad had said. "That's just what they call the system. It's only a series of books."

I didn't know why my dad seemed so sad about what had just happened; it would have been much more in his nature to give the guy a brusque "Thank you, we're not interested" and close the door.

But then my dad had said to my mother: "I was in the Army with that fellow. We were in Italy together."

The rest was left unspoken. Here we were—our family having a leisurely dinner on a balmy summer evening—and here my father's old Army friend was, driving around with addresses next to him on the front seat, undoubtedly knowing, in 1955, that the surest way to find everyone when they were at home was to show up at suppertime. Now the man was on his way to his next cold call. My father was making a good executive-level salary, with his paycheck being handed to him every Friday; his fellow soldier was chasing down people who had mailed in coupons, hoping to score a commission.

"For a moment I didn't remember him, and I don't think he knew it was me right away," my dad said to my mom. "It took a few seconds for it to click in."

All of a sudden I had felt bad for having put the envelope in the mail. No one was blaming me and my dad wasn't angry, but I felt bad.

"The poor devil," my father had said, the street outside our house now free of traffic.

Tonight in Nashville we decided that the evening was getting late, and we got up from the table by the pool and headed inside.

We passed the man who was going over his paperwork. A couple of mosquitoes hit the light and there was a series of quick, sharp, burning sounds as they died.

The man looked up as we walked by. He smiled pleasantly at us and said, "Good night."

"Good night," I said, and he went back to his work.

"So what do you think?" Ronnie said. "Do you think anyone's going around saying that they once pissed next to you?"

"Very funny," I said.

"I'm serious," he said.

"No, you're not serious," I said.

Ronnie had been ragging me on and off all during the trip about being recognized from time to time. The little exchange with the waitress back in the St. Louis hotel coffee shop seemed to have revitalized his inclination to jab me. Now, having come in from our late-night stop at the motel pool, the three of us were sitting around his room, and he was at it again.

"I could tell people that I've pissed next to you," he said.

I told Ronnie that he could make himself far more well known than I would ever be. All he would have to do is pay for it.

"What are you talking about?" he said.

"Become the national TV spokesman for your company and you won't be able to walk through an airport," I said. "Tell your advertising agency to put you on the air and people will get all misty-eyed at the very sight of you."

Which was true. Fame, if that is what you're after, can be very easily purchased. A Victor Kiam or an Orville Redenbacher is every bit as recognizable as a Paul Newman or a Burt Reynolds. If your company's ad agency is willing to swallow hard and roll over and follow your directions to film you and buy saturation-level airtime for you, before long strangers will become tongue-tied and self-conscious as they walk up to you and ask you for your autograph.

"I was reading a book once," I said, "and the person who wrote the book said that when it comes to fame, in a specific town there's really no difference between Frank Sinatra and the local weatherman. Either everyone in town recognizes you or they don't."

"Ah, I was just kidding you," Ronnie said.

"Hey, I know my limitations," I said. "I realized a long time ago that I would never get past a certain plateau. It was the week James Taylor made the cover of *Time* magazine."

"James Taylor was on the cover of *Time?*" Michael, who had been listening to all this, said.

"I think it was 1970 or 1971," I said. "It was the first time anyone our age made the cover of *Time*."

"Didn't we all make it once?" Michael said. " 'The Student Generation' or something?"

"That doesn't count," I said. "I'm talking about one person. I picked up *Time* that week and I got really depressed. It was like I had lost a race I didn't even know I'd been in. There was James Taylor on the cover of *Time*, and in an instant I knew that I'd never get to that level."

"You thought that?" Michael said. "What kind of person goes around thinking that he belongs on the cover of *Time*?"

"I told you, I hadn't really thought about it," I said. "Not until I saw James Taylor. My whole life I had been seeing presidents and kings and actresses on the cover of *Time*, and it never affected me one way or the other. They were big shots and they were on the cover of *Time*. It made sense. They weren't my age, so I didn't feel competitive. And then—I guess it must have been when we were twenty-three, twenty-four—there's James Taylor. It was like everyone our age took off from a starting line at the same time, and James Taylor won."

"You weren't really depressed," Michael said.

"I was pretty down," I said.

"But why would anyone ever put you on the cover of *Time*?" he said.

"No one ever would," I said. "That's what I'm telling you. I'm not a person who would ever even be considered for the cover of *Time* magazine."

"Neither am I," Michael said. "But I certainly never felt bad about it. I never even thought about it."

"Well, you're thinking about it now," I said. "There comes a moment when every person faces the fact that he's not going to make the cover of *Time*. For me, that moment came in 1971. For you, it came tonight."

"Fine," he said, laughing.

"I'm going to sleep," Ronnie said.

Michael and I got up to go to our own rooms. Out in the hallway Michael was unlocking his door, and he said to me, "Don't feel bad."

"About what?" I said.

"Think how James Taylor feels," he said. "Every day of his life, he wakes up knowing that he'll never be on the cover of *Time* again."

I don't know if Michael called Debby Forbes that night; I never asked him, and even now I still don't know. It seems unlikely. That late at night, how would he explain why he was calling her?

But I do know that he takes things very seriously, and that while some people might be capable of being casual or flippant over something like how he had felt after reestablishing contact with Debby back in St. Louis, Michael is not such a person. I guess it really doesn't matter when it was that he first called her from the road, or even how many times he called her. But sometimes I still find myself wondering if he called her that night.

Around 3 A.M. I woke up and couldn't sleep. I walked around my room, then went to the window and pulled back the drapes. Down below was the pool, still lit up, vivid blue in the midst of blackness. Michael was sitting by the pool, all by himself.

The salesman was gone. It was just Michael. He was sitting in one chair with his feet up on another.

I knew that what was happening was a very significant thing for him. Michael would never let himself pretend that the way he had reacted to seeing Debby was a minor matter. A great part of what he thought about himself was invested in the fidelity he felt as a husband toward Ellen. It was nothing he ever talked about. But I know Michael as well as I have ever known a person in my life, and when I saw him sitting down by the pool in the middle of the night I instinctively understood why he was awake.

When we were growing up in Bristol, Michael's family had a big reel-to-reel tape recorder. On the night in 1959 that Floyd Patterson first fought Ingemar Johansson for the heavyweight championship of the world, we set up the tape recorder next to the radio in Michael's room and ran a tape all during the bout. I guess we must have figured that it was historic and that we would keep it.

At one point during the fight, as Johansson was nearing his surprising and brutal victory over Patterson, the radio announcer's excited voice cried: ". . . and the championship may be going now!"

For some reason we thought that was the most dramatic moment of the broadcast. The fight wasn't televised, so we couldn't see it; on the tape from the radio broadcast there were graphic accounts of the knockdowns themselves, and the sounds of the referee counting. Somehow, though, those seven shouted, portentous words—". . . and the championship may be going now!"—were more gripping than the descriptions of the punches. The announcer's voice had been quavering. For days after the fight Michael and I had backed the tape up again and again, just so we could hear those words. The message in those words mesmerized us.

At three o'clock in the morning in Nashville I looked down from my window and saw Michael by the pool. He didn't know I was there, and to this day I have never told him. It was late and I was tired and I don't know why those words from across the years kept sounding in my head. I saw my friend, and that announcer's voice kept repeating: ". . . and the championship may be going now!" Finally I went back to bed.

Thirteen

WHEN WE ARRIVED IN ATLANTA it was still the three of us. When we left, we were four.

"What is this, a convention?" Ronnie said.

We were in the elevator of the Hyatt Regency Atlanta. We had just checked in; we were still carrying our bags as we rode up to our rooms.

The woman to whom he had directed his question was dressed in shorts and a T-shirt, on the left side of which was pinned a plastic-covered nametag. Actually, there were seven or eight women in the elevator, all apparently in their twenties or early thirties, all wearing the tags.

"You aren't dentists?" the woman answered him.

"Dentists?" Ronnie said.

"Do you sell the equipment?" the woman said.

I looked at the tag that the woman next to me was wearing. This wasn't a convention, exactly.

"We're all here to take our boards," the first woman told Ronnie.

The tags indicated that the women were in Atlanta to take the certifying tests that would make them licensed dental hygienists in the state of Georgia.

"You're not from here?" Ronnie said.

"I'm from Philadelphia," the woman said.

"Buffalo," said another woman.

"Providence," said a third.

The elevator door opened and a few women got off. I looked out the glass window and down into the atrium lobby below. As I recalled, this was the hotel that was responsible for starting the trend that made elevators with opaque walls an endangered species.

"Why would you need a Georgia license to practice up there?" Ronnie said.

"Everyone who's here for the boards wants to move South," the woman from Buffalo said. "But you can't even apply for a job in a dentist's office here until you pass your boards. You really can't even get an interview. They won't talk to you unless you're already certified."

"You don't want to be worked on, do you?" the Philadelphia hygienist said to Michael.

"Pardon me?" he said.

"It's part of the boards," she said. "We have to go out and find people and bring them to the boards so that we can work on their teeth."

"You're kidding," I said.

She handed me a stack of preprinted cards. The cards said that a free dental examination would be given to the bearer if he or she showed up at a certain building at a certain time.

"I need them back," she said. The elevator was stopping at her floor. I returned them to her.

"They make you find your own patients?" Michael said.

"I spent all day yesterday at a shopping mall handing these things out," she said.

She and two friends started to depart the elevator car. Just before she got out she turned around to Michael, reached for his mouth, grasped his lower lip between her thumb and forefinger, and pulled the lip gently away from his bottom teeth. She took a look inside.

"Nice," she said.

The next morning I got to the pool just before 10 A.M. The night before, on the way back to our rooms from dinner, we had asked the desk clerk what time the pool got sun. He had said there was full sun on the pool deck from ten until after five.

When I got there, though, the pool was in shade; the sun had not yet risen above the top of the building. I started to sit down on a lounge, but at the last minute I saw that it was covered with ants. I mean covered; the lounge was painted white, but about one square foot of it was brown with ants.

It was pretty sickening. I looked closely and saw that someone had left some food between the slats, and the ants had congregated. I moved over to another lounge and sat at the foot of it, waiting for Michael and Ronnie.

A man came out of the hotel, looked up to see that the sun was blocked by the building, and started to select a lounge anyway.

"You probably don't want that one," I said, gesturing at the ant lounge.

He looked at me quizzically, then saw what I was talking about. "Oh," he said. "Thanks. Thanks a lot."

A family—husband, wife, two children—came out bearing towels and pool toys. "You probably don't want that one," I said.

I don't know why I'm like that. It was as if I was on sentry duty. I felt almost an obligation to be the warning system against the ants. I'm always like that. As soon as I saw the ants, it became incumbent on me to stay there and let people know what lay in wait for them. It was as if were I to leave, and then to come back later and find someone lying there with ants crawling all over him or her, it would be my fault.

So I sat lookout. And I always used that same sentence. The words never varied. It was as if "Don't sit on that one" would have been too much of an order; "Please don't sit on that one" would have made me a supplicant.

So every time it was "You probably don't want that one." Feigned casualness, as if it was an offhanded thought—hey, I'm just sitting around here anyway. As long as I'm here, I might as well tell you.

The "probably" was the key—you can sit on that one if you want to. But you probably don't want to.

Probably.

I stayed at my post and warned people away until a custodian came by on his morning rounds. I told him that he should take a look at the lounge next to me.

Actually, what I think I said was: "You probably ought to take a look at that lounge there."

Sometimes I wonder about myself.

Michael came out, followed a few minutes later by Ronnie. Michael and I were talking when Ronnie arrived; he took one look up at the sky—the sun was still hidden by the tower of the hotel—and he turned and hurried back inside.

We followed him; he hadn't even spoken to us. When we caught up with him he was speaking angrily to a clerk at the front desk.

"We were specifically told that the pool got sun at ten o'clock," he was saying. His voice was rising.

The clerk appeared not to know how to respond.

"We made a special point of stopping at the desk last night," Ronnie said. "We asked the person about the sun, and we asked for a time. We were told ten o'clock. If you people don't know what time the sun hits your pool, then you should tell your guests that you don't know."

This was absurd. What was the clerk supposed to do? Move the building so the sun would shine correctly?

"I know the sun is on the pool deck in the morning," the clerk said, trying to be conciliatory. "We have lots of people who go to the pool before lunch."

"But we were told ten," Ronnie said. "Look." He pointed to the clock behind the desk. "It's quarter after."

Michael was shaking his head in disgust. "Come on," he said to Ronnie.

Ronnie glared at him.

"What's wrong with you?" Michael said. "What's this guy supposed to do about it? You can't come down here and complain about the sun like it's your room-service order that's late. The guy can't make the sun move faster." But Ronnie's world had come to that; if something displeased you, then you found someone to chastise for it.

A woman in her early thirties, on her way to the pool and wearing a terry-cloth robe over her swimsuit, was observing us. If Michael and I were a little embarrassed by Ronnie's behavior, she seemed amused. She was smiling.

"Do you always get what you want?" she said.

Ronnie looked over at her. "You talking to me?" he said.

"Yeah," she said. She had a little Jimmy Cagney tough-guy thing in her voice. It sounded like a joke at the time.

I went up to my room. I opened the drawer of the desk across from the bed, pulled out three pieces of hotel stationery, and sat down to write a letter to Hannah.

In the letter I told her about all the places we had visited. I told her about some kittens I had seen at a roadside fruit stand on the way from Iowa to Kansas City; Hannah loves kittens. I told her about an ice-cream place in Missouri that serves chocolate sundaes that are eighteen inches tall.

In the letter I asked her if she was reading during the summer; she knows how important I think that is. I asked her if she was making any new friends at the shore. I asked her if she was getting a lot of sunny weather.

I told her I loved her, and at the end I wrote, "Say hi to Mom."

I had clipped a comic strip from the morning paper. It was about a little girl who puts a "Do Not Disturb" sign on her door to keep her parents from coming in when she's talking to her friends on the phone. Once, as a joke, I had brought Hannah a "Do Not Disturb" sign from one of my reporting trips. She had hung it on her doorknob and let it stay there. But she virtually never closed the door; the sign said to stay out, but Hannah never seemed to think that Nancy or I represented any threat to her privacy. A "Do Not Disturb" sign on a door that was never shut. I sat at that desk high up in the Atlanta Hyatt and thought about a lot of things.

Then I folded the comic strip and put it, along with the letter, in a hotel envelope. I would mail it when I went down to the lobby.

It was only after I had sealed the envelope that it struck me: I had known Nancy for so many years before Hannah had been born. Nancy and I had shared so many terrific and happy and close times, times that Hannah wasn't around for.

And now our lives had reached the point where, at the end of my long letter to Hannah, I asked her to say hello to "Mom." As if Nancy were some distant relative of mine, a person I knew slightly, a person to whom I felt obliged to pass on my regards. When I first knew Nancy, when I knew I wanted to marry her and share my life with her, I wonder if I would have believed it if I could have looked ahead: Someday you two will have a child, and it will be far easier for you to write a letter to that child than it will be for you to write a letter to Nancy. Someday you will feel closer to the child. Someday you will have screwed things up sufficiently that you will, without really thinking twice, blithely ask this child to pass on your regards to Nancy. A virtual postscript: Oh, say hi to Mom.

I left the room without calling either Michael or Ronnie. I went out for a long walk. I wanted to walk as fast as I could and as far as I could; I wanted to walk until I was too tired to think.

When I got back to the hotel I went to the pool. Now the sun was hitting the pool deck full-force. I saw Michael standing by the deep end.

"Guess what," he said, nodding over toward Ronnie.

Ronnie was stretched out on a lounge next to the woman from the lobby—the woman who had asked him if he always got everything he wanted. With her terry-cloth robe off, it was clear that she was a person who was used to being stared at in the sun. A few feet away from us a couple of men in business suits, apparently out here on a break from a meeting inside the hotel, were speculating to each other about whether her figure had been enhanced by cosmetic surgery. "Has to be," I heard one of them say. "Too perfect to be real. She made the decision she wanted to look like that." They couldn't take their eyes off her.

"What's the deal?" I said to Michael.

"When I came out, they were already lying there together," he said. "I walked up to talk with them and it sounded like Ronnie had already given her his whole Dun and Bradstreet."

"I take it she was interested," I said.

"You might say so," he said. "She was asking him how many people worked for him."

"Where'd they get drinks at this time of the day?" I said. Ronnie and the woman were both sipping on tall pink cocktails, the kind that often have paper parasols sticking out of them.

"She got them," Michael said. "She's part of that dental thing. She went inside and got the drinks for both of them."

"She's a dental hygienist?" I said.

"From Detroit," Michael said. "She wants to move down here because she's sick of the Michigan weather."

"She's a little older than some of her colleagues," I said. If I'd had to guess, I would have said that the woman with Ronnie was thirty-one or thirty-two. Other women from the dental boards, including several who had been in the elevator with us the day before, were sunning themselves and splashing in the pool; many seemed to be in their early twenties.

"Yeah, she was sort of making fun of them to Ronnie," Michael said.

Across the way, Ronnie was hanging on the woman's every word. The two of us walked over to where they were talking.

"Hi, again," she said to Michael.

"This is Ben," he said.

She sat up and extended her hand. "I'm Gail Donlon," she said. "I'm down here from Detroit."

"So I heard," I said. "You're here to take the dental boards?"

"I've been here a week," she said. "Your friend Ronnie is the first sign of intelligent life I've been able to find."

I felt my eyebrows rising. She casually laid her hand on his arm. I saw that he had a cigar burning in an ashtray down on the pool-deck surface.

"You must have had a lot of people you could talk to," I said. "All the others who are here for the boards."

She looked over at the other women in the pool.

"You mean the tee-hee girls?" she said.

Ronnie laughed that chortle laugh of his. He sounded as if he was ready to foreclose on a destitute widow on Christmas Eve.

"That's what we call them," he said. He reached for his cigar.

"We do, do we," I said.

"I was telling Ronnie about them," Gail said. "They giggle all the time. All day and all night. After a week it's driving me crazy."

"Tee-hee girls," Ronnie said, coughing happily through the smoke.

Michael and I went for a swim. From the pool we could see Ronnie and Gail deep in conversation.

"We'd better tie a boulder or something to him," Michael said. "Otherwise he just might float away."

"He does seem rather pleased," I said.

"When I first walked over she was asking him what it was like to run a whole company," Michael said.

"Is that what he told her he does?" I said.

"Well, he said that he was chairman," Michael said.

"Did he explain that since Sidney Steele died, the chairman doesn't run Steele International?" I said.

"I don't think she's interested in an organization chart," Michael said. "She knows he's married to the money. She doesn't care who calls the shots."

"He said he was married?" I said.

"Oh, yeah," Michael said. "He explained the whole thing. About Marilyn's dad dying, about him taking over as chairman—everything."

"She doesn't seem especially upset that he's spoken for," I said.

"She hasn't exactly fled from the pool deck, has she?" Michael said.

A poolside waitress had come on duty; Ronnie called her over, and she nodded and walked off, presumably to fetch more drinks.

In the pool, some of the tee-hee girls swam past us. If they were overcome by longing for our four-decades-old bodies, they did a very good job of hiding it.

"It's amazing," I said. "Unless I'm missing something, these women don't even know we're here. And look at Ronnie." His new friend had found another excuse to place her hand on his arm.

"I never realized he was so irresistible," Michael said.

"Maybe it's the smell of the cigar she's attracted to," I said.

"Right," Michael said. "Either that, or he's hypnotizing her with one of his stories about how he beat a cartel of gumball merchants out of their rightful commissions during a closeout sale in Toledo."

When we got out of the pool, both of them had their eyes closed. They were baking in the sun.

We walked up behind them. They didn't yet know we were there.

"It is so hot," Gail said.

Ronnie grunted. He was sweating a lot.

"I feel like I'm wearing a snowsuit," she said.

Her bathing suit consisted of four square inches of shiny fabric.

A moment passed.

"I wish I could just take it off," she said.

"Let me know when you do," Ronnie said.

She shifted on her lounge. Their eyes remained closed.

"Maybe I'll just pull my top down and put some No. 25 block on my nipples," she said.

For anyone else, that would have been enough. But Ronnie just smiled and continued to let the sun hit him.

"I think that is so great," Gail said. "That you're still close enough with your high school friends that you'd want to spend the summer with them."

Another heat-driven grunt from Ronnie.

"I mean, with all the success that you've had, that you'd still have something in common with them," she said. "I think that is so nice."

I thought Michael, standing next to me, was going to gag.

"I wish you would have gone to my high school," she said.

"Yeah?" Ronnie said.

"I really do," she said.

"What would you have done?" he said.

She giggled. If I didn't know better, I might have thought that she was a tee-hee girl.

"Probably taken you into the boys' room a lot and rubbed up against you," she said.

"Hey, Ronnie," I said, and he opened his eyes. "I think this woman may be on the verge of flirting with you."

To our great surprise, Ronnie informed Michael and me that he wouldn't be having dinner with us that night.

So we wandered down the street and found a nice, dark steak house. We were seated immediately—the place was half empty—and at a table fifteen feet away from us were three elderly couples.

Their waiter, a guy in his twenties, said to them in a loud, animated voice:

"Well, are we out for the prom tonight?"

The women at the table laughed gaily, if a little too quickly. I looked over to see that one of the men was smiling slightly, but the other two weren't.

"So can I offer you some pre-prom cocktails?" the waiter said. "I will have to see some identification, though."

The women laughed again.

"I hate that," I said to Michael.

"They're having a good time," he said.

"Don't count on it," I said.

"What's wrong?" he said. "The waiter's making them feel special."

"Oh, come on," I said. "If you live to be seventy years old, you've probably earned the right not to be patronized by some guy who doesn't know anything about you."

"Something on your mind?" he said.

The waiter said to one of the women: "Now, I know that *you're* not old enough for a hard drink."

We ordered steaks and salads. About halfway through our meal a couple was led to the table next to us. They appeared to be in their thirties. The tables in the restaurant were close together, and we couldn't help but hear their conversation.

This was their first time out together. He was a lawyer. At one point the woman asked the man what he liked to do in his spare time.

"I really enjoy sailing," he said.

Michael hit his fork against his plate. I think he did it purposely.

"Yes?" I said to him.

"Have you ever sailed?" Michael said.

"Quiet," I said, looking over at the couple.

"I'm being quiet," he said. "They can't hear us. Have you ever sailed in your life?"

"I've been on a sailboat once," I said. "Maybe twice."

"Right," he said. "I think that's how it is for everyone. Everyone has gone sailing a couple of times."

"So?" I said.

"So why does everyone in the world say that their hobby is sailing?" he said. "In every personal ad in every magazine in America, every person lists their hobby as sailing. Every contestant in the Miss America Pageant says that she likes to sail. Somebody's got to be lying. Otherwise you'd have total gridlock on every lake in America."

Next to us the lawyer said to his dinner companion, "Do you ski?"

In the morning Ronnie wasn't in his room. We found him alone in the coffee shop.

"What's up?" Michael said to him. Ronnie was nursing a cup of coffee and looking more than a little glum.

"You get stood up last night?" I said to him. "Special meeting of the Junior League, and your new friend had to brush up on her *Robert's Rules of Order?*"

He didn't seem to be in any mood for jokes.

"Why don't we get out of here," he said. "Let's pack and hit the road."

I would have thought that perhaps he was feeling remorseful about something, but among the emotions that may or may not occasionally flow through Ronnie's heart, remorse has never been chief among them.

"I cannot believe that she stole from me," he said.

"That woman?" I said.

"It's such a meaningless thing for her to steal," he said.

He told us that they'd had dinner, and had drunk a couple of bottles of champagne, and had gone back to his room. She had spent the night.

Under different circumstances that would have been the morning's breaking news. What Ronnie does with his life is his own business—I make it a point not to ask him what the story is with him and Marilyn—but as far as I knew, this was the first time during the summer that any of us had ventured into this particular territory. I was sure of it: I knew I'd had no late-night guests, and there was no question that Michael hadn't, either.

But the fact that Ronnie and the woman from the pool had spent the night in his room, while significant on about a dozen different levels, was pushed aside by the apparent fact that she had stolen something from him.

"The thing is, I liked her," he said.

He told us, and in some detail, the specifics of what had happened after they returned to his room from dinner. I could have done without the play-by-play; maybe it's a function of age, but I don't have an overwhelming desire to hear that stuff from my friends at this point in my life. If his report was accurate, her demeanor out by the pool had been downright demure compared to the way she acted when they were alone. "About four o'clock in the morning she woke me up again and tried to get me interested," he said. "I told her, 'Fine. But why don't we just call the paramedics for me now to save them a little time later.' "

For Ronnie that wasn't a bad line, but he said it with an absence of mirth.

"You know that medallion I carry?" he said.

The medallion was a good-luck thing, something that Ronnie always carried in his pants pocket. He'd been carrying it all his life, or at least for as long as I'd known him.

"I keep it on the table next to my bed every night," he said. "That, and my watch. Around seven o'clock this morning she said she was going to go back to her own room. I offered to take her to breakfast, but she said no thanks. I went in to use the bathroom, and when I came out she was dressed. She kissed me goodbye and then she left.

"And then I took a shower, and I was thinking what an amazing night it had been. I got out of the shower and I walked back into the room and got dressed, and I reached for my watch, and the medallion was gone."

"You're sure you didn't lose it?" Michael said.

"Nope," Ronnie said. "She was asking me about it the night before. When we got back from dinner and I put it on the table, she asked me

148 · *Bob Greene*

what it was. That's the creepy part. She probably knew right then she was going to take it."

"So how much could it be worth?" Michael said.

"Nothing," Ronnie said. "Three or four dollars. It's a piece of metal I won at a carnival thirty years ago. The watch is worth fifteen hundred dollars. And she took the medallion."

"Are you positive you didn't put it somewhere else?" I said.

"I looked everywhere," he said. "I got down on the floor and looked under the bed. I took the sheets off. I moved the furniture around. It's not there. She took it."

"So you're out three bucks," Michael said. He was trying to sound flippant and trying to dismiss it, but I could tell that he thought it was pretty creepy, too.

"The way I figure it, she's got to be a kleptomaniac," Ronnie said.

"You're a psychiatrist now," I said.

"I'm serious," Ronnie said. "I've been sitting here thinking about it. You've got to be sick to steal something that little. The watch was right there. The watch I could have understood."

"You'd have understood it if she'd taken your watch?" Michael said.

"The watch was worth something," he said. "The medallion . . ."

"Maybe she thought the medallion was more personal than the watch," I said.

"What do you mean?" he said.

"I don't know," I said. "Maybe she wanted something to remind her of you. Like a souvenir or something." I tend to view life as *Rebecca of Sunnybrook Farm*.

"That doesn't make any sense," he said.

He looked around the lobby of the hotel, as if searching for something.

"My wallet was in the room," Ronnie said. "She could have taken the wallet. She didn't."

"Write it off to experience," Michael said.

"I just don't know why she did it," Ronnie said.

"She probably doesn't know why she did it, either," I said. "If she knew why she did it, she wouldn't do it."

I figured that Ronnie's consternation was partly because he had never run into this particular flaw in a person before. I had to admit, I hadn't either. You meet alcoholics and cocaine users and liars, and at least you're accustomed to that kind of human frailty. This woman, though . . . I could tell that Ronnie was truly upset. He didn't get it. He had lived enough years to think he was past this kind of surprise, and he genuinely didn't get it.

"People have cheated you in business before, right?" Michael said, trying to put it in the context of conventional deviousness.

"This is different," Ronnie said.

Fourteen

PACKING IN MY ROOM, I heard a knock at the door. I assumed that it was Michael or Ronnie, ready to leave Atlanta. I kept putting stuff into my suitcase, and then there was the sound of a key in the lock, and of the door opening.

"Oh, I'm sorry," the voice said.

It was the housekeeper assigned to my floor; she had her cart with her. She appeared to be in her fifties, wearing a Hyatt uniform.

"I didn't hear you, so I just came in," she said.

"That's okay," I said. "I'm thinking of checking out of here anyway."

My television set was on. WTBS was broadcasting *King Creole*, one of the early Elvis Presley movies. The housekeeper's eyes went right to the screen.

"You like him?" she said.

"Very much," I said.

"How long have you liked him?" she said.

"Oh, forever," I said.

The scene on the screen was an argument between the Elvis character—Elvis was playing a rebellious young busboy/singer—and his father, a timid pharmacist.

"He sure was handsome when he was young," the housekeeper said.

"Sit down if you want," I said.

She hesitated, but then sat in one of the room's two chairs.

On the TV, the Elvis character angrily told his father that he wasn't going to continue in his footsteps and be meek and unsuccessful. He was going to go where the cash was instead. "Money talks," the Elvis character snapped to his father.

"If that's not the truth," my visitor said, talking to the screen.

There was a time when she and I might have had few common

reference points. But that was in the America before television. Now it doesn't matter where you grow up, or under what circumstances—one thing you can count on is that you are seeing and hearing the same images as the rest of the country. That doesn't mean your life is going to turn out the same as anyone else's. But somewhere in your consciousness, you'll share those images. I don't think we'll fully understand the importance of that for decades to come.

"Does he sing in this one?" she said.

"Sure," I said. "Stick around. In a minute or two he goes down to the nightclub and sings."

Those of us who are alive now—at least those of us who were born before the mid-1950s—are the only people in the history of the world to straddle television. We were around when there was no television, and we saw it arrive, and now we live in a time when a world without television would be literally unimaginable. People born after us, including our younger brothers and sisters, have absolutely no idea what it was like before there was such a thing as TV.

In 1952 or 1953, before my family bought our first TV set, television was mainly a rumor. I was only five at the time, and of course I didn't know that I was missing anything—you can't miss something if you aren't aware that it exists. But some friends of my parents—their name was Finn, and they had two sons, the older one my age—had become one of the first families in Bristol to buy a set. My parents would go to their house and watch; back then, or so I am told, families actually had discussions over whether they should buy a TV, or whether it was just a frivolous fad that would soon pass.

One weekend afternoon—I don't remember this, but my parents always told me it was true—I went with them to the Finns' house, and while the adults talked I played with the Finn boys. The Finn boys had been sitting in front of the television daily; it doesn't take long to learn how to stare at a TV screen. Other addictions seem to move with glacial slowness compared to the TV addiction: It can grab you in the first minute.

So the Finn boys and I were playing out in their front yard, and Danny Finn hid behind a tree, and he jumped out at me with one finger pointing and he yelled: "Bang! Bang!"

And I—or so I have always been told—looked back at him and said: "Boo!"

What the hell, I was only a kid. But the Finn boys had been watching Hopalong Cassidy and Roy Rogers and the other cowboy shows every day. I had never seen a cowboy show. The Finn boys knew from TV that cowboys emerged from behind trees and boulders and banged away at their enemies with guns. We didn't have a TV; if you wanted to scare someone, you acted like a ghost.

For a while there, you probably could have divided the country into those two categories—the kids who were learning their play habits from TV, and the kids whose play habits were still learned from stories and games around their homes. Hey, what did we know? If you've never seen a cowboy shoot a bad guy, you don't know "bang" from "boo." It's hard to conceive of that now: an America in which some children had seen television shows and most other children hadn't.

In my hotel room at the Atlanta Hyatt, the housekeeper said, "Who's that who's running the nightclub?"

"Walter Matthau," I said.

"I thought I recognized him," she said. "He sure is young, too."

"Well, it's an old movie," I said.

Ronnie's room was two doors down the hall. About fifteen minutes after the housekeeper had left my room, I could hear him whooping. It was the kind of noise that some football fans make when their team scores a touchdown in the final seconds of play.

I walked down to his room. The door was open; the housekeeping cart was propping it in place.

I edged my way around the cart and went in. The same woman was working on his room.

"Now tell me again where you found it?" Ronnie said.

He was holding the medallion.

"It was caught between the frame and the mattress," she said. "It was stuck right in there."

She turned to see me.

"Oh, hello again," she said. "Did you need something else in your room?"

"No," I said. "I know this guy."

Ronnie looked like he was going to hug her. Suddenly she was his best friend. "So you worked on Ben's room, too?" he said to her.

"You mean old King Creole?" she said.

Then:

"I thought you were checking out, King Creole."

"We're not checking out," Ronnie said before I could answer.

So we stayed one more day, and the following morning, when we met in the lobby to leave for the airport, Gail, with her bag packed, was with Ronnie.

"Gail's going to ride up to New York with us," Ronnie said.

As if he were merely going to give her a lift to the corner. As if she wasn't going to get on a jet airplane with us and fly for hundreds of miles to another part of the country.

He was smoking one of those cigars again; he seemed almost giddy. It was as if, by virtue of the housekeeper's discovery of the medallion, Gail had presented to Ronnie the most romantic and beneficent gift a woman could bestow: She had demonstrated that she was not a thief.

"I just always love going to New York," Gail said. She was wearing a tight summer jersey dress made out of a thin material that showed off her tan, and she was being stared at from all over the lobby.

"And where are you going to be staying?" Michael said to her, trying to make a joke, but Ronnie and Gail were already walking toward the front door of the hotel, and appeared not to hear. Her arm was hooked lightly through his.

We both hesitated for a second before following them.

"Kind of restores your faith in people, doesn't it?" I said.

The flight attendant came back to make sure all of us had our seat belts fastened as we began our descent into New York.

"I still have trouble believing it every time I land here," I said, looking out the window at the skyline of Manhattan.

"I've only been here I think three times," Michael said.

"I'm here all the time," I said. "But I always feel like I should ask someone's permission to enter the city. Like I should have a ticket or something. It's the only place that makes me feel that way."

Ronnie and Gail were up in first class. At Hartsfield Airport in Atlanta he had pulled out some upgrade stickers. He asked Michael and me if we wanted to use them, too, but we both said no almost before we'd had time to consider the offer.

On the drive from the Atlanta Hyatt to the airport, there had been a lot of silences in the car. Ronnie and Gail would talk, and it was as if by that very act an unseen "mute" button had been pressed that automatically quieted Michael and me. It was as if all of a sudden we were wary of being considered interlopers. When we did talk, Gail would turn around—she was in the front seat with Ronnie—in an effort to demonstrate interest in what we were saying. The whole thing felt pretty awkward to me.

So I didn't mind the fact that they were in the front of the plane while Michael and I were in the back. We had told ourselves that at some point during the summer we were going to visit New York. We just hadn't anticipated that there would be an extra person with us.

The wheels touched down at La Guardia, and some music started playing inside my head. It wasn't coming from anywhere; it wasn't on some tape in the plane. It was the same music I heard every time I landed here.

On a hunch I said to Michael, "What's going through your head right now?"

" 'New York, New York,' " he said.

"Right," I said.

I'm not even a fan of the song, but every time I get off a plane and walk through La Guardia, those opening bars play in my ears: "Dah, dah, dah-dah-dah, dah, dah, dah-dah-dah . . ."

"Frank Sinatra or Liza Minnelli?" I said to Michael.

"Frank Sinatra," he said.

"Me, too," I said.

It isn't just New York where that happens to me. Most of the songs are tunes I never think of unless I'm walking off a plane and into an airport. In Los Angeles it's always the initial verse of something called "Promised Land." I have no idea what the first few words leading up to the germane syllables are, so in my head it's always: "Doo-doo-doo-doo, L.A., California . . ." In Houston it's an old Dean Martin ballad that I hear as soon as I look down from the airplane and see that unlikely forest of dark green trees surrounding Houston International Airport: "Goin' back to Houston, Houston, Houston . . ."

In Detroit it's the mournful Bobby Bare dirge, "Detroit City." In Denver it's "Get Out of Denver"—the Bob Seger version, not the Tina Turner. In Pittsburgh it's a country song about cheating hearts that I know for a fact I only heard once, because I've been listening for it ever since, hoping to hear it again: "They could call us the Pittsburgh stealers, stealin' happiness and cheating anytime we can." In Miami it's the final phrase of the theme song from the fifties TV show *Surfside Six*: ". . . in Miami Beach!" Cleveland is a snatch from the Peter Townsend solo "Sheraton Gibson": "Cleveland, Ohio, you've blown my mind . . ."

A lot of times I'll walk off a plane and into an airport, and I'll wonder if any of the mature-looking and apparently serious-minded business travelers on every side of me are secretly hearing in their heads the same song I'm hearing in mine. It seems unlikely, but maybe not. I'll be walking through the big airport that's located between Seattle and Tacoma, and I'll be intensely curious about whether one or more of those somber fellows in gray suits and Burberry coats are also hearing Perry Como's peppy voice singing: "The bluest skies you've ever seen are in Seattle . . ."

Ronnie didn't seem to be hearing anything. He was looking around La Guardia impatiently for the driver of the limo he had called ahead to order before we left Atlanta.

"I think at this airport they wait for you down by the baggage claim," Gail said to him.

"It's so nice to have someone along with us who knows the lay of the land," I said to Michael.

"Sort of like a trusty wilderness guide," he said.

Michael and I walked along Fifth Avenue late that afternoon.

"How many cities do you do this in?" he said.

"What?" I said. "Walk?"

"Right," he said. "Go for walks."

"Well," I said, "if it's quicker than driving or taking a cab . . ."

"I'm not talking about walking to get somewhere," he said. "I'm talking about just going out to walk around."

The answer was: very few. In New York, though, whenever it gets to be late afternoon I almost feel an obligation to go for a walk. It's not that I'm expecting anything to happen—it's more like that it's part of the rules. This is New York, and you're supposed to be out and about.

"It's probably a holdover from old movies," I said to him. "Everyone bustling and hurrying and rushing to get someplace."

" 'The Bronx is up and the Battery's down,' " he said.

"Yep," I said. "That kind of New York."

"What play was that from?" he said.

"I think it was called *On the Town*," I said. "Famous play."

"It was the spring play our junior year at Bristol," he said.

"I thought that was *Brigadoon*," I said.

"That was sophomore year," he said. "Tina Kleinhuizen had the lead."

"Why are you thinking about plays?" I said.

"Because my Aunt Rose used to go on those Broadway Theater Weeks to New York," he said. "The ones that the Columbus papers used to sponsor."

"I remember," I said. "Norman Nadel used to accompany the people who signed up."

"I don't know Norman Nadel," Michael said.

"He was the theater critic of the Columbus *Citizen*," I said. "He'd sort of be the scoutmaster on the trips."

"You want to head back to the hotel soon?" Michael said as we crossed Fifty-ninth Street.

"In a few minutes," I said. We were supposed to meet Ronnie and Gail for dinner. That had suddenly become an automatic set of words in our vocabulary. "Ronnie-and-Gail." I didn't much want to think about it.

"Sometimes my Aunt Rose would sing a few bars from that song in

On the Town," Michael said. "And when she sang it the phrase wasn't 'wonderful town.' It was 'hell of a town.' "

"I think maybe it was 'hell of a town' in the play, and 'wonderful town' in the movie," I said.

"I think that was probably it," he said. "Like they thought that 'hell' might be okay on Broadway, but that it was too dirty for neighborhood movie theaters or something."

We could see the Plaza. That's where we were staying. Ronnie's idea.

"My aunt really seemed to get a kick out of singing that lyric," Michael said.

"That was the purpose of the Columbus *Citizen* Broadway Theater Week," I said. "You got to go to New York with Norman Nadel, and when you came back you got to let everyone else know that you saw a play that had the word 'hell' in one of the songs."

"Sort of jaunty," Michael said.

"I can just see your Aunt Rose playing mah-jongg in Bristol and bursting out with 'hell of a town.' "

We waited for one more light to change; the hotel was straight ahead.

"I've never seen a Broadway play," Michael said.

"You've been to off-Broadway plays?" I said.

"No," he said. "I've never been to any plays in New York at all."

"To tell you the truth," I said, "I haven't, either."

"You haven't?" he said. "But you're here so much more than I am."

"I've just never gone," I said. "I wouldn't feel comfortable."

"Why not?" he said.

"I just wouldn't feel like I belonged," I said. "I don't think I'd be able to concentrate on the plot. I'd just be sitting in my seat thinking: I'm at a Broadway play."

Michael laughed. "Would that be so bad?" he said.

We walked up the steps that led into the Plaza's main lobby.

"Maybe not," I said. "It just seems like it's too late to start."

"I can check the theater listings in the New York *Times*," Michael said.

"See if *Brigadoon*'s playing," I said.

Michael shook his head and laughed again. We headed for the house phones to call Ronnie's room.

"You figure Norman Nadel made out pretty well with the Ohio ladies on those theater trips?" Michael said.

"It wouldn't surprise me," I said. "Hey. New York."

When we had checked in at the Plaza, Ronnie had gone out of his way at the front desk to make it clear to Michael and me that he and Gail were registering separately, in two different rooms. Ronnie doesn't embarrass easily, and he can be pretty obtuse, but I think he was getting the picture that we thought he ought to go a little easy. Or at least make a token effort at giving that appearance.

Now we waited for them in the lobby before dinner. They emerged from the elevator together. Before Ronnie could say anything, Gail said, "We've been shopping for the last two hours. Where did you guys go?"

I found that pretty amazing—seventy-two hours ago in Georgia we had been complete strangers to her, and now, in New York, we were "you guys." She seemed to have adjusted to it considerably more seamlessly than we had. With a bright smile she said, "Do you want to head down to the Oyster Bar for drinks?"

"Is that close to here?" Ronnie said.

"It's in the hotel," she said. "Right down the other hallway, by the gift shop."

"What about that Mickey Mantle place?" Ronnie said.

"It's like a jock hangout," she said. "Like a sports bar."

She turned to Michael and me and said, "We were walking along Central Park South and Ronnie saw Mickey Mantle's name on a restaurant and his eyes lit up."

Her voice had a tone of playful exasperation—the signal it sent was: That Ronnie! He never changes, does he? It was the tone of voice you'd use when you were talking about a person you'd known all your life. As totally inappropriate as it was in this particular situation, I had to, in a perverse way, admire Gail for it. When the week began, she'd been hanging out with the hygienists in Atlanta, and here she was at the Plaza.

"What'd you buy when you were out shopping, Gail?" Michael said. "Just detergent and Clorox and paper towels?"

She was smooth enough not to let him get to her. "Right," she said. "That and some powdered milk."

She glided her hand into Ronnie's. "So anyway," she said to us. "I was telling Ronnie that only tourists go to a place like Mickey Mantle's. We should go down to the Oyster Bar for cocktails, and then decide where we want to have dinner."

She paused.

"Ben," she said, addressing me by name for what I think was the first time, "I know that you're in New York a lot. Where do you suggest?"

"Mickey Mantle's," I said.

"Definitely Mickey Mantle's," Michael said.

You can be forty-three years old and standing with harps and violins playing in the elegant lobby of one of the most famous hotels in the world, and still you're dipping her pigtail in the inkwell of your desk. It's nothing to be proud of, I suppose, but then in this case it was nothing to lose a lot of sleep over, either.

"You guys are so funny," she said.

"We guys," Michael said.

"You're sure you can get us in there?" Ronnie said. "That's not even your network."

"We can get in," I said. "I know a guy."

This was the next day; after dinner at Mantle's, Ronnie and Gail had split off and wandered up by Rockefeller Center. Ronnie wanted to know if there was any chance we could see the NBC television studios.

"Let me call Jack," I said.

Jack McRae was a field producer I used to work with on stories; he'd been hired away by NBC, and now he was an inside producer at the *Later with Bob Costas* show. When I was up late at night sometimes I'd see his name crawl by on the credits.

I called him at NBC, got bounced around the phone system a few times, and finally was connected with him. There was noise in the background, and his voice had that harried yet focused sound that you hear so often around television broadcasts. It's a voice that, beneath the specific words, carries the message: I'm very busy so say exactly what you want in one sentence.

"We start taping at one," Jack said after I'd explained why I was calling. "I'll leave your name at the guard desk. How many people with you?"

Thus Michael and Ronnie and I arrived at Rockefeller Center—Gail had gone out shopping again, this time by herself—and we walked down the long first-floor corridor. At the guard desk we had to wait for a moment; several high school kids were being told that, no, there were no seats available for that night's Letterman show.

Disappointed, the kids headed for the NBC Store a few feet away so that they could buy *Late Night* T-shirts and baseball caps to take home with them; at least they'd be able to display artifacts of having been here.

I told the guard that Jack McRae was expecting me. Without looking up he dialed an extension on his telephone, then handed us building passes and told us to go to the third floor.

It was funny; I noticed something about Michael and Ronnie, and for a second I couldn't figure out what it was, and then it became clear: They were walking gingerly, almost as if they were attempting not to make noise. Ronnie especially can bluster his way into any restaurant or office building, but something about being in the NBC headquarters seemed to make him strangely humble.

On the third floor Jack McRae was waiting for us by the elevator doors.

"Hey, Ben," he said. I introduced my friends, and even as Jack was shaking hands with them I knew their names weren't registering in his brain. Had I asked him five seconds later whom he had just met, he wouldn't have a clue. On days when he was putting a broadcast together, no information other than information pertinent to the show stuck. The false majesty of network television was such that this kind of quirk was acceptable, even expected; had Jack worked in a department store or a brokerage house he would not be excused for failing to pick up on people's names, but at NBC he could get away with it. It came with the job, along with the pension plan and the medical benefits.

"We're taping four shows in a row today," he said, walking down the corridor and knowing we'd follow. "We're already in the middle of the first one. You can stand in the back of the room."

There was a red light flashing over a light brown wooden door. Jack pulled the door open; it was cool inside. The big studio was dark, save for the set, which was lit by harsh spotlights.

"Stay as long as you want," Jack whispered, and then walked off.

Michael and Ronnie and I stood behind the cameras. Up in the lighted area, Costas, in an overstuffed easy chair, was having an animated conversation with Garth Brooks, the country music singer. Brooks was talking about his current hit album.

Michael and Ronnie were transfixed. I had read a quote once—I think it was from Steve Allen. Allen had said that once a person has been televised enough, it's as if the person gives off a glow wherever he walks. People look at the person as if there are bright rays emanating from him. So it was with Costas this afternoon; Michael and Ronnie had seen him do so many sports broadcasts on TV that today they were seeing the invisible glow. I could tell; they were staring at him as if it were a privilege. They'd have denied it if I had asked them. Maybe they didn't even know. Seeing the glow is an involuntary response.

Costas and Brooks kept talking, and during a commercial break Costas got out of his chair and walked over to exchange a few words with Jack McRae, who was holding a clipboard. Even though Michael and Ronnie had met Jack only minutes before, he seemed to take on a new stature in their eyes simply on the strength of this little production meeting with Costas.

"This would be some job to have," Michael whispered.

In realistic terms, Jack McRae's job was not all that much different from any middle-management job in America. He took care of details and had meetings with his bosses. But because the job was at the NBC television network, its allure was amplified in the eyes of strangers. That was the reason so few people ever willingly walked away from network TV jobs; the amplification of the allure was a magnet with a fierce pull. I knew the feeling.

Costas went back to his chair (a chair that Michael and Ronnie would think about having seen with their own eyes every time they watched *Later* from now on; even the allure of furniture is amplified when it is connected to network television), and near the end of Brooks' half hour the wooden door behind us opened, and a production assistant escorted Meryl Streep into the room. Streep was up next; she had a new movie coming out, and she was going to do *Later* as part of her publicity tour. Brooks finished and shook hands with Costas, and Streep was led to the chair and hooked up to a microphone. We watched Costas talk to her for a few minutes, and then we returned to the hallway outside.

On the walls were color portraits of the various *Today* show casts through the years. Over to the left was a big picture with Dave Garroway and Jack Lescoulie and J. Fred Muggs, the monkey; there was a picture from the Jim Hartz days—Hartz smiled next to a young, dark-haired Barbara Walters; there was a picture from the Tom Brokaw–Jane Pauley years, with Gene Shalit featured prominently; there was one with Pauley and Bryant Gumbel and Willard Scott. As we looked at the pictures, men and women carrying paper cups of coffee walked past us, talking about parking problems and restaurant prices.

The juxtaposition was sharp; on the walls were the pictures of the men and women who, through the years, had been daily guests in the households of America. Through the corridors walked the network employees to whom this was a job and a paycheck; somehow the on-air personalities in the portraits represented something different to them than they did to the rest of the country.

For all the stories in the newspapers about financial troubles at the networks, the NBC television network still meant something very important to those of us who grew up with TV. Right down the hall from Costas' studio was the room from which *Today* was broadcast every morning; *NBC Nightly News* came out of the same room. Out of these rooms and into the air and into every city and town in the land. All the years of *Saturday Night Live* had come out of this building, and the Letterman show, and Michael and Ronnie were still so silent, even though we were no longer inside the *Later* studio.

The two of them kept looking at the wooden door. I knew what they were thinking. They wanted to go back inside. I understood completely. For the same reason that Michael had said he envied Jack

McRae's job, he and Ronnie didn't want to depart this hallway. For whatever reason—and it may have had something to do with that invisible but quite real glow that Steve Allen had spoken of—they instinctively felt that something good existed inside that room, and that by leaving it behind they would be cheating themselves.

The sidewalks outside Rockefeller Center were crowded and the day was hot and Michael and Ronnie said very little on our way back to the hotel.

"Can I help you gentlemen?" the uniformed doorman said.

"No, thanks," I said. "We're fine."

The doorman didn't seem to know how to proceed. He stood next to Michael and me, and then he said, "Were you waiting for someone?"

"No," Michael said. "We're just hanging out."

This was at night; after returning from NBC, Ronnie had left with Gail to have dinner at the Four Seasons. Michael and I had stayed behind, and now we were sitting out on the wide flight of stone steps that led down from the lobby of the Plaza to the sidewalk facing Fifth Avenue. We'd been sitting on the steps for about half an hour.

It felt sort of like when we used to sit out on the front stoop at Michael's parents' house in Bristol. We'd talk for hours then. Michael's parents lived on Lincoln Road, and even on busy days there wasn't much traffic on Lincoln. It was a residential street surrounded by other residential streets, and unless you were heading home or to a friend's house, you probably wouldn't end up on Lincoln, except by mistake. On some of those nights Michael and I would see only one or two cars the whole time we talked on his stoop. Sometimes we'd sit on that stoop until past midnight.

So, objectively speaking, this was different; out in front of us the Manhattan traffic was heavy, and the streets were filled with people, and horns honked constantly. Men and women passed us on the wide steps—some were leaving the hotel, some were arriving.

"I really felt funny this afternoon," Michael said.

Just then the doorman came back. He had disappeared after speaking to us, and now he was accompanied by a hotel security guard.

"Is there something we can do for you?" the security man said to us.

"No, sir," Michael said.

"Is there a reason you're sitting here?" the security man said.

"It's just a nice night," I said.

"Are you guests of the hotel?" he said.

"We are," I said.

"May I ask to see your keys?" he said.

"No problem," Michael said. He stood up, reached into his right front pocket, and handed his room key to the security man, who examined it.

"There are several bars and lounges inside," the security man said.

"We're fine out here," Michael said.

So the security man and the doorman left, and I asked Michael why he had felt funny at NBC.

"I just felt rubeish," he said.

I looked at all the people on the street.

"I mean like a rube," he said.

"I know," I said.

"All those people working at NBC, and they didn't even think it was a big deal to be there," he said. "To me, the NBC television network is a big deal. New York's a big deal.

"When I went away to college," he said, "there was this film festival on campus freshman year. And one of the films they showed was *Breathless*."

"With Jean-Paul Belmondo," I said.

"Right, and Jean Seberg," Michael said. "Here we all were, college kids watching this movie, and I remember Belmondo had this thing where he'd run his thumb over his lips."

"I think he was imitating Bogart," I said.

"I don't know," he said. "But I thought it was really cool. I thought it would just be a matter of time before I was out of the Midwest and in Paris and making cool faces into storefront windows. Watching my reflection like Belmondo."

"But?" I said.

"But it never happened," he said. "It's not going to happen. I'm not Paris and I'm not New York. Maybe that's why I felt sort of bad today. You always tell yourself that you haven't made it to New York yet. The emphasis is on the 'yet.' And this afternoon I realized that I'm never going to make it to here. It's just not going to happen."

"Is that so terrible?" I said.

"I don't know," he said. "I looked at those people at NBC and I felt like a hick."

"There's no need to live here," I said. "You should never live in any town that doesn't have a Main Street."

"What are you talking about?" Michael said.

"There's no Main Street in Manhattan," I said.

"How do you know?" he said.

"I checked it out once," I said. "There's no Main Street. I was testing my theory. It really works. Any town you'd want to live in, there's a street called Main Street. Any town you wouldn't, there isn't."

Some people were arguing loudly down below us on Fifth Avenue, but they moved on. Whistles were blowing; men and women were waiting for cabs that weren't there.

"I wonder what room at NBC *Peter Pan* came out of?" Michael said.

"You thought about that this afternoon?" I said.

"Yeah," he said. "I was thinking that in one of those rooms Mary Martin flew through the air being Peter Pan, and it went out into the sky and came into our houses in Bristol and we stared at it and loved it."

"There's probably not a person we saw in the building today who was working at NBC when that happened," I said. "Not a person who remembers what room it was broadcast from."

"I remember what room I was in when I saw it," Michael said.

There were some ceremonial flags hanging from poles in front of the hotel; a slight breeze had come up, and the flags made a soft, flapping sound as they hit the poles.

"It was our living room," Michael said. "We all sat on that long couch."

"The light green one, right?" I said.

"Yeah," Michael said. "What an ugly couch."

On the stairs of the Plaza, we watched the summer night.

"You feel like going in yet?" I said after a while.

"Not really," he said.

So we didn't. Midnight wasn't so long away.

In the morning we headed for Boston on the shuttle. Ronnie had persuaded us to drive out to Cape Cod for the weekend.

Gail was still with him. We hadn't seen them the night before. When Michael and I had finally gone back into the hotel we rang his room, and there was no answer. In the morning he'd said that they had gone to some clubs after dinner and had come back to the Plaza around 2 A.M.

"What clubs?" Michael had asked him.

"I don't know," Ronnie had said. "Some places Gail knew about."

"So we're not talking about the Elks Club," Michael had said.

"Fuck you," Gail had said, smiling because she knew that at this point what Michael or I thought didn't matter.

During the flight Ronnie and Gail sat together on the left side of the plane, and Michael and I sat across the aisle from them. Whatever the morality of what was going on with them, it had already taken on an oddly domestic tinge. Ronnie had bought the New York *Times* at La Guardia; as we flew toward Massachusetts he read the business section while she read the feature section. She sipped orange juice, he coffee, and they appeared lost in whatever stories they were reading. They could have been a quiet married couple on their way to their annual vacation at the shore.

"How many days ago was it that he met her in Atlanta?" Michael said.

"There've been World Series that have lasted longer than they've known each other," I said.

"Are you going to feel comfortable with all of us going to Cape Cod together?" Michael said.

"Who knows," I said.

"She looks different," Michael said.

She did look almost staid on this bright, cloudless morning. Probably the clothes. Nothing flashy now; today she was dressed as if she were on her way to the PTA's summer national convention. If not a mother on the governing board, at least a music teacher.

"If she catches Ronnie looking around the beach, she'll probably tell him to quit staring at other women," I said.

Ronnie unbuckled his seat belt and walked to the front of the plane. He slipped a credit card into one of those public phones; when the phone's machinery had verified the card, he lifted the receiver out and carried it back to his seat.

"I'm calling the office," he said to us as he sat down.

It wasn't a comment he had to make; it was a piece of information that could have remained unspoken. Most of the times on the trip that Ronnie had gone off to make his business calls, he hadn't felt compelled to explain to us what he was doing. Maybe he wasn't quite sheepish about Gail's presence, or embarrassed, but clearly on some level he knew that her being along was making a difference in the dynamic of the summer. When he told us that he was calling his office, it was the first words he had spoken to us on the flight. Maybe that was the point.

He sat down and punched the numbers.

"You know," he said to us after thirty seconds, "you can never get a dial tone on these things."

He tried again. We could hear him talking to his secretary: "Hi, it's me." Then: "Talk loud, I'm on a plane."

And then all the color went out of his face and I thought he was going to be sick. His voice changed; when he next spoke it was higher and it was shaking.

"Tell them I'll be there as quickly as I can," he said. "I'll call you back as soon as I land in Boston. Please don't leave the desk."

He put the phone on the seat and closed his eyes.

I leaned across the aisle.

"Ronnie?" I said.

He turned toward me, his eyes wet.

"It's my dad," he said.

Fifteen

IT TOOK US most of the day to get down to Sarasota. As soon as the shuttle landed in Boston, Ronnie and Michael and I went to pay phones and started calling airlines. Even though we were in Logan Airport, we figured it was quicker to check out flights by phone than to stand in line at the various ticket counters.

Ronnie's dad had been rushed into surgery; that was the extent of the message his secretary had given him on the phone. Ronnie's parents had moved to Florida about five years before. Mr. Hepps had stayed in Bristol for several years after his retirement, but he said that he felt like he had become a different person once he stopped working. That's what he told Ronnie: that he no longer felt totally at home in Bristol. Without a job to go to, he felt that people didn't know what to say to him, or how to treat him. Even people his own age—even other people who had retired.

The very fact that he would confide in Ronnie about this was indicative of the change. Mr. Hepps and Ronnie were never an especially close father and son—Carlton Hepps was the senior vice president of a big real estate firm in Columbus, he was one of the Bristol fathers who made that freeway commute every day, and for most of our growing-up years he seemed a distant figure not just to us, but to Ronnie. Mr. Hepps was a dark-blue-suit, white-shirt guy, and whatever he might have been thinking he seldom expressed. At least not around the house. Not to Ronnie.

So when he had told Ronnie that he no longer felt content in Bristol, the unspoken message was that things had truly shifted. He was talking to Ronnie as he would to a friend—which, Ronnie knew, probably meant that the friends Carlton Hepps had had at his office were no longer available to him, at least on a ready emotional level. Mr. Hepps had worked with some of those people for forty years. Perhaps that is the reason he was uneasy speaking to them about why he felt so foreign in his own town. How do you tell the people you know best that you no longer feel welcome?

In any event, Ronnie's parents had moved to a condominium on one of the keys near Sarasota, where by all accounts they were relaxed and happy, and took special pleasure during the winter months watching the weather reports from the North as they sat on their balcony overlooking the Gulf of Mexico and had cocktails in the warm breeze while the sun dropped slowly toward the water line.

Michael hung up the phone and said he'd found us a Delta flight that would take us nonstop to Orlando, from where we could catch a connection into Sarasota. Gail rode with us—in that one second everything had changed, but we weren't going to just leave her in the Boston airport—and this time she sat next to Michael on the flight. I didn't know whether Ronnie would feel like talking, but I took the seat next to him just in case he did.

My own parents are okay—their health is holding up. I talk to them at least once every week, and I'd kept it up during this summer. They're no longer in Bristol; they're down in South Carolina now, and the geographic distance effectively guarantees that we don't see each other very often. In the back of my mind I always know that one day the inevitable phone call is going to come—my version of the call that Ronnie had just been a part of. Knowing that, I do my best not to think about it. Thinking about it isn't going to delay it or prevent it.

"He's probably in the operating room right now," Ronnie said.

I didn't know what to say. Ronnie has never been a person who I assumed was in need of much commiseration; his attitude has always signified that he is quite capable of taking care of things by himself.

"If I'm lucky, he's in the operating room," Ronnie said.

Meaning the obvious; meaning that if things had gone very badly, the trip to the operating room might have been futile.

"Whenever I think of your dad, I think of that oil painting in your living room," I said.

In Ronnie's parents' house—their old house, the one in Bristol—there was a framed painting of his father in uniform. Ronnie's dad must have been twenty-five or twenty-six years old when he served in World War II.

"Didn't your dad get that painting in Italy?" I said.

"That's the story," Ronnie said. We had always been told that an Italian village artist had painted the portrait during the war, and that Ronnie's dad had rolled it up and brought it back to Ohio with him. The painting was a part of Ronnie's house, but it never seemed to have any real-life connection with the man we knew as Ronnie's father. We'd joke about it—when Ronnie's dad would get mad at us, we'd salute the oil painting. But the fact that the chilly, dignified, incurably aloof businessman who was Ronnie's dad was once the soldier in the picture . . . we knew it was true, but it didn't quite register.

"Did your own dad talk much about the war?" Ronnie said.

"He had some scrapbooks," I said. "Once he came home from work and my sister and I were going through them, and he said to be careful we didn't tear any of the pages. But then he walked right out of the room. I think he wanted to let us learn whatever we might learn from the scrapbooks themselves. Rather than talking to us about it."

"It really wasn't ancient history to them, was it?" Ronnie said.

"Think about it," I said. "When were we in first grade? 1953? 1954?"

"You know that stuff better than I do," he said.

"Fifty-three," I said. "That oil painting was in your living room and the scrapbooks were in our den, and the war had only been over for eight years."

"Eight years?" Ronnie said.

"They came home from Europe in '44 and the war ended in '45, and then we were born," I said. "I remember, there was this book that was very popular in elementary school. It was written for kids; there was always a waiting list for it in the school library. As soon as boys learned to read pretty well, they all signed up for it. It was called *The Battle of Britain*."

"I think I read that," Ronnie said.

"Everyone did," I said. "It seemed like this old historical thing, like an account of Waterloo or the Civil War. But for our parents, the Battle of Britain was something that they'd lived through just a few years back."

"The model airplanes, too," Ronnie said. "We were like six years old. I can remember the smell of the glue, and how slimy the decals felt when you soaked them in water."

"I was terrible at that," I said. "I'd always get the glue on the plastic wings, and it would eat through."

"Spitfires," Ronnie said. "I think the Spitfires were British planes. And the Messerschmitts were German."

"We were gluing those model planes together," I said, "and some of the men who had flown the planes during the war were still in their late twenties or early thirties."

Across the aisle, Michael and Gail were talking. I decided not to say anything about her to Ronnie. It was going to be a touchy enough situation to deal with when we got to Florida.

"When I was very young," I said to Ronnie, "there was the unveiling of a new military jet out at Port Columbus. I forget what the plane was, or why it was being unveiled in Ohio. My dad drove me up from Bristol to see it. It was a boys' thing. My mom and sister didn't come. I don't think my dad invited them.

"And we got to Port Columbus, and there was actually a drape or a cover of some kind over this new jet. It was really hot out; it was early evening. Out on the runway were all these dads and all their young sons. I realize now that most of the dads must have been World War II guys.

"There was a military honor guard standing at attention. They were holding their rifles and standing so stiff. I got the impression they'd been there for a while. We all gathered around. We were waiting for the cover to come off the jet.

"So I was standing with my dad, and all of a sudden this one soldier in the honor guard fell face-forward right onto the concrete. Right onto his face. They rolled him over and he was bleeding from his nose. I could see his face. He was so young under his cap.

"My dad said that the soldier had had too much heat. He said that the soldier had fallen properly—he said that soldiers are trained to stay at attention even when they fall. I don't know whether that was true or not, but he did fall flat onto his face. My dad seemed to approve of the way he had fallen. They gave him some smelling salts, and a few minutes later some medics took him away in a car.

"Then they unveiled the jet. I can't even tell you what it looked like. I remember that everyone applauded; I remember my dad telling me what kind of jet it was, and I remember that he really liked it.

"Isn't that funny? All these years later, I have no idea what the jet was. But I remember that young soldier falling so hard onto his face."

Ronnie said, "I don't think my dad ever took me to Army stuff."

"My dad didn't either, except for that one time," I said.

The flight attendants were coming around with lunch.

"Did your parents take the oil painting of your father with them when they moved to Florida?" I said.

"They must have," Ronnie said. "But it's not hanging up. Their condo is much smaller than their house in Bristol was."

"I wonder what the painting would look like to us now," I said.

"Probably like a kid," Ronnie said. "I'm almost twenty years older than the soldier in the painting."

There was a pillow behind his head. He reached over to pull down the window shade, closed his eyes, and turned away from me. When the flight attendant arrived with lunch, she asked if my friend was asleep. I said yes, even though I wasn't sure.

———————

The seventh-floor corridor was chilly to the point of discomfort. It seemed to have nothing to do with the bright, sweltering day we could see through the windows, or the palm trees down below.

"You sure you want us to be here?" Michael said.

"I do," Ronnie said.

The nurses walked past us, not paying much attention. I don't know what it is about hospitals; we're living in some of the most security-conscious times of the century, yet you can walk through hospitals without anyone asking you what your business is there. Probably the doctors and nurses are so busy, they don't have time to think, much less to wonder about the people around them.

"I'm sorry," Ronnie said, his voice nervous. "I knew I was going to forget this. Did you write down the room number my mom gave me?"

"It's 712," Michael said.

"I'm sorry," Ronnie said again.

"Stop it," I said.

Gail had taken a cab ahead to the hotel. I think she was feeling more than a little discomfited being along with us now; certainly she didn't want to be at the hospital. We'd told her that we would meet her as soon as we could. No use blaming her for this; whatever Michael and I felt about her presence on the journey, she'd been invited. Ronnie had asked her to come along. She'd had no way of anticipating this particular detour.

We got to 712.

"We'll wait out here," I said.

Ronnie stared at the outside of the wooden door. It had a vertical, oversized metal handle, the kind of handle you'd never see on a door at someone's home.

"I don't even know whether you're supposed to knock or not," Ronnie said.

"I don't think anyone would mind if you just walked in," I said.

"My dad's not the kind of person who likes being walked in on," he said.

So Ronnie knocked, and within a second or two a nurse pulled the door open, and right behind her was Ronnie's mom, red-eyed and older than I'd ever seen her. But then, I hadn't seen Mrs. Hepps in many years.

Michael and I found a lounge area at the end of the hallway. Three couches were arranged in a U shape around a television set. The set was tuned to a baseball game; men and women, all of them visitors, filled almost all of the space on the couches.

There was enough room for us to sit down. Along with the others, we pretended to watch the ball game. No one here had any interest in the contest; no one here had any reason not to stand up and switch the channel. But all of us feigned attention to the televised competition as if we had purchased tickets. Once in a while a doctor or a relative of one of the people on the couch would come around the corner and gesture, and the person would rise. Mostly, though, we looked at the baseball players.

An hour or so later, Ronnie came to get us.

"He's awake," Ronnie said.

Then:

"He wants to see you."

I don't know why I was so surprised. Maybe it wasn't the fact; maybe it was just the words. "He wants to see you." There was a certain vulnerability to that, a certain implied plaintiveness. I don't think Carlton Hepps had ever expressed a desire to see any of us in his life. Carlton Hepps didn't want to see people; people wanted to see Carlton Hepps. I was imagining that blue business suit, that white shirt.

"You're sure?" Michael said.

"I told him you were here," Ronnie said. "It was his idea."

So we walked with Ronnie back up the hallway, and we followed him through the door with the long metal handle, and there, flat on his back in a skinny bed, was Carlton Hepps with two tubes running into his nose and two more tubes running into his arms and his face looking as if it had been dusted with gray powder.

"Hello, boys," he said.

And then, as if realizing what we were thinking before we could think it: "I apologize for the voice. My throat is very dry."

He sounded as if his throat was a stretched balloon. He couldn't have moved in the bed even if he'd wanted to; the various tubes had him pinned in.

"They tell me I got lucky," he said.

Apparently something had burst in his intestines; apparently thirty minutes more of a delay in getting him to the hospital and we wouldn't be talking to him.

"You all must be hungry," Mrs. Hepps said, as if this were her kitchen back in Bristol and she was somehow obliged to offer us snacks.

"We're fine, Mrs. Hepps," Michael said. "We ate on the plane."

"I guess I threw your trip out of whack," Carlton Hepps said from beneath that tangle on the bed.

"Dad," Ronnie said to him. Somehow it sounded odd.

"Well, they tell me I'm going to make it," Carlton Hepps said. "So you can head on back to the airport. Continue on."

"Dad, we're not going anywhere," Ronnie said. "Not for a while."

I don't know whether Carlton Hepps intended for us to see the relief on his face when he heard Ronnie say those words, but there was no mistaking it.

"Well, your mother will appreciate the company," Mr. Hepps said, deflecting the emotion.

"Florida is no place to vacation at this time of year," Mrs. Hepps said.

"Mom, we're not here for the climate," Ronnie said.

"It's so good to see you boys," Mrs. Hepps said.

The nurse had left the room momentarily.

"God, I'm so dry," Mr. Hepps said.

"Shall I ring for some more ice water?" Mrs. Hepps said.

"No, there's still some in that pitcher," Mr. Hepps said, trying to be in charge.

Then:

"Son?"

The word seemed to blindside Ronnie.

"Would you mind?"

So Ronnie poured some ice water from the brown plastic pitcher into a plastic cup. He carried it over to his father's bed. Carlton Hepps inched his head up ever so slightly, and Ronnie reached behind to adjust the pillows so they would give support. Then Ronnie, balancing his weight on a chair by the side of the bed, lifted the cup to his father's lips.

Slowly, carefully, like a new parent feeding his baby for the very first time, Ronnie tilted the cup until he could tell that the water was trickling into his father's mouth.

"Is that too fast?" Ronnie said.

"Just give me a second," Mr. Hepps said, swallowing.

"Take your time," Ronnie said, in a voice that betrayed a premonition that nothing would be quite the same ever again.

We were staying at the Colony, out on Longboat Key, about ten minutes from downtown Sarasota. The place is an expensive tennis-oriented resort during the spring and winter months, but we'd called at the last minute and had been quoted good rates for the next several days. Apparently the demand wasn't as great during the summer, when people up North didn't have to head for Florida for sunshine.

Ronnie had told us he was going to have dinner in his dad's hospital room, so Michael and I took a cab to the Colony, where Gail had already registered for all of us. We had two units, each with two bedrooms, overlooking the Gulf of Mexico.

We found Gail sitting out on the terrace of one of the units; she was gazing out at the water.

"You okay?" Michael said to her. That's him; no matter what he thought about her continuing presence, he realized how out of place she must be feeling. Or at least how he assumed she must be feeling.

"I'm fine, Michael," she said. "How's Ronnie's dad?"

Michael held his right hand in the air and waggled it back and forth in a gesture of uncertainty. Which was probably as good a report on Mr. Hepps' condition as any. If we had been relieved to arrive and find him alive, there was still no indication of what his future might hold.

"Is Ronnie going to sleep at the hospital tonight?" she said.

"No," I said. "He'll be here after dinner."

She smiled at Michael. "You guys don't need to babysit me," she said. "I'm fine here."

What an unusual thing for her to say, yet she seemed to understand that Michael felt the obligation to look after her. We went to our own unit, put our bags away, then took a stroll around the grounds.

"Look at that sunset," Michael said.

"Let's walk," I said.

We hiked over the beach, toward the water line. A few guests of the resort were watching the sun go down, but the sand was surprisingly deserted. Michael kicked off his shoes and held them in his hands, and then so did I, and we followed the shoreline, not knowing exactly where we were headed. In a few minutes we were off the Colony property and walking past some damaged old trees. The only sound was of the Gulf coming in toward us, then rushing back.

"Little different from New York," Michael said.

"Was that just last night?" I said.

"Big country," he said.

He picked up some stones and threw them toward the water as we walked. "Seeing Ronnie's dad like that . . . ," he said.

I didn't say anything, and he knew I was waiting for him to go on.

"I don't think I'd let my friends see my dad like that," he said.

"You think he would have been embarrassed?" I said.

"Dad?" Michael said. "No. He never embarrassed easily. I just wouldn't have brought my friends. It's too private."

"Do you think about him a lot?" I said.

"It used to be every day," Michael said. "It's isn't anymore."

A man and woman who appeared to be in their sixties walked toward us from the other direction. They each wore those floppy white hats that people favor in full sunlight, even though the day was approaching dusk. "Hello," they said in unison as they passed, and we said hello in return, and they continued on their way and we continued on ours.

"Do you remember the Country Playhouse?" Michael said.

"Summer-stock place," I said, "about halfway between Bristol and Columbus."

"Do you remember my dad acting there?" he said.

I vaguely did recall that Michael's dad had done some acting, although I'd never seen him perform.

"He did it for three or four summers," Michael said. "I must have been nine or ten. Our family went to watch him every time he was in a show. I think about it now, and it was such a brave thing for a man in Bristol to do."

Obviously Michael had thought about this before; "brave" is not the first word you'd come up with if you were remembering something like this for the first time in years. "Brave" is a word that comes to you after some reflection.

"Bristol dads could play golf in the summer or play softball or have cookouts," Michael said. "But here was my dad, and he ran that grocery store, and he went out to the Country Playhouse and acted."

"He was never a professional, was he?" I asked.

"No, and that was the thing about the Country Playhouse," Michael said. "Almost all of the actors and actresses were professionals. They were in Equity, or whatever you call it. But one or two actors every show could be non-Equity. And there was my dad, every summer, trying out for the smallest speaking part in the shows."

There was a wooden pier jutting into the water, and I asked Michael if he wanted to sit for a while. He just kept on walking, and I kept pace.

"For the two weeks before a show would open, Dad would bring the script for the play home with him after work," Michael said. "He would have checked it out of the Bristol Public Library. And he'd run through the lines with my mom. She'd sit there with the script. They'd be in the living room, and she'd read every part except his. By the time the play opened, he would know every line of every part. And so would she."

"It sounds like it made him happy," I said.

"Oh, I don't know," Michael said. "I remember one summer, he went to the first rehearsal on a Saturday afternoon, and when he came home for dinner he seemed real low. He and my mom were talking in the kitchen, and they didn't know I was listening. He said that he'd rehearsed with the actors all morning, and that they'd broken for lunch and that they hadn't asked him to join them. He told my mom that he'd gone out to a restaurant and eaten lunch by himself."

"Well, you know how people are," I said. "They'd probably just met him."

"I know," Michael said. "They weren't from Ohio. They didn't live there. They traveled around the country on the summer circuit together. It was their real job."

"Who knows?" I said. "They might have assumed that because your dad lived there, he had people to eat lunch with."

"That's just it," Michael said. "I think that's why it would have been so important for my dad to be invited. Those actors represented what my father would never have. He lived in Bristol and he ran his grocery. That summer theater was probably the closest he ever came to letting himself dream."

"Was he good?" I asked.

"I think he probably was," Michael said. "I remember going to see him act one night. The theater was an in-the-round thing, in this big old tent. It was raining that night, and you could hear the rain against the top of the tent. He was saying the same lines I'd heard him rehearse in the living room with my mom, but instead of her answering back, the real actors were answering back. And they were all in costumes, in character. My dad was playing a police lieutenant. Or a plainclothes detective, I think it was. I remember being proud of him. And the sound of that rain on the tent."

"Did he keep doing it every summer?" I said.

"He stopped and I don't know why," Michael said. "By the time we were in high school, he wasn't doing it anymore."

We'd been walking for about twenty minutes. Without saying anything to each other we turned around so that we were heading back down the beach in the direction of the Colony.

"Now I wonder what the men he worked with at his store thought about it," Michael said. "Or what they must have said to him."

"Did he ever talk about it?" I said.

"Later on?" Michael said. "No. And I never brought it up. But there were some bureau drawers around our house, and my mom would carefully clip out the reviews of the plays, and she'd never throw them out. I'd go in those drawers years later, and the reviews would always be there, wrapped for safekeeping in Saran Wrap."

"He got reviewed?" I said.

"Just a line or two, if at all," Michael said. "Sometimes the reviewer would say, 'Samuel Wolff, local grocer and amateur thespian, showed energy in a supporting role,' or something like that. Other times he'd just be listed in the cast of characters. You know, in the agate type. But my mom would save those, too. Even when they misspelled his name."

"They got his name wrong?" I said.

"Oh, yeah," Michael said. "One *f*, or an *e* on the end. She still kept them."

Up ahead, we could see the Colony.

"I guess it was his way of getting out," I said.

"Getting out, without ever leaving," Michael said.

We cut across the sand, toward the main Colony building.

"The first couple of months after he died, if you'd ever told me there would be a day that would go by when I wouldn't think about him, I wouldn't have believed you," Michael said.

"But now it happens all the time. Two or three days will pass, and then I'll think about him, and I'll realize that for those two or three days I haven't thought about him at all. God, I guess you can get used to anything."

We were sitting out on our deck when Ronnie pulled in. Michael had taken the downstairs bedroom and I had taken the one upstairs, and we'd walked over to Tastebuds, the Colony's food shop, and had them heat up a pizza for us. So we were eating and watching the moon over the Gulf, and we heard footsteps on the little roadway beneath us. Ronnie had arrived, and was going to the unit he and Gail were checked into.

It must have been less than five minutes later when there was a knock on our door. I answered; Ronnie was standing there.

"She said she was tired," he said. "She said she wanted to sleep."

"Come on in," I said. "You hungry, or did you eat at the hospital?"

"They brought me a tray in Dad's room," he said. "I didn't have much."

"Here," Michael said, sliding the box of pizza toward him. "This isn't bad."

There had been only two chairs on the deck, but we brought a third one out from the living room, and we sat there for the next couple of hours. "He got worse after you left," Ronnie said before too much time had passed.

Michael said, "Surgery, when you're his age . . ."

"He was crying," Ronnie said, for which we had no ready response.

We waited, and Ronnie continued. "I don't think I've ever seen my father cry," he said. "He was telling my mom and me about how he'd been feeling fine this morning, and about how all of a sudden he'd doubled over, and I could tell that even as he was reviewing the day with us he was in a lot of pain. And that's when he started crying, and I don't think it was the pain that did it. I think it was knowing that everything changed today."

"How's your mom?" Michael said.

"I don't know," Ronnie said. "She was talking like nothing's happened. I think that's the only way she can deal with it. My dad was crying, and she asked him if he wanted some water or something, and he said no, he wasn't really listening, and she said that she felt like a cup of coffee. And then, out of nowhere, she said that back at their place she still had the coffeemaker she'd gotten with S&H Green Stamps.

"She was talking about her coffeemaker, and about how it's lasted all these years, and about how it had only cost her three books of S&H Green Stamps. She said how careful she always was when she pasted the stamps in the books. She's saying all this while my dad is lying there crying."

"It's been a long day for her, too," I said.

"She turned to me and said, 'They really valued your business back then,' " Ronnie said. "She said, 'Companies don't really value their customers anymore.' And Dad's crying."

"I guess she's trying to hold on to something," I said. "I guess that's what she's doing."

"You know what I was thinking when he was crying in that bed?" Ronnie said. "That he never was reckless or never went out on a limb in his life. Everything he's ever done has been planned and careful and safe. And he's lying there crying tonight, and I'm thinking that even if you play it by the book every day of your life, you're going to end up scared and crying in some hospital bed anyway."

"They all played it by the book," I said. "That's not bad. That's good. Our dads all pretty much played it by the book. Maybe when you manage to make it through a depression and a world war, that's what comes naturally to you. Maybe being able to finally play it safe is almost a relief."

"You know what living life on the edge was for my dad?" Ronnie said. "Eating Mister Mustard."

"What?" I said.

"It was this hot kind of mustard," Ronnie said. "It was a brand. Mister Mustard. I guess it had horseradish in it or something. It burned your mouth. On purpose. Like an adults-only mustard. Sometimes when he'd grill hamburgers, he'd give the regular bottles of catsup and mustard to the rest of our family, and then he'd pull the Mister Mustard off a top shelf for himself. Like it was contraband."

"He didn't want you to have any?" Michael said.

"It wasn't that," Ronnie said. "It was like eating Mister Mustard was crossing over onto dangerous ground. He was the man, and the grownup, and the father, so he could eat it. Life on the edge."

Ronnie got up and went inside, and I thought I heard him crying from behind the bathroom door. When he came back out, though, he wasn't, and I didn't ask.

I didn't sleep so well, and in the morning I was up early. I walked around the grounds of the Colony, watching the tennis pros wetting down the courts, and the pool attendants getting the piles of towels ready for the guests, and the bakery delivery drivers carrying boxes of bread and rolls into the restaurant.

The day was bright and hot, and I went down to the beach where Michael and I had started our walk the night before. In those first hours of daylight, it almost looked like a different place, with the water stretching out forever and the sand reaching toward the horizon farther than I could see. I pulled my shirt over my head and took off along the beach.

The sun was harsh enough that I had to squint, and twice I walked into the water just to cool off. After the second time I came out dripping, and there was a young woman watching me.

She was tan with short brown hair, wearing gym shorts and a Duke University T-shirt, which she had sweated through.

"You look like the Old Man and the Sea, Mr. Kroeger," she said, and she flashed me a perfect white smile that could have been something in a toothpaste ad. I had no idea who she was.

She waved quickly and started to run down the beach. That's why she'd been sweating; she was out for a morning run. I watched her until she was out of sight.

By the time I got back to the Colony, Michael and Ronnie and Gail were eating breakfast. They'd picked up some sweet rolls and orange juice at Tastebuds, and they were out on our deck.

"You going over?" I said to Ronnie.

"In about half an hour," he said. "I just called the hospital. He didn't have such a good night."

Gail retrieved the paper bags the pastries had been in, and carried them inside to the kitchen wastebasket. She was subdued and tentative this morning. Nothing like the drumbeats of mortality to throw cold water on a racy summer adventure.

"The worst part is feeling so helpless," Ronnie said.

"You've talked to the doctors?" I said.

"I talked to them a little after you guys left yesterday afternoon, and a little on the phone this morning. I'm supposed to sit down with the surgeon this afternoon."

"It's about the least fun thing in the world," Michael said. "You sit there listening to them, and you know from the way they're talking that they've been through this same speech a thousand times before, and you want to interrupt them and say, 'Hey! This is one of my parents you're talking about!' But you know that everyone they see on that operating table is someone's parent. Everyone on the table is someone's mom or someone's dad.''

The first time that someone died and I was aware of it was when I was in the second grade, and we were in Miss Ruman's classroom and the principal came to the door. Mr. Brandenberg never did that before; he was always a voice on the PA system, we never saw him in the classrooms, but he said something to Miss Ruman, and Miss Ruman turned pale, and then she went to the desk where Irene Robbins was sitting and took Irene's hand. Irene didn't seem to realize anything was wrong; she was smiling, as if Miss Ruman had picked her out for something special, something good.

So Miss Ruman held Irene's hand and walked her out of the classroom, and the three of them, Miss Ruman and Mr. Brandenberg and Irene, disappeared down the hallway, and the school nurse came in to sit with us because there were no substitute teachers available on such short notice. When Miss Ruman came back she had us bow our heads on the desks and say a prayer, and she told us that Irene Robbins' mother had died suddenly.

I had only seen Irene Robbins' mother two or three times, waiting outside the school doors at the end of the day to pick Irene up and take her home. Probably I'd seen her more than that, but the two or three times were all I remembered; all the moms were there every afternoon when school let out, and Irene's mom, in my mind, was just one face among the many. One part of the composite Bristol mom.

But even though I didn't really know her, her death broke my heart. Besides making me so sad, it made me angry; why did Irene have to be without a mom? I suppose now that the anger was really fear. If Irene's mom could die, any of our moms—my mom—could die. That was a little too close to the bone to think about on a conscious level, though.

So what I was was mad. That was the year that *Superman* was so big on TV; we all watched the show after school every day, with the "Faster than a speeding bullet!" opening culminating with the shot of George Reeves in the Superman uniform blended together with a shot of a waving American flag, and the theme music swelling up like something out of a military parade, only much better.

And after school on the day that Irene Robbins' mother died, I walked around the block where our house was, pretending inside of me that I was Superman, hearing the theme music in my head, and telling myself that I was going to make Irene's mother be alive again. It wasn't that I believed it; I knew that I wasn't Superman, and that even Superman couldn't bring people back to life. So I don't know what it was exactly—but I walked around hearing the Superman music, and if

I knew it wasn't real, I also knew that I wasn't doing this out of any sense of fun or happy make-believe. I guess it was just the need to think that someone could do something; the need to think that the principal couldn't just come to the classroom door with the news that someone's mom was dead. Someone had to be able to change something like that.

I walked around and around the block the whole afternoon, so angry as I heard the theme music in my head, and that night at dinner my parents talked about death and what it meant, and the next day in school we talked about the same thing, and that next afternoon I walked around the block again, trying to convince myself that Superman could make things different. But that second afternoon I didn't walk around the block for quite as along, and the third afternoon I didn't walk around the block at all, and the next week Irene Robbins was back in class and I don't know if I ever told her how bad I felt about her mother.

Around one o'clock that afternoon I went for a swim in the Gulf. I was surprised at how far I could walk out with my feet still touching the sand on the bottom; I expected it to get deep right away, but I must have been thirty yards out and I was still walking, my chest and head still above the water line.

The Gulf felt clean and cool. Away from the beach I could look back on the Colony as if I were an invisible observer. Some kids were playing volleyball on the beach, and boat-rental guys were signing out some of those paddle machines that you sit on and pedal, the ones with high bicycle-like seats and four huge plastic wheels; a lone fisherman trolled at the end of a dock.

Ronnie had gone back to the hospital right after breakfast. He was being uncharacteristically apologetic; he told Michael and me that he didn't know just how long he'd have to be staying here, and we told him that it didn't matter, we liked the place. We'd probably been moving around too much as it was, and it was nice not to constantly be thinking about getting back into the car or going to the airport.

"I just really don't know how Dad is," Ronnie had said. "And I can't leave until I do."

"We're fine," Michael had said. "Don't think about us. We're hardly in a hurry." Ronnie's father was going to be all right or he wasn't; nothing Ronnie could do was going to change the outcome, or hurry up the timetable. He knew that this was different from anything else he'd ever gone through. Out in the chilly water on the blazing afternoon, I looked at the panorama of the people back on the beach as if it were all a painting.

I must have been doing this for about fifteen minutes when I realized that I was alone, and that I was hearing whistles. There had been about a dozen others out in the water with me, but now they were gone. I could see a lifeguard from the Colony gesturing vigorously, and I realized belatedly that he was gesturing to me.

As soon as I tried to make my way in, I understood why. Without my noticing it, the water had turned choppy and rough; what had been so placid was now stirred up. It took some effort to make it back to the shore. I turned around right before I got there and saw that the waves were coming in fierce and high.

"Thanks," I said to the lifeguard as I reached the beach. "I guess I didn't hear you."

"We were going to come after you in a few minutes," he said. "Things change so quickly here. The water can trick you."

Michael was on the sand, reading a copy of the Sarasota *Herald-Tribune* and eating a hot dog he'd bought at the snack bar up by the pool. "Ronnie called," he said. "He doesn't want us to wait on him for dinner if he's not back."

I dried myself off and sat down next to him.

"How did he sound?" I said.

"A little scared," Michael said.

"It's hard to blame him," I said.

The lifeguard had been right; the water was roiling up, it was decidedly darker than it had been even fifteen minutes before, and the spot in the Gulf where I had been standing was now churning with angry tide.

"When your dad's gone, it hits you for the first time that you're the oldest male in your family," Michael said. "It's a feeling there's no way to get ready for."

"Does it take you long to get used to?" I said.

"You get used to it," he said. "But you don't like it. At least I don't."

"Still?" I said.

"I've thought about it," he said. "It's like when you're growing up, and your parents are both alive, you sort of assume that your life is like some circus, and there's always a safety net below you, and the safety net is your mom and dad. You don't think of it that way at the time, but that's how you feel.

"And then when your dad dies, you realize that the safety net is gone. You're all alone. You're your own safety net now. Even if you're not ready for it and you don't want to be it, you're your own safety net."

It had been such a clear and cloudless day, but suddenly it was like evening in the afternoon. The sky was dark gray and rain started coming down hard. The boat-rental men were tying up their craft, and people were running toward the units where they were staying. The raindrops made a sharp, rattling sound against Michael's newspaper, which he left behind as we joined the others, running toward the buildings. I thought I saw lightning over the water.

"It comes and goes real fast this time of year," one of the pool attendants yelled to us as we ran by.

We were moving quickly enough that I wasn't sure what he yelled next, but what I think I heard him say was, "It'll fool you."

Sixteen

"DO YOU LIVE IN FLORIDA, Mr. Kroeger?"

I'd been looking at the water while I walked. This was the next morning; when Ronnie had come back from the hospital he'd said his dad wasn't doing so well, so we'd all had an early dinner at the Colony's restaurant and then gone to bed. Now, early in the morning again, I was walking on the beach just as I had the day before. I could see how people get used to this; the sound of the water, and the sight of the sand stretching out ahead, combine for an exceedingly pleasant way to start a new day.

The voice belonged to the young woman in the gym shorts and the Duke T-shirt. She'd been running; apparently this was her daily routine, too.

"I'm sorry," I said. "Do we know each other?"

"I watch the news," she said. "Plus, you were on our campus two years ago."

"Duke?" I said. "I don't think I've ever been to Duke."

"I haven't either," she said. "It's just a shirt. I'm in grad school at the University of Tennessee."

I had been there; we'd done a story about reports that college students were smoking more cigarettes than ever, despite all the health warnings, and we'd spent a day at Tennessee getting quick quotes from students. The story never aired; it was one of those ideas that a producer in New York gets all excited about because he's read it in the New York *Times*, so he spends thousands of dollars sending crews to report it, and then realizes that he doesn't really want it anyway. We'd flown to three campuses in the South; three days out of my life, for a story no one ever saw.

"Did we interview you?" I said.

"No," she said. "You interviewed some people from my dorm. There was a story in the paper about you guys being on campus."

"I didn't see it," I said. "It must have run after we left."

That's usually the case. The presence of a network crew in a small town or on a college campus generally ends up on the front page of the local paper, but by the time it goes to press we're in another town, where again we'll be in the paper after we've left. It's a pretty pointless practice; there's no real reason for us to be written about in the paper— we know far less about the town than the local reporters do. But because they're there every day, and we've flown in on an airplane accompanied by cameras with the network logo on them, we're considered news. It always makes me uncomfortable when the local reporters show up to interview us. I always get the feeling that they resent the assignment—that they're pissed off because they're stuck in town, and they have to interview reporters who they feel really aren't any better than they are. Actually, no local reporter has ever been less than cordial; maybe I'm reading my own feelings into this. But if I were working in a small town, and my boss assigned me to interview a visiting reporter, I'd go into the interview with a grudge.

"I've always liked your work," she said.

I hear that once in a while, but not so much lately.

I was tempted to ask her to name one story of mine she remembered—I don't know why I always distrust praise about my TV work, I never used to distrust it when someone said something nice about my newspaper stories—but she beat me to it. "Back when I was in high school I saw that series you did on crimes against old people, and it made me cry," she said. "After that I found myself looking for your stories."

The crimes-against-the-elderly series was, indeed, highly emotional, and I had been proud of it. Finding the people to talk to, and then making them at ease enough to tell their stories on camera, had been difficult and time-consuming, but the end result had been one of those rare series of stories—even as you see it being broadcast in the control room, you know that viewers in every town in the country are stopping what they're doing and being riveted by what's on the screen in front of them. Pieces like those are what make network news so valuable and unique; at the same exact instant, men and women all across America are being moved by the same story. The impact of the series had very little to do with any words I wrote; the power was in the faces and voices of the elderly Americans recounting, sometimes in flat tones, sometimes in tears, what had happened to them when they were victimized by criminals who regarded their advanced years only as an added convenience, a means of facilitating the robbery or the home invasion.

Still, she'd said she had been in high school when she had seen the series, and it wasn't necessarily a topic you'd expect most high school students to stop and think about. Old age, and the problems that accompany it, are fairly simple matters to ignore when you're young. Old age doesn't seem like something that's ever going to happen to you.

On the beach, as if reading my mind again, she said, "There was one woman in that series who reminded me of my grandmother. She was the one you showed those pictures of."

I remembered the elderly woman in question. She'd been mercilessly beaten by a robber who had crawled in the window of her apartment. To illustrate her spoken words, we had used color police photos that were taken of her right after the attack. My producer and I had debated for several hours about whether to show the photos; they were so painful to look at that we were afraid we might, perhaps correctly, be accused of insensitivity. In the end, with the elderly woman's endorsement, we'd gone with the pictures; we decided that if the point of the series was to let people know about the awful nature of what was being done to the nation's older men and women, we shouldn't be afraid to be graphic.

Apparently our decision had been the right one; here this young woman on the beach was, six or seven years later, remembering the woman in the interview. Television, for all its transitory aspects, can leave a very permanent mark in millions of memories when the material is compelling enough.

"I saw that poor lady and I thought of my grandmother, and I couldn't sleep that night," the young woman on the beach said. "That's when I started looking for your work. When I saw you walking yesterday, I thought you might be down here for a news report. Is that what you're doing?"

"No," I said. "I haven't been on the air all summer."

"I didn't think I'd seen you lately," she said. "So what are you doing here? Is this your home?"

"No," I said. "It's a long story."

"Do you have time to tell me?" she said.

Mr. Hepps was asleep when Michael and I got to the hospital.

I had been surprised that Ronnie wanted us to come. He had called our unit at the Colony right after lunch. Michael was out at the pool, but I was inside, getting out of the sun for an hour or two and reading some magazines, and I'd answered the phone. I'd asked how his dad was, and he'd said so-so, and as a courtesy as much as anything else I had said, "Would you like us to come by this afternoon?"

"I really would, if you wouldn't mind," Ronnie had said.

It was unlike him. Ronnie has never been a person who is quick to acknowledge that he needs anything, especially anything of a nonmaterial nature. So when he said that he'd like us to come, I realized just how much his father's illness was affecting him.

I walked to the pool to look for Michael. He was sitting with Gail; I don't know what they were talking about, but whatever edge he seemed to have felt about her traveling with Ronnie seemed to have softened. As I approached the pool I could tell that their conversation was a friendly one.

"Ronnie just called," I said, and repeated the message.

"I'll get dressed," Michael said.

It went without saying that Gail would stay at the Colony; she didn't have to bring it up, and neither did we. While Michael was taking a quick shower I called a cab, and within fifteen minutes it was waiting by the main building to take us to the hospital.

Mrs. Hepps was in the hallway near her husband's room. She appeared even more wrung out than she had when we'd seen her in the hours just after his operation. "Thank you, Ben," she said. "Thank you, Michael."

She said that she'd just come up from the cafeteria in the basement, where she'd had a sandwich. "The nurse said that she would bring me a meal with Carlton's, but I needed to get out of the room for a few minutes," she said. "I slept there last night, sitting up in a chair."

Ronnie had stayed with his dad while his mom had eaten lunch. Mrs. Hepps opened the door to the room; in that half second as she pushed it open, you could tell that in a terrible way the room already felt like home to her. She pushed open the door with a proprietary bearing—it might as well have been the door to her condominium.

We followed her in. Ronnie was in the chair, which was a few feet away from the bed; there were three chairs in the room, but this was the only one with any padding, the others were like low-budget office furniture, so I assumed this was the chair in which Mrs. Hepps had slept. Ronnie didn't get up; he just nodded at us.

His dad was asleep. The tubes were still running into him, and his head was resting on its right side on the single pillow. I felt a little bit like I was violating something private, looking at Mr. Hepps while he slept, but for whatever reason it seemed important to Ronnie that we be there. So for fifteen or twenty minutes Michael and I stood off by the door, just lending our presence.

Ronnie finally got up and walked out to the hallway with us.

"He's been like that for a couple of hours," he said. "The nurse said he's going to be sleeping most of the time for at least the next few days. I don't know what to do."

"There's nothing to do, except to be here," I said.

"But that means you guys are stuck here in town," he said.

"It's not exactly hardship duty," Michael said.

"I know," Ronnie said. "I just don't know what the timetable on this is going to be."

"Will you stop thinking about that?" I said.

"I don't want to leave my mom alone with this right now," he said.

"You shouldn't," Michael said.

We reentered the room, where Carlton Hepps lay silently, his eyes closed tightly. His wife was gazing at his face, as if trying to discern an expression. She didn't look up when we came in.

"You've really never listened to Taylor Dayne?"

Mary was talking. That was the name of the young woman from the beach—Mary. The nicest American name. You don't hear it so much anymore.

She pulled the Walkman headset from over her own ears and handed it to me. We were sitting by the Colony pool late that afternoon.

"Here," she said. "Just listen to this one song."

"Taylor Dayne's the blonde who wears the sequined bras, right?" I said.

"So you have seen her," Mary said.

"I think I saw her on MTV," I said. "She's horrible."

"What did you hear her sing?" Mary said.

"I don't know, but it was bad," I said.

"How long ago was it?" she said.

"Maybe two years," I said.

"This is the new album," Mary said. She placed the headset in my hands. "This is much better than her first one. Just give it a try. Just give it a chance. I know you'll like it."

"Unless she got Brian Wilson to write the songs for her and Mike Love and Al Jardine to sing backup, I don't want to hear it," I said.

"Open yourself up to new horizons, old-timer," she said, reaching across and putting the headset over my ears herself.

That had pretty much been the tone of it since I'd met up with her after coming back from the hospital. On the beach in the morning I had told her I'd get together with her later in the day; she'd been waiting for me by the Colony's pool when we returned from visiting Ronnie's dad.

It had taken us only a minute or two to get past the "Mr. Kroeger" bit; when she'd referred to me that way in the morning I think part of it may have come from a reluctance to assume too much familiarity with a person she'd never met, but most of it was for effect—she wanted to be invited not to be so formal. We'd easily fallen into gentle kidding about the number of years between us; the Taylor Dayne conversation had evolved from a mostly serious soliloquy I had delivered about the deceptive depth of some of the old Beach Boys music.

"I know that the songs seem silly and frivolous," I had said to her. "Most of them are car songs and summer-in-the-sun songs. But when you think about Brian Wilson, about his life, it's almost enough to make you cry."

"He was the lead singer, right?" she'd said.

"And he wrote the songs," I said.

I told her that the Brian Wilson story had always fascinated and saddened me. Here was the man who established the fantasies for a whole generation of young Americans; his songs about surfing and cruising and hanging out with your best friends defined part of the adolescent American dream. For those of us who grew up in the landlocked middle of the country, Brian Wilson—the Brian Wilson whose seemingly autobiographical three-minute records came booming out of our car radios—represented the perfect American life under the perfect California sun.

It wasn't until years later that I began to hear about the truth. Brian Wilson—who wrote some of the happiest songs in the history of post-fifties American music—was a lonely, fearful young man, deaf in one ear from a slap delivered by his father when he was a child. The man who wrote and sang about endless days of surfing was deathly afraid to go near the water; he did not swim. The man who through his songs made aimlessly cruising the streets a symbol of cheerful youthful abandon became so petrified of driving a car that eventually someone had to take him everywhere beyond walking distance. We had all thought that Brian Wilson was writing songs about the way he lived his wonderful life, I'd said to Mary; the fact was, he was writing songs about the life he desperately wished he could have.

"I guess that's how it always is with artists, isn't it?" she said.

"I don't know about always," I said. "But when you're driving around with your friends and 'Surfin' U.S.A.' comes on, you don't think of the guy who's singing it as an artist. You think of him as someone who's having a better time than you are."

"Did you ever meet him?" she said.

"No," I said. "But he's been inside my head for most of my life. There's this one song he wrote—'In My Room.' When it first came out I just thought of it as a really pretty song. It was a slow song, and they'd play it at dances so you could dance close with someone. But think about it—of all the rock-and-roll songs there ever were, all the songs about girls and love and old cars, I think that's the only song there's ever been about going into your room and closing the door and feeling safe. That must have been such a hard thing for him to do—to decide to record that song. It must have been like admitting to the world that he was scared and he was lonely and that the only place he ever felt really okay was behind the locked door of his bedroom."

"Did people feel sorry for him when the song came out?" Mary asked.

"I don't think anyone really thought about it," I said. "It was just a slow song to dance to. He must have felt like he was hiding in plain sight. He told the world this big secret, and no one really got it."

"At least not at the time," Mary said.

"Nope," I said. "Not at the time."

So now she slipped the headset over my ears, and I listened to Taylor Dayne for about thirty seconds, and I handed the headset back to her.

"Tell you what," I said. "Wake me up when you're done listening to this, and we'll talk some more."

She laughed and poked my arm. "Forget it," she said. "You can wait twenty years, and like Taylor Dayne when she's an oldie."

"I doubt it," I said.

We both tilted our heads up toward the sun and talked. She was down here visiting her grandmother—the same grandmother, it turned out, she had thought about when she'd seen my series about crime against the elderly. Her grandmother was a widow who lived in a condominium on Longboat, and Mary came to stay with her for a few weeks every summer.

"I like Longboat Key," she said. "It's quiet."

Her eyes remained closed as she spoke. Her hair was pulled back off her forehead and her face was brown from the sun.

"It's a pretty old crowd," I said. "More your grandmother's age."

"I don't like a lot of action," she said. "I think I'm past going to bars where they serve Jello-O mixed with vodka in paper cups."

We talked about the summer trip that Michael and Ronnie and I were on—at first she thought I was kidding, but then she became intrigued by the whole idea—and we talked about her life at the university, where she was a graduate student working toward a master's degree in English literature. She was twenty-three, she said; as an undergraduate she had been a varsity athlete, a member of the Southeastern Conference champion women's 400-meter-relay track team, but had realized that she would never be fast enough to qualify for the Olympics.

"Did you try?" I said.

"Believe me, it wasn't in the cards," she said. "There were at least fifty runners around the country with better times than me."

"So you've stopped competing?" I said.

"I still love to run," she said. "But now I just do it for myself." At the university, she said, she worked as a teaching assistant part-time, to help pay the bills. She said she liked how it felt to teach.

She asked me about my job—about the specifics of what I do. It's not very often that people want to know about the mechanics of putting a story together. Usually they're more interested in what Dan Rather or Tom Brokaw is really like, and usually when I'm asked that kind of personality-column question I give the most honest answer I can: "I have no idea."

But Mary wanted to know about the real stuff, and I found myself happy to tell her. I didn't think I'd been missing doing stories during the summer; certainly I hadn't been feeling any pangs of regret over taking the time off. But as I told her about the process of having edit-packs shipped to you at a remote location so that a story could be cut and relayed to network headquarters on deadline, and about the importance of having a cameraman who is willing to really put out on a piece instead of just getting the shots that are the minimum requirement, and about how a glitch in the audio track can render a whole week's work virtually useless, I could hear the enthusiasm in my own voice. I was a little sheepish about seeming so eager to tell her these things, and more than once I said to her, "Is this stuff boring you?"

"Yeah, right," she said. "I seem pretty bored, don't I?"

We must have talked for a couple of hours. Some music was playing just above audible level over the loudspeakers by the Colony's pool, and I thought I could hear the Gulf washing up against the sand. Our eyes were still shut against the sun, and it was nice to hear a voice other than Ronnie's or Michael's. When she laughed I liked the sound of it— the music and the waves and the sound of her voice.

It was time for me to meet up with Michael, but I really didn't want to stop talking with her. Earlier in the day Michael and Ronnie and I had been discussing what we might do for dinner, and part of me wanted to ask her if she was free, but I didn't know how appropriate that would be.

So instead I said, "Well, thanks for coming by."

"Thanks for having me come by," she said.

We stood up. She slipped her T-shirt over the top of her bathing suit. She put her white athletic socks back on, then laced up her running shoes. Out past the pool railing the afternoon sun glistened off the Gulf, heading toward sundown.

"I guess you're probably having dinner at your grandmother's to-night," I said.

"I guess you guess wrong," she said, grinning once more. "Where do you want me to meet you?"

Still thinking about her, I was in a pretty good mood as I walked into our unit. Michael was sitting on the couch, looking more than a little dispirited.

"You okay?" I said.

"Ah, I just called home," he said.

"Problems?" I said.

"Ellen says the money's running low," he said.

This was the first time that subject had come up since the beginning of the summer. For Ronnie, of course, money just wasn't a topic; the cost of the trip was not something that had a remote chance of concerning him at all. I had sat down before leaving on our journey and figured out how much of my savings the summer would consume. It was going to eat up a goodly chunk, but I had determined the summer would be worth it—it had better; this was, after all, my idea. So I knew pretty much what my bank account was going to look like come September, and I was prepared for it.

I hadn't thought about Michael's finances since that first week, when Ronnie had all but insisted on paying for Michael's trip, and Michael had implicitly accepted. Actually, I figured Michael would get his family through the summer fairly easily; the way I understood it, his paycheck from the Bristol Board of Education kept arriving at his house all summer, even though he wasn't teaching. He'd told us that was the way it worked for all teachers in the school system.

"She's out of money?" I said.

"She's not out," he said. "The paychecks come every week. I just think that without me there, she feels sort of fragile in that way. I think she looks at the amount on the paychecks and realizes that's all there is."

"What did you say to her?" I said.

"I told her I'd come home if she wanted," Michael said.

That one stopped me. "And?" I said.

"She said no," Michael said. "She said that she and the girls are fine. She knows I'm having a good time, and she says that's what she wanted for me in the first place. And she said she knows that even if I were to come home, the paycheck wouldn't get any bigger. She kidded me and said that it's probably best that I stay out here—she said if I came home there'd be one more mouth to feed."

"But she's going to get through until the end of the summer all right?" I said. "I mean, with the money?"

"Of course," he said. "The money's the same as it always is. It's just that depositing the checks and balancing the checkbook without me there, I think it's hitting her just how close to the bone we live."

If the news about Ronnie's dad had been like a splash of ice water in the face of our jerry-rigged fantasy, then Michael's call home was another. This was fine out here, this was what we had wanted. But even when you're moving through the country at will, in the company of the people you like the best, you can only pretend that what you've left behind is somehow frozen in a blissful, static state. The world you've taken a leave from changes, too; that world might not be on the road with you, but it changes.

There was a knock at our door. I went to answer; Ronnie was outside.

"Have you seen Gail?" he said.

"She's not at your place?" I said.

"No," he said. "I guess she must have gone up to St. Armands Circle to check out the stores or something."

"Your dad doing better?" Michael said.

"He's awake," Ronnie said. "He's having a lot of pain. I think that first day, the anesthesia hadn't really worn off."

"Are you going back there tonight?" I said.

"Not tonight," he said. "Why don't we all have dinner. I told them I'd see them first thing in the morning."

"I may be bringing someone along to dinner," I said.

"Someone from the pool?" Michael said.

I didn't know he'd seen Mary.

"I was walking around earlier," he said. "I saw you talking at the pool. Who is she?"

I gave them a brief version of the story.

"She's beautiful," Michael said to Ronnie. "Just really beautiful."

"What's the deal here, Ben?" Ronnie said. "Are you handsomer than we think you are?"

"Cut it out," I said. "Never have been. I've always ranked a distant third to you guys."

"Then what is it?" he said.

"I don't know, Ronnie," I said. "Maybe I'm just a potential war story."

"You really think that?" Michael said.

"I don't know," I said.

"And you're going to invite her to come to dinner with us?" Ronnie said.

"If you don't mind," I said.

"What, you're being polite?" Ronnie said. "You're asking my permission?"

"Well, you know me," I said.

"Sometimes I'm not so sure, Ben," Ronnie said, laughing. It wasn't a mean laugh, and Michael joined in, and in a moment I did, too, although perhaps not quite as ardently.

We made reservations at a place called the Columbia. Gail had, indeed, been shopping at St. Armands Circle in the afternoon; she had seen the restaurant, and some people had told her it was a Sarasota-area institution, so at seven-thirty we were led to our table.

Mary had called me around five-thirty, and I'd invited her to join us. I offered to pick her up on our way over—Ronnie had rented a car after the first day—but she said it would be just as easy to meet us there. She showed up about five minutes after we arrived.

She looked like a sprinter blessed by the sun, lithe and tan and full of energy. "Hi," she said when she saw me, lighting up with that smile. There was nothing flamboyant or overwhelming about her, but the maître d' who brought her over seemed momentarily more contented just to be in her company. I understood the feeling.

You might have thought she'd feel a little awkward in this circumstance—she knew only me, and not all that well—but she was instantly at home. "Hi," she said, favoring Michael and Ronnie and Gail with the smile. "I'm Mary Hamrick. I think what you're doing is so great."

Apparently she was referring to our trip. There had been moments when I had thought that "great" might not be the precise adjective—in the afternoon, when Michael was talking about his worrisome phone call back home, and when Ronnie was in his dad's hospital room while the woman who for some reason was traveling with him shopped on St. Armands, the most apt term I would have come up with was "selfish"—but mostly, all these weeks into the summer, I would still have agreed with her. The warmth of the day was still inside me, and Michael and Ronnie were the two best friends I'd ever had, and our only obligation, at least right now, was to savor the night. Soon enough, I knew, our lives would be returning to something else.

"Nice to meet you, Mary," Michael said. "I'm Michael Wolff. This is Ronnie Hepps. And this is Gail."

Michael seemed to omit Gail's last name as if by reflex; he seemed to be aware that to point out she wasn't married to Ronnie might raise questions better left unspoken.

At the pool in the afternoon, I hadn't said anything to Mary about Gail. I had told her all about Michael and Ronnie, and our personal histories; she knew that Michael had a family in Bristol and that Ronnie had a family in Cleveland and that I was no longer married. So there were a lot of things she could have said when Michael made the introductions. What she did say was: "Hi, Gail."

We all ordered drinks, and I found myself talking mostly to Mary. Once I thought I noticed Michael appearing kind of low again; I thought about how he and I felt when Gail had joined us in Atlanta, how we had thought the dynamic of the trip had been altered and refashioned by the presence of a stranger. Now here he was, having dinner with his two friends, each of whom was accompanied by a woman.

We were at the table for more than two hours. We all got pretty loose, and Michael perked up a little bit, and as Mary was finishing her swordfish she said, "You know, until about a year ago I was a strict vegetarian. I wouldn't eat anything that was ever alive. But now I'll eat fish and poultry. Still no red meat."

"When did you start this?" I said.

"Which part?" she said.

"No meat," I said.

"It was back when I first went away to college," she said. "Freshman year. I talked to some people in my dorm, and they convinced me there was really no need to eat meat. And I thought about it, and I stopped, and I really haven't missed it."

"That's got to drive parents crazy," I said. "The 'I don't eat red meat' syndrome."

"What's that mean?" Ronnie said.

"It's just a symbol of how parents lose control of their kids within forty-eight hours of when the kids go off to college," I said. "A parent raises a kid for eighteen years. Pot roast on the table, steaks on the grill at summer cookouts, Big Macs and Quarter Pounders every week. The kid never says a peep. Then the kid comes home for Thanksgiving vacation freshman year, and the family sits down to dinner, and the kid says, 'I'm sorry, Dad. I don't eat meat.' "

"But the dad should be happy," Mary said. "It's healthier."

"That's not the point," I said. "The parents have got to wonder, 'What's going on here?' The kid's in their house for almost two decades, and after ten weeks at college the kid comes home aghast that anyone would ever dare to serve a lamb chop at that dinner table. Got to drive the parents nuts. It's just the first sign that everything's going away."

Mary was laughing. She said to Ronnie, "Do you eat red meat?"

"Exclusively," he said.

Mary was taking it all in. She knew I wasn't making fun of her; she knew that we were all merely savoring the night. Savoring all of these nights. She put her hand on my shoulder and said, "There must have been some mistake in our house. My mom and dad seemed to be pleased that I was eating food that was good for me. I guess they didn't understand the terrible symbolism of it all."

"Anybody want some dessert?" Ronnie said.

"Just bring me a plate of raw hamburger," Mary said.

"You want some whipped cream with that?" Ronnie said.

"That, and some gravy on the side," Mary said. "I've seen the light."

Ronnie seemed to like this; Ronnie seemed relaxed. Somewhere, just a few layers down, he knew that two or three miles away his father slept in that hospital bed. He hadn't forgotten. He was only trying to put it away for a couple of hours. I couldn't blame him for wanting to do that. Savor the night. Savor every night that you can.

We sat on the beach around eleven o'clock. Ronnie had driven us back to the Colony after dinner; he had asked Mary if she wanted to be dropped off somewhere, and she had said no, she'd just come back with us.

Ronnie and Gail had gone to their unit, and Michael had gone to ours. Mary and I had walked out near the water. We held hands and talked.

"So is this a serious thing with them?" she said.

"I don't really know," I said. "We haven't asked him that much about it."

I had explained to her how Gail had happened to be present on the trip, and she said she hadn't been able to discern at dinner how Ronnie and Gail felt about each other. "There's not much there," Mary said. "As far as I can tell."

"I have no idea what Ronnie's situation at home is," I said. The beach late at night was empty; in either direction from us there were no other people in sight.

"So you don't know if this is a threat to his marriage?" Mary said.

"I would doubt it," I said. "I think it's probably just part of the summer for him."

"Do you approve of that?" she said.

"What do you want me to say?" I said. "No?"

"Say what you think," she said.

"I think Ronnie is one of my oldest friends, and I think there's a lot of things I don't know about his life, and I think he's going to do what he wants to do," I said.

"Do his folks know that this woman is down here with him?" she said.

"No," I said. "That's all they need to hear. In the hospital."

She rubbed the palm of her hand slowly against mine. "Thanks for dinner," she said. "This whole day has been great."

"You're leaving?" I said.

"No," she said. "I just hadn't thanked you."

"Well, thank you, too," I said.

"For what?" she said.

"For the day," I said. "For your company."

We stood and brushed the sand from our clothes. Still holding hands we walked back toward the Colony buildings. I was wondering what to do, but she made it easy. When we got near the building where our unit was, she led the way without saying anything. She walked right to our door. I pulled the key from my pocket and opened it.

The door to Michael's bedroom was closed. There was no light coming from beneath it. Mary walked up the stairs, toward my room, and I walked right behind her.

We lay on the bed, light from the moon cutting across the room through a small window.

"So how are you doing, Mr. Kroeger?" she said.

"I don't know," I said. She unbuttoned my shirt, starting at the bottom, and when it was all the way open she put her head on my chest and she said, "I hope you don't think I'm stupid, Ben."

"Stupid?" I said. "Why would you say something like that?"

"Because I'm here," she said. "Because I'm so available to you."

"I like you being here," I said.

"Good," she said.

We didn't say much. I held on to her, and she held on to me, and she kept running her hand over my chest, and then after a while she got up and walked over to the window and, where I could see her against that small shaft of light, she took her shirt off. Just that. Then she came over to the bed again and she held me again and I could feel her chest against mine.

I guess Brian Wilson isn't the only one. I guess Brian Wilson isn't the only person who ever felt a little scared and a little lonely and who just wanted to close his door and shut out the rest of the world. We didn't know it back then, but maybe that was the whole lesson. You never know it about anyone. Maybe that was the lesson.

She pressed even tighter against me and said, "Do you want to fall asleep by yourself? If you do, you can tell me to leave."

"No," I said. "Don't leave yet."

"I won't," she said. "I don't want to."

You never know it about anyone. I could feel her hair against my chest, and I could feel her breath, soft and warm, her breath whispering across my chest, no words, just her breath, like an even signal from somewhere near her heart.

The next afternoon, while Ronnie was at the hospital, I tried to give Hannah a call at the beach house in Delaware. I'd been trying to reach her again for a few days, but it seemed like anytime I'd phone, the answering machine was on.

This time, though, I was surprised. Nancy answered on the first ring. For a moment I wanted to believe that it was like all those years when hearing Nancy's voice on the other end of a phone was the most routine thing in the world for me. My wife's voice.

Today, though, it was: "Oh. Hi." As if I were interrupting something. We talked briefly, and I asked if Hannah could come to the phone.

Nancy hesitated for a second, then said, "Hannah? It's your dad."

She came to the phone, out of breath and excited. "Hi, Daddy," she said. "It's raining. We're going into town to see a movie."

I asked her how things were going, and she spoke in that rapid tempo that tells you she's in a big hurry to be doing something else. "Daddy?" she said. "Can you call after we get back from the movie? I don't want to be late."

I was happy for her; I was happy she was okay and was having a good time and was too busy to talk to me. That's how a child should be in the summer; too busy to talk on the phone.

But I didn't know; the combination of everything in the last few days was catching up with me. Ronnie's father, and the sound of Nancy's voice and of Hannah in a hurry . . . Mary had gone home around four in the morning, with promises that we would talk again today, but now I was tired and I was needing something and I wasn't sure quite what.

"That's fine, Hannah," I said. "You enjoy the movie. I'll talk to you a little later."

After I hung up I started to walk outside toward the Gulf, but then I returned to the phone and made another call.

"Mom?" I said when my mother answered in South Carolina.

We talked for about ten minutes. She put my dad on, and I told him about the trip, which I knew he did not entirely approve of. In my dad's world, you don't run away for the summer. When I gave him a rundown on Carlton Hepps' condition in the hospital, he expressed sympathy and asked me to be sure to give Carlton his very best wishes, but I could tell that there was just the slightest hint of something in his voice. Not gloating; not pleasure. I think it's just that when you get to my father's age and Carlton Hepps' age, every time you hear about another of your contemporaries recuperating from a big operation you silently congratulate yourself that it's not you. In a way it must be the new scorecard once you reach that age. You can't compete over job promotions or big houses or money anymore, so you compete over being healthy. Or even, I suppose, over being alive.

He handed the phone back to my mother. "Are you all right?" she said.

I hadn't mentioned a word to her about feeling a little melancholy today. "Why do you ask that, Mom?" I said.

"I know when you say 'Hello' whether you've got something on your mind," she said.

I guess that's what you give up when you grow up and face the world on your own. You give up having someone know how you're feeling from the sound of the first word out of your mouth. Although you don't really give it up. You just don't always remember it's there.

My mother has always been able to sense when something is wrong. When I was young, she would make a point of being around in case I needed to talk about it. I seldom did. I don't think I ever told her I was aware she was noticing. But the fact that she knew when I felt troubled helped me, even when I could not acknowledge her vigilance.

My father seemed always to be at work. He was the executive vice president of Licata Manufacturing, a producer of machine parts over in Columbus. The job consumed his life. He was meticulous about the details of his work. I don't know how much he knew about me. He was home every night for dinner, and we talked at the table. We talked about my day at school, and we talked about his day at the office, and the traffic went by on the street outside our house, and I'm not sure how much he knew.

"I'm really fine, Mom," I said now, from the telephone in our unit at the Colony.

"Your father says he wants to ask you something else," she said.

My dad got back on the line.

"So you saw Carlton Hepps in the hospital yourself?" he said.

"A couple of times," I said.

"Does he have a private room, or is he in with a bunch of strangers?" my dad said.

"He's got his own room," I said.

"Oh," my dad said. He sounded just the tiniest bit disappointed. "Well, that's good for Carlton. He was never the kind of guy who liked going second-class."

"He's got a real nice room, as a matter of fact," I said. "View of the water."

"All right, then," my dad said. "You give him our best."

"I will, Dad," I said, and hung up.

I don't know why I told my dad that Carlton Hepps could see the water from his hospital room window. Carlton Hepps' window looked over the parking lot. There was no water for miles.

"You got a minute?"

It was a curious thing for Michael to say. He's never had to ask me if I have time to talk. I took it to mean he was nervous about what he was about to relate.

"Sure," I said. "You want to talk here?" We were in the living room of our unit at the Colony.

"Why don't we go down to the beach for a while," he said.

So I locked the door behind us, and we headed up the beach in the same direction we'd gone the first day. There were some fishermen out on the water, and a couple of pleasure boats, and a Coast Guard cutter.

"Ronnie offered me a job," he said.

Whatever I had been expecting, that wasn't it. With Michael, it would have been needless for me to ask him if he was kidding; I knew he wasn't kidding. So I said, "When?"

"This morning," he said. "You were still sleeping. I got up and went over to the restaurant for some breakfast. He and Gail had eaten, and she left the table and Ronnie stayed. So I joined him."

Michael said he had talked to Ronnie about what might happen in the fall—how we'd all be heading back to our jobs and our real lives, and how he'd be teaching another class of Bristol High School students.

"And out of nowhere, Ronnie said, 'You ought to come work for me,' " Michael said.

"Do you think he's been planning this?" I said.

"That's the thing," Michael said. "I don't think he has. I think it just popped out of his mouth. But he meant it."

He said that he and Ronnie had sat at the table and talked for almost an hour. Ronnie had a specific job in mind for him, at a specific and very large salary. In fact, the salary was nearly triple what Michael was making at the school.

"And he wasn't just talking," I said.

"No," Michael said. "He said it was time I made some money."

"So what do you think?" I said.

"I think it's awful, and I think I may say yes," Michael said.

He said that Ronnie had pointed out to him the difference between how the two of them lived—"as if I hadn't noticed," Michael said— and had said how much he was enjoying being with Michael this summer. "He said there wasn't any reason why I couldn't let my family live a lot better, and he said it would be great seeing me every day."

"Seeing you every day?" I said.

"Yeah," Michael said. "The job's up in Cleveland."

I suppose that should have been obvious; I suppose that should have gone without saying. But the idea was so new to me, I hadn't digested it enough to realize that of course Michael would have to leave Bristol.

"Could you work for Ronnie?" I said.

"That's a big question," he said. "That would change everything, wouldn't it?"

We both knew the answer. Ronnie's friend as a kid; Ronnie's friend again this summer. Employee in the fall.

"Did you say anything to him about that?" I said.

"Of course," Michael said. "That's one of the first things I said to him. And he said, 'Michael, this is me. Don't be ridiculous.' "

"But?" I said.

"I thought about it," Michael said. "I thought about all of the people we went to school with whose kids I teach, people I see every day at the grocery store or the bank or the drugstore. All of them with better jobs than I have, making more money than I make. And I asked myself whether seeing them every day is all that much worse or all that much different from working for Ronnie."

"What did you decide?" I said.

We were way up the beach from the Colony. Michael laughed briefly. "Of course it's different," he said. "Ronnie as my boss?"

We kept walking, and I said, "What are you going to do?"

"I told him I'd think about it," he said. "I'm going to call Ellen and talk to her about it."

When I didn't answer, he said:

"Do you know what Ronnie told me? He told me that there are so many stupid people making so much money, there's no reason in the world that I should be living the way I do."

"I think that may be Ronnie's way of attempting to give you a compliment," I said.

"Yeah, I know," Michael said. "You know what else he said?"

I waited.

"He said his only concern was that I might not have the killer instinct. He said no offense, but the only question mark was whether I was too nice a guy to make it in his business."

"He used those words?" I said.

"Uh-huh," Michael said.

"What did you say?" I said.

"I told him that I thought I had the killer instinct," Michael said.

"You did?" I said.

"Yeah, I did," he said. "Ben, I felt myself wanting the job."

Sometimes, if you look way out across the water, where it meets the horizon, you can give yourself the illusion that you can see the earth turning. That if you look hard enough, you can see the world change.

Seventeen

I WAITED FOR MARY out on the second-floor balcony of our unit at the Colony. She'd called to say she would be coming by.

Michael had gone with Ronnie to the hospital. Two more days had passed; it was late in the afternoon, and the sun was still bright, and in the morning we'd be leaving. Mary and I had seen each other again last night. I'd liked the evening as much as I had the first one. Sometimes life will catch you unawares.

I stood on the balcony, part of me having the irrational urge to stay here a few more days. That made no sense; the whole point of the summer was to keep moving. And now that Ronnie's dad was out of immediate jeopardy, it was time for us to go.

I heard Mary before I saw her; I know that she didn't see me. I heard the tires of her bike rolling against the pebble surface of the winding driveway that runs through the Colony. I hadn't been looking for her on a bike; I was expecting a cab or a car. But it made sense. She was a jock, she was obsessive about her daily runs and about doing her workouts, so of course she'd use her visit as an excuse to get in a little more exercise.

She was in her gym shorts and a plain white T-shirt. Even though she'd been pedaling for several miles down Gulf of Mexico Drive from her grandmother's place to the Colony, she looked fresh and she didn't seem winded. Her short hair was disheveled in the warm salt breeze.

I was surprised by how happy I was to see her. She hopped off the bike; she still didn't see me up on the balcony. She was looking for a place to stash the bike before coming around to the stairs leading up to the unit. I watched her, and it reminded me of another time and another place, back when the idea of someone I cared for coming to see me was new and when such an idea seemed so unlikely as to be unreal. She found a tree to rest her bike beneath, and I saw her and I thought of that.

For a long time when I was growing up, the thought of being alone with a girl who cared for me seemed like a miracle, and like all miracles the prospect of that one seemed unreachable. If my life was shy and insular until I was thirteen or fourteen, one of the side effects of that social silence was the absolute conviction that no girl would ever like me as more than anything but a friend. This was not even something that I particularly dwelled on or lamented over. I regarded it as a decree of nature. It was like being skinny or fat or short or whatever; the cards are dealt to you before you have any conscious awareness that you're even in a game, and some deficits are just too deep to make up. At least that's how it seems in those years when you are first becoming aware of who you are.

The entry of Wendy Bishop into my life coincided with the unforeseen surge of self-confidence that ended the most solitary years for me; Wendy came along at the same time I was making the reserve basketball team, and writing my first stories for the school newspaper, and becoming accepted by the same people who only a year or two earlier had routinely slighted me. I still don't know whether Wendy's acceptance of me was a product of those things, or whether Wendy's being with me helped give me the self-assurance to accomplish those things. But Wendy changed everything. Wendy made me feel that maybe I was okay.

Wendy was a year younger; Wendy was the kind of girl I once would not have believed would have deigned to so much as glance at me. Wendy was physically beautiful and smart in every way that mattered and one of the best-liked girls at Bristol. At first I was so unsure of her apparent interest in me that I thought it was some kind of cruel joke; the Wendy Bishops of the world, up until that point, had no time for a person like me.

But it was real; to this day I don't know what Wendy saw in me, but evidently she felt she wanted to know me. Wendy made my life different, and of all the good memories I have of my time with her, one always stands out in bold and sharply focused detail.

On summer and early-autumn weekends, my parents would often go out of town on Friday night and not return until dinnertime Sunday— little weekend vacations. On those weekends, Wendy would come over. It was mostly innocent; I don't think anything that went on would have startled our families. It was the dream I had dared to allow myself just a few years earlier—it was the girl I wanted to be with most, making me know that she wanted to be with me.

And of all the wonderful memories I have of those weekend afternoons with Wendy, perhaps the ones that remain the most enticing are the memories of the anticipation. Wendy would ask me on the telephone the night before whether I was sure my parents would be gone; then she would tell me a time on Saturday afternoon when she planned to come by.

I would open my eyes for the new day Saturday morning thinking about it before I was even fully awake. My morning would be spent knowing that in four hours—then three hours, then two hours, I was involuntarily looking at the clock every few minutes—she'd be there. Yet on those Saturday mornings I always held in reserve the most slender doubt—the doubt that she would for some reason abandon her wish to be with me, and that she would not be arriving after all. That's how I would know that the wonderful thing had gone away, or so I feared; I would not know by her telling me, I would know by the fact that one Saturday she would say she was coming and she would not arrive.

So twenty or twenty-five minutes before Wendy would be due at my parents' house I would start looking out the front window. Five minutes before her arrival time, I would already assume she was late; if the exact minute came and she was not within view, I would have the empty feeling that she was not coming. She always did come; sometimes she was five or ten minutes late, but she always came, and the specific sight that would inevitably fill me up with a feeling of happiness was when she would come into view, rounding the corner down by the mailbox, walking unselfconsciously toward our house in the middle of the block.

That would be the best moment, that would be the moment of my contentment: when Wendy would turn left at that corner and head toward my house and I would see her walking up the street. I never told her about any of this; I never revealed to her just how fervently I awaited her afternoons at my house, how I looked for her through the window and worried that she would not come. As much as I trusted her—and I trusted her just about completely—there are some things you can't tell anyone.

Everything changes; everything goes away. Wendy never failed to show up when she said she would, but eventually she stopped saying she would. It happens to everyone; the first, best thing to happen to you eventually disappears. I wouldn't trade a moment of those afternoons, though. Wendy made my life better, and when she was with me I never had thoughts of parties where people were having a happier time than I was.

Sometimes even if you think a memory is far behind you, you understand that it will never truly be gone. Now, late in the afternoon at the Colony, I watched as Mary walked through the parking lot toward the outdoor stairs. She didn't know I could see her, and I knew I wouldn't tell her. Some things you don't tell anyone. I heard the sound of her feet on the wooden steps that led up to the door, and I was glad.

"So you're out of here, chief?"

Mary was in the kitchen as she called to me; we'd sat together on the balcony, then had watched the early-evening news.

"Isn't this where I came in?" she had said during the broadcast, sharing a big armchair with me, and I realized how curious this must seem to her; she'd first become aware of my existence by watching the news, and now we were together watching the news, me right now just another news consumer like everyone else in America.

"Just think of it as a Home Shopping Network featuring human beings," I had said, nodding toward the newscast. "Pick one out and place your order. See anyone you like?"

She had looked at me, then at the screen, then at me again and had said: "Think they'll give me a deal on a trade-in?"

"Depends on what you're looking for, I guess," I had said, taking the bait.

"I don't know," she had said. "Maybe something a little younger."

"Is that right?" I had said.

"Yeah," she had said, digging an elbow into me. "Or maybe a woman."

She had laughed at the expression on my face and had elbowed me again, Abbott-and-Costello style, and she'd jumped out of the chair and gone into the kitchen.

I heard her open the refrigerator door, and that's when she called out her question: "So you're out of here, chief?"

"In the morning," I called back to her. She already knew that; we had discussed it the night before, and we had discussed it again on the phone before she'd come over today. She was trying to keep the tone as light as possible, as if nothing really mattered. Hence the "chief"; like it was all a nimble joke.

She returned to the living room, carrying two glasses filled with ice and two cans of Hires Root Beer. "You enjoying the day here?" I said.

"Great," she said. "Next-best thing to having a good time."

She was echoing something I'd told her about. The first evening we were together, she had asked me every half hour or so if I was enjoying myself; she'd actually seemed not to be sure. So I had thrown the "next-best thing to having a good time" line at her, and then had explained that it's what my dad always used to say. Which was true; he had used that lame line all the time, and it had stuck in our family.

She hadn't given any indication that she was paying any attention when I'd said that to her; we had been at the restaurant table with Michael and Ronnie and Gail, and it was loud in the place, and I hadn't even been sure that she'd heard. But now she dropped that line on me. I sort of liked that she had remembered.

"Brought you something," she said, handing me one of the glasses and one of the Hires.

"You hungry at all?" I said. "There's a barbecue out by the beach."

We carried our glasses with us. A big tent had been set up overlooking the Gulf. We stood in the buffet line, filled our plates with ribs and chicken and cole slaw, and found an unoccupied table. There were white tablecloths and fancy silver, even though it was an outdoor affair, and it felt kind of elegant.

The sun was almost down, and no one hurried us, and as the dusk turned to full evening we sat and talked for hours. There's no way to explain why you're comfortable with one person and not with another; if there were, life wouldn't be so mysterious.

"Is your grandmother feeling abandoned, with you spending so much time over here?" I said.

"My grandmother's great," Mary said. "She doesn't ask me any questions. I think she's glad to get me out of the house, if you want to know the truth. She really doesn't need me to help her. When I come down here in the summer she's the one who's doing me the favor. She doesn't charge me to stay with her, so I get a free trip to Florida."

"But as long as you're in Florida, she doesn't mind you not spending every minute with her?" I said.

"Not hardly," Mary said. "She's got a friend who comes by, and I think he feels more at ease when I'm not there."

"A friend?" I said.

"Yeah," she said. "A man who lost his wife a few years ago, and who has a place in the next high rise over."

"It never changes, does it?" I said.

"What?" she said.

"I can just imagine the guy," I said. "Checking with your grandmother in the morning to see if she knows what your plans are. And when you leave the house, your grandmother calling him to tell him the coast is clear."

"Actually, that's pretty much how it is," she said. "It's cute."

"Cute?" I said.

"I'm sorry," she said. "That is a little patronizing to them, isn't it?"

"Seriously, think about it," I said. "Think about how you felt about boys you liked when you were a kid. And about how you were embarrassed for your parents to know. And think about your grandmother with him . . . does she refer to him as her friend, or is that your word for it?"

"That's what she calls him," Mary said. "That's what he is."

"That's nice," I said.

"I know," she said. "I don't think she's being coy when she refers to him that way. I think she's just being accurate."

"That's really about the best thing you can call another person, isn't it?" I said.

She reached over and took my hand.

"Other than 'chief,' you mean?" she said, and then, right there, with all the people sitting at their tables, she leaned over and kissed me on the cheek.

"I miss you already, and you're still here," she said.

"Are you going to want me to stay until morning, or would you rather I left?" Mary said.

We were in my room; her arms were wrapped tightly around me, and she lay with her head nestled against my neck. The night had grown cooler. I had turned the air conditioning off when we had returned to the unit, and the window near the bed was wide open. The wind through the screen was steady and mild; Mary had kicked the blanket off the bed, and we were covered only by the clean white top sheet.

"I want you to stay," I said. "I'm just a little concerned about Michael."

To her great credit, she did not point out to me that Michael was a grown man, and would survive waking up to find her here. We'd heard him come in about forty-five minutes after we did. Undoubtedly he knew we were upstairs.

"You really watch out for his feelings, don't you?" she said.

"It's just that I don't think he needs to get up for breakfast in the morning and find us sitting around," I said. "This trip was supposed to be Ronnie and him and me. I don't want to make it any more difficult."

"He really seems like a fine person," she said.

"He's the best person I've ever known," I said.

Even as I was saying that, she seemed to catch herself. "That's so presumptuous of me," she said. "To tell you something about someone you've known for your whole life."

"That's okay," I said. "I like hearing what you think."

I don't know what it was that Mary was providing that I welcomed so much, but in these last few days I had felt more at ease than I had the whole trip. It wasn't that the trip hadn't turned out to be everything I had expected; it had. But the time I had been spending with Mary was making my days and nights feel complete.

I looked at her, and she flashed that smile back at me in the half-darkness, and being with her was just so much fun. Maybe that's why I found myself questioning how I was feeling. I was raised—a lot of people were raised—to believe that having fun is not a good enough reason to do anything; having fun is not a sufficient excuse. If the best you can say about something is that it's fun—or so the inner voice has always told me—then you're being shallow and without consequence.

You go through your life spending so many bad hours with so many people you don't want to know; with Mary I found myself wishing that she wouldn't stop talking to me, wishing she would keep telling me stories about herself and asking questions, even the sound of her voice pleased me, it was eager and it was quietly energetic and it always had a herald of laughter in it, a hint that if something she heard in the next ten seconds were to gladden her, she was ready to fill the air with the sound of her delight. Maybe having fun means more than simply having fun, I thought to myself; maybe having fun is a measure of something, sort of like taking the temperature of how you feel about a person. Maybe it is not something to be so easily devalued.

That's what I was thinking as we lay together and talked. What I said was: "Maybe it's best if we meet to say goodbye in the morning. I just don't want Michael to feel any worse."

"I think you're right," she said. "But I don't want to leave right this second."

"Then don't," I said.

Sometime later in the night she stood up and walked to the bathroom to get a glass of water.

"Have you always used Crest?" she called.

I walked in to see her looking at the tube of toothpaste. I was bewildered by her question.

"Yes," I said. "Why?"

"I've just always wondered if people ever change," she said. "All the millions of dollars spent on advertising, and I bet you most people stick with the same soap and toothpaste and brand of chewing gum they used when they were kids."

"Maybe, but in my case there's a different reason for the Crest," I said.

"What?" she said.

"Bristol was one of the cities for the Crest test," I said. "It really was. We all got free toothpaste for a year or two. They came in plain white toothpaste boxes, and you didn't know if you were getting real Crest or some dummy toothpaste. Every month or so we'd go down to the school nurse's office and pick up our toothpaste. There were coded letters on the boxes, and the nurse had a record of which toothpaste each of us was supposed to be given."

"Which one did you have?" Mary said.

"I don't think I ever found out," I said.

"Did you have a lot of cavities as a kid?" she said.

"As a matter of fact, I did," I said. "But I don't know if I was using Crest or not."

"So you have this brand loyalty to a toothpaste that you don't even know if you were using in the first place," she said.

"I bet this is one conversation you never had before," I said.

"Count on it," she said.

Later, in the darkness, she said, "Why do you like being with me?"

I was tempted to tell her about all of the things I had been thinking. Instead, I said, "There's a song that I always thought was great, and it never became a hit. The song was called 'Don't Look for Love, Love Looks for You.' "

The words came out before I realized what I was saying. I wondered how to defuse the moment, but she beat me to it.

"Not that we're talking about love here, right, chief?" she said.

"I've just always felt that was a good thought," I said. "That when you go out and try to make something great happen, you always end up disappointed. The great things always happen when you're not looking for them."

We lay there for a while more, and we both knew that before long she'd have to be heading home.

"I guess love is sort of like having a good time, isn't it?" she said.

"What do you mean?" I said.

"Sometimes the next-best thing is good enough," she said, holding me.

We went to say goodbye to Mr. Hepps.

"Sit down, boys," he said, motioning to the chairs in his hospital room. "Take a load off."

He was very thin and he looked exhausted, but the doctors had said he was going to get out of there all right. He and Mrs. Hepps had insisted that Ronnie not stay any longer. So there we were, just after ten o'clock in the morning.

Mary had finally gone back to her grandmother's at around 4 A.M. As I had walked her out of our place at the Colony I realized that her way home was via her bike; I had told her that I'd put the bike in the back of Ronnie's rental car and drive her down. She said no.

"I like riding the bike," she said. "I think a lot when I'm riding."

When I had told her that the middle of the night was no time for a person to be riding by herself, she'd laughed and said, "This isn't Central Park, Ben. This is Longboat Key. I'm fine. I do this a lot. Believe it or not, I was taking care of myself quite well even before you arrived here."

What she also meant was that she'd be taking good care of herself after I'd moved on. So I promised her I'd talk to her before we left, and she kissed me good night, and I watched her hop on that bike and ride down the path that wound through the darkened buildings of the Colony.

And now, barely six hours later, we sat with Carlton Hepps. He was going to need full-time nursing care at home for a while, and the doctors wanted him to come back to the hospital for evaluations every few weeks. I could tell from his voice that in a way he felt safe here; in a way at home he was going to feel vaguely unprotected. Once they hook you up to post-surgical monitors, it must be a little scary when you find yourself suddenly unmonitored and wondering how you are.

"If there's anything at all you need, Dad . . . ," Ronnie began.

"I don't need anything," Mr. Hepps said. "Anything I need, I've got your mother here."

And then, as he seemed to sense we were going to depart, he began to tell a story.

"You know," he said, "when I was a young man I had a friend named Red Lawrence. He was my best friend, I suppose you would say. And when Red was twenty or twenty-one, his father had a severe stroke, and was left virtually helpless. Red's mother was no longer living.

"So Red dropped out of college and he devoted himself to helping his father. Some of the things Red had to do . . . suffice it to say that he had to do everything. He had to change his father's catheter. He had to clean up after his father every time his father moved his bowels. He had to feed his father with a spoon. He had to bathe his father. We were so young. I got together with Red one day after all of this had happened. I was still in school, and I told Red that I didn't know how he was doing it. I just didn't know how he was managing to do it.

"And Red told me that there was no secret to it. You do it because you have to do it. You learn to make yourself do it. It has to be done, and if you're the only one in the family to help, then you learn very quickly. No one pictures himself doing that, but when it happens you do it because there is no alternative."

None of us knew quite how to respond. Mr. Hepps was sending a message with that story, but perhaps even he did not know the precise nature of the message. We wished him well, and said we had enjoyed seeing him, which really sounded absurd when it came out of our mouths, and we said goodbye to Mrs. Hepps and then Michael and I left the room so that Ronnie could say so long in private.

We were in the hallway for about five minutes before Ronnie came out. We didn't know if he wanted to talk about it with us, but all he said, softly and quickly, was, "Let's go."

We loaded the rental car at the Colony. I'd seen all of our suitcases in so many parking lots during the summer that I would have known instantly had we forgotten one in the rooms.

"So maybe I'll talk to you sometime?" Mary said. She had walked down the beach to say goodbye; she was in a T-shirt and the bottom of her swimsuit, barefoot in the gravel lot.

"Well, I hope so," I said. Both of us were trying to sound as if none of this had really meant anything special, and by trying to sound that way we were only demonstrating the opposite.

Mary laughed.

"What?" I said.

"When I was at my grandmother's this morning, I was going over in my head what I was going to say to you when I said goodbye," she said. "And when I looked at my grandmother in the kitchen I remembered what my brother and sister and I used to say whenever we used to have dinner at Grandma's when we were little."

Ronnie got into the car, behind the wheel. Gail climbed in next to him. I was surprised she was still here, but then there wasn't much I could really figure out about that, anyway.

"When our parents would take us to Grandma's house for Thanksgiving or Christmas dinner, there would be a certain thing we would be expected to say at the end of the evening, before we went home," Mary said. "It was supposed to be polite, but we learned the words by memory, and it became sort of a family joke."

"What were the words?" I said.

Mary scrunched up her nose. When she spoke it was in a high-pitched, nasal voice, like she was imitating a ten-year-old: "Thank you very much for the lovely occasion."

I looked at her, not feeling like laughing at all. "That's what you said, huh?"

She looked straight back into my eyes. "That's what we said."

"Ben, you ready to go?" Ronnie said.

"I guess so," I said, lying.

Mary and I looked at each other for another few moments, and then I got into the back seat, where Michael was already waiting, and Ronnie pulled away, too fast, like he always did.

Eighteen

RONNIE HAD CHOSEN DALLAS. When we asked him why, he had merely said, "I've never been to Dallas." What I found myself thinking was that Dallas provided a lot of miles between Ronnie and that hospital room. We weren't just up the road from Sarasota; we were halfway across the country. And Dallas didn't feel anything like the west coast of Florida.

"This looks like a moonscape," Michael said as we drove along the Stemmons Freeway. The flight from Florida had been a long one. At DFW Airport we'd made our customary stop at the rental counter, and now I was driving toward our hotel.

"Do you know where you're going, Ben?" Ronnie said.

"The front desk gave me directions when I called from the airport," I said. This was one of the rare occasions when I was the driver; not only did I not relish the task, but Michael and Ronnie had made it clear all through the summer that they'd just as soon handle the duty. I felt that I should drive once in a while, though, so here I was.

"I thought the hotel was supposed to be before downtown," Gail said from the back seat. Now apparently she, too, felt free to criticize my driving and navigation.

"It is," I said. "This isn't downtown. This is just freeway."

"Look at that place," Michael said.

"That's it," I said. "That's the hotel." What he had seen was the Loews Anatole complex—a modern gargantuan hotel-and-shopping-plaza compound that seemed to be a ludicrous parody of the Texas stereotype generally, and of Texas as it had been in the boom years particularly. The Loews Anatole leapt out of the prairie like some huge work of surrealistic art dropped down from the stratosphere; it was so outsized as to seem impossible, the simple chore of filling the place with guests seemed like a formidable challenge. This had been Ronald

Reagan's headquarters at the convention that nominated him for a second term in 1984; Reagan and his White House staff had taken over the tower section of the hotel. The man, the city, the hotel, and that moment in history had seemed precisely right for each other.

I pulled into the parking lot and a valet car hiker at the front door handed me a ticket. In the soaring lobby, few people wandered. Apparently we had hit the hotel during a slow week. We were registered and on our way to our rooms within three minutes.

We'd agreed to meet back in the lobby an hour later. I threw my bags onto the second bed in my room and turned the TV set on. The three network newscasts were just beginning. The message light on my phone was unlit, as it almost always was this summer. Traveling for my job, there was seldom a time when I'd walk into a hotel room to find the message light dark. Usually it was blinking urgently, beckoning me to call the assignment desk or a headquarters producer right away. I was finding it calming and agreeable this summer, not being greeted by that blinking red light. I was finding it very easy to get used to. I switched the channel from the news to a *Sergeant Bilko* rerun, and at the appointed time I went back downstairs to meet the others.

"You're not going to be doing the driving all night, are you?" Ronnie said.

"I think I am," I said. "I'm sort of liking this."

"I can't take it," he said. "You drive like somebody's grandpa."

We were in a Texaco station near a Dallas suburb called Highland Park. From the looks of it, this was a fancy area. We'd all had dinner in the top-floor restaurant in the tower at the Loews Anatole, and right after dessert Gail had said she was tired, which was getting to be a pattern. But the three of us wanted to drive around and check out Dallas.

In one of the big windows of the gas station was a poster offering music tapes to customers. The poster was a vividly colored, stylized rendering of high-performance cars from the fifties and sixties—the legend at the top of the poster, in letters that were supposed to look like fat neon, said: "Cool Cruisin'."

The tapes that were for sale featured old car songs by Jan and Dean, by the Stingrays, by Bruce and Terry. The idea was that if you bought gas at this station, for an additional $1.99 you could buy a "Cool Cruisin' " tape and re-create the cruising atmosphere of yesteryear.

Which seemed a little odd—the things we used to take for granted being offered as a service-station premium. Cruising the streets of Bristol had never been considered a sinister activity by the parents of those of us who did it, but neither had it been endorsed. Our parents thought it was wasteful and lazy and nonproductive—we were cruising in our cars instead of studying or working, listening to the car radio instead of doing something constructive. Now here we were, middle-aged targets of marketeers who had realized—probably correctly—that there was a considerable customer base in America composed of people who wouldn't mind spending a couple of bucks for a taped promise of a return to the streets of their hometowns. I looked at the poster and wondered what we would have thought of this back then—if cruising had been packaged as an authorized, officially sanctioned activity, for sale to grownups in carryout form by a giant petroleum company, we might have chosen not to cruise.

I paid for the gas and we pulled out into the Dallas night. It was a few minutes after ten. We were just looking around.

"Which way do you want to go?" I said.

"Take a right up there," Michael said. "I want to look at the houses."

So I headed into an expensive-looking neighborhood. "I bet these go for a million apiece," Michael said.

I slowed down so that we could look at one particularly spectacular house.

"More like two million," Ronnie said.

"Unbelievable," Michael said, staring.

In the driveway of the house were about a dozen men. They were young—college age, definitely older than high school but with that look and bearing that tell you they're not worried about holding down jobs just yet. They were loud in the night—they were bellowing and making those barking sounds you hear on some sportscasts and talk shows. Some were holding cans of beer, others were passing bottles back and forth.

I had pulled to a complete stop.

"I think even two million's low," I said to Ronnie. I wondered just what a person had to do for a living, how high a person had to have risen, to be able to reside in such a place.

The men in the driveway were looking back at us. I guess I didn't blame them; we were strangers parked in front of the house.

"Probably the son of the owner and his friends," Michael said.

I pulled away from the curb and drove up the block. We looked at other houses in the neighborhood for five or ten minutes. Nothing matched that one.

"You want to head back to the hotel?" I said.

"If you do," Ronnie said, yawning.

"Do me a favor," Michael said. "Go by that house one more time. I love that place."

So I swung around the block and drove up the same street in the same direction as before.

"Boy," Michael said as I slowed again. "What a beautiful, beautiful place."

"What the fuck are you looking at?" one of the men in the driveway hollered.

It caught us by surprise. They hadn't spoken to us before.

"Get the fuck out!" another one yelled.

"Guess we aren't welcome," Michael said.

"Okay," I said. "Let's take off."

I started to accelerate and I had driven about twenty feet up the street when the rock hit the trunk of the car. It had that sharp, hollow sound, like a log hitting a metal drum.

"Move your asses!" a drunken voice from behind us screamed.

Then, before any of us could even think to react, the back window shattered. The sound was even louder.

"God," Michael said.

"Are you okay?" I said, my voice sounding peculiar to me. Michael was in the back seat alone; I turned around briefly to see that some of the glass had sprayed onto him.

Ronnie had his head out the front window, looking back down the street.

"The little fuckers are throwing rocks from the yard," he said.

"Get your head back in," I said to him.

"Fuck you!" Ronnie screamed back at them.

"Go, Ben," Michael said.

Another rock hit somewhere on the car. I couldn't tell where, but I heard the people back in the driveway whooping and laughing.

The summer before junior year, we painted street-address signs. It had been a scheme of Ronnie's. Early every morning we would go to the towns near Bristol—Millview, Rockton, a couple of others—and we would pick out a street. We would be carrying cans of white spray paint and black spray paint, and also a set of metal stencils that had the numerals 0 through 9 cut into them.

We would work our way up the selected street. Every house had its address either adhered to the mailbox with decals or displayed on the front lawn with a sign . . . something. So at each house we would see what the address was.

Then we'd go down to the curb right in front of the house. On each curb we would spray-paint a white rectangle. We had a stencil for that, too. We'd do the rectangles first. After the rectangles dried we'd start again. With the stencils we would paint the addresses on the rectangles, using the black spray paint for the numbers. We got pretty good at it; we could do an address in a matter of seconds.

As we finished each address, we'd walk up to the front door, all three of us. We'd ring or knock. When someone answered—usually a woman—one of us would say:

"Ma'am, we're working this summer painting street addresses." At which point the woman would invariably tell us thank you very much, but she wasn't interested.

"But we've already painted yours," one of us, usually Ronnie, would say.

The woman would not quite understand. Ronnie would repeat himself. The woman would say that she hadn't asked us to paint her address on the curb.

"You're not obligated to pay us," Ronnie would say. "But if you like the job we've done and feel like giving us something, we'd be grateful."

The woman would walk down to the curb with us and examine our handiwork. I must say, we gave value. The women would generally be impressed.

"Well, how much do you charge for this?" they would ask.

"Anything you think is right," we'd say. "Some people give us a dollar, some people give us two or three dollars."

About 90 percent of the time, the person in the house would give us something. When we were finished with one block we'd move on to another.

It was probably illegal—I don't think you can just go around painting on people's curbs. Today? Never mind the legality of the painting—in a lot of big cities, it's illegal for teenagers to even carry cans of spray paint.

But we made good signs. I think we did it mainly because it was an adventure. We didn't know who we were going to meet every day. We liked the idea of walking up to doors.

One day this girl—she was about our age—invited us in. She was wearing a pair of very short red shorts. Nothing happened; she was just flirting a little bit in her kitchen, and we were flirting back.

When we walked out, there were five guys waiting for us. They appeared considerably tougher than we were. They were gathered on the girl's front lawn.

"What are you doing with Sandy?" one of them said to us, although I don't, in fact, recall whether the girl's name was actually Sandy.

He was the boyfriend. We'd seen these guys off and on during the day. They had been watching us paint.

They were setting us up for a fight, and we were outnumbered, and even if we hadn't been, these guys could have taken us one-on-one.

"Hi," I said, friendly. I wasn't trying to disarm them for a sucker punch or anything, this wasn't some feint before I lunged at the guy. I was plain scared.

"We've been doing this all summer," I said, knowing that my voice was shaking a little bit. "This is a real good neighborhood for us."

The five of them stood their ground, staring us down, moving a little closer. It sounds cartoonish now, but it wasn't then, they were five guys we'd never seen before and it was just them and us.

"So you guys live here?" I said. "You like it here?"

"Hey, fuck you guys," Ronnie had said to them. "You want to fight, we'll fight. You've got us beat. Five against three. But don't stand there like you're going to do something. We weren't with your girlfriend. We're just working."

"Get out," the main one of them had said. "Don't come back."

"That's fine," Ronnie had said. "We're gone."

We'd walked toward Ronnie's car, them watching us.

"Don't let us see you here again," the talker had called to us.

When we had gotten to Ronnie's car we drove away toward Bristol. No one said anything in the car for a couple of minutes.

Then Ronnie had said, "Shit, Ben, how could you do that?"

"Do what?" I had said, knowing exactly what he meant.

"I'd rather get beat up than be like you were," he had said. Then, in a whining voice, he had mimicked my words: "Hi! We like working in your neighborhood! This is a real nice neighborhood!"

Michael, who had been silent during the exchange in front of the girl's house, had laughed a little at me in the car, which wasn't like him.

"Aren't you embarrassed?" Ronnie had said.

"For what?" I had said.

"Oh, come on," he had said. "How can you back down like that? That's sickening."

"I was just trying to talk to them," I had said.

"You were just trying to beg them not to hurt you," he had said.

The thing that made me feel the worst was that he was right. It had been a tiny moment; it really hadn't meant anything. Except I'd reacted one way, and he'd reacted another.

Ronnie has probably forgotten all about that summer day with the spray paint and the stencils. But I think about it sometimes. They had been out there waiting for us, and I had acted like a coward. Worse; I had acted like a coward who'd do just about anything not to fight.

The best I can remember, we didn't paint any more signs that summer.

———

"Are you sure you're all right?" I said to Michael. I had driven quickly away from the big house in Dallas, and now we were pulled over on a side street.

"I'm fine," he said. Most of the back window was still hanging together in shards. "I'm not cut or anything. I can't believe they did that."

"They were drunk," Ronnie said.

"Maybe they thought we were casing out the house to rob it or something," Michael said.

"Come on," Ronnie said. "They're just a bunch of drunk college kids being complete assholes."

"What, are they nuts?" I said.

"The rocks weren't that big," Ronnie said.

"You just can't go around throwing rocks at people's cars," Michael said.

"They can," Ronnie said.

"What do you mean?" I said.

"You saw the house," Ronnie said. "Obviously they know they can do anything they want."

"I don't think so," Michael said. "I think we ought to call the police."

Ronnie laughed. "Do you really think the police are going to do anything to those guys in that neighborhood?" he said. "The guys in the driveway will say that we were harassing them and that they were just trying to chase us away."

"But look at the car," Michael said. "Look what they did."

"The rental insurance will cover it," Ronnie said. "We'll get a new car in the morning."

"So they should be able to get away with it," Michael said.

"I didn't say that," Ronnie said. "I said it would be useless to call the police."

"Then what are you suggesting, Ronnie?" I said.

"We'll just take care of it ourselves," he said.

I turned to look at him. I hoped he wasn't saying what I thought he was.

"You don't want to fight them?" I said.

"Fight them?" Ronnie said. He had a happy, faraway look in his eyes. "Of course not. We can't fight them. We're forty-three years old."

He grinned at Michael and then he grinned at me.

"We're going to do something much more immature than that," he said.

———

I was parked outside the front door of the 7-Eleven. Three or four other cars were in the lot.

"Here he comes," Michael said, looking toward the store.

Ronnie emerged from inside, carrying a big paper grocery bag.

"Here," he said, getting back into the car. "I got four dozen for each of us."

He reached into the bag and began to pull out cartons of eggs.

"We're not doing this," Michael said.

"The girl at the counter thought I was crazy," Ronnie said. "She asked why I would need more than a hundred forty eggs at this time of night."

"What did you tell her?" I said.

"I said they were for a project," Ronnie said.

"A project?" I said.

"She seemed to buy it," he said.

"I don't know about this, Ronnie," I said.

"Just drive back the same way we came," he said.

I did. I followed the same streets, but two blocks before the big house I took a right and parked the car at the corner of a quiet side street with big, leafy trees. We got out.

"All right," Ronnie said. "This way."

Silently, we walked up the street toward the big house.

"They might not even be here anymore," I said to Ronnie.

"Shh," he whispered. "Keep it down."

There was another side street, this one right before the big house. We headed down it.

"Now this way," Ronnie said softly.

There was some shrubbery with a break in it. Ronnie led us through the opening. We were cutting through someone's backyard. Each of us was cradling our four cartons of eggs in our arms.

"What are we supposed to say if someone sees us back here?" Michael whispered.

"Say we're milkmen," Ronnie said.

Within seconds we could hear the voices. The young men were still in the driveway of the big house.

"Okay," Ronnie said. "Right over there."

We were at the rear of the property next to the big house. There was a freestanding garage large enough for three cars. Through a row of trees dividing this property from the lot with the big house on it, we could make out the shapes of the young men. We couldn't see them clearly; the tree line mostly hid them. But the driveway where they stood was brightly lighted, and we could tell where they were.

We were in darkness. "We do this quick, and then we go," Ronnie whispered.

He opened all four of his cartons. Michael began to do the same. We were close enough to each other that, even without direct light, I could see my friends' faces. These were not the faces of people you would expect to find getting ready to do what we were about to do. These were the faces of men you'd see at a corporate pension fund planning meeting, or on a commuter train at the end of a weary day downtown. Responsible people. I could feel a smile beginning.

Ronnie dumped all the eggs from his cartons onto the grass, so he could reach them easily. We did the same.

We all looked at each other.

"This is really stupid," Michael said, trying not to laugh.

"I know," Ronnie said, his own smile even wider than before.

He picked up an egg.

"Now," he whispered.

He heaved the egg over the tree line. Before it could land he was throwing another.

I held one of mine. I tried to calibrate where the people in the driveway were standing, then sent the egg in a high arc over the trees. Next to me Michael was grunting as he threw his.

We could hear them landing. "What the fuck . . . ," a voice yelled.

"More," Ronnie whispered.

We were standing up, all three of us, hurling the eggs one after another. Now all of the people on the driveway were shouting; we couldn't tell where the eggs were landing, but from the angry sounds of the voices, at least some of them had to be hitting their marks. The people had no idea where the eggs were coming from, at least not yet. We kept heaving them, now not even thinking of precision, just throwing them in quick succession in towering, erratic lobs over the tree line. I could hear Ronnie and Michael huffing a little with the exertion, and I guess I could hear myself, too.

The eggs cracked hard as they hit the driveway, egg after egg after egg, and now the people on the driveway were really screaming, it was raining eggs, and Ronnie said out loud, "Let's go!"

He started running back through the yard, in the direction of where we'd parked. Michael and I followed him, and then Michael stopped, noticed that he had an egg in his hand, turned back toward the tree line and slung it high. We were running hard, and we saw the break in the shrubbery, and we sprinted through it and jumped into the car. We were all breathing unevenly and we were trying to stifle our laughter.

I put the key into the ignition and we pulled away, back in the other direction, toward the hotel. Ronnie reached down to the floor of the car and said, "Look. We forgot to take one carton." He put the package of eggs in his lap.

"Turn the car around," he said.

"What are you talking about?" I said, driving fast out of the neighborhood.

"Turn it around," he said. "Go back to the house."

"Ronnie . . . ," Michael said.

"Drive slowly until you're a block away," Ronnie said. "Then turn the headlights off."

Well, as long as we'd taken it this far . . .

I circled around until we were on the street that ran past the big house. I stopped a block away. I pushed the headlight button in until the lights were off.

Ronnie, next to me in the front seat, said: "As fast as you can."

I stepped on the accelerator. There was no other traffic on the block. We were picking up speed as we approached the driveway. I was looking straight ahead as I drove, so I couldn't see much of anything, but right before we got to the house I did see that they were all still standing there, and there was stuff on the surface of the driveway, and as we raced past them I could hear Ronnie, as he leaned out the window, yelling "Pussy!" as he threw one last egg, and then I could hear them shouting again.

I flipped the headlights back on with one hand, and steered with the other, and within ten minutes we were in another part of town and I stopped the car.

We got out and leaned against it. We could barely breathe, we were laughing so hard.

"Did you hit anyone with that last one?" I said to Ronnie.

"Who knows?" he managed to say; he was laughing so uncontrollably that for a second I thought he was weeping. "I doubt it."

"Could you see anything?" Michael said, he, too, barely able to get the words out.

"Not much," Ronnie said. "Lot of broken eggs. Lot of guys in surf jams and baseball caps."

That started us up again, and Michael sat on the grass next to the car, howling he was so happy. I hit the grass, too, and then Ronnie did. We were in another residential neighborhood, under a streetlamp, and I figured that in a minute or two someone in one of the houses would come out to see what was going on.

" 'Pussy'?" Michael said.

"It was the first thing that came out," Ronnie said.

Michael lay flat on his back, not even having the energy to sit; he looked up at the stars and shook with his laughter, unable to talk anymore. I looked at him, seeing him so filled up with ridiculous delight, and that made me laugh all the more, and in a second or two all three of us were lying on the grass in this town we didn't know, howling like happy children in the night, never going to be children again, but howling in the night anyway, joyful and tired and too happy to be ashamed, looking up through wet eyes toward the summer stars.

I drove us back to the Loews Anatole, and we walked into that big lobby, and standing near the front entrance, looking like she was waiting for someone, was Debby Forbes Waggoner.

Michael's face lit up. "Was your plane on time?" he said.

He walked over to her and they hugged.

"Just got in," she said to him. "We left St. Louis right after dinner."

Ronnie and I stood together a few feet away, as if forbidden to move.

"Am I missing something here?" he said to me.

"I don't understand this," I said.

"Did you know she was going to be here?" he said.

"Michael didn't say anything to me," I said. Debby looked just as pleased to see Michael as she had at her surprise birthday party in St. Louis. "Hi," she said in a friendly voice, waving at us.

"Hi, Debby," I said, feeling dumb. I had no idea what was going on.

"The kids are upstairs in the room," she said to Michael. "I can go check on them, and then do you want to get something to eat or drink?"

"Great," he said. She went to the bank of elevators and called to him, "Meet you down here in five minutes."

She disappeared into the elevator car. After a few seconds I looked at Michael, who was all but glowing.

"Something you want to tell us?" I said to him.

"I'll see you guys in the morning," he said.

Nineteen

"GAIL'S LEAVING?" I said to Ronnie.

"She says she'll be back," he said. "She's just going to go for a while."

"When did she tell you?" I said.

"When we got back last night," he said. "In the room."

"I guess it was pretty awkward for her when we went down to see your dad," I said.

"She says she'll be back," he said again, not wanting to say much more about it.

That wasn't all it seemed he'd just as soon not discuss. Ronnie and I had met for breakfast near the health club and jogging path behind the hotel. I had brought up the job he'd offered Michael—I'd been as low-key as I could about it. I'd said, "So I hear Michael has got some decisions to make before the school year starts"—and Ronnie had said, "I don't know what decisions you're talking about." That's his way. He declares something off limits, and you know it's not open to conversation. For whatever reason, the fact that he'd asked Michael to come to work for him was something he didn't choose to go into with me.

Now he was letting me know that Gail was departing, at least temporarily. I can't say I was surprised; the only thing that surprised me was that she was planning to eventually rejoin us.

"If you don't mind my asking, I'm a little curious about what this is all about, anyway," I said. "You and her."

"You're curious about me?" he said. "What about Michael? What the hell is Debby doing here?"

We hadn't seen Michael yet this morning. Or Debby. Neither of us had any idea what was going on.

We waited for our breakfast to arrive. "You must have had some hint she was coming here," Ronnie said. "He wouldn't keep it from you."

"I told you last night, I didn't know anything," I said.

There was music playing from a radio somewhere in the restaurant, and a voice was saying that the anniversary of Marilyn Monroe's death was coming up. It was the same kind of story you hear and read every year at this time—all the shopworn Monroe anecdotes, and the quotes from people who allegedly knew her, and some songs from her movie sound tracks. The announcer signed off the way so many announcers always sign off on their annual Monroe stories: "It was August 5, 1962—a day that no one who was alive then will ever forget."

"What I remember is Allan Shoop," I said.

"There's a name I haven't heard in a while," Ronnie said. "Why would Marilyn Monroe remind you of him?"

Allan Shoop was a little guy in our class, a good tennis player, a kid none of us really knew that well. On that August day in 1962 I had been walking by the Bristol tennis courts, and Allan had been standing by himself on an empty court. Someone he'd been supposed to play with hadn't showed up. He called over to me and asked if I'd hit with him.

We both knew that I'd provide no real competition—later Allan would become a star on Bristol's varsity—but I guess as long as he was there he needed someone to hit with, so we knocked the ball back and forth for about half an hour. Then we decided to go to the Toddle House for hamburgers.

"Allan and I were walking down the street toward the Toddle House," I told Ronnie, "and he had this weird thing he did. I don't know if you remember this, but cars back then had these plastic ornaments on the front—one on each side, mounted on the hood on top of the headlights."

"Big things?" Ronnie said.

"No, they were little, about the size of quarters or half-dollars, and they were encased in metal circles," I said. "They stuck up from the hood. And we walked down the street, right by the courts, and Allan would look around to make sure no one was there, and then he would take the butt of his tennis racket and knock the ornaments out."

"Right off the car?" Ronnie said.

"See, the plastic parts were just pushed tight into the metal circles," I said. "So he'd hit a circle real hard with the end of his racket, and the ornaments would fly out. The metal circles would stay on the car."

"What did he do that for?" Ronnie said.

"I don't know," I said. "He said he collected them. He stuck the ornaments in his pockets."

"Allan Shoop didn't strike me as someone who would do that," Ronnie said.

"Me, either," I said. "Anyway, he was knocking the ornaments off the cars, and this one car had its radio on."

"The car was turned on?" Ronnie said.

"I don't think so," I said. "I think back then you could turn the radios of some cars on even if the engine wasn't running, but you weren't supposed to do it because it would run the battery down. But the radio in this car was definitely playing. And the newscaster said that Marilyn Monroe had just been found dead in California."

"What did you do?" Ronnie said.

"Nothing," I said. "Allan kept knocking the ornaments out, and we got to the Toddle House and had our hamburgers, and that was it. I guess you really never do forget a day when something historic happens."

"So Marilyn Monroe dying that day wasn't all that big a deal to you," Ronnie said.

"Yeah, but every time I think of her dying now, I always think of Allan Shoop, too," I said. "They're always together in my mind. The day she died, I think that was the only time in my life I ever really talked to Allan Shoop. Slamming those decorations off the hoods of the cars. I remember the look in his eye. I guess you never know about someone."

We found Michael eating ice cream with Debby Forbes Waggoner and her two children.

"You remember Rick," Michael said. "And Caroline." As if Ronnie and I had stood around making conversation with the children when we'd been at the surprise birthday party. The best I could recall, we'd never even been introduced to the kids.

"So what are you guys doing here?" I said to them. Rick was eleven; Caroline, who looked just like her mother, was seven.

"Mom calls it a getaway weekend," Caroline said. It occurred to me that this was, indeed, the weekend; for us, such distinctions had pretty much lost their meaning this summer. There was an old song called "Seven Day Weekend." Three very appealing words.

Michael shot me a quick glance; I sensed he would have preferred as few questions being asked about Debby's trip as possible. I knew then, if I'd had any doubts, that Jack Waggoner had not come along with his wife and kids for the weekend.

Rick Waggoner's ice-cream cone was dripping onto the front of his shirt. "Here," Michael said, reaching over with a paper napkin and cleaning up the spill. Then: "Here," handing the boy a fistful of paper napkins of his own, in case of more spills in the immediate future.

Amazing. I had no real idea of what Michael was up to, but he's the only person I know who would meet a married woman in a hotel on the road and have no problem with the woman bringing her children. No problem with it? He probably preferred it this way. This way he could assure himself that nothing untoward was going on; this way he could sleep with a clear conscience through the night.

Maybe. I saw the way he and Debby looked at each other. It was as warm as the way they had looked at each other more than twenty-five summers before in Bristol. Maybe he could sleep through the night.

The way we ended up at Chuck E. Cheese's was that Ronnie had to take Gail to the airport—he said it like a loyal husband seeing his wife off as she goes to visit her family. Debby's kids were getting bored, and there was a Chuck E. Cheese's on the way to DFW.

"I'm sorry if I've been in the way," Gail had said. She'd been waiting in the lobby with her suitcases; Ronnie was due down from the room momentarily.

"That's okay, Gail," I had said. I didn't want to contribute to this charade by continuing to act as if her attendance with us in the days and nights since Atlanta was something that Michael and I considered a routine, demure part of our summer plans. The fact was, I'd just as soon have had it be the three of us the whole way; Gail's being along had changed the alchemy of the journey, and even though Ronnie remained unforthcoming about his reasons for wanting her with him, the fact was that I knew Ronnie's wife and kids, and I was getting tired of pretending that this was something conventional. On the other hand, Debby Forbes Waggoner's unanticipated arrival had made the mix even more complex, and I was beginning to feel that I really didn't understand anything.

So, standing with Gail, I said, "I guess I'm just a little confused about all of this. I guess I'm just looking out for my friend."

"Ben," Gail said, "there are parts of your friend that are very unhappy."

Her words surprised me. Not necessarily the declaration that there was sadness somewhere inside Ronnie, although on the surface he is one of the least sad people I have ever met. But there is sadness, I suppose, inside all of us. It just wasn't something that I would have expected her to pick up on. It wasn't her problem.

"So maybe I'll see you somewhere on down the line," she said.

Ronnie came walking across the lobby from one direction and, from the other, came Michael, Debby, and the two kids.

"You ready?" Ronnie called to Gail.

And Michael said, "Rick and Caroline say they're going to go crazy if they don't get out of the hotel." Rick and Caroline; I wondered if saying their names so casually in this setting felt as alien coming out of Michael's mouth as the sound of the words felt going into my ear.

"I can drop you somewhere, but I need the car," Ronnie said.

So it was that he pulled into the parking lot of Chuck E. Cheese's. Ronnie and Gail and I were squeezed into the front seat; Michael and Debby and her children were in the back, the window still cracked from the night before.

The children got out and ran across the parking lot ahead of us and waited impatiently at the front door. They were still young enough to be a little reticent about going into a place by themselves. Even a Chuck E. Cheese's.

"You know, I've got this sales rep who works for me," Ronnie said before the rest of us got out. "And he swears that the best place in America to meet women is at a Chuck E. Cheese's."

"What are you talking about?" Michael said.

"It's true," Ronnie said. "Well, I don't know if it's true—but it's true that he says it. He says that all of these sales guys who hang around bars and cocktail lounges are wasting their time. He says that every Chuck E. Cheese's in America is full of bored, frustrated women with time on their hands. He says that it's a secret gold mine."

"Ronnie," I said, "the women at Chuck E. Cheese's are with their children. Most of them are married."

"I'm just telling you what he says," Ronnie said. "He's on the road all the time. He always makes a point of going into a Chuck E. Cheese's for lunch. He says that when he was younger he used to go into singles bars, but even the best ones couldn't hold a candle to the average Chuck E. Cheese's. Not at night, though, he says—he says the dads are there at night. He says the prime time to meet women at Chuck E. Cheese's is on weekday afternoons."

"A real Norman Rockwell tableau," I said.

We climbed out of the car, saying so long to Gail—another halting scene, I don't know where you're supposed to learn the etiquette for something like that—and she and Ronnie drove off toward DFW Airport.

We went inside Chuck E. Cheese's. It had the familiar calliope, arcade-game, pinball sound. Debby's kids ran to the Skee-Ball machines. We found a table big enough to accommodate all of us.

All around us, dozens of children were scampering between the game machines, climbing into the net cage with the soft plastic balls to jump around, watching the mechanical animals sing along with the taped music, begging their moms to buy more tokens for the various attractions. The mothers—usually it was one mom by herself, sometimes two sat together—doled out the tokens, or gave their kids quarters, which the machines would also take. Some of the moms smoked; most just sat silently eating Chuck E. Cheese's house pizza or munching on a Chuck E. Cheese's hot dog.

"I can see it," Michael said.

"What?" Debby said.

"What Ronnie was talking about," Michael said. "I can see it being true."

Debby started laughing out loud. She has one of those happy laughs that makes everyone around her start reflexively smiling, too. She was looking at the menu that was posted on the wall.

"Look," she said, nodding at the menu. "They serve wine coolers here. I can just picture it—some guy walking up to a mom who's sitting next to the Space Invaders game and saying in this real suave voice, 'Buy you a drink?' "

"If the mechanical animals ever sing a slow song, they could even dance," Michael said.

It was a nice couple of hours. Debby kept her eyes on the children as they roamed around the restaurant. Michael asked us what we wanted, then went to the counter and placed our orders and paid for them. I was going to offer to chip in, but then I realized this was one of the few times during the summer that Ronnie hadn't been there to pick up Michael's tab; the last thing he needed in front of Debby was for me to insist on paying.

After a while, the children left the games for a few minutes and ate their own lunch. Debby asked them if they were ready to go back to the hotel, but they said no; they wanted more tokens.

"Are you in a hurry?" Debby said to me.

"Not really," I said. "We don't have anywhere we have to be. We don't even have a ride, anyway. Actually, I kind of like it here."

Rick went to a basketball-shooting machine that was right by our table. The idea was that you put your token in the slot and then shot miniature basketballs at a miniature basket until, as a clock ticked down, your time ran out. The more rapidly and more accurately you shot, the more prize tickets came out of a second slot. Rick, a thin, quiet kid, kept getting better each time he tried. You could see it on his face—he was at that age when coordination and athletic skill mean so much, and even though it was only a game in a restaurant for kids, he didn't want to be bad.

A man of about seventy brought a small boy over to try his hand at the basketball game. The boy kept referring to the man as "Grandpa"; the grandfather was the oldest person in the place.

"Rick," Debby said to her son, "do you want to let the little boy have a turn?"

"That's all right," the grandfather said. "We'll just watch for a few more minutes. Then we'll try. Tucker can learn something by paying attention to how this young man does it."

Rick turned around, seemingly startled at the words.

"You're very good, young man," the grandfather said to Rick. "I think you may have a future as a basketball player someday."

Rick's face flushed, clearly pleased.

"You watch closely, Tucker," the grandfather said to the younger child. "This is the way to do it when it's your turn."

Michael leaned toward Debby and me and, in a soft voice so that only she and I could hear, said, "You never know how important a moment like that may be."

He watched Rick shooting some more, then continued: "When we were kids I was trying to get good at baseball. I was okay, but I could never really get the hang of it. One day we were playing over at the diamond on the corner of Washington Street and Elm . . ."

"By the junior high school," I said.

"That's the one," Michael said. "I was playing second base. I'd had a pretty good day. The game ended when the batter hit the ball to me, and I fielded a hard grounder and tossed it to the first baseman for the out. And we were leaving the field, and do you remember Neil Stewart?"

"About three years older than us?" Debby said.

"Right," Michael said. "His dad was watching the game. Neil wasn't playing; I think his dad just liked to watch baseball."

"Wasn't Neil's dad a pro ballplayer when he was young?" I said.

"Yes," Michael said. "Remember? He was the only person in Bristol who ever played professional sports. I think it was just the minors, for a year or two when he was right out of school, but people knew that he'd been a ballplayer.

"And when I walked off the diamond that day, he was watching, and he said, 'That was a real good performance out there today.' He told me he'd liked the way I'd charged the ball instead of waiting for it to come to me. He said to me, 'You keep working on that and you're going to be a ballplayer.' "

"I don't remember you playing baseball, Michael," Debby said.

"I didn't," he said. "Not in high school. That day when Neil Stewart's dad said that, I must have been twelve or thirteen. By the time we got to high school I wasn't good enough for the varsity. But it didn't matter. I just remember how good I felt that day. He hadn't had to say anything. Even if he thought I'd played okay, he could have just kept it to himself. But he told me. I don't know if he was just a nice man, or if he was in a good mood that day, or maybe there's even a chance that I really did play great that day. But I just floated home. Isn't it something, how something like that will stick. I don't think I ever talked to him again. I'm sure he didn't even know my name. His voice had a kind of drawl to it. I remember exactly how it sounded. 'That was a real good performance out there today.' "

Next to our table Debby's son was still shooting, and the little boy and his grandfather were waiting. "Rick," Debby said, "take a break. Let him play for a while, and then I'll get you some more tokens."

Her son still had a few seconds on the clock. He didn't look away from the hoop as he fired ball after ball at it, and he didn't acknowledge having heard Debby; he was concentrating. But after the timer had run down he stepped away so that the grandfather could put a token in the slot.

The little boy, nervousness in his eyes, stepped up to the game.

Michael said to Debby's son: "Rick?"

He looked over.

"You might want to give that boy some pointers," Michael said. "I think it's his first time."

Rick, with a flicker of something like adult pride in his face, picked up one of the balls and showed the boy how to hold it. "You've got to keep your eyes on the basket," he said. The little boy stared up at the hoop. Rick had been so shy every time I'd seen him; I didn't recall him saying much more than "hello." Now, though, he was talking; his voice was high and assured as he knelt next to the younger boy and said, "Don't get flustered if you miss. Just think about the next shot."

Debby, gladdened, glanced over at Michael. But Michael didn't notice just then. He was looking at the two boys, seeing the one showing the other how to shoot the basketball, and perhaps seeing something else, too.

"He must have left this in here before he went to the airport," Michael said.

We were in his room at the hotel. When Debby's children had finished playing the games at Chuck E. Cheese's we had called a cab to take us back to the hotel. Debby and her children had gone to their room, and I had stopped off at Michael's. On top of his dresser was a piece of Steele International stationery; embossed underneath the corporate logo were the words "Ronald G. Hepps. Chairman of the Board."

Michael looked at it. "He came in for a few minutes earlier this afternoon," he said. "I didn't notice he had this, but I guess he forgot it when he was here."

I didn't know that Ronnie was traveling with corporate letterhead. I hadn't seen it all summer. I wondered why, in this summer that was supposed to be free from business responsibility, Ronnie had felt compelled to stow the letterhead stationery in his suitcase?

The piece of stationery was covered with handwriting. I knew at once that the writing was Ronnie's; I didn't recall having seen his writing, except on a credit-card stub or in brief jottings on a notepad, all summer, but this was definitely a version of the severely diagonal slant that he had used to fill school assignment papers back when we first knew each other.

"Should we be looking at this?" I said.

We already were. "Dear Gary and Jody," it began. Those were his children.

"I have not been very conscientious about writing to you lately, for which I apologize. Mom has informed me that you are enjoying camp this summer. I am also enjoying the summer, although as you know it is a rather unaccustomed one for me. To-day I think I am going to go to a golf driving range, and then to-night or to-morrow we will probably leave Dallas. Oh, I have neglected to tell you that Dallas is the town where we are visiting this week. Gary, Mom informs me that she has ordered new wallpaper for your bedroom, which should be installed before you return from camp. Jody, Mom informs me that your cactus plant is thriving. Well, I must go now, but due to the fact that we are traveling all around the United States, I will attempt to come to the East Coast before your camp is over so that I can see you both. I love you both and miss you. Love, Daddy."

"Well," I said, feeling as if I had looked into someone's night-table drawer.

"I guess he forgot to mail it," Michael said.

"No, he didn't," I said. "Look at the top."

Above the Steele International logo Ronnie had hand-printed the word "FAX," all in capital letters, followed by a telephone number with a Pennsylvania area code.

"He faxed a letter to his kids at camp?" Michael said.

"Evidently," I said.

"My," Michael said.

There is something about seeing a personal letter not meant for your eyes that, in large ways and small, can be powerfully revelatory. You almost always come away with an unexpected glimpse of the person. In Ronnie's letter, for instance, the voice was so markedly formal; the voice in the letter did not sound like Ronnie's voice. It sounded as if he were exerting himself. Little, unintentional things surprise you: Where did the "to-day" come from? And the "to-night" and the "to-morrow"? The hyphenated construction of those words is something archaic, something that generations back at the turn of the century might have used but that has been out of common application for decades. Where did Ronnie pick up that quirk, and why did it stick with him? The whole sound of the letter . . . there were facets of Ronnie here that you never heard out loud.

Many years ago I spent a summer in Wisconsin at camp. At this particular camp, we lived in a dormitory. There was a boy at camp—he was about my age, I think I was twelve that summer—who was profoundly deaf, and could speak only in guttural notes that were often impossible to decipher. His name was Billy Furman. He seemed to be a nice boy, and many times during that summer I found myself wondering at how difficult the camp experience must be for him, and how brave he and his parents were to venture it. He was the only boy at the camp with an observable disability of any kind.

One day I had forgotten something in my room—now I have no idea what it might have been—and I ran from the athletic field back to the dorm to retrieve it. The dorm was deserted, or it was supposed to be. I dashed into my room, grabbed whatever it was I was looking for, and started back out of the building, when I heard a sound.

It was a voice. I listened and I recognized it as the voice of an older camper—a large, unpleasant boy who had a reputation as a meanspirited person. If you saw him coming your way you would alter your course, just to avoid an unhappy encounter.

He was standing half inside a doorway three rooms down from mine. It was Billy Furman's room. I could hear the words the older boy was saying:

"Ah, this is sweet. This is real sweet."

I looked out of my room. He was holding a piece of paper in his hand, and looking directly into Billy's room. He had found the paper on top of a desk right inside the door of the room.

"This is a real love letter," he said. "Ah. Mushy."

He raised a hand and, still looking into that room, he snapped his fingers. He paused, then snapped them again, then, louder, again.

"You can't hear a fuckin' thing, can you?" he said.

I saw him walk all the way into the room. I moved down the hallway, so I could see in.

Billy Furman was sitting on his bed, looking out the window at the campgrounds. The older boy was standing over him, just a few feet away, snapping his fingers again and again; Billy had no idea the older boy was even in the room.

"You can't hear a fuckin' thing," he said, over and over.

I saw him reach down and touch the back of Billy's neck. Billy, startled and frightened, recoiled. When he looked around he saw the older boy holding the piece of paper.

Billy reached for it, but the older boy yanked it away. Billy made a sound.

"Real pretty," the older boy said, looking at the piece of paper again.

Billy said something that sounded like "Please."

"Dear Mommy and Daddy," the older boy read, mocking.

Billy tried to say something; it sounded like "I don't feel well."

The older boy continued to read aloud, holding the piece of paper out of Billy's reach.

I couldn't stand it. I was afraid the older boy would beat me up if he knew I was there, but I couldn't stand it. I said, "Stop it," and the older boy turned around and saw me in the doorway, and I said, "Just stop it!"

He looked at me for a long moment. Then, for whatever reason, he dropped the piece of paper to the floor and walked out of the room.

Billy hurried over and picked up the piece of paper. He examined it as if to make sure that it hadn't been harmed. Then he said something to me that sounded like "Thank you."

I stood there with him. As if having made a decision, he handed me the piece of paper.

It was a letter, an uncompleted letter. It did, indeed, start out "Dear Mommy and Daddy." The handwriting was beautiful, and so was the language; in the letter he described the loveliness of the campgrounds, and the lunches and the dinners we'd been having, the counselors he liked, and activities he'd been participating in. I can still see that handwriting—it was so perfect, it could have won a penmanship contest. All the thoughts that were locked up inside that boy, all the things he was thinking, came pouring out in the letter. All the words he might have told the rest of us, he had put in his letter to his parents. Because he couldn't speak well, because he couldn't hear what we said, we didn't know what he was thinking. We didn't know what was in his heart. But here it was, and the letter was as yet unfinished.

I read up to the point at which he had stopped writing. I didn't know what to say. So I handed him the letter, and smiled and nodded my head, as if to show approval. He smiled back, said the words that may have been "Thank you" again, and went back to sit on his bed.

In the hotel room now, Michael folded Ronnie's letter up and put it in his pocket and said, "I ought to give this to him as soon as he gets back."

"He'll probably want it," I said. "It shouldn't be too long before he's here."

"Do you want me not to be asking you about this, or what?" I said.

Debby smiled. "You can ask anything you want," she said. "I'm not sure I can answer."

Michael was up in his room taking a shower. Debby and I were walking in a big park behind the hotel. It seemed to be part of the health-club complex. Her children were running up ahead of her, and we were keeping track of them from a few feet back.

"Michael hasn't told me how you happened to be here," I said.

"Oh, he's called me a few times from various places you've been," she said. "I'm sure you knew that."

"Well, I thought he was probably calling," I said.

"I was just really surprised at how glad I was to see him when you all showed up at my birthday party," she said.

"I'm starting to think we shouldn't have even come," I said.

"Now why would you say that?" Debby said.

"Because here's Michael in Dallas with you, and I'm quite sure that Ellen doesn't know about it, and I'd have to assume that your husband doesn't know why you're here, either." I sounded like a country minister, and a rather stern one at that.

"Then you'd assume wrong, Ben," she said. She called ahead of her: "Rick! Slow down! Let Caroline catch up with you."

We were heading across the grass in the direction of the sun. "He knows?" I said.

"I would never have come here without telling Jack," she said. "He's aware that I'm seeing the three of you."

"You're not here to see the three of us," I said.

"He knows I'm seeing Michael and the two of you," she said.

"And that's okay with him?" I said.

"I explained it," she said. "I'm here with his blessing."

Her children had stopped to throw rocks into a small pond. Debby and I sat on a stone bench.

"I can't think of many husbands who would give that kind of blessing," I said.

Debby laughed. "Well, I don't think Jack would have if I'd come without the kids."

I looked at her.

"Ben, I'm very happy with my life," she said. "I love my husband and I love my children. Coming here this weekend is not like anything I've ever done."

"Then why are you doing it, Debby?" I said.

"Because when I saw the three of you walk into that party in St. Louis, it made me remember how much I'd loved who I used to be, too," she said. "It has been so long since Bristol for me. Bristol is not something I held on to. But I loved that place, and I loved who I was, and I loved Michael. I would never do anything to harm my marriage, and I would never do anything to harm Michael's marriage. But when the three of you left St. Louis the day after the party, I found myself being really jealous. Seeing the three of you reminded me of what my life used to be like before everything became so set and so complicated. And when you drove off from St. Louis I felt that you were taking that with you."

"I just hope that Michael isn't getting himself in too deep," I said, surprising myself a little.

"I don't think there's any danger of that," she said.

"I wish I was as sure as you are," I said.

"Look, Ben," she said. "The three of you have been out on the road all summer. It may even be starting to seem normal to you. But what you're doing isn't normal. It's great. It's wonderful—it's the opposite of normal. I've never heard of anyone doing what you three are doing. It would have been easy for me not to come this weekend. But I wanted to—I wanted to see what this felt like. Don't worry—I'm not going to stick around. But if anybody should understand why I'd want to be here, you should."

"Your husband must be quite a person," I said.

"He's a very good man," she said. "I told him that if three women from his high school should ever take a summer off and drop in on him, he has my complete permission to join them for a couple of days."

"Somehow I doubt that's going to happen," I said.

"You never know," she said with that laugh. "This could catch on."

The children had become tired of skipping the stones across the water, and were walking through the park again.

"Other way, kids," she called. "Back toward the big building."

Obediently, they turned around and scurried in the general direction of the hotel.

"I don't know if you're aware of the effect you're having on Michael," I said. "It's been a long time since he's felt there's anything very special about him."

"That's part of what makes him so special," she said. "He truly isn't aware of it."

"I just hope you know what you're doing," I said.

"So do I," she said.

————

That night I dreamed I was back at work. In the dream it was September and I was on deadline with a story that I didn't think was worth doing and that I knew probably wouldn't get on the air; in the dream I called Ronnie because I felt like talking, but his secretary said he was in a meeting, and so I called Michael at the high school, but the woman who answered the phone in the principal's office said that teachers were not allowed to accept phone calls during school hours.

In the dream the woman in the principal's office said the only exceptions were in cases of emergency, and she asked me if this was an emergency, and I said yes, I had to talk to my friend. She asked me what the nature of the emergency was, and that's when I woke up. It wasn't September; it was heading into August, and I was in my hotel room in Dallas, and when I looked at the clock next to the bed the bright numbers on the display panel said that it was 3:32 A.M. It was some time before I was able to fall back to sleep.

Twenty

THE NEXT WEEK we vowed to drive without caring where we were going, without hurrying or feeling we had to reach any particular stop by day's end. This was after Debby and her children left. We drove slowly; we got out of the car a lot. We took back roads and bought sandwiches at roadside cafes and sat by the car on the grass at the edge of the highway and ate our lunches in the sun, washing the bread and the meat and the cheese down with cold soda pop from filling station vending machines. Anytime one of us asked if we shouldn't be moving along, another one of us would ask why. We slept in small motels where the owners thanked us for our business and urged us to stay over another night.

In Sanger, Texas, we met a man who made guitars by hand. He said it took him up to six months to craft a guitar from raw wood to finished instrument. Ronnie took his phone number and address and said he might get in touch with him later to order one. In Myra, we saw a barber pole in the shade of the main street, and on the spur of the moment parked the car and went inside to get haircuts. It was a two-chair shop with one barber; he said his partner had retired. So we took turns, one of us in the barber chair while the others read old magazines that were stacked atop a space heater that was turned off for the summer. In Marietta, Oklahoma, just over the Texas border, we went to a laundromat and washed our clothes alongside some young house-wives from the town.

Oklahoma in the beginning days of August was dry and hot. Ronnie had gotten a splinter in his hand somewhere along the way, and he was afraid it was becoming infected, so in Ardmore we stopped at a clinic where the nurse removed the shard from his finger and dressed the wound. She asked what brought us to town, and we told her, and we ended up taking her to dinner at a chicken place about five miles down the road. In Duncan we watched some kids play baseball, and when their game was over they let us toss the ball around on the dusty diamond.

In Altus the afternoon was so scorching that we went into the town movie theater just to sit in the air conditioning. The movie was more than a few years old—Gene Hackman in *Hoosiers*—and two of us had already seen it. On another day I might have wondered about the happenstance that had brought this particular movie to this most unlikely of venues, but I was so grateful to get off the baking streets outside that I just sat back in the cool, dark theater and relished the film.

Outside of a town called Willow we went fishing in a tiny creek; we bought poles from some old men who were only too happy to sell them, and we caught nothing. When we were finished we gave the poles back to the men. They thought we were asking for a refund, but we told them we had no further need for the rods, and said to go ahead and sell them again. They looked at us as if we were daft. In Elk City we had milk shakes.

Once in a while we'd pick up a local newspaper, and I would look at the date on the front page and realize that the summer was getting on. In Woodward, we mailed postcards. In Alva there was a burst water main in the middle of town, and we sat on the trunk of the car as the children in their shorts and bare feet romped delightedly through the flooded street, and the volunteer firemen worked diligently to repair the break. They did, to the sound of cheers from the adult onlookers, and boos from the kids.

"You okay?" I said to Michael.

We were parked at a rural hamburger stand one windless evening. We'd carried our dinner out to the car in white paper sacks, had laid the food out on the hood, and had eaten standing up. We'd been driving most of the afternoon, and no one wanted to sit anymore. This way we could stretch our legs at the same time we had our supper.

"Fine," Michael said.

"Oh," I said.

"You sound surprised," he said.

"I am a little bit surprised, to tell you the truth," I said. "I was expecting you to be all down about Debby going back to St. Louis."

He hadn't been. From the lobby entrance of the hotel in Dallas I had watched him as he'd put Debby and her children in a cab for the airport. I couldn't hear what they were saying to each other; I'd seen Debby kiss him on the cheek, and I'd seen him stand there, looking at the cab until it was out of view. Since then, though, he had been in

high spirits; if anything he was the opposite of morose, he seemed to be highly enjoying our travels through the Texas and Oklahoma countryside. He didn't seem to have his mind on anything gloomy. I wouldn't have bet that.

"You knew she was going to go home," Michael said.

"I didn't know anything," I said. "I didn't know she was meeting you in Dallas . . . when did you arrange that, anyway?"

"In Florida," he said. "I called her from there."

"Well, I didn't have any idea," I said. "I didn't have any idea she was going to join you, and I still don't really know what that was all about."

"She said you talked to her," Michael said.

"I did," I said. "But I don't know what to make of what she told me."

"Look, I'm not Ronnie," he said. "There was no way Debby and I were going to go to bed. I've got to go home at the end of the summer."

"Stranger things have happened," I said.

"The very fact that she dropped everything and flew down to see me was a lot better than anything that could have happened like that," he said. "It told me a lot more about how she felt about me."

"And how would you define that?" I said.

"Well, I guess she loves me a little bit," he said. "That's what she told me."

"And you?" I said.

"I guess I love her a little bit, too," he said. "But I don't think that's bad. What would be bad, I think, is if we did something to screw each other's lives up. We didn't do that. She helped me remember some things about myself I'd almost forgotten. I'm not going to feel guilty about having seen her."

" 'Seen her'?" I said. "Debby put her children on a jet airplane and flew to Texas and checked into a hotel and spent two days with you."

"And?" Michael said.

"And I just think it's a little bit weird," I said. "A woman and her two kids traveling to meet someone."

"That's weird?" Michael said. "And Ronnie putting that dental hygienist friend of his in a beachfront resort while he sits by his father's hospital bed, and never mentions to his dad that there's a woman waiting for him ten minutes away—that you don't think is weird?"

"They're both weird, Michael," I said, smiling and shaking my head to let him know I wasn't trying to knock him. "Everything's weird."

"And your Sweetheart of Sigma Chi back at the Colony—that's not weird?" he said. "I thought I was done listening to my friends in the next room with college girls twenty years ago, if you don't mind my saying so."

"Number one, she's in graduate school," I said, seeing that he was starting to laugh. "And number two, you're right. It is somewhat weird."

Ronnie was coming out of the men's room of the hamburger stand across the parking lot.

"So graduate school doesn't count as college?" Michael said, his grin spreading across his face, pleased that now he had the upper hand.

"I prefer to think of it as the gateway to a doctorate," I said.

"Give me a break," he said.

"It's a joke," I said. "Everything's weird, Michael. Everything's weird. I'm glad you're glad that you saw Debby."

Right before Ronnie got within earshot of us, Michael said, "I don't know what I'm going to do about that job offer of his."

"I've been wondering about that," I said.

"Do me a favor," he said. "Let's not talk about it in front of him, okay?"

Ronnie tossed the car keys to Michael from ten feet away. "Your turn," he said, and within a minute we were off again.

Late that night, on a two-lane highway that we seemed to have to ourselves, Michael said, "Sorry if I jumped down your throat."

Ronnie was asleep in the back seat. Michael drove; I sat in the front passenger seat.

"About Debby?" I said. "No problem. It's really none of my business anyway."

It was pure Michael. I had intruded into something that meant a great deal to him—and he was feeling the need to apologize for having snapped back at me. Having snapped back in the mildest possible way, at that.

Way up ahead we could see the lights of an all-night service station. "We're running low," Michael said, looking at the gauge. "I'm going to stop."

So we pulled into the lonely station on this black Oklahoma night. One attendant—a teenager with a wary face, accustomed to being outnumbered by strangers—sat behind a glass wall.

"Do you remember back in Nashville, when you asked me if I'd told Ellen that I'd seen Debby?" he said.

"After the birthday party?" I said. "I believe you told me that you hadn't."

"I'm going to tell her now," he said. "I think she'll understand. After St. Louis I was feeling a little guilty for what was going through my head. But I'm not feeling guilty anymore. I'm feeling good. I want to be honest with Ellen.''

"So you're going to invite Debby and her husband to your house?" I said, not being able to resist.

Michael laughed. "Let's not get carried away here, okay?" he said.

"I'm staying out of this," I said.

The wary teenager came through the door, checking us out like a border patrolman.

"Life's a strange old thing, isn't it?" Michael said, turning off the ignition.

The Litany of Adult Experiences came about after we saw some poor business guy getting yelled at by his drunken wife one night in a Wendy's.

The business guy—he was wearing a short-sleeved white shirt and a tie and he was about our age—was sitting across the table from his wife. They were waiting for their meal to arrive; it was unclear how much she'd had to drink or where she had been doing her drinking, but whatever inhibitions she might have had about raising her voice in a public place were long gone.

She was complaining about the house in which they lived; she was complaining about his salary. She was complaining about their friends—or rather, their lack of friends; she was complaining about the town where they lived. He sat there, miserable, letting it run its course. It was evident he had been through this before.

"And I have to stop what I was doing this afternoon, and for what?" she said to him. "So you can take me to dinner at a damn Wendy's!"

At our booth, Michael said, "How'd you like to be that guy?"

I said, "When he was eighteen, she probably looked great to him."

Michael said, "What do you think he would have done if he could have looked twenty-five years into the future."

Ronnie glanced over at the guy, seemingly trying to envision him twenty-five years back. Ronnie didn't say anything for a few seconds. Then he announced to us:

"You know, they ought to let you go to your high school graduation, let you go to your all-night senior party, and then the next morning shoot you in the fucking head."

We started cracking up at that, which at least diverted attention momentarily from the businessman and his wife. After a moment I said, "I don't think something that drastic is necessary. I think you could accomplish the same thing by giving everyone a list when they turn eighteen."

"What kind of a list?" Ronnie said.

"A list of everything that's going to happen to you in the next fifty or sixty years—so you don't have to actually go through it. Stuff that you never think about when you're a kid."

"Like what?" Michael said.

"I don't know," I said. "Like . . . like cops are going to start looking young to you."

"Oh, yeah," Ronnie said. "That kind of thing."

So, for the next day or so, we became obsessed with compiling our list—which we promptly named the Litany of Adult Experiences.

We would be somewhere, talking about something completely different, and Michael would say: "You're in a public place and you ask them to turn the music down."

And Ronnie would pipe in: "You think it's frightening how hard football players hit each other."

No one would have to say out loud that these were intended for inclusion in the Litany of Adult Experiences. We'd know it without having to put it in context.

"You get glasses," Ronnie would say.

"That's too easy," Michael would say. "How about this: Whenever you buy glasses, you order two pairs, because you know for a fact that you're going to lose one."

At a stoplight I said: "You're proud that you always are asleep by midnight on New Year's Eve."

Michael said: "You leave concerts and ball games early so that you can beat the traffic."

Ronnie said: "You become compulsively interested in articles about the causes of lower back pain."

We never wrote any of this down—we just couldn't stop throwing the suggestions into the air. We were ordering lunch one afternoon and the waitress was repeating our food selections; Michael interrupted her.

"Your barber trims your eyebrows," he said.

"You hate teenage boys," Ronnie said.

"You forget where you put your keys," I said.

There was no rating system; no scores awarded to each item. Beside a motel pool one morning, Michael said: "You deal with the fact that your sister is a grandmother."

"Whose sister is a grandmother?" I said.

"Mine is," he said. "Lois—my older sister. Her son just had a son."

"Lois is a grandmother," I said.

"You ask someone for the name of a good podiatrist," Ronnie said.

As we kept this up, I think we began to half believe that if the list was really complete and comprehensive, then any young men to whom it was given truly would be able to elude life's vicissitudes. There was no other way to explain our devotion to the project for those couple of days. The car blew a tire one evening; as we stood in a service station waiting for it to be changed Michael got a thoughtful look on his face and said, "You feel cold all the time and put on sweaters."

"Your idea of heaven on earth is retirement," I said.

"You can't remember the last time you slept all the way through the night," Ronnie said.

And so it continued. "You miss old cars and think the new ones all look alike," Michael said.

"A pretty young girl smiles at you on the street, and you're flattered until you realize she thinks you're harmless," Ronnie said.

"You don't understand the music," I said.

We stopped in a small-town public library; I wanted to see what it was like. We stood and examined the books, and suddenly Ronnie said: "You think it might be a good idea to look for a younger doctor."

"You worry that the oil in your car might, indeed, be a quart low," I said.

"You read the obituaries every day and the first thing you look for is the ages," Michael said.

We told each other that we were going to stop making the list; we realized it was beginning to dominate the trip. So we would quit for a couple of hours. It would be behind us. We'd be having a perfectly normal conversation.

Then Michael would say: "When it snows your first concern is whether there's a kid in the neighborhood who can shovel it for you."

Ronnie would say: "You have to think for a second when someone asks you how old you are."

I would say: "You consider buying a certain car but then decide not to because you think it's too fast for you."

On the third day of this we made a hard-and-firm rule: no more. We were serious; we knew we had to cut it out.

Twenty minutes later I said: "Younger people call you 'sir' and you realize they're not kidding."

Ronnie said: "You get out of the hot sun."

Michael said: "You worry about gum disease instead of cavities."

After that we told ourselves that it had been okay to do it that one last time; after all, this was supposed to be a summer without regulations. But, we told ourselves, this was a self-imposed regulation, for our own good. No further additions to the Litany.

That night I lay in bed in my motel room. The phone rang. I picked it up.

Ronnie's voice said: "You have old suits in your closet you don't remember ever having worn."

I hung up. I lay awake, staring at the ceiling. I dialed Michael's room. He answered the phone in a weary voice.

I said: "You complain that there's not one show on prime-time TV that appeals to you."

Through a yawn, Michael said: "You don't have another drink at a party because you know in advance that it will make you feel bad in the morning."

Gradually, we did stop. We'd go a whole day without reviving the Litany. Maybe one of us would break down; maybe Ronnie would say: "When new neighbors move in, you wonder if they're the right kind of people."

But we managed to beat it. Three or four hours later I would say: "You think younger people at work talk too loudly." The others wouldn't pick up on it, though. This was over; the fever had broken. We were finished with this.

We crossed the state line into Kansas.

"Your new boss was in sixth grade the year you graduated from college," Michael said.

"Stop it," I said.

"You think the way young people dress is an absolute disgrace," Ronnie said.

In a town called Wellington, on the way to Wichita, Ronnie said there were some calls he had to make. He'd pretty much stayed away from telephones in the days after Dallas; all of us had. But now he said he had some things he needed to take care of.

We parked the car outside a hardware store. Inside, the owner said Ronnie could use the pay phone on the back wall. We'd been riding for a while, and Michael and I decided to walk around the area while we waited for Ronnie.

Off the main street we turned onto a side road, just wandering. "I think I have to take that job, Ben," he said to me.

"Have you talked about it with Ellen?" I said.

"She's not real excited about it," he said. "She wants to stay in Bristol."

"And Ronnie wouldn't let you work out of Bristol?" I said.

"Not for the kind of money he's going to pay me," he said.

There was a yard with a big, leafy tree in front of the house. "You think they'd mind if we sat here?" I said.

"I guess we'll find out," Michael said, and we settled onto the grass. It felt about fifteen degrees cooler in the shadow of the tree.

"You haven't really told me what the job is," I said.

Michael shrugged. "It's basically a sales job with a title," he said. "The way Ronnie explained it, I work out of their headquarters and I come up with plans to merchandise their stuff, and if the people above me like it the sales guys on the road try to do it."

"That doesn't make any sense, Michael," I said to him. "You've never done anything like that in your life."

"I know," he said. "Ronnie says that if you're good at it, you're good at it."

"Killer instinct, huh?" I said.

"Killer instinct," he said.

"How can he give you a job like that without having any idea whether you can do it?" I said.

"You want to know what I think?" Michael said. "I think he's doing it because he doesn't want the summer to end."

"Meaning?" I said.

"Meaning that about a month from now you're going to be back at your news bureau in Washington, and I'm going to be back in my classroom at Bristol High School, and Ronnie's going to be back in his office," Michael said. "And I don't think he wants that to happen. Ronnie doesn't say much about how he feels, but I think he's loving this summer. And I think having me work with him is his way of trying to make the summer go on."

"But what about you?" I said.

"Me?" Michael said. "Me, for the first time in my life I make a good living."

"You like the job you have now, though," I said. "You're great at it."

Michael picked up a long twig from the base of the tree. He snapped it in two and tossed the first piece across the grass; after the piece landed he threw the other piece toward it, trying to hit it. He came within an inch or two.

"Do you know what's going to happen if I don't take Ronnie's job?" he said. "The summer's going to end, and we're all going to say how wonderful it was, and we're all going to go back to our towns and our jobs. And for the first week or two we'll call each other every day, or close to it. It'll be like a conversation that we never quite ended—we'll think of something that happened during the summer, or of some place we went, and we'll pick up that phone.

"Pretty soon, though, that will stop. The calls won't come as often. And within six months this summer will become a story for each of us to tell. You'll be on the road somewhere, and you'll meet someone, and just to make conversation you'll say, 'I did something last summer that I'll never forget.' Or Ronnie will have to break the ice at some business meeting, and he'll say to the other people in the room, 'What did you

244 · *Bob Greene*

do last summer?' And then when they're finished talking he'll say, 'I think I can top that.' And he'll tell them about this summer, and it will be like a little victory for him. A little edge up during the meeting.

"And every time anyone talks about the summer, they'll talk about you, and they'll say 'You may know that name—he's a television correspondent.' And they'll talk about Ronnie, and they'll say that he's the chairman of Steele International. And they'll talk about me and say, Michael, he's a great guy. He's back in Bristol, and he teaches at the school, and everyone loves him."

"That's not the worst thing you can say about a person," I said.

"Ben, we're forty-three years old," he said. "I'm sure that as a member of the cast of characters in somebody's anecdote, I sound real appealing. My life isn't an anecdote. I've got two little girls, and I've got a wife who depends on me, and I have no prospects of ever making anything more than a teacher's salary. And in ten years I'm going to be fifty-three, and in ten years after that I'm going to be sixty-three, and there's going to come a time when I'm too old to be a teacher anymore. I've never had a chance like this before. Am I scared I won't be any good at the job? I'm scared to death. Am I scared I won't like it? You wouldn't believe how scared I am. But I'm scared of a lot of things, Ben. I'm scared of the fact that without this I have no prospects of ever giving my family the kind of life they deserve. I'm scared that if something happened to me, they'd have nothing to fall back on. I'm scared that when I'm asleep and Ellen looks over at me, she thinks she took a wrong turn somewhere in her life."

"Don't even say that, Michael," I said.

"I mean it!" he said, suddenly almost angry in this unfamiliar yard where we'd never been before and would never be again. "Look, I've been thinking about all the bad things that might happen if I take the job. I don't think there's been an hour when I haven't thought about it since Ronnie brought it up. Forget about whether I'll be good at it or not—I honestly have no idea whether I'll be good at it. But whether I'm good or I'm not, there's something humiliating about this anyway. Any way you cut it, it's charity. For whatever reasons, Ronnie is doing this as a favor. And every day I walk into the office I'll know there's not a person who looks at me who doesn't know that."

"And you may do it anyway?" I said.

"If I don't, I'll be standing in that classroom every day, and I'll feel terrific about the kids I'm teaching, and then after school I'll go home," he said. "And as usual the bills will be on the kitchen counter and they'll be more than the paycheck, and as usual the girls will be talking about the trips to Hawaii and Europe their friends are taking, and as usual Ellen won't mention that the women she sees at the grocery are moving into big new houses and buying expensive new cars. And this summer will already be a long-ago story, and in the story I'll be this nice guy with this nice job. And every day we'll be getting older, Ben."

We sat there for a minute or so saying nothing.

Finally I said to him, "I don't know what's right. But never think that Ellen feels she took a wrong turn somewhere. She knows she didn't, Michael. And you must know that she didn't."

"Someone sure took a wrong turn," he said.

When Michael and I were first old enough to be allowed to roam around Bristol on our own—six years old, maybe seven—we were on our bikes one warm spring Saturday. It was one of those days that make you feel free; even early in the morning you can sense that you're going to be late for dinner.

Now it is hard to recollect just how exhilarating it was to be out by yourself when, during all the years before, you had never been permitted beyond an adult's sight. Michael and I felt like adventurers; we felt that, on those bicycles, we could go just about anywhere and see just about anything.

We had ridden by the high school baseball field that day, and by Swendell's Ice Cream Shop, and by Gebhardt's Drugstore. We hardly stopped at all; we supposed there was so much to see. We looked straight ahead over the handlebars—never taking our eyes off the road, as our parents had enjoined us—and we rode in single file, one of us directly behind the other. But we talked ceaselessly; we had to raise our voices to be heard, one of us in front, one of us in back, and we provided a nonstop narrative of the day.

We were riding up Sturdevant Avenue when we saw a crowd of kids gathered in a yard two hundred feet or so ahead. Michael, in front, saw this first; he called out excitedly to me. We stood up on the bikes, giving us greater leverage on the boxy hard-rubber pedals; we sped up the avenue, past the white-fronted two-story homes, until we got to the crowd.

I remember feeling startled, and then sick, at what we saw. In the yard, two dogs were fighting. Except that is not quite accurate. A big German shepherd—we had seen it around that neighborhood many times, in Bristol you know not only the people and the houses but also the dogs—had a little white dog in its mouth. The white dog we had seen before, too. It wasn't a poodle but it had that kind of look—small and frisky and cute.

The name of the big dog was Queen. Queen was famous in the neighborhood just for being so large. We weren't aware of the name of the little dog. Queen belonged to a career Army officer a block away from this house; the little dog belonged to an older lady at the end of the block, a lady whose children were grown and out of school, and thus a lady we did not know.

Queen was shaking the little white dog as if it were a toy. Perhaps it had been a real fight for a few moments when it had begun; now the white dog was inert and silent in the German shepherd's mouth. We had been there for fifteen seconds and no part of the small dog had touched the ground.

The only sound was the gnarl coming from deep in Queen's throat. The people in the yard—all youngsters, but almost all of them older than us—said nothing. They weren't there to cheer; in fact, they seemed not to know what to do. The voice of one eight-year-old boy rose out of the crowd: "Don't, Queen." Queen did not listen.

Behind us a Bristol police car pulled to the curb. Apparently someone from one of the houses had called. The officer had not turned on his siren; sirens were virtually never necessary in Bristol, and two-man cars were never used. But a second police car pulled up after the first, and both officers walked swiftly into the yard.

Queen, seeing the humans moving across the lawn, dropped the white dog. Once the white dog was on the ground, Michael and I could see that its stomach had been torn open. Its white fur was covered with red, and its entrails were protruding. I thought I was going to vomit. The little dog, still making no noise at all, attempted to crawl toward Queen. The little dog could not walk, but it was using its front paws to try to pull itself closer to Queen. Perhaps it wanted to continue whatever fight it had been able to muster at the beginning; perhaps the nascent movement toward Queen was a gesture of surrender. One of the police officers held Queen by its collar.

The officer closest to the small dog got down on the grass and looked closely. "Jesus," he said.

"It's Mrs. Crane's," a boy in the crowd called.

Another boy: "That little dog was just running around the yard."

The officer looked toward us and said, "Out of here, now. All of you." Then: "I mean it. Now!"

Everyone scattered, bikes hurrying away. But the crowd moved only to the end of the block, and formed again. I could hear boys talking in awe: "Did you see how Queen picked her up?" "I thought Queen was going to swallow her." "I heard Queen killed a cat up the street once."

Gradually the other kids dispersed. Michael and I stayed, though; we remained at the end of the block, not wanting to disobey the police officers. We could still see them. One was kneeling next to the little dog, whose owner, the lady from the opposite end of the block, had appeared in a housecoat and in tears. The other continued to hold Queen's collar.

Within fifteen minutes Dr. Burton Rath, who ran Bristol's only veterinary hospital, arrived in his car. He carried a bag, just like an M.D. making a house call. Michael and I wheeled our bikes up toward the house again. We had to find out what was going to happen.

We could hear Dr. Rath as he examined the little dog. "Oh, my," he said sadly. The little dog did not move, but we could see that its eyes were open.

He picked the little dog up and carried it to his car. The lady from the end of the block followed him, and they drove off, and then the two police officers led Queen to one of the cruisers and put the shepherd in the back seat and they drove off, too.

There were various stories about what happened to the little dog. Some kids said that it died on the operating table; some said that it had to be put to sleep. Others swore that they saw it again; they said that miraculously the little dog recovered, but that the lady at the end of the block never again permitted it to face the dangers outside. The kids said they saw the little dog by peeking in the lady's front window.

Queen, on the other hand, became a Bristol legend. Queen was talked about with wonder and an ignoble kind of respect. By virtue of coming close to disemboweling the white dog, who could put up no resistance, Queen became the champion dog of the town. Not in a celebratory or buoyant sense. But Queen had proven itself beyond any doubt to be one tough animal; no matter that the proof was delivered to a smaller animal who was unable to defend itself. People talked quietly when they saw Queen from that day on; people looked at Queen as they might look at a rugged football star. Queen's owner, the Army man, convinced people that Queen was not a danger to human or animal; Queen had only hurt the other dog, the Army man said, because the other dog had started it. That became part of the fable: "Queen was only defending herself." Children who had been there and knew different even began saying that.

I remember the absolute quiet in the neighborhood after the veterinarian took the little dog away. Michael and I had stood there, each with one foot on a pedal, one foot on the ground. The commotion was over and the big dog had won, and life went on. We were too young to ever have heard the term "survival of the fittest," but we learned about it that day. The big dog will beat the little dog every time, and the big dog will be a hero to some, and no one will be quite sure what happened to the little dog.

We rode our bikes home just after the noon hour. We didn't feel like being out any longer. The big dog was always going to win.

Now, in Wellington, Kansas, I sat with Michael under the tree.

"Have you decided that you're going to take the job for sure?" I said.

"Not for sure," he said. "But I don't see how I have that much of a choice."

We sat there and I thought back to the fight between the dogs. Once in a while in the weeks and months after the fight we would be talking about it and Michael would ask me: Why did I think the little dog, in such pain, had tried so hard to crawl toward the German shepherd? Was it a sign of a willingness to fight on? Was it a symbol of submission? I don't think we ever figured it out.

"We'd better go," he said on this Kansas afternoon. "Ronnie's probably finished with his phone calls."

I would see Hannah soon.

I'd been thinking about the possibility of that ever since I'd read the letter that Ronnie had faxed to his children. The prospect of seeing her enlivened me in a different way than anything else had all summer.

Ronnie was waiting by the car when Michael and I walked up the sidewalk to the hardware store. "Did we keep you waiting?" I said.

"No, I just finished up," he said. "Lot of calls."

"Did you call your dad?" I said.

"He seems better," Ronnie said. "It's hard to tell from his voice, though. That's still pretty raw."

"So how did you know?" Michael said. "Was he telling jokes?"

"I can't recall my dad ever telling a joke," Ronnie said. Come to think of it, I could never remember Carlton Hepps telling a joke, either, or even trying to say anything funny. Ronnie's dad just wasn't a joke-telling guy.

"Did he say he was feeling better?" I said.

"Not in so many words," Ronnie said. "But he acted a little put out when I asked him some detailed medical stuff. I asked if he was still having trouble with the catheter, and he said, 'I think a subject like that should be broached by me, not you.' When we were in Florida he worried aloud with me about the catheter day and night. He even asked me to speak to his urologist about it."

"And you find that encouraging?" Michael said.

"He sounds more like himself when he talks like that," Ronnie said. "When he doesn't want me in his life. That's a terrible thing to say, but it's true. The dad I know doesn't need to confide in me. That was one of the scariest things in Florida. I knew he was despondent because he kept telling me stuff."

Ronnie probably didn't want any curbstone analysis of his family situation. So Michael and I both just said we were happy his father seemed to be improving.

"My mom says hi," Ronnie said. "And listen—do either of you have any objections if we fly to Pennsylvania next?"

He said he had called Marilyn; she was planning on going to their children's camp for Parents Day. Ronnie wanted to go, too. "I haven't seen them since we left, and I don't want to wait until September," he said.

It was exactly what I'd wanted to hear. My arrangement with Nancy was that she and Hannah would spend the entire summer together— Nancy thought it was best that way, and Hannah had said that she wanted to be at the beach house all summer. I had said that was okay, if it was what Hannah really wanted. But before I'd left on our trip I had told Nancy that, should we be traveling anywhere near the Delaware beach, I planned on seeing them. She said of course; she said that would be no problem.

Eastern Pennsylvania was right next door to Delaware. I planned on calling Nancy and Hannah that night to tell them about our plans. I felt nervous—I felt like I'd felt when I had first been going out with Nancy, and I would hesitate by the telephone before I'd call her for a date, because I'd be so afraid she'd say no.

Except now I was afraid she'd say no on Hannah's behalf. It wasn't going to happen, of course—how could she? But somewhere there was that fear: I'd call and say we were coming, and Nancy would say they were busy, and I'd ask to speak to Hannah about it, and Nancy would say that wasn't necessary, she was Hannah's mother and she made the decisions for Hannah.

I don't know where that came from. Nancy has never been like that. It's inside me somewhere, though. I was afraid we were going to go East and when we got there I wouldn't be allowed to see my daughter.

It was my turn to drive for the next few hours.

We were about to get into the car. Across the street there was a drugstore.

"I think I'm going to sit in the back seat and read," Ronnie said.

Then he said:

"Michael, you want to stop in that store and get me a *Sports Illustrated* and a *Business Week?*"

We were all standing outside the car; none of us had opened the doors yet. Michael hesitated only a fraction of a second; I don't think anyone else would have noticed it. But I did.

Then he crossed the street to buy Ronnie magazines.

We got the convertible in Wichita. Ronnie saw it; it was sitting in the lot of a National Car Rental place. A white Chrysler LeBaron with a red top.

We had the top down before we were out of the lot.

"This is pretty dumb," Michael said.

He had a point. The reason we'd been in the National lot in the first place was to return the car we'd rented in Dallas—the one that replaced the car with the shattered window. We'd be flying to Pennsylvania in the morning and we wouldn't need a car; the hotel had a courtesy van to the Wichita airport.

So Ronnie was turning in our Dallas car, and that's when he saw the white convertible, and within five minutes we were driving through the outskirts of Wichita with the top down.

"Had to do it," Ronnie said. "First convertible of the summer."

It was. It was the first convertible in which I'd ridden in years. And it was funny; a car is just a car, but being with Michael and Ronnie in a convertible felt different. We'd ridden in convertibles all the time when we were first driving—most of my summer memories from Bristol have a convertible figuring in somewhere—but at some point that stopped. Convertibles went away. I hadn't realized I'd missed them.

"You feel a little naked in this," Michael said. He was in the back seat, and his voice got lost in the wind. So he raised his volume: "You feel like everyone's looking at you."

A lot of people were. I didn't recall that convertibles used to be considered especially showy; they were nice and they were admired, but I don't think you used to feel garish for riding around in one. Tonight, though, in Wichita, we were drawing stares. It was almost as if we'd gone out on the streets with our shirts off.

Ronnie drove slowly through residential neighborhoods. If we were going to enjoy the night, highways were out of the question; anytime we drove over thirty miles per hour we couldn't hear each other.

Ronnie looked at the built-in tape deck. He found a commercial street and drove to a records-and-tapes outlet. He threw the car into park, left the motor running, went into the store, and emerged with a plastic sack. Back in the car he removed a tape and stuck it into the machine.

The Beatles' "From Me to You" blasted through the car, and wafted through the night air to the sidewalks bordering the street. I picked up the cassette box that had held the tape. It was a Beatles greatest hits collection.

Ronnie reached forward and turned the sound even higher. This was something; this was a time machine.

He took a hard left onto a wider street. We weren't going anywhere special; we were driving in our convertible. "From Me to You" was replaced by "She Loves You," which was followed by "Please Please Me."

"I did something pretty stupid when I was in college," Michael said from the back seat. "Actually, I hate to admit this, but I think it was right after college. There had been this Beatles concert at Shea Stadium . . ."

"It was televised," I said. "Not live, but televised."

"Right," Michael said. "And a couple of years later, there was this little ad in the back of *Rolling Stone* magazine saying that you could buy a live album of the concert. Today everybody would have videotaped the thing, but back then you saw the show and after it was over the music was gone."

"The album must have been a bootleg," I said. "There's no regular album of that concert."

"Wait," Michael said. "That's what I'm getting to. The ad said that the live album cost five bucks. So I sent a check for five bucks to some post office box. And about five weeks later I get a postcard back. It says that the Shea Stadium album is temporarily out of stock, but that they'll send me one as soon as the new ones come in. And it's signed by someone named Cinnamon."

"Cinnamon?" Ronnie said.

"Right," Michael said. "Cinnamon. Handwritten, no last name. I just felt so hip getting a card in the mail from someone named Cinnamon that I didn't complain or ask for my money back. I just kept waiting for the album. Never came. Never got my five dollars back."

"You think Cinnamon was screwing you over?" Ronnie said.

"That's the thing," Michael said. "If I'd gotten a form letter from some executive at a record warehouse saying the album was out of stock, I might have asked for a refund. You know, a typed letter on stationery signed by a guy with a first name and a middle initial and a last name. But this postcard from Cinnamon . . . I don't know, I'd seen the ad in *Rolling Stone* . . ."

"The old *Rolling Stone*," I said. "With the paper cover."

"Paper cover folded over two different ways," Michael said. "Anyway, I'd seen the ad in *Rolling Stone*, and I'd gotten the postcard from Cinnamon, and I kind of had this mental picture of Cinnamon, in her bell-bottoms and loose top and long hair, sitting in the warehouse, looking every day for my copy of the Shea Stadium album to come in, so she could send it to me the minute it arrived. I trusted old Cinnamon. Album never came."

"By sending you the postcard, they were probably fulfilling some postal regulation," Ronnie said. "Some mail-order legal requirement."

"Don't say that," Michael said.

"Cinnamon was probably some fifty-year-old shipping clerk named Sol," Ronnie said.

"Cut it out!" Michael said, laughing. "I'm still waiting for that album. Cinnamon's probably still there, refusing to quit until my album comes in."

On the tape deck, "A Hard Day's Night" began. It was loud in the open car and then dissipated quickly into the evening air.

"I always sort of thought that this would be the song they opened their concert with if they had a reunion," I said.

" 'A Hard Day's Night'?" Michael said. "Why?"

"It just seemed to me like the song they'd choose," I said. "It's not like it was their most famous song. But every time I'd think about a reunion concert, I'd envision the curtain going up, and the four of them standing there, all those years older than when we'd first seen them, and the crowd screaming and standing and crying, and the Beatles looking at each other, ready to start, and then John Lennon hitting the guitar and that one chord sounding and then the first words . . ."

"I'm glad that they never had a reunion," Michael said.

"Why?" Ronnie said. We were driving up a street we had already been on earlier, but it made no difference.

"Because everybody has reunions," Michael said. "Every band that ever had a hit gets together and does a reunion tour and makes a reunion album and does a reunion TV appearance. We didn't know it at the time, but one of the best things the Beatles ever did was to get out when they got out, and then never to perform together again. It was like they were here, and they were great, and then they went away and they never stepped on our memories."

"You really wouldn't have wanted to see them perform again?" Ronnie said.

"Oh, sure," Michael said. "If they'd done a reunion concert, I would have watched just like everyone else. On closed-circuit or on network TV or whatever. That's what makes it all the more impressive that they were smart enough never to do it. They must have known that if they'd done it even once, the memories of them would be altered forever. They wouldn't be those four kids who came along out of nowhere. If they'd had a reunion concert, the memory would have turned into four older men doing their old hits on a stage. It's better they never did it. The memory's purer."

We were stopped at a red light. This was a quiet neighborhood; the only other car on the street was a family Jeep stopped on the other side of the intersection.

"If you go by your theory, we shouldn't be here," I said to Michael.

I was turning toward the back seat so I could see him. "I guess we're a reunion, too, aren't we?"

"Yeah, but the Beatles shouldn't be like us," he said. "The Beatles knew that they should always be this perfect frozen moment in time. They shouldn't be like everyone else. They should just be out there, like Santa Claus. Out there and good."

I heard him say those words as we waited for the light to change. Whatever it was that had happened to us when we were young— whatever the events were that, in memory, were so important to us now—there were voices that had accompanied those memories. The voices, in close harmony, had been the voices of those four young men we'd never met. I knew I would be hearing and thinking about those voices for the rest of my life. Out there and good; Michael was right. Those four men, strangers to us, were always going to be out there and good.

The light turned green; Ronnie stepped on the accelerator and our car moved forward and we passed the Jeep coming the other way, inside of which we could see a mother and a father and three Wichita children, out for a drive on an August night. "Do you think that the people who just missed being around for the Beatles understand this at all?" Michael said.

"If they thought about it they would," I said. "We just missed James Dean, and we understand what that was all about. There's always someone who's a reference point to one huge generation of people, and the succeeding generation just misses him. Someone just missed Rudolph Valentino, and someone just missed Rudy Vallee . . ."

"Rudy Vallee?" Michael said. "Not the same thing."

"I bet he was for someone," I said. "Someone just missed him, and someone just missed Frank Sinatra, and we just missed James Dean, and someone just missed Elvis and the Beatles. Everyone just misses someone."

"I Should Have Known Better" had been playing on the car's tape deck, and it faded out and then there was the soft, insistent sound of a repetitive guitar chord, and as if having been instructed we fell silent. The evening had turned to full night, and there was just a touch of chill in the air, and the song we were hearing was "Things We Said Today."

It was never a huge hit; it was a song on a relatively minor Beatles album called *Something New*, released at the end of the summer of 1964. I don't know why "Things We Said Today" spoke to us so intensely; I suppose that is part of the magic of music—a song insinuates itself into your life, and becomes a part of you, and you never know exactly why.

That August of '64, cruising in other cars in another town, "Things We Said Today" narrated the last days of summer for us. The song was about realizing how much you have, even as you have it, and knowing that you're in the middle of precious times. Tonight we were together again, and those voices from all those summers ago sang to us in the night.

> You say you will love me,
> if I have to go.
> You'll be thinking of me,
> Somehow I will know . . .

Did we really understand back then? Did we even partially apprehend that the moments we were living through then would someday enrich our lives in ways so important that we would hardly be able to verbalize them?

Ronnie drove and none of us spoke.

> Me I'm just a lucky kind,
> Love to hear you say that love is luck . . .

Probably we couldn't have known; probably it was just a song. Even back then, though, even when we were just three friends on the threshold of a life we could barely imagine, that song had the ability to silence us. Even back then we would listen quietly as if someone were telling us something of consequence.

So tonight Ronnie drove on, down streets where children were growing up and people were sensing stirrings of romance and family secrets were forming. He drove down streets to which we'd never return, and we felt a little out in the open in that white convertible, three friends on a summer night. Hardly anyone else was out: a man and woman walking hand in hand, and on the other side of the street five kids laughing as they hurried somewhere on foot. In the car, from all those summers back, the voices sang.

> Someday when we're dreaming,
> Deep in love, not a lot to say,
> Then we will remember,
> Things we said today.

It ended, and a moment passed, and then Michael said:

"I hadn't realized it was such a short song."

Depends on how you measure, I thought. How long is a song? This one had been playing, in our heads and in our hearts, for almost thirty years.

Twenty-one

HANNAH WAS DUE in the morning.

We'd flown from Wichita to Philadelphia. Ronnie had a business associate who lives in Wilmington, Delaware, not too far south of Philadelphia, and he was away for the month of August. He'd offered to loan Ronnie his house. It turned out to be more like an estate.

We arrived around dinnertime. Three members of the household staff were waiting for us. The place looked like one of those mansions in a whiskey ad; enormous, gently rolling green expanses of yard in front and in back, a winding driveway leading up to the house from stone gates on a wooded road, a pool and a tennis court and—I don't know what else you'd call it—a veranda behind the house. It felt like something out of a United States Lawn Tennis Association brochure from the 1930s.

"Old money," Michael said as we drove into the roofed entryway by the front door.

"Not really," Ronnie said. "My friend's a liquidator. He closes out failing companies, marks the distressed merchandise way down and sells it to wholesalers. He bought this place in early '88 from a guy who took it in the throat when the stock market crashed."

"That's sweet," I said. "A real wholesome, inspirational success story."

Ronnie shrugged. "The guy who owned the house was hurting. My friend moved fast and got the place at about half of market value."

"That ought to be the official slogan for the new American business ethic," I said.

"If you don't like it here, you can always stay down the road at the Days Inn," Ronnie said, a little sharpness in his voice.

"No, I'm sure I'll like it here," I said.

Now I sat in a second-floor guest bedroom, looking out the leadedpaned window over the sloping back lawn. From Kansas I had reached Nancy at the beach house. At first she hadn't been sure how convenient it would be to bring Hannah to see me, but after some hesitation she'd said that tomorrow would be fine. She and Hannah would be driving up in the morning, and would return to the beach tomorrow night. The Delaware shore was only an hour or so away.

Marilyn Steele Hepps was on a plane from Cleveland, due to arrive at about midnight tonight. In the morning she and Ronnie would drive to their children's camp near Philadelphia, then bring their son and daughter here. They'd gotten permission from the camp; the official Parents Day was two days away, and they'd be taking the kids back for that.

From my window I could see Michael exploring the grounds. Tonight I didn't feel like going down and joining him. I thought I'd just read for a while, then turn in early. Hannah tomorrow. I was eager and I was fidgety and I was happy. Happy in advance. I wonder if she knows that? She's eight years old, and I wonder if she knows how happy I am just thinking about seeing her?

There was a breakfast table out on the stone patio, and that is where I found Ronnie and Marilyn a few minutes after eight o'clock the next morning. A maid was just bringing them a pot of coffee when I came out the double glass doors in back of the house.

"Marilyn," I said.

"Well, look at you," she said.

The last time I had seen her was in Cleveland, when I'd had dinner at their house and had tried to explain what this summer trip of ours was going to be about. That was in early June; not so very long ago. Yet as I saw her and Ronnie sitting next to each other at the breakfast table, my first instinct was that this was like one of those visual quizzes in old puzzle books: What's Wrong with This Picture?

Maybe it was just that we had been on the road for so many weeks; maybe it was the recent memory of Ronnie with Gail. But as Ronnie spread some jam on a piece of toast and Marilyn half rose out of her chair to kiss me on the cheek, I had this sudden impression that there was no connection between them. I felt as if I were looking at two people who happened to be sitting next to each other on a bus.

"You were asleep when I got in last night," she said. "We sat and talked down in the living room with Michael, but we didn't want to wake you."

"So your flight was on time then?" I said.

"It was actually a little early, if you can believe that," Ronnie said. "Michael went out to the airport with me to meet her."

It's hard to define exactly how Ronnie seemed—a little stiff, a little restrained. I don't think, back at the beginning of the summer, I would have noticed it. But the Ronnie at the breakfast table this morning was just a few degrees tighter than the man I'd been spending every day and every night with. I'd say something and he'd hesitate before answering. I didn't get the impression that it was because of any guardedness over having been with Gail. At least that wasn't the bulk of it. Whatever I was sensing in Ronnie was much more than that. Having Marilyn there, he was behaving almost as if there was a stranger at the table. Not someone he didn't like; just a stranger.

I knew that if I was going to learn anything about what was going on, it wasn't going to be now. The glass doors from the house opened again, and Michael came walking out.

"Good morning," he said. "Marilyn, I'm surprised you're up so early. That was a pretty late night last night."

"I can never sleep well in a strange bed," she said.

Ronnie was reading the sports section. "So when you guys have some time," Marilyn said, "I want you to tell me all about your summer."

"I'm not sure where we'd even start," Michael said.

I heard her before I saw her.

"This is so cool!" Hannah's voice said.

I'd been waiting in the backyard; Nancy had said they'd be arriving around 10 A.M. So I had breakfast and read the newspaper that Ronnie left behind. He and Marilyn had departed for camp, and I didn't expect to see them again until midafternoon.

And then there was her voice. I turned in the direction it was coming from. In red shorts and a turquoise T-shirt she came running around the corner of the house.

"Daddy, look at this place!" she said.

I couldn't help smiling at that. I guess she was glad enough to see me, but I ranked second to the setting. Which was how it should be, I supposed. A dad should be a constant, something solid in the background, something for all the new people and places to move past as he remains a steady presence. I was nowhere near as constant as the ideal dad ought to be. I wished I was; I wished every day of my life I was. When a daughter sees something that amazes her or pleases her, though, she should be sure enough of her dad that she can exult over the amazing, pleasing thing and be confident that her dad isn't jealous of the attention—and by that measure, we seemed to be doing all right, at least for the moment.

"Daddy, who lives in this place?" Hannah called from the edge of the grass.

"I'm not really sure, to tell you the truth," I said.

Nancy had come around the corner of the house right after Hannah. As she heard me say those words, she rolled her eyes.

"Well, I'm *not* sure," I said to her. "Some friends of Ronnie's. How are you?"

"I'm fine," Nancy said. "The roads were a little crowded." She was as genuinely pleasant as always and she looked as pretty as always. And as always after I haven't seen her in a while, I thought to myself: How odd. I was married to this person and now I'm not. I used to see her face next to mine the first thing after I opened my eyes each morning.

Or I did on those mornings when I was home. "Hey, Daddy!" Hannah called. "Watch how good I've gotten!" She sprinted out into the yard, ran down the slope of the lawn, and did three cartwheels in a row, one turning right into the other.

"Where'd you learn that?" I called.

"I've been practicing," she shouted to me. "Watch again!"

She stood straight up, raised her arms above her head like a ballerina, and started her running approach again. "Be careful," I heard myself calling.

"Ben, she's careful," Nancy said. "I watch her. She does this every day."

"I'm sorry," I said. "Old habit."

I'd always been protective of her; when she was a baby and was learning to walk, I would follow one step behind her, all around the house, my hands ready to catch her should she stumble. On the days and nights when I was home, that is. I guess you really shouldn't be allowed to consider yourself protective when you're there only when your schedule permits; there's something inherently contradictory about that.

"Did you see?" Hannah called from down the slope.

"Great!" I yelled to her. "Come on up and say hello!"

"I'll be right there," she called. "Watch me do more!"

She was running up the hill toward me, her hair blowing behind her, and I could see her glad eyes. Right before she got to me she launched into another cartwheel, and I fought the urge to caution her, and she flipped twice, legs over hands, until she ended up right next to me.

"Cool, huh?" she said, out of breath.

"Cool," I said, meaning: I love you.

She skipped instead of walking; I think, when I look back on that day, the skipping is what I'll remember. It was just so filled with joy, and I don't think she was even aware she was doing it.

I first noticed it when we were walking across the back lawn to the tennis court. I held her hand, and she was telling me about her summer, and I looked down at her and I saw that she was skipping across the grass. It wasn't very pronounced; it was just a little jump in her step, almost like an imitation of a pony, or a cartoon pony. It was a sign that she was still very much a kid, and not yet conscious of the ponderous, somber carriage that most men and women adopt once they realize people are watching. Hannah didn't care; even when she saw I was looking she just grinned and tugged at my arm so that I would walk faster.

The stories she told me, too, were altogether absent of that self-editing that we all learn to do—the self-editing that is intended to remove all the enthusiasm, all the wonder from our voices. We edit ourselves once we realize that people may judge us harshly for being too unsophisticated; we edit ourselves once we understand that to appear jaded is to tell others that we are worldly, that we have seen things.

Hannah had seen things, all right. She was brimming over with news. "Dad?" she said. "I have this friend Jenny?" I'd noticed that once in a while she was falling into that cadence eight-year-old girls often reflexively use when they're telling stories to each other; the unseen question mark after each phrase. I liked hearing it.

"Do I know Jenny?" I said.

"No no no," she said, the words repeated in rapid succession, a new verbal habit I knew without asking she'd picked up from friends during the summer. "Jenny's mom and dad have a house near ours." Ours. Meaning Nancy's beach house.

"So Jenny's mom and dad have this attic? And they've made it into a bedroom for Jenny and her brother? And we can climb up into it on a ladder, and there's a window in this wall where we can look right down into their living room!"

"So it's more like a balcony than an attic," I said.

"No no no," she said. "It's an attic. But it only goes halfway across the top of their house. So we can look out the window. We throw pillows down into their living room!"

So soon, I thought, she'd feel no need to tell that kind of story. She was going to meet a lot of people and go to a lot of houses in her life; soon enough each house would just be another house. She wouldn't think to notice. She wouldn't bother to tell anyone. I felt something in my throat, and I looked at her skipping along next to me, and I said, "What other things do they have in her house?"

"Well," Hannah said, "they have this really cool couch in their living room? That turns into a bed when they have people stay over? And Jenny's grandmother was there one week, so they let her grandma sleep up in the attic with Jenny's brother, and Jenny got to sleep on the foldout couch."

"Did Jenny like that?" I said, wanting to listen to her voice all day.

"Of course!" Hannah said. "And then when her grandma left . . ."

Nancy was walking behind us. I turned around and caught her eye. She smiled and made an exaggerated motion with her arms pumping up and down and her mouth open, like it was an exertion to try to catch up with us. Moments like that, I always wonder how we managed to screw things up so badly between us; moments like that I always wonder whether it's totally beyond repair.

"Can we play on that court, Daddy?" Hannah said.

"Well, we don't have rackets," I said. "Let's see if they've got anything there."

We stepped onto the hard, hot green surface of the tennis court. No rackets were in sight, but some balls were caught between the sides of the court surface and the green chain-link fence.

"Go to the net on the other side of the court," I said to Hannah.

She skipped over there. "That's right," I said. "Okay. Now come up right to where I am."

We met at the net. "I'm going to throw the ball to you," I said. "If you catch it, we both take one step back on our side of the court. Then you throw it to me. If I catch it we each take another step back. We keep going, moving back a step each time one of us catches it."

I tossed her the ball. "Good," I said. "Now a step back."

We kept moving away from each other and from the net after each successful catch. When she'd miss one I would say, in an announcer's voice: "The referee has ruled that Mr. Kroeger's throw to Miss Kroeger was bad. Miss Kroeger will be given an additional chance." And, as she was waiting for the long throws: "The crowd is cheering, an international television audience is watching, some pigs in a pen next to the court are snorting at Miss Kroeger . . ."

"Daddy, what pigs?" Hannah called to me.

"Miss Kroeger apparently does not see the pigs," I said in the announcer's voice. "Apparently she does not know about the famous invisible pigs, so much a part of the tradition of this wonderful game . . ."

Hannah bent over, laughing and saying, "Daddy, I'm trying to concentrate!" and I saw Nancy looking at us, but I couldn't read her expression.

We played the game for about half an hour—"The pigs are snorting so loud, they're drowning out the crowd, and if Miss Kroeger can catch this ball she's the champion"—and then we went up to the house to get ready for lunch.

Hannah was running across the grass ahead of us. I walked next to Nancy.

"I hope I didn't take you away from anything you needed to do today," I said.

"No, Hannah really wanted to come," she said. "This is fine."

"You're sure you have to go back tonight?" I said. "There are plenty of rooms here."

We walked together. She said, "We really do need to get going tonight, Ben."

"But you can stay for dinner?" I said.

"Yes, I've told Hannah we're having dinner here," she said.

"This is one of the best days I've had all summer, and it's not even noon yet," I said, trudging across the lawn. "Maybe when Ronnie and Marilyn and their kids get back, you and I can find some place to just sit and talk for a while."

She didn't answer, so I said, "I'd like that."

"Look, Hannah's going right into the house," Nancy said. Then she called, "Hannah! Wait for us!"

"It's all right," I said. "The house is ours for the next couple of days. We have free run of it."

"She just shouldn't be walking into a house where she's never been," Nancy said.

So Hannah waited and we caught up with her. About half an hour later, when lunch was almost ready, I heard her voice singing from the den of the house.

I looked in. She was sitting on the floor, and she was singing a song she must have learned from her friends during the summer. It was one of those songs that are meant to be sung in rounds, each person starting a verse a few beats after the person before. The song was about a frog. I stood in the door, listening:

> Froggie on the rock so small and green,
> Happiest frog you've ever seen . . .

She didn't know I was there. Her back was to me. She was singing away, her voice doing its best to stay in tune.

> Along comes another frog, oh so big,
> First little froggie jumps on a twig . . .

I could tell she was reading something. I looked; it was a copy of *Seventeen* magazine. Whoever lived in the house must have been a subscriber. I remembered that younger girls often read *Seventeen*; the name of the magazine, or so I had been told, was kind of a subliminal lure to girls who weren't yet seventeen. It made them feel older to read it.

I saw my daughter sitting there reading the magazine filled with fashion tips and bathing suit ads and advice on how to deal with boys; her back was still toward me, and she still wasn't aware of my presence, and as she read *Seventeen* she continued with her little girl's song.

> Little froggie lands on a lily pad,
> Big froggie follows, oh so mad . . .

I walked away quietly, not wanting to disturb the moment. There were people in the dining room, just about ready to sit down at the table, but I waited before going in because I didn't want anyone to see my eyes.

Ronnie and Marilyn and their children arrived back from camp, and in the afternoon we went swimming. Actually, only the kids went in the water. The rest of us kept an eye on them from chairs on the pool deck.

After everyone had had enough sun, we all gathered in the living room of the house. There was ice cream and lemonade for the kids, and we sat around talking. A big color TV set was on.

Ronnie had the channel changer in his hand. He zapped around, looking for something he liked, and an image of Mick Jagger appeared on the screen. The show was a taped concert; the audience reaction shots indicated that the concert had been held in Japan.

Ronnie put the zapper down. Jagger and the rest of the Rolling Stones moved across the Tokyo stage, singing "Start Me Up" and "Jumping Jack Flash" and "Satisfaction." I imagined it must have been quite a payday for the band.

"Okay, Dad, enough," Ronnie's son said.

"What?" Ronnie said.

"Turn to something else," his son said.

"I don't want to," Ronnie said.

Hannah, too shy to challenge Ronnie directly, looked at me and said, "Can we watch Nickelodeon?"

Michael was laughing out loud. "Too much," he said. "When we were kids our parents used to try to make us turn the Rolling Stones off when they were on TV. And now our kids are trying to make us turn the Rolling Stones off."

"Come on, Dad," Ronnie's son said.

Ronnie's little daughter had been sitting close to the TV, staring at the electronic image of Jagger as if she was trying to figure something out. Finally she turned to her father and said, "I think I've seen that man somewhere."

"Really, Jody?" he said. "Where did you see the man?"

She looked at Jagger some more. Finally she said:

"At a birthday party?"

Marilyn said, "You saw that man at a birthday party, sweetie?"

"I think so," the girl said, becoming a little quiet as she sensed that everyone was looking at her.

"Whose birthday party?" Marilyn said.

"I think it was Elizabeth's," Jody said.

"What was the man doing at the birthday party?" Ronnie said.

"Making balloon animals," Jody said, looking again at Jagger with the stage makeup on his face and the outlandish costume. "And doing magic tricks."

Very late in the day, when we were deciding what to do about dinner, Hannah was running in the backyard with Ronnie's son and daughter. It was one of those rare hours of one of those uncommon days when you think nature has granted you a miracle: the sun was just far enough down that its harshness was abated, and the soft light it cast over the setting made the children seem backlit. The beauty of the moment just about turned you weak.

"There's a video camera in the house," Ronnie said. "Someone get it quick."

There it was: the immediate notion to reach for a video camera anytime a pleasurable minute seems imminent. That notion is threatening to change everything. Within a period of a few years, video cameras have gone from being novelties, to useful tools, to something quite different: They have become a replacement for memories themselves.

Not capturers of memories; substitutes for memories. I have been to so many gatherings—anniversaries, retirement parties—where the entire course of the afternoon or evening is organized around the video camera. At least in the days of home movies, you had to wait a week or two for the film to be processed, and then every time you showed it you had to spool it through the sprockets on the projector; the inconvenience of home movies provided a necessary, paradoxically welcome distance between them and the events they recorded.

Now the videotape is the memory. Whatever difference there is between the tape and the moment has been entirely and inexorably blurred. When there is a gathering of friends and family, and a video camera is present, nothing that happens when the camera is turned off is considered to have really occurred. The gathering is the videotape;

the videotape is the gathering. I attended one fiftieth wedding anniversary at which the speeches were made, the songs were sung—and then everyone hurried to the closest TV set with a VCR attached, where the tape was popped into the machine and forty people gathered around to watch. As the anniversary couple held hands on the TV screen, a grown niece called out: "Oh, do you remember that?"

Remember it? It had happened twenty minutes before.

So on this gorgeous late afternoon I watched Hannah racing with Ronnie's children on the lawn, and her peals of laughter and the sight of her scrambling down the gentle hill that led to the woods were a gift from God, and Marilyn Hepps emerged from the house with the camcorder and I said, "Why don't we just enjoy this and not take pictures."

"You don't want me to make a tape?" Marilyn said, honestly puzzled.

"No," I said, my voice sounding quiet to me. "Can we just remember this?"

"But that's what the tape is for," Marilyn said. "It makes it easier to remember."

Hannah was doing one of her cartwheels, her hair golden in the lovely light, her form splendid and limber against the line of the trees, a little girl growing up.

"I can remember this," I said, looking at my daughter.

There was a place called Jitterbug's; it was a takeoff on an old fifties drive-in, and Ronnie thought the kids would enjoy it. It was just ten minutes down the road, Ronnie said, and that's where we were planning to have our dinner.

We were all going to go to our rooms to clean up and to change, and as we entered the house Marilyn said to Ronnie, "Weren't we supposed to cover the pool at the end of the day?"

"Oh, that's right," he said. "I promised them we'd do that."

In front of all of us he called: "Michael? The canvas has to go over the pool."

In the bedroom where I was staying I put on a fresh shirt for dinner. I could see the pool from the window. There was Michael, a figure by himself in the distance, closing the pool for the day. I was far enough away that I could not see his face.

"What a cutie."

The waitress was looking right at Gary, Ronnie's son. She was wearing roller skates and snapping her bubble gum, which appeared to be part of the planned atmosphere of the place. I always assume that there's a bound computer printout back in the kitchen of establishments like this, officially instructing the waiters and waitresses what to do: blow bubbles at least once a minute, address all customers as "honey" (for waitresses), run your comb through your hair as you take orders (for waiters) . . .

Somewhere there must be a software program that verifies a projected profit margin for all fifties drive-in knockoffs if enough of the suggested criteria are met enough of the time; I envisioned a planning committee in Hart, Schaffner and Marx suits sitting around a boardroom table and discussing the relative merits of metal malt canisters vs. plastic ketchup and mustard squeeze bottles: "Are the canisters really necessary? They're much less cost-effective than the squeeze bottles, and they're prohibitively labor-intensive if we have to make the milk shakes one at a time." "Granted—but if you have the squeeze bottles without the canisters, you're running a potential risk. There was a study done at Princeton that established beyond any doubt that each period utensil eliminated contributes to a dramatic downward curve in net income per store, leading to diminished returns that override the savings accrued through elimination of the malt canisters. Gentlemen, if you will examine the spreadsheets we have distributed to you . . ."

"How old are you, cutie?" the waitress said, a pink bubble forming through her lips.

"Tell her, Gary," Marilyn Hepps said.

The boy looked down at his paper place mat.

"Go ahead," Marilyn said.

"I'm ten," he said, eyes averted.

"Look at those eyes," the waitress said. "Those eyes are going to break a million hearts!"

"What do you say, Gary?" Marilyn said.

"Your eyes are making me swoon!" the waitress said, as I tried to imagine the guideline in the printout: "Flirtation is encouraged, but our studies show that in terms of tip ratio per customer, such flirtation is most revenue-generative when directed at children of the primary patron; every index corroborates that the primary patron, especially when he/she is the parent of the child at whom the flirtation is directed, is actually more likely to reward the server with a gratuity in recognition of the flirtation toward the child than for an equivalent flirtation toward the parent himself/herself, this being ascribed to a positive regenerative projection/identification on the part of parents aged thirty-plus with the child in question . . ."

Ronnie excused himself to go to the men's room; I followed a few seconds later. The waitress' gambit seemed to have worked; standing in front of the mirror, Ronnie said to me: "This is goofy, Ben, but I was really liking it when the waitress was telling Gary he was cute. I mean, I was getting as much of a kick out of it as if she'd been telling me I was cute."

"What are you doing to Michael?" I said.

"Michael?" he said, turning to face me.

"What's this about?" I said. "The thing with going to fetch the magazines in Kansas day before yesterday. The thing with closing the pool today. What are you doing?"

"I'm not doing anything," he said. "The pool today, he was the only one of us who didn't have his family with him. The magazines, I didn't think he'd mind."

"It's rotten," I said. "It stinks, and you ought to stop it."

"What are you getting at?" Ronnie said. "You're losing me."

"You know exactly what I'm getting at," I said. "You offer him a job, you offer to change his life, and all of a sudden you're ordering him around. You're treating him like a servant. Stop doing it."

"Number one, you're reading too much into it," he said. "And number two, please don't tell me what to do."

"I'm not reading anything into it," I said.

"Michael can say no," Ronnie said.

"You've been paying Michael's bills all summer," I said. "He's not going to say no to you. You'd better think about it. This is not some guy who brings your car around in the morning. This is your friend. Don't do this."

"I think you're overreacting . . . ," he started to say.

But I was already on my way out of the men's room.

I was sitting at the table with the others by the time Ronnie got back.

"Hey, Dad," his daughter Jody said to him, pointing to the pocket of her blouse. "The waitress gave me a hot-dog pin!"

"That's good, sweetie," Ronnie said, not looking at me, not looking at Michael.

The sun sets late at this time of year. We finished dinner and drove back to the estate, and even after eight o'clock there was still light, and only hints of evening.

The children ran footraces in the backyard, starting at the veranda (they checked to make sure that at least one foot was touching the stone deck, so that no one would get a jump on anyone else), ending down past the tennis court.

"Makes me a little homesick," Michael said. Looking at the children, he was thinking of his girls. That gave me an idea, but I decided to hold it until the morning.

"You know, when my grandfather was dying, he asked to see me," Michael said. "I was really a little kid at the time—I can barely remember this. But my parents took me into his room. It was very dark. And he held my hand—I remember he had this small, bony hand, but he held my hand hard—and he said, 'I want you to think about going into the field of electronics. Will you promise me you'll think about that?' "

"Electronics?" I said.

"I don't think I even knew what electronics were," Michael said. "Later, after my grandfather was dead, my father said that they'd talked about it right before my grandfather asked to see me. I guess my grandfather was convinced that electronics were the wave of the future, and that I'd be on the gravy train if I studied electronics."

Down by the tennis court, the children touched a pole, turned around, and began the second leg of their race, up toward us.

"You know what I think it is?" Michael said. "I think maybe when you're getting ready to die, it must occur to you that after you're gone you can't tell anybody anything again. Think about it. You go through your life making all these decisions and taking all these responsibilities, and then they're all gone. Maybe at the end you want to suggest something to someone you love because you know if you don't say it, it's never going to get said."

"Did he tell you that he loved you when you were in his room?" I said.

"No," Michael said. "Or if he did, I don't remember it. All I remember is him holding my hand and telling me the future was in electronics, and that I should study so that I could get a good job."

"Maybe that was his way of telling you he loved you," I said. "Worrying about your future, and hoping it was a good one."

The children were screeching and puffing as they approached the finish line. The race was neck and neck.

"Do you think we'll ever do that?" Ronnie said. "Be grandfathers on our deathbeds, making suggestions to our grandchildren about what to do with their lives?"

"I don't know," I said. "It's a hard thing to picture, isn't it?"

"I think he thought about himself being gone, and he was worried that no one would tell me what good things I could do," Michael said.

With dusk finally driving out the last of the light, I saw that Nancy had walked away from the others on the veranda, and was sitting on the grass over by a corner of the house. I joined her.

"Can I sit with you?" I said.

"Be my guest," she said, nodding to the piece of lawn next to her. So stilted and stiff; once we could have guessed each other's next words, every day.

"Hannah seems like she's doing great," I said.

"It's been a very good summer for her," Nancy said. "I think it's good that she's been away from Washington. Living at the shore has shown her there are other ways of life out there."

"Does she miss her friends?" I said.

"Some of them have come to visit on weekends," Nancy said. "She's made a lot of new friends at the beach."

"She told me about the girl with the house with the attic," I said. Trying to prove that I'd been listening to Hannah's stories; trying to demonstrate that I could catch up fast, that I was a quick study. I endeavored to come up with the name.

"Jenny," Nancy said.

"Right," I said. "Jenny."

Now the children were playing ring-around-the-rosy. I didn't want this to stop. "You're sure there's no way at all you and Hannah can spend the night?" I said.

"We really can't," Nancy said. "I told you—we have to get back."

"It's just that this is so nice," I said. "Look at them having so much fun. This is the way people should live all the time."

Nancy let out a breath. "You couldn't live like this for a week," she said. "By tomorrow you'd be thinking that you'd seen the kids do the very same things today, and by the next day you'd be making excuses for having to go somewhere."

I didn't want to fight. "I'm not so sure," I said to her. "A day like today is pretty hard to beat."

"This summer is perfect for you," she said. "Tomorrow you'll get in the car with your friends, and by midnight tomorrow night you'll be sleeping in another town, and the next day you'll be somewhere else. You'd like it if your whole life could be that way. Go somewhere new every day. Pretend that the day before didn't happen, and the people didn't exist."

I probably could have thought of a more flattering way for her to put it, given the chance. What I said was, "I'm just saying that today has been terrific, Nancy, and I wish it could last longer."

She said nothing for a few seconds and then she said, "I'm getting married, Ben."

Oh. Let a mountain collapse on top of you, let every assumption you have be proved a lie, let every secret hope be stepped on, but don't show anything. Don't show that you feel anything; don't even show that you're surprised. Seems to have been my irreparable credo since I was a kid, and the funny thing is, I don't even know where it came from.

"When?" I said.

"Sometime this fall," she said. "Sometime before Christmas."

Don't show anything; don't betray a sign. Whatever's hurting, keep it hidden. Save it until you're alone.

"Do I know him?" I said.

"No," she said. "He lives in Boston. He's a physician. A pediatrician."

"How did you meet him?" I said.

"I have a life, Ben," she said. "I met him."

"This summer?" I said.

"No," she said. "I've known him for a while."

"Does Hannah know him?" I said, wanting to change the words even before they'd left my mouth. "I mean, obviously she knows him, but do they get along all right?" I said, feeling sick.

"She likes him," Nancy said. "You'll always be her dad, but she really does like him."

You'll always be her dad. Like an upbeat chapter in some best-selling guidebook to no-fault contemporary divorce. I wanted to hide. I wanted to scream.

"You say his practice is in Boston?" I said.

"Yes," she said.

Then:

"We'll probably be moving there."

We. Moving.

Don't let anything out; don't let anything show. Not that it ever worked that well for you.

"Well, I guess I ought to say congratulations, but I have to admit that would sound pretty strange," I said.

"I asked Hannah not to say anything to you until I told you," Nancy said. "She didn't, did she?"

"She didn't say a word," I said, seeing her playing ring-around-the-rosy across the way, all fall down.

There were lightning bugs in the night.

"I don't know when the last time was that I saw those," I said.

I was standing with Michael. After my talk with Nancy, she had gone back to join Ronnie and Marilyn; now Michael and I watched the children with their glass jelly jars, running after the fireflies. Full night was here.

"There must be lightning bugs where you live," Michael said.

"I'm sure there are," I said. "I just haven't noticed, I guess."

Maybe it's because lightning bugs are essentially a children's diversion; when you're a kid lightning bugs are part of summer, they're a nightly signal that it's almost time for you to go to bed. It's funny—

Michael was probably right. Of course there must be lightning bugs outside the house where I live in Bethesda. I just don't recall having seen them.

"There's one!" Gary Hepps called, out on the lawn. He and his sister chased the flickering light in the darkness; Hannah, a little hesitantly—or so I imagined—followed them, her own jelly jar in her hand.

"Look how many there are," Michael said.

Like tiny beacons, the lightning bugs beckoned for a moment, then lost their illumination, then beckoned anew from a different patch of the air. "We used to fill whole jars with them," Michael said. "I don't think we even considered that they were living things."

I still didn't know why Ronnie had been treating Michael the way he had. Was he testing him? Checking him out to see whether he was malleable enough to heed prosaic directions? If so, it was a needless exercise; if Michael were to accept Ronnie's job, it would be with a full understanding that now Ronnie was his employer and superior. We all knew that.

But if there was a bullying imperative inside of Ronnie that compelled him to belittle even Michael—then the question became much more baleful.

"I got one!" Jody Hepps cried from the lawn. Her hand was over the mouth of her jar. "I got one in here!"

I thought about Michael; I thought about me. Often I have wondered what would have happened to me had I never left Bristol. There was something about the town, when I was a boy, that whispered to me that I must get out. As much as I loved the town, I comprehended even then that if you grew up there, you would never be acknowledged as having accomplished anything if the things you achieved were all achieved in Bristol. It was a perverse equation; when you are young the people you want most to respect and admire you are the people in your town, yet you find out that the only way they will truly hold you in esteem is if you leave.

The three children came running up the lawn, shouting about Jody Hepps' lightning bug. They showed the jar to Ronnie and Marilyn and Nancy; Michael and I walked over to look.

"Does he have a name?" Marilyn said to Jody.

"Mathroy," Jody said.

"Your lightning bug's name is Mathroy?" Ronnie said. "I never heard of that name."

"I just made it up," Jody said.

"There's another one!" Hannah yelled. She ran down the slope, following the light, and then she shouted out in triumph as she ran back to us, a firefly in her jar now.

Thirty or forty seconds passed.

"He won't light up," Hannah said.

She waited some more.

"He still won't," she said.

"They must not like it in captivity," Nancy said to her. "They must not be able to light up in the jar."

I knew the feeling, I wanted to say; I knew how hard it was to light up when you're trapped in the jar. Your only chance to light up is once you have escaped. But what I said to Hannah was, "Maybe you should let him go."

She removed her hand from over the top of the jar. The firefly fluttered out, darting back toward the woods, and as it flew it lit brightly.

"He's saying thank you," I said to Hannah. "He's making his light go on to say thank you for letting him go."

"But look at Mathroy!" Jody said. "Mathroy's in my jar, and he's lighting up!"

The firefly in Jody's jar was, indeed; every second or two its whole body would glow in that jar.

"See!" Jody said. "He's doing it again!"

"I guess some of them can do it," Marilyn said. "I guess some of them are able to light up in captivity after all."

I looked over at Michael. That's you, my first friend; that's you, lighting up after all, against all odds lighting up and making everything around you bright. You'll never know just how much I admire you. You'll never know how much I like the person you turned out to be, and how much in so many ways I wish I could be like you.

Hannah put her hand on Jody's arm.

"Jody?" she said. "Could you let Mathroy go?"

"Let him go?" Jody said.

"Could you?" Hannah said. "I think he'd be happier."

"But he's lighting up," Jody said.

"I just think he'd be happier if you let him go," Hannah said.

Jody gave an exaggerated sigh, then abruptly turned the jar upside down. It took the firefly a few moments to figure out what to do. But then it soared downward, out of the jar, and once in the open air shifted its direction and sailed away from us, joining all the others pulsing with nature's innocent fire in the darkness.

The children waved goodbye.

"Bye, Mathroy," Hannah called.

"Bye, Mathroy," Jody and Gary called.

"Do lightning bugs make a noise, Daddy?" Hannah said to me.

"They don't really have to," I said. "They're so beautiful, they don't have to do anything but light up the night."

She was falling asleep when Nancy led her by the hand to the car.

"It's been a long day for you, hasn't it?" I said.

Hannah nodded.

"You can sleep on the way back home," I said, that last word sounding all wrong.

Her eyes were closed tight by the time Nancy got done fastening her seat belt around her.

"Drive safely," I said to Nancy, of all the things to say.

I looked through the open passenger-side window at my sleeping daughter. I wished her summers of joy, and friends to cherish all her life, and I thanked God for her, and she didn't stir, she was sound asleep. On the seat next to her was her lightning bug jar, empty, the firefly she had given its freedom now fluttering through the night somewhere beyond the house. I had this urge to tell Nancy that I'd ride a few blocks with them and then walk back, but I knew that would make no sense. So I watched as they drove off and when the red taillights had vanished down the road I was alone.

Twenty-two

"HEY, SCOTTIE!" Gary Hepps called. He was scrambling out of Ronnie's rental car even before we had come to a full stop, and was dashing away from his parents to join one of his friends across the campgrounds.

"It's nice to be needed," Marilyn said.

This was early the next morning. Ronnie and Marilyn were going to spend Parents Day at the camp; Michael and I had ridden up with them. Later, after the special events of the day were finished and the kids had returned to their cabins, Marilyn would be flying back to Cleveland.

But we were going to Bristol. I'd thought about it, and I'd figured that we owed it to Michael. At least for one day; at least so he could see Ellen and the girls. Ronnie hadn't had any objection.

Now, though, on the campgrounds in the morning, we stood on grass damp from the overnight dew, beneath an unclouded sun that felt like it was going to be sending down ninety-degree heat by noon. All around us were boys and girls in identical purple shorts and white T-shirts with the camp's logo—a purple, winged eagle—printed on the front.

"That's a real campy, outdoorsy touch," I said to Ronnie, nodding toward the lit cigar that was in his mouth.

He grunted. He didn't seem enamored of being up this early, and of being surrounded by screaming children.

"Maybe you can hire one of the campers to carry an ashtray around for you," I said. "Do your bit for the environment. Keep your ashes off the grass."

"Spare me," he said. "This is going to be a long day."

Marilyn was walking Jody over to where her counselor was waiting. "Come on, Ronnie," she called back to him. "We're supposed to have breakfast in the lodge."

"Maybe they have room service," I said to Ronnie.

"I don't have a room," he said.

"There's a cellular phone in the rental car," I said. "Just have them bring your food to the front seat."

"Very funny," he said, and then followed Marilyn's retreating figure through the sea of purple and white.

In Michael's den in Bristol, his daughters fought for space on his lap as he told them stories about the summer. We had arrived in the middle of the evening, after flying from Philadelphia, and Ellen and the girls had waited up.

"Dad, did you go to any more Chicago Cubs games?" Leslie said.

"We haven't been back to Chicago," he said to her. "We just went that one night."

Hearing him say that, it already seemed like a long time ago. Laura, his other daughter, balanced herself on one of his knees and said, "Were there horses at the camp you saw this morning?"

"I didn't notice any horses," Michael said. "Ronnie, do they have stables there?"

"I think down the road," Ronnie said. He and I were sitting on a pair of chairs across the room. "I don't think there are stables on the campgrounds."

"Kelsey and Barb are away at camp," Leslie said to Michael. "Their camp's in Maine. They sent me a postcard."

It didn't need explaining; Kelsey and Barb had to be two of her friends. "Can we go away to camp next year?" Laura said.

Ellen, sitting next to Michael and holding his hand, spoke to their daughters before he could: "Next summer is a long time away," she said.

Michael had seemed almost to blossom when we walked into his house; when he first caught sight of Ellen and the girls the kind of look came onto his face that you used to find on the front of corny old greeting cards depicting a boy coming down the stairs on Christmas morning. Watching him together with them here, I couldn't help but feel I was seeing people who were exactly where they were meant to be, in the company of exactly who they were meant to be with. I'd seen a lot of things over the summer, but most of them had to do with moving through places and moving on. This was different; this was something abiding and firm, and maybe it was just because I was tired after a long day, but I felt privileged to be here.

Ellen told the girls that it was past their bedtime, but she didn't seem to mean it, there was a tone in her voice that was asking to be challenged, and when the girls did challenge it she and Michael said, well, all right, this was a special night. They could stay up.

So we all sat around together, Michael looking anchored on that couch, and we talked until past midnight. At one point Ellen brought up a controversy about four-way stop signs that apparently were supposed to be installed on their corner; from Michael's reaction I could tell that this was something they had discussed over the phone during the course of the summer.

"I thought you said that had been overruled," Michael said, sounding annoyed.

"I thought it was," Ellen said. "Now they're saying the signs are going up at the end of next week."

"That's just no good," Michael said.

"You don't want stop signs here?" Ronnie said to him. "What's the difference?"

"If they put four-way signs up, that means there'll be cars backed up in front of the house all the time," Michael said. "We're going to constantly have people stopped in front of our yard."

"At least it sounds like you won't have any speeders on the street," I said. "If they have to stop."

"That's what the city of Bristol is saying," Ellen said. "They're saying it's for safety reasons. But people don't speed on this street anyway—there's a stop sign one street back and another sign one street up. You don't need a four-way stop here."

I could tell it was important to her. If I'd heard of this dilemma when I was five hundred miles away, I might have dismissed it as trifling— compared to a lot of the world's problems, this one didn't sound too burdensome. But here on Michael's quiet street on this noiseless summer night, I could understand why it mattered. Michael's house was just a few feet from the corner. With a four-way stop, especially during busy times of the day, it would seem as if Michael's family always had visitors—strangers parked temporarily at their doorstep.

"So when did the city change its mind?" Michael said.

"It was in the Bristol *News* this week," Ellen said. "The mayor overruled the streets and parks committee. They're supposed to vote on it at the town council meeting tomorrow night."

"What time?" Michael said.

"The same time as always," Ellen said. "Seven o'clock."

Michael seemed to consider something, and then to make a decision. Laura tugged on his neck and said, "Dad, can you find out who my teacher's going to be next year?"

"Hey, you know I can't do that," he said. "You find out on the first day of school."

"But you're a teacher," she said. "I know you can find out."

"I'm in the high school, not the elementary school," he said. "And even if I could find out, I wouldn't. That wouldn't be fair to the other boys and girls—for you to know and them not to know."

"But, Daddy . . . ," she said.

"You wouldn't want me to break the rules," he said. "And besides, you don't have that long to wait. It's not really 'next year' you're talking about, is it? School starts in just a few weeks."

Which I knew, of course; I guess I just didn't want to think about it. Ellen insisted that Ronnie and I stay with them, and although we'd made reservations at the Holiday Inn Ronnie got on the phone and canceled our rooms, and within half an hour Michael's house was dark and the street outside was still silent and I lay awake, listening to the calm.

"I know you don't want to hear it," I said to Ronnie, "but that was a very nice thing you did."

"Shut up," Ronnie said, his customary form of acknowledging a compliment from me.

"Fine," I said. "But it was."

When I had gotten up for breakfast at Michael's house—I had slept in the guest bedroom, Ronnie had slept downstairs on the foldout couch—I had showered and gone to the kitchen. Just as I'd been about to walk in, I had heard Michael and Ronnie talking.

"So I'm sorry," Ronnie had said.

"You don't have to be sorry," Michael had said.

"I was way out of line," Ronnie had said. "I don't know why."

"It's forgotten," Michael had said.

With anyone else, I would have doubled back to where I'd come from, and would have pretended all day that I hadn't heard. With them, though, I could walk into the kitchen, knowing it was all right. They stopped the conversation as soon as they saw me, and instead we began talking about what we were going to do during the day. But they knew I'd overheard.

Now it was the afternoon, and Ronnie and I were walking through Bristol. We wanted to give Michael as much time alone with his family as we could—which meant getting out of the house.

"You didn't tell him that I'd brought it up, did you?" I said.

"What?" Ronnie said.

"The other night," I said. "What I said to you in the restaurant."

"What restaurant?" he said. He was going to play it this way. Whatever made him feel more comfortable.

"I just hope you didn't tell Michael that I'd gotten on you for being that way with him," I said, giving it one more try.

"I don't recall you and I having any conversation like that," he said. "I must not have been paying attention if we did."

"Whatever," I said. "I just think that was good, what you said to him this morning."

"I don't know what you're referring to," he said.

We were walking up Rankin Street, past homes with screened-in porches and basketball hoops in the driveways. People out on their lawns waved hello to us; some kids were tossing a Frisbee, and Ronnie called "Nice catch" to them, and one of the boys, pleased to be noticed, yelled, "Thank you." Sprinklers were on, affording a soft background murmur, and I could feel the sidewalk under my feet and I said to Ronnie, "You know, every time I come here, I swear, I breathe easier."

No sarcasm now. "I know," he said. "Me, too."

I suppose it's not just Bristol; I suppose a lot of people feel that way about the town in which they grew up. For a town to feel this good to you, so many years after you've left—you've got to have grown up in a very lucky way.

"There was this song, when I first went away to college," I said. "It was this soul song. I think it was by a guy named Chuck Jackson."

"I don't think I know that name," Ronnie said.

"Doesn't matter," I said. "All the people I knew at college loved the song. It was called 'It's an Uphill Climb to the Bottom.' A real sad, blues thing. All of the people at college said that it expressed their feelings perfectly. About what it's like to feel so low that the bottom looks high."

A mail carrier, on his afternoon rounds, wearing shorts and a pith hat, passed us and said, "Good day, gentlemen."

We said hi. "I guess you want to romanticize your life when you go away from home for the first time," I said. "You're a freshman in college and you want to tell yourself that whatever pains you're feeling are sort of monumental and heroic. But I have to laugh a little bit at the idea now—a bunch of suburban kids sitting in a dorm room, nodding their heads to 'It's an Uphill Climb to the Bottom.'"

"I'm sure the song was about emotions, not about where you came from," Ronnie said.

"Yeah, I know," I said. "But look around us." We were at a corner from which we could see freshly mowed lawns in all directions, and American flags displayed next to six or seven front doors, and, at the end of a driveway, neighborhood kids washing their bicycles, with soapy water trickling in foamy rivulets into a street paved with red bricks.

"Some uphill climb," I said.

"You can feel bad anywhere you live," Ronnie said.

"Still," I said. "We were so blessed," surprising myself with my choice of the word.

"Don't I know," he said.

We'd been walking for another half hour or so when, from a side porch, we heard three voices—two male, one female—yell, almost in unison, "Get up, Jack!"

It was momentarily startling, and we turned to look in the direction of the sound. When I saw the color TV screen through the mesh walls of the porch, I knew immediately what it was.

Within a second of the "Get up, Jack!" there was a loud cheering from the porch.

"Come on," I said to Ronnie. We walked over the lawn.

On the porch were four older couples—the house belonged to William and Florence Moore, whose son Ed had gone to school with us. When we got within a few feet of the porch Mr. Moore caught sight of us, looked for a moment, and then said, "Ben Kroeger?"

"Hi," I said, waving. "How are you, Mr. Moore. Hi, Mrs. Moore."

"We're watching the senior golf tournament," Mr. Moore said. "Come in and join us. Nicklaus just got a birdie on seventeen."

"So I heard," I said, laughing.

"Really, come in," he said. "Who's that with you?"

"You remember Ronnie Hepps," I said. "We were in Ed's class."

"Oh, of course," Mr. Moore said. "I'll be sure to tell Ed that I saw you. He's up in Detroit, you know, with Chrysler. Finance division."

"He was at our reunion," I said. "I saw him there. We had a nice talk."

"Well, both of you, come in here," Mr. Moore said. "Trevino's in the clubhouse with a one-stroke lead, but Jack can catch him on the last hole."

Mr. and Mrs. Moore let us in through the screen door, and introduced us to the other couples. "Ronnie, did I hear your dad was in the hospital down in Sarasota?" Mrs. Moore said.

The Bristol grapevine is as efficient as CNN, and occasionally faster. "Yes, Mrs. Moore," Ronnie said. "I just spoke with him on the phone this morning. He's home now, and feeling much better."

"And your mother is all right?" Mrs. Moore said.

"She's great," Ronnie said. "Thank you for asking."

I don't know why the sound of that exchange was so pleasing to me, but it was. It had the timbre of home to it—it told me where I was, the same way that the shouted "Get up, Jack!" had a few minutes earlier.

I'd been hearing "Get up, Jack!"—invariably directed at television screens—all my life. Jack Nicklaus grew up in central Ohio, the most famous athlete to come out of our area. I've never met Nicklaus—I don't even know where he lives now, I think maybe in Florida—but to people from the middle of Ohio, he's always been regarded as a neighbor. Since I was a kid, "Get up, Jack!" never needed any translation. It meant that somewhere in the world, Nicklaus had stroked a putt toward the hole; back here in central Ohio, people were yelling for the ball to roll all the way to the flag.

None of us had to really know him; it was enough that we had grown up under the same Ohio skies, breathing the same Ohio air. It was enough that Jack must have grown up listening to the records played by the disc jockeys on WCOL just like we did, and getting the sports scores every night from Jimmy Crum on Channel 4 just like we did (although he probably knew Jimmy Crum, he probably could call Jimmy on the phone before the newscast and get the scores early), and eating doubleburgers at a Big Bev drive-in just like we did.

"Aw, no," Mr. Moore called out, and the others on the porch let out disappointed groans. "In the rough."

Nicklaus had just hit his drive on eighteen; the ball had hooked left and landed twenty feet off the fairway. On the screen the electronic image of Nicklaus, a sardonic half-smile on his face—"What can you do?" the smile said—tipped his golf cap to the cheering members of the gallery. It occurred to me that I didn't even know what city the tournament was being played in.

It didn't really matter; through all those tournaments before, and all the tournaments that would come, Jack's exact location in the United States or beyond wasn't the important thing. The important thing was that he was one of us—or so we flattered ourselves, so we hoped that he regarded himself—and he was out there doing well, and we were watching him, watching him and telling that ball to get up, roll into that cup.

"It's been good to see you, Mr. Moore," I said. "Thanks for having us, Mrs. Moore." And to the others: "Nice to have met you."

"You don't have to leave just yet," Mr. Moore said, his eyes on the TV.

"We're due back somewhere," I said, and Mr. and Mrs. Moore stood up to shake hands and say goodbye.

"Ronnie, our very best to your dad and mom," Mrs. Moore said.

"Thanks," he said. "They'll appreciate that."

"Ben, I don't think I've seen you on the tube lately, have I?" Mr. Moore said.

"No," I said, "I've been taking the summer off."

"So you're not in town here doing a story, then?" Mr. Moore said.

From the TV set, I could hear the announcer say that Nicklaus was addressing his lie. "He's taking his time," the announcer's voice said. Jack always did; he always took his time.

"No story," I said to Mr. Moore. "I'm just in town passing through."

Ronnie wanted to go back to Michael's, so we walked there. Michael and Ellen and the girls were gone; they'd left a note saying they were at the grocery, and were going to stop at Swendell's for some ice cream after that. The note said they'd see us later.

Ronnie had some phone calls to make, but I didn't feel like sitting around the house. So I headed out again. I walked toward the high school, and I saw that the main gate on the fence surrounding the football field was open.

I passed through the gate, as I had on so many autumn Friday nights. The stadium, with its white painted exterior, was across the sun-washed parking lot. In the lot were three long yellow buses, each with the words "Bristol City Schools" painted on its side. The sight of the buses brought immediate pictures to my mind: sports teams excitedly departing for away games; thirteen-year-olds boarding the buses for that Bristol rite of passage, the seventh-grade spring overnight trip to Oak Meadows State Park.

The signs above the entranceways to the stadium, I would have sworn, had not changed. They looked as if they had been created in Mr. Runson's woodworking class, and maybe they had. On the piece of gray lumber hanging over the center tunnel, "Reserved Seats" had been burned into the body of the wood; the tunnel to the right bore a sign burned with "General Admission," the tunnel to the left a sign with "Students."

I walked through the general admission tunnel. On the quarter-mile track that surrounded the football field, about a dozen Bristol boys, bare-chested in the sun, were running laps. This was early football practice, informal August workouts before the season began. In the front row of the stadium was a young man I didn't recognize, maybe twenty-four years old, wearing a white Bristol Athletic Department shirt. An assistant coach, keeping his eye on this ritual the way young Bristol assistant coaches had for generations.

In the tunnel I did notice one thing that had changed. The blue wooden door to the trainer's room had undergone a rechristening. No longer did it carry the modest legend "Trainer"; rather, painted on the door in white block letters were the imposing words "Sports Medicine." Sports medicine or not, I envisioned a harried, sweating trainer in that underlit, musty old room, wrapping tape around scores of ankles, some of whose owners doubtless did not require the tape, but who would never willingly set foot on the Bristol field without that visible declaration of their manhood and athleticism.

"Hey, Coach Griffin," a boy on the track called to the man in the first row of seats. The boy held up a white Bristol helmet with a blue stripe down the center. "How about putting a Walkman in here? Then I could go dancing down the field."

He and a few of the other boys had finished their laps, and now they were doing wind sprints on the track. They were full of the eagerness that comes with the knowledge that a season is about to start. Some of the players were running up and down the aisles of the stadium, to the top and then back again. "Lift your knees up," the assistant coach called to them. "The point is conditioning, not just to get it done."

He saw me there. "Mr. Kroeger?" he said.

Mr. Kroeger. A Bristol football coach—he's calling me Mr. Kroeger.

"Ben," I said, walking over to him and extending my hand. "My name's Ben."

"I'm Brian Griffin," he said. "I've only been at Bristol for two years. What brings you here?"

"Just stopping by," I said.

"You're not here to do a big story on our team, huh?" he said, kidding but not.

I probably should have known that I could count on hearing a lot of that while we were in town. Be grateful for small favors, I told myself. At least here they know you.

"I'm not working," I said. "I'm just here."

I walked down the three stone steps at the front of the stadium, crossed the track, and made my way onto the field itself. It was solid green; the chalk yard lines had not yet been rolled onto the grass. I went out to where I guessed the fifty-yard line would be come September, then turned around and faced the stadium.

Fifteen rows. I counted. That surprised me. All the emotional magnitude that stadium carried in Bristol—and it was only fifteen rows high. Fifteen rows of splintery wooden benches.

Yeah, but I bet it delivers damn close to a 100 share, I thought to myself.

That's the language of mass entertainment; specifically, it is the language of network television. A program's share is the percentage of sets in use; if a particular show gets a 15 share, that means that 15 percent of all people in America with their TV sets turned on were watching it. On such numbers are advertising rates set; on such numbers are careers in the entertainment business made or destroyed.

Fifteen rows in the Bristol High School stadium—but what happens in that stadium, and on that field, reaches and touches more families in Bristol than the highest-rated program on ABC or CBS or NBC. The stadium has always been the main gathering point in Bristol, the main emblem of the individual public fortunes of the families of the town. If your son becomes a star halfback, this is where he will hear his ovations, and this is where you, as his parent, will receive your congratulations from the parents of other Bristol boys, and where you will wonder just how many of those congratulations are heartfelt. If you are a fifteen-year-old falling in love, this is where you will take your date on a crisp October night, wondering whether everyone in the stands notices that you are with this particular wonderful person, and hoping that they do. If you are a teacher or a cop or just a longtime Bristol resident, this is where you will see the town's human history—or the part of that human history that somehow feels the need to gather by the hundreds—pass before you and change.

I stood on the fifty-yard line in the sun. You don't have to be a football player to feel that a part of your personal history is in this stadium. I looked at the fifteen rows of seats. They were empty, save for Coach Griffin, and I kept looking.

Two memories:

In our junior year in high school the quarterback on the Bristol football team was Frank Laggitt. There is a Frank Laggitt in every high school class in America, every year—the star, the best, the one who has already risen far above everyone else.

Sitting in the stadium on football Friday nights, we would all watch Frank Laggitt. During the week, Frank Laggitt was one of us—he sat in physics class, and he was really quite decent and very smart, and he walked the hallways with us. But the Frank Laggitt on the football field on Friday nights was separate from us, he had achieved something we had not. We were in the stands watching, and Frank Laggitt, in his blue-and-white Bristol uniform, was on the grass floor of the stadium, with the whole town looking on with respect and hope and approval.

Often, in the stands on those Friday nights, I would think about what it would be like to be in the end zone, and to have Frank Laggitt see me and throw a pass in my direction. In my mind, I was always waiting for the pass in one precise spot in the end zone—this was in the north end zone, by the fence separating the high school from the junior high school—and I would envision Frank Laggitt seeing me free there, and lofting a pass toward me. In the fantasy the ball was never unreachable, I did not have to chase after it or leap into the air for it—in my daydreams the ball was always a perfect, soft spiral, and it always found me, it twirled into my waiting arms, and somewhere, muffled, I could hear the voice of F. W. Terman, the Bristol athletic director and game-night PA announcer, saying my name, saying over the stadium loud-speakers that the pass was complete, that Frank Laggitt had hit me in the end zone with the pass for a Bristol touchdown.

Even years later, when I had accomplished a few things, sometimes that scene would play itself out and I would find myself wondering why. No matter how well I had done, no matter what honors I had received, sometimes out of nowhere, in some strange city where I had been sent for my work, I would imagine myself moving laterally across that end zone, toward the west sideline, and there the ball would be, and down the field I could see that Frank Laggitt, having released it, was looking at me, waiting to see what would happen. The football would float toward me, the spiral identical in all the daydreams over all the years, the spiral so familiar to me that it was almost a friend, and I would pull the ball into my arms and clutch it to my chest and wait for what I knew was coming—F. W. Terman's voice—and I would know that I had made the catch and that all of the people in the stands at Bristol stadium had seen me, and they couldn't take that away from me, the score was on the board and they had seen it all.

And:

This was much earlier—I was much younger, this may have been the first time I was ever inside the Bristol stadium.

Bruce Wells and I had come to the stadium on a Saturday morning during the summer. I think we were seven. It was an extraordinary feeling for us to be there by ourselves; we knew that Bristol stadium meant something. Bruce challenged me to a race around the track. One time around, first person across the finish line the winner.

The track was a quarter mile. I had never run in a long race before. We crouched down on the cinders, and Bruce said, "On your mark, get set, go!" and I dashed off. I ran as fast and as hard as I could. In fifteen or twenty seconds I realized that I had a huge lead.

I knew something must be wrong; I sensed it. Bruce was back behind me, loping along at a modest pace, and I turned to look at him and I saw he was not worried. I didn't know what my mistake had been, but I was sure I had made one.

Confused, I kept sprinting. Within a few minutes my chest began to burn and my throat began to feel scorched. I sprinted on, though, as fast as my legs could take me, but my legs could no longer take me very fast. We weren't a third of the way around the track when Bruce chugged past me. He wasn't breathing hard. He was moving steadily. With one settled step after another he was past me and then ahead and then far, far ahead, one little boy in front of another—I was watching his back, my lungs ached, my legs felt like they could do no more.

Someone had told Bruce. I didn't know who, but someone had told him the secret. I walked the last half of the oval, and even that hurt, and Bruce was waiting for me, and he said: "You can't run so fast at first or you'll wear yourself out."

Someone must have told him that.

Now I was on the fifty-yard line in August. I looked up into the stands. Fifteen rows; that's all. The dreamed-for voice of F. W. Terman, announcing a touchdown pass that no one in Bristol could ignore or deny. Bruce Wells waiting at the finish line, a child with a lesson: You don't have to sprint to win the race.

It was warm on the field as I stood there with my thoughts. You don't have to sprint to win the race. This is not the only race in the world. It only seems that way, for such a long time when you are young.

The five of us sat on folding chairs in the town council chambers: Ronnie, Ellen, the two girls, and me.

"Daddy!" Laura whispered toward Michael.

He turned around, smiled at her, and held one of his fingers to his mouth to signal her not to talk during the meeting.

Mayor Singer—I always have to hold back a grin when I see or hear those words, Paul Singer was a guy three or four years older than we were, he and his friends used to play wiffle ball in the street in front of my house, and now he's the longest-serving mayor in Bristol history—was preparing to call the meeting to order. The mayor had lost most of his hair over the years, and while he was always a stubby teenager, now he weighed more than 250 pounds. He looked at Michael from behind the blond-wood façade of the podium where the council members sat. Paul—the mayor—was in a light blue summerweight suit.

"Haven't seen you much lately, Michael," the mayor said, friendly.

"Well, I've been gone," Michael said. He was standing at a lectern facing the mayor and the council members.

"So I hear," the mayor said. Our trip was hardly a secret in Bristol. "You'll have to tell me about all of this sometime."

The five council members—I knew all of them—made some small talk with Michael. This hearing was not going to have any of the intimidating formality of a congressional inquiry, or even of a big-city council meeting. With the exception of Ronnie and Ellen and the girls and me, there were only two people present in the gallery—older women, the Delaney sisters, who, I gathered from a Bristol policeman I'd spoken with briefly on the way in, come to every town council meeting just to break up their evenings once a week.

"We'll start with the pledge," Mayor Singer said.

All of us rose, and faced an American flag displayed by the far wall, next to a window looking out on Main Street. We recited the Pledge of Allegiance—Michael's daughters saying the words louder than the rest of us—and then we sat again, and the mayor said, "Ladies and gentlemen, we have a number of items on our agenda tonight. It seems a shame to make Michael Wolff and his family spend such a beautiful summer evening sitting indoors, so I've taken the liberty of inviting Michael to speak to us first. He called me this morning and said that he'd like to be here, so if no one has any objections, we can hear him now."

The council members nodded their assent. "If I don't say yes, he'll flunk my son next year," said a councilman named Curt Beatty, trying to make a joke. Michael, who had worn a coat and tie tonight, waited at the lectern for permission to begin.

"Michael has come here to address us on the proposal for a four-way stop at the intersection of Harding and Oak," Mayor Singer said. "As the council knows, after considerable discussion, it had been agreed that four-way stop signs at that intersection would prove advantageous in ensuring that traffic on the surrounding streets maintains a moderate average speed. As a homeowner in that neighborhood, though, Michael has some objections to our plan. So before we vote, I'd like to let Michael have his say."

Michael had prepared notes. He looked down at them, cleared his throat, and began to talk. His voice was a little constricted, a little nervous. Even though he knew every person on the council.

"Mr. Mayor," he said, "council members . . . As many of you are aware, my family and I live in a house at 238 South Harding, next to the intersection of Harding and Oak. We have lived there for more than ten years, and we like the neighborhood very much. . . ."

He explained to the council that one of the things he valued most about the block where he lived was the tranquil feeling: "Because we are not a main thoroughfare, ours is not a block where there are constant traffic jams. There is a steady flow of cars most of the day, with additional traffic during commuting hours in the morning and the late afternoon. As the council knows, there are two stop signs on Oak—one on each side of the intersection."

Next to me in the gallery section, I could see Laura and Leslie looking at their dad. The sight of their father in an official setting, presenting his thoughts to figures of authority in a businesslike manner, seemed to beguile them.

"If there was a traffic problem on our street, I would know about it," Michael said. "I submit to you that there is no such problem. I understand how, in theory, it might sound prudent to install two more stop signs on the corner, in the name of safety.

"To do so, though, would be to rob our block of one of its best features—its peacefulness and sense of privacy. With stop signs on Harding—one directly in front of my home—the effect would be to create a constant succession of cars at a complete standstill. If any of you have ever looked out your window to see a car driven by someone you didn't know stopped in front of your house, you can understand that this can be very disconcerting."

Ronnie, sitting next to me, whispered, "You can always throw eggs at it."

"Quiet," I whispered back.

Michael was looking at his notes again. "I don't have any statistics on something like this," he said. "And obviously I'm not an expert on traffic flow. But if I thought that my block was in any way unsafe, I would be the first person to call for a four-way stop. My family—and from everything I know, the other families on our block—are very happy with our street. If you decide to put the four-way stop in, you'll probably never think of your decision again. I realize that, in the grand scope of things, it seems like a very minor matter. But I would appreciate it tremendously if you would at least reconsider your decision. I honestly feel that, in a way we would sense every day, life on our block would be made less pleasant if the four-way signs go up. Unless this is a matter that the council feels very strongly about, I would ask you to think about leaving things the way they are."

He paused, as if not quite sure what to do next.

"Thank you all for listening to me," he said, and then sat down.

"Thank you, Michael," Mayor Singer said. The mayor addressed the other council members: "I believe that the signs were supposed to go up in ten days or so. It seems to me, though, that this is not a matter of such pressing concern that we have to rush on it. With the council's assent, I'd like to have our public safety people take another look at that corner. Maybe we're right and maybe we're wrong. But does anyone have any objections to tabling this until we can hear from the public safety folks?"

There was no formal vote. The council members simply said that was fine with them.

Through the window next to the flag, I could see that late dusk was coming to Main Street. Tonight felt so different from so many of our nights during the summer; tonight—with Michael trying to preserve something the rest of the world would never even notice, with his children looking toward him with this lovely expression of pride in their eyes—seemed rooted and constant. Seemed essential.

"Michael, are you back in town for a while now?" Mayor Singer said. I looked at the mayor, behind the Bristol city seal, and all I could see was him in the street in front of our house, circa 1957, swatting that wiffle ball with his friends, older boys at play in the neighborhood.

"Just for a day or two," Michael said. "The summer's not over yet."

"Well, I envy you," the mayor said. "From what I hear, it sounds like a hell of a time you're having." He looked over at the council stenographer. "Make that 'a whale of a time,' " he said to her.

"Thank you for hearing me out," Michael said. "If I'm not pushing this, do you know when you'll have your decision?"

"I would guess we'll make the draw by early September," the mayor said. "You'll be home by then?"

"Yes," Michael said. "I believe I will."

"It's still open," Ronnie said to Michael. "Don't feel you have to make up your mind right now. It's open whenever you decide you want it."

"You know how much I appreciate that," Michael said. "But Ellen and I talked about it most of the night last night, and all day today. I don't think it would work, Ronnie. Not for me and not for you."

We were at Swendell's—the second ice-cream trip of the day for Michael and Ellen and the girls. We'd decided to walk over from the town council meeting; Swendell's is just a block and a half from City Hall. Now we were sitting at one of the wooden picnic tables outside, the girls eating cones, the rest of us drinking chocolate sodas.

I don't think it had come as any huge surprise to Ronnie when Michael had told him he wouldn't be taking the job in Cleveland. It certainly wasn't a surprise to me. I had a hunch that maybe Ronnie was feeling secretly relieved. I would have been, under the circumstances; Ronnie's life, I sensed, would only be more complicated with Michael as an employee. But Ronnie kept stressing that Michael's decision didn't have to be final.

"If school starts up, and you're feeling like you might want something different, what I said still goes," Ronnie said. "I'd love to have you with me. I think you'd be good."

It sounded off-key; it sounded formal, like a pitch Ronnie might give a potential client he had met ten minutes before. I figured part of it was because he was still feeling bad about the way he had treated Michael during the last week.

Ellen called to the girls, who had wandered over to talk to a couple of their friends: "Laura? Leslie? Finish up. It's been a long day."

Then she turned to Ronnie.

"Blame me if you want," she said. "I just don't want to turn our lives upside down. We belong here. This is home for us."

"I know," Ronnie said. "It's not a question of blaming anyone. I just think that you and Michael should be able to live any way you want to." I could tell that he wasn't going to get into the area of specific finances; he didn't need to, and to do so in front of Ellen would have been somehow wrong.

"I've thought about it every day since you first brought it up," Michael said. "I had all these visions of what it would be like. I saw myself sitting in an office in your building, and flying around the country working on deals, and taking customers to restaurants. It was nice to think about, but every time I would dream up one of those scenes, the person in there wouldn't seem to be me. Does that make any sense? He would look like me and he would have my voice, but he wouldn't be me."

In a way, I think Ronnie's job offer to Michael may have been just another part of the summer fantasy. It was meant to be anything but that—it was meant to be a way to take the best part of the summer, the friendship and the closeness, and to carry it into real life once the summer was gone. But Michael seemed to understand, maybe more than any of us, that such an arrangement would never work; whatever it was that we'd given ourselves during these weeks and months, it wasn't renewable come autumn. That had been our agreement before we'd set off back in June. Come September, this would end. At Swendell's, we worked on our sodas.

The smell was almost sweet, and it was something I remembered from Bristol summers long ago.

It was the smell of freshly poured blacktop on warm streets, and it always spoke of renewal, of people fixing things before those things could have a chance to really fall apart. There was an accompanying sound—the sound of gravel hitting the undersides of cars. The gravel would always be poured at the same time the blacktop was. The smell and the warmth and the sound of the gravel; they were all here tonight.

I'd gone out by myself after we had gotten back to Michael's. In the morning we would be leaving again. I had half expected Michael to tell us he was remaining behind, but he had said he didn't want to miss the conclusion of this trip of ours, and Ellen had encouraged him to stay with us. I was glad; somehow, for Ronnie and me to finish the summer alone would have violated the spirit of what we had embarked upon.

So they were all back at Michael's, and I walked through Bristol. Not many cars out tonight; the ones that drove along Dodge Avenue stirred up the gravel, and it was nearly musical, that sound on an August night mixed with the scent of the new blacktop.

There was a traffic light ahead, at the corner of Jefferson Street. As I approached it, I thought I could hear other sounds—a vaguely electrical buzzing, followed by a mechanical clunking. I got closer, and the noises got louder, and I knew what they were.

Mounted on a wooden pole at the intersection was a metal box, painted dark green. On the box, in raised letters, were the words "City of Bristol." The noises were coming from inside the box. The traffic light would be green, and the buzz would be steady, and then there would be the second noise inside the box, like metal dropping onto metal, and the light would change to yellow. Buzzing briefly, then metal to metal again, and the light would go to red.

It must be like this everywhere—but from the time I was a boy, Bristol has been the only place I've ever noticed it, the only place where that series of sounds in the metal boxes has seemed to be always in the background, always a part of the surroundings.

Maybe it's because so many of the places I go are so congested; you wouldn't notice the noises in the boxes if there was a lot of traffic. Or maybe it's just that when I go places now, I am not attuned to even listen for such sounds.

At the corner I paused by the traffic light. No cars to mask the sounds; nothing but that buzz in the night. I stood by the metal box for five or six cycles through the catalogue of colors, and I felt in some way soothed by the sounds, and I was just as glad that there was no one around to see me.

When I left I found myself heading toward the stadium again. A block away I could see that the field lights were not turned on. There would be no reason for them to be; no football games for another month. Some safety lights were shining from the fence around the stadium, just so the area would not be in total blackness, and the streetlights cast a short glow, too.

When I got to the fence the gate was still unlocked. I walked through, until I was on the track.

The stands, across the football field, were dark now. I looked toward the end zone. In the deep evening I couldn't tell precisely where that spot was, the spot I used to dream about back when this stadium was the center of the universe, when nothing that happened in this stadium seemed like it could ever be unimportant. Tonight I looked toward that spot in the end zone where the dream pass from Frank Laggitt always came floating into my arms, and I didn't need a lot of light to find that spot; I had spent years finding that spot in the dark.

I knew I should get back to Michael's; everyone else was probably in bed by now. I wasn't tired, though, and I knew that even if I went back I would not be able to sleep.

The cinders of the track were underneath my feet. I began to run, slowly at first, and I could hear myself on the track better than I could

290 · Bob Greene

see, the lights were very dim and far removed. But I kept running, I felt myself speeding up, and what breeze there was pushed warm against my face. You don't have to sprint to win the race, you don't even have to be in the race at all, but I urged myself harder, all the way around the track, I was gulping for breath but I would not let myself slow down, and I was sweating through my shirt and my legs began to ache but still I wasn't tired, I did not want to stop, until finally, after I had been once around and was halfway through my second circling, I gradually slowed my pace, and I let my steps become shorter, and then in that stadium with the tower lights turned off I was walking on the track, regaining my breath, and when everything was steady again I left to join the others through the same gate I'd come in.

Twenty-three

WHEN WE DECIDED to fly to California, I think we all sensed that there was more to it than just wanting to go somewhere we hadn't yet been during the summer. We are about as un-California as people can possibly be; maybe California sets the trends and California defines a considerable part of the national culture, but that state and that life always seemed so far removed from us. I'm not sure whether, as kids in Bristol, we were conscious of the irony of cruising Ohio streets to songs like "California Girls" and "California Sun" coming out of our car radios; probably we didn't give it much thought. But we were never California; we never would be.

When Ronnie made the suggestion, he didn't get any arguments from Michael or me. Day by day we were moving steadily through August, and although none of us talked about it yet, there was this sense of something getting ready to end. We didn't quite feel like we were into those days when everything had to be rushed and crammed in. But we knew it was coming, not too far up the road, and going to California seemed like something we ought to do.

We flew to John Wayne Airport in Orange County. The plan was to drive up and down the coast for five or six days, more if we were especially enjoying it. Ronnie said it would be nice to spend time on the famous beaches abutting the Pacific Ocean; Michael said he liked the prospect of being on the far edge of the continent.

It went beyond that, though. With August hurrying by, and September waiting for us, and the summer destined to soon be something in the past tense, California seemed to serve a purpose for us. What we were sensing was an impending sunset. So we landed in California, where American sunsets say their best goodbyes.

In a cafe at an outdoor mall near Huntington Beach, we ate cheeseburgers and looked at the water. After dinner we saw a small crowd gathered near the exit of the mall's movie theater complex. As the customers left one of the theaters, they were being stopped by a three-man, two-woman crew equipped with a video camera. We watched to see what was going on.

A high-school-aged girl who had just come out of the theater stood in front of the camera. One of the women in the video crew said to her: "So how did you like it?"

The girl said, "I . . . uh, I . . ."

She turned to her boyfriend.

"I don't know what to say!" she said to him. "What should I say?"

"Thank you very much," the video woman said. She made a notation on a clipboard she was carrying. She said to the high school girl's boyfriend, "How about you?"

He shifted back and forth on his feet, stared into the camera, and said: "It was fantastic! The best movie I've seen all year!"

One of the men in the crew materialized out of the background with several documents. "That was very good," he said. "If you could sign these releases, we'll be happy to consider you for the commercials."

Seeing this, the other people leaving the theater got the idea. A woman in her forties said to the cameraman, "Can I try?"

The cameraman shrugged. He motioned with his head toward the crew member with the clipboard.

"Did you like the movie, ma'am?" the clipboard woman said.

The woman who'd just seen the movie, animated and loud, threw her arms in the air and said, "Incredible! Fabulous! I'd see it again!"

"Not yet," the clipboard woman said. "Wait till we're set up." She told the cameraman to aim his lens at the woman.

The woman from the audience said, "Now?"

"Anytime," the cameraman said, his eye pressed to the rubberized rim over his focus mechanism.

"I thought . . . ," the woman said excitedly. She stopped. In a normal voice, she said to the woman with the clipboard: "I'm sorry. I forgot what I said the first time. What would you like me to say?"

"We can't tell you what to say," the clipboard woman said.

"You can't?" the woman from the audience said.

"No, ma'am," the clipboard woman said. "The people we use in the commercials are expressing their own opinions."

The woman from the audience stood there.

"What you said before was excellent," the clipboard woman said.

The woman from the audience composed her thoughts, then said, "Okay, I think I remember."

"We're rolling," the cameraman said.

The woman peered at his lens. "It's fabulous!" she cried. "So good! I'm coming back!"

The man with the documents came forward. "I can do it again if you didn't like it," the woman from the audience said to him.

"That was fine," the clipboard woman said, answering for the document man. "That was perfect."

Ronnie, taking all of this in, said, "So that's how they do it."

"I never saw that before," Michael said.

"We're in California," I said. "I guess that's where they do all of them."

We'd seen the commercials on TV hundreds of times—happy people streaming out of a movie theater, saying how much they'd adored the film they'd just seen. It was an effective way to drum up enthusiasm for a movie; there have been times when I've been persuaded to see a particular movie because of commercials like that. I suspect that a high school kid saying that he laughed so hard he thought he was going to puke (I actually saw a kid say that in a commercial once) might sell as many tickets as an endorsement from a newspaper critic who thought the director's overview of life was intriguing.

Michael said to the woman with the clipboard, "Excuse me. When will this be on the air?"

The clipboard woman, having heard this a thousand times before, did not look at him as she said, "Probably next weekend. This was a sneak preview. The film opens next Friday."

It's a science, I suppose; the studios must have a whole slew of marketing strategies for their new films, and what these people were doing obviously was one small part of the plan for this movie. It's hard to blame the studios. These days if a movie doesn't get talked about in its first few days of release, it's pretty much dead.

In the mall at Huntington Beach the commercial camera crew had found a young man who—a quick learner—had volunteered to say "Awesome flick!" about the film he had just seen, "Awesome flick!" being just about the perfect testimony in the eyes of the commercial crew (not only was it uncontradictably laudatory, but it was so short that it could be easily used in a commercial in conjunction with other audience endorsements). Ronnie, watching the young man talk to the camera, said to us, "I wonder if they'd let me do one."

"You want to say that you liked the movie?" Michael said.

"Yeah," Ronnie said. "It would be good to be in a commercial."

"You haven't seen the movie," I reminded him.

"Do you think they care?" Ronnie said.

"What would you tell them?" Michael said.

"I don't know," Ronnie said. "I think I'd say that it's the funniest movie I ever saw. That I laughed so much my fillings fell out."

"What if it's not a comedy?" I said.

"What do you mean?" Ronnie said.

"We don't know that the movie is a comedy," I said. "We don't even know the title of the movie. What if it's a thriller?"

Ronnie walked over to the man with the release forms.

"Let me ask you something," Ronnie said to him. "This movie— could you tell me a little about the plot?"

The next afternoon we sat on the sand at Laguna Beach, watching people surf.

"Just so it doesn't take you by surprise," Ronnie said to us, "I talked to Gail last night. I asked her to meet me."

"And?" I said, not immediately coming up with any better reply.

"She's coming," he said.

"Right now?" Michael said.

"In a few days," Ronnie said. "Before we leave California."

He didn't seem to be asking for our consent, so I didn't say anything else. Obviously he had his reasons.

"You talk to your dad?" Michael said. I think there was an edge there. As in: You talked to Gail, did you bother talking to your dad?

"He's doing better," Ronnie said. "He says he feels pretty good."

Some kids who had just walked past us with their surfboards had made it to the water line, and now they were paddling out into the Pacific. Soon I couldn't see their faces; they were dots on top of the water, they could have been colors on a California surfing poster for sale in an Ohio shopping strip. I wonder who we would have been, I thought. I wonder who we would have turned out to be had we been born in this town instead of our own.

We drove south, and the next day, in La Jolla, we stopped at a service station. We all wanted to use the rest room and make phone calls. There was only one pay phone, and a man was using it. We leaned against our rental car, waiting for him to get done across the way, and finally Michael said, "I'll go stand behind him. Maybe he doesn't know anyone's waiting."

Michael walked across the parking lot, and after a few minutes the man left the phone, and Michael made his call—he'd told us that he was going to check in with Ellen and the girls—and when he returned he was shaking his head.

"I don't think I've ever seen anyone do that," he said.

He explained. When he had approached the pay phone, the man had been in the midst of writing on the adjacent wall. "He didn't hear me coming up behind him, and he was writing as I stood there," Michael said.

"What did he write?" Ronnie said.

"It was really stupid and really crude," Michael said.

"Well, what did it say?" Ronnie said.

"I feel stupid even saying it," Michael said.

We waited.

"The guy was writing 'Suck me now,' " Michael said.

Ronnie started laughing. "Come on," he said.

"I'm serious," Michael said. "Those words."

"Did he write his phone number or something?" I said. "Was it one of those deals?"

"No," Michael said. "And it's not like I interrupted him and stopped him from writing anything else. He was talking on the phone, and he wrote those words, and he put the pen back in his shirt pocket and finished the conversation and hung up and started to walk away, and that's the first time he saw me. He had no way of knowing that I'd even been there when he did it."

"He looked pretty normal from here," I said.

"That's the first thing I thought," Michael said. "He looked like a business guy. He was wearing a pair of nice slacks and a business shirt and a tie. He looked like a guy who makes a good living. And he's talking on the phone and he writes that."

"I've seen a million things written on a million walls, but I've never caught anyone writing them," Ronnie said.

"That's what's so bizarre," Michael said. "I mean, you see that stuff on walls every day. But you don't envision anyone actually taking out a pen and writing it."

"Or if you do you envision some mental case," Ronnie said.

"Can you even imagine writing something on a wall?" Michael said.

"What, something dirty?" Ronnie said.

"Not necessarily," Michael said. "Just writing anything at all."

"I have to see this," Ronnie said.

He went over to make his call, and when he came back he said, "Yep. Right by the phone."

I went last. Looking at the words, I thought: Here's a man, he could be your mortgage officer or your pharmacist, and there's something in his mind that makes him write those words on a wall. Such a strange thing. Does he do this every day? Does he even think about it when he's doing it? So much going on in the world we travel through, so much that we'll never know.

Gail arrived a couple of days later. After stopping in a different city up and down the coast every night, we had stayed put in Marina del Rey. The tranquil sight of the boats bobbing in the harbor, the sun glinting off the Pacific, the breezes that tempered the heat of southern California in August . . . we knew it was going to be hard to do any better than this beautiful town by the sea.

So late one afternoon she was there. "Need your teeth cleaned, boys?" Michael and I heard a voice say, and we turned around from where we'd been sitting by the pool and she was walking across the deck with Ronnie. He'd driven out to LAX to pick her up.

What do you say in a situation like that? "Welcome back, Gail"? We said hello and we asked her how she was doing, and after a few minutes she borrowed Ronnie's key and went to his room. When she came back out she was wearing a variation of the minuscule bathing suit that had jarred the men at the pool in Atlanta the day we'd met her.

It had the same effect here. I noticed that all of a sudden most of the men in the vicinity of the pool were making excuses to walk past us. Somehow I thought that people in California were jaded when it came to bodies in bathing suits, but by the reaction Gail was getting she might as well have been the only woman in Greater Los Angeles.

She seemed slightly different than when she had left us in Dallas. In Dallas there had been just a hint of discernment on her part that being with Ronnie on the road might not constitute the ideal place for her. Now, though . . . this is probably a weighted word, but she seemed a bit triumphant. I didn't know exactly what had been said between her and Ronnie after we'd gone to Florida to see his dad, and in Dallas just before she'd departed, but her attitude now was almost as if she'd won some sort of victory.

I guess I shouldn't have been surprised. When Ronnie and Marilyn had passed within five yards of each other in Delaware, the temperature seemed to drop twenty degrees. Clearly whatever was going on in their marriage was not a cause for rhapsody, and it was pretty apparent that it had been that way well before Gail Donlon had appeared. Still, I'd just seen Ronnie with his children, I'd just watched him walking across the grounds of their summer camp with them and Marilyn. This seemed a little untoward, a little coarse.

It was hard to blame Gail, though; she didn't owe anybody anything, and I assumed that she hadn't found her way to Marina del Rey on her own. A smile on her face, she got up from the lounge where she was lying in the sun, ran a comb through her hair, then sat on Ronnie's lap. Without a word Michael dived into the pool and swam toward the far end.

"So, Ben," Gail said. "How have you been?"

A white bird was making lazy patterns overhead. Michael tore a corner off a piece of bread, waited until the bird was close to us, then tossed the bread into the air.

The bird, apparently not interested, ignored the offering. The scrap of bread fell to the boardwalk.

"I thought sea gulls were supposed to like that," Michael said.

"I'm not sure that bird's a sea gull," I said.

"Maybe it's just not hungry," he said.

Ronnie and Gail were out on a boat he had chartered for the afternoon; Michael and I were checking out Marina del Rey, taking a long walk along the water. It had been two days since Gail's arrival, and we hadn't seen much of Ronnie since.

"The way I look at it, it's pretty much a matter of who takes your phone calls," Michael said. "As ridiculous as it sounds, that's what it comes down to."

We'd been talking about his decision to continue teaching at Bristol. I had wanted to know how confident he was that he was doing the wise thing. I thought he was, but I hoped that, five or six months down the line, he wouldn't be looking at his paycheck in the faculty lounge and wondering whether he should be sitting in a private office at Ronnie's headquarters building.

He'd assured me he was fine with his decision; he'd said that after he and Ellen had talked about it, he'd never had a second thought. Now he was explaining his theory about phone calls.

"Here's what I figure," he said. "Let's say I would have taken Ronnie's job. So I'd be in my office, and I would call someone—say the president of the Lazarus department store in Columbus. And my secretary would say to the president's secretary that it was Michael Wolff calling, and that Michael Wolff was a vice president of Steele International. Chances are, the president of Lazarus would take the call."

"Maybe," I said.

"For the sake of argument, let's just say he would," Michael said. "Okay. Now let's say in September I come home from a day at the high school, and I pick up the phone and I call the president of Lazarus. And his secretary asks who's calling, and I say it's Michael Wolff. And she asks who I represent, and I say that I'm a teacher over in Bristol. He's not going to take the call. He's going to figure I have a complaint about a piece of merchandise, or a question about my bill."

I had been trying to count the boats in the marina, but I'd soon realized it was futile. So many boats, side by side, moored in the water;

where do so many people get so much money? It could have been a freeway at rush hour.

"So it's really absurd, isn't it?" Michael said. "I'm the same person, whether I'd have taken Ronnie's job or not. But with the job certain people would have picked up the phone right away when I called. Without the job, they won't. Seems like sort of a stupid thing to disrupt your life for."

"Well, it's not just that," I said. "There's the money."

"Yeah, I know," Michael said. "I haven't forgotten. But since I've decided to stay in Bristol anyway, I prefer to concentrate on the phone-call angle, if you don't mind. If I think about the phone calls, I don't have to think about the money I'm passing up."

There was a honking from out on the water. We didn't pay any attention, but the honking persisted. We stared in the direction of the noise. Standing up in the back of a huge fishing boat were Ronnie and Gail. They were waving at us. Apparently the charter captain was driving.

"A nice effect, the cigar and the ocean air," Michael said.

The captain took a hard turn and directed the boat farther out into the Pacific. That was a lot of boat for just two passengers. Who weren't even fishing.

"I was getting dressed this morning," Michael said. "I'd just come out of the shower, and there was this big full-length mirror on the back of the bathroom door. I didn't realize it was there until I looked into it. There I was, absolutely naked. And I'm standing there thinking: All of us spend all of these hours worrying about what our bosses think of us, and what our neighbors think of us, and what our co-workers think of us, and whether we're making as much money as we should. We do all that worrying, and when it comes down to it each of us is just a bag of bones."

I had to admit, that one caught me by surprise. "Well, there's a real cheery thought," I said.

"No, I'm serious," he said. "I don't mean it as something sad. It's really funny, if you think about it. The chairman of the board of IBM and the lady who cleans his office at night. Bags of bones. The Kingston Trio. They were great singers, but they were also three bags of bones."

I was laughing in spite of myself. "I really don't think we ought to dwell on this," I said.

"I never thought of it before, but that mirror caught me unawares," he said. "I'm going around making plans about my life, and there's this bag of bones looking back at me from the mirror. I hope they don't have mirrors like that in the White House. I don't think the President should ever have to think of himself in those terms."

"Somehow I don't think he does," I said. "Can we drop this? As it is, I don't think I'll ever listen to a Kingston Trio record in quite the same way again."

"But it's true," he said. "And forget the Kingston Trio for a second. Think about the Supreme Court."

"No, I won't," I said, knowing that he was just trying to get me to laugh some more.

"Kind of puts things in perspective for you, doesn't it?" he said.

"No, it does not," I said. "Now stop it."

"Tommy Lasorda," he said.

"You're cracking up," I said.

"How can you say that?" he said. "This is one of the sanest observations I've ever made."

"I wouldn't tell anyone else if I were you," I said.

"Aretha Franklin," he said. "Don Meredith."

Later, on our way back, I said, "So you really are satisfied that you're doing the right thing this fall."

"Absolutely," he said. "I mean, Ronnie's a bag of bones, too, so why should my bag of bones have to report to his bag of bones? How is that fair?"

Then:

"Yeah. I'm actually kind of looking forward to getting back to work."

There is something especially enticing about a pool that's built right next to a body of water. The pool would seem to be redundant, but somehow swimming in the pool while seeing the ocean just yards away gives you an extraordinary feeling, like one of those uncommon meals during which you take the time to taste every bite. Especially at night; especially when the pool is lighted, and you can just make out the moon on the ocean across the way, and there are moments when you can't be sure whether what you are hearing is the gentle, cleansing sound of the water circulating through the pool or the muted lapping of the waves from the ocean beyond. It's as if you are in both places at once, getting the best of both.

We had the hotel's pool to ourselves. This was around 11 P.M. Ronnie and Gail, following their afternoon at sea, had gone out to dinner, and now they had rejoined us and the four of us were in the shallow end. The water was warm, and we drank from icy cans of beer, which we rested on the edge of the pool deck. Gail swam a lap and that is when Ronnie said to Michael and me, "I'm not sure I'm going home."

Which I suppose should not have taken us totally by surprise, but it did. Whatever it was that Ronnie was doing this summer, I had not given serious thought to the prospect of its changing anything after

September came. Everything out here was supposed to be temporary and fleeting; that had been the agreement.

"What are you talking about?" I said.

"I'm talking about not giving this up," he said.

I think Gail knew that Ronnie was going to tell us this; there was no other reason she would pull herself out of the pool by the deep-end ladder and take her beer to a chair by the fence overlooking the ocean. With her up there Ronnie could say what he was saying in private.

"I'm going back to Cleveland, but I don't think I'm going back to my house," he said.

"Not because of Gail," Michael said.

"Well, I like Gail," he said. "But no, not because of her."

"Then what, Ronnie?" Michael said. I seldom heard his voice rise like that. "What?"

Ronnie let out a sigh. He wasn't saying any of this lightly; that I could tell.

"Michael, it's a very good thing that you can go home every night and be happy," he said. "I'm not being sarcastic in the least. I envy you that. Not everyone is as lucky as you."

And he began to tell us the story of his marriage. Some of it I had assumed from the cool distance that had been apparent between him and Marilyn when I'd last seen them at the big house in Delaware: They hardly talked, he told us, their evenings consisted mostly of long silences and one of them staying awake to watch television while the other one went to bed, even when the television show held no particular interest. There were arguments, and occasional scenes at parties, and Gail was not the first woman with whom he had kept close company. Some of it I would rather not have known. He and Marilyn no longer slept together, ever. He thought there might be a chance that she was seeing someone. He wasn't sure. The worst part of that, he said, was that he didn't particularly care.

This was more than he had to tell us. I had the feeling that in some way he was almost asking our permission for what he was doing.

"So you're moving out," I said.

"I think I am," he said.

"Have you told Marilyn?" I said. "Does she know?"

"Not yet," he said. "I'm going to wait until the summer's over."

"Your kids?" I said.

"It's not like I'm going to be moving out of town," he said. "I can see them all the time."

"Your job?" Michael said.

"The company still has to be run," he said.

I let that one go. Michael didn't.

"The name of the company is Steele International, not Hepps International," Michael said, not even trying to be diplomatic.

"I'm quite aware of that," Ronnie said. "And the chairman of Steele International is Ronald Hepps."

I didn't know if he was drunk, or deluding himself, or what. I did know that this was the first time in my life I had ever heard him refer to himself in the third person. And "Ronald," at that.

Ronnie sensed our unease. "Look," he said. "All this summer you've heard me laugh. I don't think there's been a day we haven't laughed out loud. Every time I heard myself laughing I realized that it sounded like somebody else. Because I don't laugh anymore, or at least I didn't. I used to, but until this summer it's like I had forgotten how.

"I can go back to that house I live in, and pretend that this summer never happened, and go back to the silences and the no laughter. I can go to the same dumb-ass parties with our same dumb-ass friends and pretend that it's fun. But I've learned this summer that I don't have to do that. I don't have to settle for that. People may think less of me for it, but that may be the price I have to pay. One of these days I'm going to wake up old. One of these days I'm going to be in a hospital bed like my father. And when that day comes I don't want to realize that I could have been happy and chose not to."

"There was someone next to your father's hospital bed," Michael said.

Ronnie turned away from him in the pool. Physically turned away.

"You don't want to think about it, but it's true," Michael said. "Yes, you're going to wake up old someday. And you'll probably wake up in a hospital bed someday. And when you do, you'd better pray that when you wake up you have someone sitting next to you and looking into your eyes the way your mother was looking into your father's eyes."

"Don't lecture me, Michael," Ronnie said.

"I will lecture you," Michael said. "Because I had a father who woke up in the hospital and there was no one but a nurse. I had a father who woke up for years and there was no one in his bed. So spare me your goddamned need for laughter, if you don't mind. And grow the fuck up."

Ronnie pulled himself out of the pool and, without speaking to Michael, walked dripping across the lighted tile deck and joined Gail at the table by the other end.

I said nothing. My silence seemed to anger Michael.

"What?" he said, snapping.

And when I still did not speak, his voice rose even more:

"Well, what?"

"Oh, hell," I said.

The pool by the ocean suddenly seemed less extraordinary; there were still two of us in that pool, but it no longer felt like we were in the pool and the ocean at the same time, like we were getting the best of both. It was just a pool, one more pool. At the other end Ronnie and Gail wrapped their towels around them and I saw them disappear up the path to the hotel.

I tried to sleep and couldn't. As I lay awake I thought about Ronnie, and what he would be telling Marilyn and their children as soon as the summer was over, and I looked at the ceiling and the fault was mine.

I remembered sitting in their dining room right after Memorial Day, convincing them what a good idea this summer trip was going to be. And Marilyn readily agreeing: Ronnie works so hard, she had said, he deserves something like this. Thank you very much, ma'am, and here's your husband back, only he's not going to be your husband anymore. Hope you don't mind. But we did have a great summer, if that's any consolation to you and the kids.

There was no way I was going to be able to fall asleep, so I got dressed and went outside again. The hotel lobby was desolate; one maintenance man was running an industrial vacuum over the carpet, and I didn't see anyone behind the front desk.

I walked past the pool, now dark, and through the gate to the boardwalk. The sailboats and yachts were secure in the water, with a pair of hired guards keeping watch.

Michael was right; if Ronnie went through with this, on the strength of whatever illusion of freedom he was taking away from the summer, then he might be fouling his life up in ways he would never be able to repair. But I was hardly in any position to address him on the merits of keeping home and hearth together. I'm not your best witness on that.

Still, I knew enough to be sure that whatever fulfillment he may have been getting out of Gail's companionship—whatever fulfillment he may have been getting out of our summer without rules—was going to evaporate and float away by the first snows of winter. And there he'd be, with what? The memories of a lot of airports and a lot of hotels, the remnants of a suntan and a batch of laughter. Which would have been fine, if he'd let it go at that. The memories were what all of this was supposed to be about. You create some memories and then you go back to what you had, to a solid base of reality. You don't let the memories become the base. It can't work.

So I say. I'd already blown it, long ago. Did I have to drag Ronnie with me? I thought of the boredom he was talking about, the nights he found so dreary with his family. There is such an impulse toward constant amusement, constant indulgence now; he wanted laughter all the time.

When Nancy and I were first going out, we spent a lot of evenings at her parents' house. One scene: They had a record player in their living room, and for some reason they had an old David Frye album that they loved. It was one of the albums on which Frye satirized Richard Nixon. I believe there may have been a track on the album on which Frye imitated Nixon as he would sound on marijuana. I'm not sure.

What I am sure about is that Nancy's parents played that album over and over, and they laughed out loud together. It couldn't have been that funny a record. Comedy albums, by their nature, have a rapidly diminishing half-life; you can only hear the jokes, and the response of the audience in some faraway nightclub, so many times before you know what's coming. As every child's father once warned as the child told a joke again and again: It's only funny the first time.

In Nancy's house I don't think the David Frye album was intended to serve the purpose of providing constantly fresh humor, though. Nancy's parents laughed every time, but I'm not sure they were even listening to the jokes. The album was in their home and they were in for the night and they were sitting together, not looking for something else. It struck me as kind of monotonous, at least then; I wondered why they did it. Now I think I know.

It was very late when I went back to my room in the hotel. I could attribute my mood to a lot of things: the news Ronnie had given us, and the impending end of the summer, and my lifelong proclivity for making everyone's problems my own.

That might have explained a lot, but it didn't explain what I did next.

The clock by my bed said it was a few minutes after 5 A.M. Eight o'clock in the morning in the East.

From my wallet I pulled the phone number I had been carrying since Florida. I dialed the number on Longboat Key. Mary's grandmother answered on the second ring. No, she said, Mary wasn't asleep. They were just finishing breakfast.

A moment later, Mary's voice was on the line, quizzical.

"Hello?" she said.

I didn't know if I'd have to identify myself, or whether she'd recognize the sound of my hello.

"Mary?" I said. "Can you talk?"

The question mark in her inflection turned into something lively and glad.

"Hey, cap'n!" she said. "Where are you?"

Just the sound made me smile.

"I believe the term was 'chief,' " I said.

"Well, it's hard to keep all you guys straight!" she said, laughing now.

It was dark where I was and light where she was. I don't know what it is, over all the years, but it still makes things better just to realize that someone is excited to hear your voice.

Twenty-four

IT WAS A SHORT HOP over to Las Vegas. I wasn't particularly eager to go, but Ronnie said he wanted to spend a few days there, and Michael seemed kind of enthusiastic about it. It was going to be his first time. And they made the classic Las Vegas argument—that it was on our way back East anyway. Las Vegas always seems to be on someone's way somewhere.

So, a foursome once again, we arrived at night. Ronnie had a contact at the Mirage, where he'd stayed on other occasions, and our rooms were waiting with champagne on ice. To the front desk, we were the Hepps party. Apparently Ronnie was no stranger to the gaming tables in this particular casino.

We walked between the rows of slot machines, crowded with players and sightseers, and edged along the craps tables. Michael kept staring, which I took to be a sign of his amazement at the surroundings—not just at the Mirage, but at Las Vegas itself. At least that's what I thought he was seeing.

"Only place like it, huh?" I said.

"I guess," he said.

"What, you're not stunned?" I said.

"I'm stunned, but not at what the place looks like," he said. "I've seen enough pictures. It's what I expected."

"Then what's that look?" I said.

"Well, I guess these are the high rollers, right?" he said.

"Some of them, I suppose," I said. "Over there, behind the ropes— I suppose those people would qualify. The rest are just regular gamblers, here to play."

"I expected them to be older," he said. "High rollers are supposed to be these worldly people who have ten or twenty years on you. Look."

I was. More than half of the people playing at the casino tables were our age or younger. Some of the men with the biggest piles of chips in front of them appeared to be in their early thirties.

"You're right," I said. "I never thought about it."

"I mean, you hear about the Las Vegas casinos, you picture . . . maybe not James Bond in *Dr. No*, but Bugsy Siegel or somebody," he said. "Somebody who can call you 'kid' and look right through you."

"But think about James Bond in *Dr. No*," I said. "The famous scene? Where he was at the chemin de fer table in his tuxedo and the woman asks his name? The 'Bond . . . James Bond' scene?"

"Right?" Michael said.

"Think about his face in that scene," I said. "He was definitely younger than we are. No way James Bond was over forty in that scene."

"I don't think I want to know that," Michael said. "Older than James Bond. What a concept."

Ronnie and Gail were directly in front of us. One of the pit bosses— he was clearly in his mid-thirties—caught sight of Ronnie and called, "Mr. Hepps! We heard you were coming tonight. Nice to see you again."

"Good to see you, Greg," Ronnie said to him. "I'll be down to do some business a little later. We're just unwinding now. Just got in."

"Anytime, Mr. Hepps," the man said. "If you need anything at all, I'm here until four o'clock." In the morning.

"Leonard working this week?" Ronnie said.

"He'll be here tomorrow," the man said. "If I see him before you do, I'll tell him you're here."

"Very good," Ronnie said. He sounded quite at home.

"Older than the pit bosses," I said to Michael.

Whoever Leonard the pit boss was, I knew I wouldn't be spending much time with him. I wasn't a gambler, at least not the Vegas kind, not the kind who traffics in chips and tokens. By the time Leonard arrived for duty tomorrow night, Mary would be in Las Vegas. When I gamble, I gamble.

Out by the fountain in front of the Mirage, Michael and I mingled with the other visitors who had come to see the place out of curiosity. Many were taking snapshots. The night was oppressively warm, even now; I know the desert is supposed to chill dramatically between sunset and dawn, but not tonight.

"I guess you can't stage-manage someone else's life," I said.

Ronnie and Gail had gone upstairs to change, and had told us that they were going to spend several hours in the casino. They hadn't invited us to join them, and we hadn't asked. So here we were, checking out the sights, as if we were at Valley Forge. Someone asked us where the white tigers were, and we said we thought they were right inside the big concourse, over there through the main entranceway.

"I don't have any interest in stage-managing his life," Michael said. "I've got enough trouble handling my own."

"I'm not saying he's right or he's wrong," I said. "But you have to admit, they seem to enjoy each other."

"Oh, come on," Michael said. "What's that mean? They 'enjoy each other.' This isn't spring vacation 1963. He's got people who count on him. They 'enjoy each other.' You actually think that he's going to stick with Gail?"

"Maybe that's not the point," I said, not even believing my own words, but trying them out anyway. "Maybe Gail's not the point. Maybe he is ready to change some things."

"Then let him go home and find out if he still wants to change the things six months from now," Michael said. "This is so selfish and so hurtful. He's feeling loose with some woman he met at some Hyatt pool, so he decides to throw away his wife and his kids. If this was a big business deal he wouldn't have made up his mind so fast. He'd consult with people and string the other side along and think of every angle and edge. He spends a couple of weeks with Gail, though, and all of a sudden the first forty-three years of his life are dispensable."

Some Japanese tourists came up and asked us where the trapezes were.

"Trapezes?" Michael said.

"Acrobats," one of the men said. "Over the casino."

"That's Circus Circus," I said. "Different hotel."

"They have acrobats in the casino?" Michael said.

"And half the time the gamblers don't even look up," I said.

"What if the acrobats fell on the tables?" he said.

"The best I can recall, there are nets," I said.

"I wouldn't be getting into this if I didn't love the guy," Michael said.

"I know," I said. "Me, too."

"I just don't want to look back, ten years down the line, and realize that I could have said something to help convince him not to do this, and that I kept my mouth shut out of some warped sense of politeness," Michael said.

"You heard what he said about how bad things are at home," I said.

"I don't care," he said. "This isn't the way to do it."

Someone behind us said the volcano was just about to go off.

"I don't see how the people who live here can stand this heat every day," Michael said.

In the morning we had a slight outbreak of the Litany of Adult Experiences. It didn't last long.

It started in the coffee shop, at breakfast.

"You worry because the waitress didn't write down your order," Michael said, providing the opening salvo.

Gail, not understanding, thought that he was complaining about our particular waitress. "I'm sure she can remember the orders," Gail said. "It's her job."

"It's not her he's talking about," Ronnie said. "It's the Litany of Adult Experiences."

"You reminisce about the price of stamps," I said.

"You read the business page first," Ronnie said.

"We'd better not get started on this," Michael said. But we already were.

"You think the neighbors are keeping their sprinkler on too long," Ronnie said.

"You use shoe trees consistently," Michael said.

"You're convinced that the car repair shop is taking advantage of you," I said.

I think we hoped that if we didn't dwell on why we were doing this, it might stop by itself. It didn't. We strolled through the casino, not nearly as congested in the daytime.

"You wake up at night and you think you heard a tile blow off your roof," Michael said.

"You're too full for dessert," I said.

"You're annoyed when people laugh too loud," Ronnie said.

In the gift shop we looked at postcards and souvenirs.

"You see that a movie is rated PG, and you realize that you're the parent who's supposed to provide the guidance," Michael said.

"You're sure the bank made a mistake," I said.

"You remember winters that were even colder," Ronnie said.

We sensed that if we kept this up, the whole day would be blown. We rode the elevator to our rooms without adding one more item to the Litany. This was encouraging. We changed into bathing suits, met at the pool, and got four lounges next to each other. We knew the sun was too intense for us to stay out more than an hour—maybe not even that.

"You consider gardening as a hobby that might be fun," Michael said. His eyes were shut, his face was covered with sweat.

"You get excited about the money you save when you buy generic drugs," Ronnie said.

"And you recommend the drugstore to all your friends," Michael said.

"You think Nova Scotia sounds like an interesting place for a vacation," I said.

For a few minutes there was silence, save for the music from the loudspeakers. It was just too hot to talk.

"You want to send soldiers places to wipe out bad governments, because you're too old to be a soldier," Michael said.

"You don't want to send soldiers places, because your kids are old enough to be soldiers," I said.

"You request paint samples," Ronnie said.

Michael walked over to the pool, dipped his entire towel into it, then brought it back and lay the wet towel on his lounge. Ronnie put one of his towels over his face.

"You're grateful that Metamucil is now available in tasty wafers," Michael said.

"What's that supposed to mean?" Ronnie said, his voice muffled from beneath the towel.

"You'll find out," Michael said.

"You go to the hardware store even when you don't need anything, because you think it's fun," Ronnie said, muffled.

"You grouse because the new butcher isn't as good as the old one," Gail said. Not bad, I thought grudgingly.

We couldn't last five more minutes in the sun. We headed inside to go back to our rooms.

There were other people in the elevator. Some had suitcases with them; they were checking in.

"You see people kissing in public and you think it's disgusting," Michael said.

"You think an iced lemonade sounds much better than a cold cocktail," I said.

"You know a judge," Ronnie said.

The other people said nothing. This was, after all, Las Vegas. Still, I could see them looking at us.

The elevator door opened.

"You go shopping for a new bathrobe," Ronnie said.

In the Delta arrival area of McCarran International Airport, I read the Las Vegas *Review-Journal* and waited for the flight to come in.

According to the paper, the city was becoming something of a magnet for Americans seeking something new. Between the lure of the gaming industry (with casinos needing employees to work three full eight-hour shifts, 365 days a year), and the dry desert air (it appealed to retirees with respiratory problems, or so the story said), and a growing reputation as a town that was welcoming to young families, Las Vegas promised to be one of the fastest-growing urban areas of the next several decades. Ten years earlier Las Vegas had been worried about Atlantic City diluting its perceived appeal and siphoning visitors away, the story said; now Atlantic City was considered a hull, a distressed territory, and Las Vegas was poised once again to become a boom town.

I looked up at the flight board. Ten more minutes.

It had been Mary's idea to come. When I had spoken to her from Marina del Rey, I'm not sure what I had in mind, but if I'd been thinking about seeing her, she beat me to it.

"Are you going to be in California for a while?" she'd said. "I got some frequent flier coupons for my birthday. I can get a free trip anywhere in the country."

"We're leaving California in the morning," I'd said. "And besides, I don't know if you want to waste your coupons on such a quick trip."

"Will you be quiet?" she'd said, and I could almost see that grin over the phone. I thought about the Crest test.

So I'd told her we'd be in Las Vegas, and when we had registered at the Mirage there was a message waiting for me saying that Mary would be arriving at 12:32 the next afternoon. I checked a flight directory to make sure that was right (years of double-checking names and numbers for stories have made me incapable of not making sure); her flight was an early-morning one out of Tampa, so she'd have to be getting up in the middle of the night on Longboat Key and somehow arranging a ride to the Tampa airport, more than an hour to the north.

And now here I was. The airport slot machines, which fascinate first-time visitors, were doing active, if not capacity, business; there are always people who truly can't step off their flights into Las Vegas—or get ready to take a flight home—without dropping money into the airport-corridor machines.

I don't know why I was feeling so eager and impatient. It's not like this was the first time I'd waited in an airport for someone I was anxious to see. I guess that's one of the mysteries—the desire to see a face that makes you happy is utterly perennial, it's one of the few things that never wear out. I would guess that the desire is just as strong at the end of your life as at the beginning. Maybe even stronger. You see it in airport eyes all the time.

Part of me was a little apprehensive. Florida had been terrific, but it had been unplanned—there had been nothing expected, nothing assumed. This might be different. I'm always wary of those potential moments when you find someone averting their glance, and you know that you're both thinking: Now why did we get ourselves into this?

But mostly I was looking at the clock and wishing the plane would hurry up. And then it was pulling toward the gate. I watched through the big floor-to-ceiling windows as it came across the runway, and there was a slight delay while the tunnel was rolled out and hooked up, and the passengers slowly disembarked, there must have been seventy or eighty of them and none of them was her. I was thinking that she'd missed her ride to Tampa, or that she couldn't get a free ticket on such short notice after all, or that something had happened to make her change her plans. But then there she was, in a white skirt and a blue man's-style shirt, even tanner than when I'd seen her last, a garment bag slung over her shoulder, and she was still twenty feet away and there was that smile.

She reached me and she said, "Viva Las Vegas, Mr. Kroeger," and it was like the sun coming up, that's all, nothing more exhilarating and renewing than that.

We were on our way to the airport parking lot when I heard someone call my name.

I looked around for the voice. "Ben!" I heard again.

Standing by a limousine, in a dark business suit of the kind favored by Las Vegas casino executives—I think they like to emphasize the distinction between them and the flashy itinerant gamblers—was Nat Rosen. I hadn't seen him in about five years.

We walked over and I introduced Mary to him. Nat was a vice president for public relations and marketing at the Las Vegas Hilton. A man in his late fifties, he had helped me out on a story I'd done for the network about how Las Vegas can make a one-night championship prizefight bring in millions of dollars in profits for the hotels and casinos. Nat had smoothed the way for my crew and me to get access not only at the Hilton, but through his contacts at other hotels all around the city.

"What are you doing, Nat?" I said. "You leaving town?"

"No, no," he said. "Gloria Estefan has been appearing in our showroom for two weeks. Her final show was last night. We just dropped her off here and got her on her plane. You need a lift anywhere? I'm going back to the hotel."

The driver came around, as if to take our bags. But I said, "Thanks anyway, but I've got a car here."

"Are you staying with us?" he said.

I said I wasn't. I told him about Ronnie's relationship with the bosses of the Mirage.

He gave me a reproachful look. With the tens of thousands of hotel rooms in Las Vegas, casino executives don't like old guests sampling the competition.

"I have to tell you, it's a great hotel, Nat," I said.

"I know, it's beautiful," he said. "No question about it."

Standing there on the curb, he seemed to be thinking about something.

"How long are you in town for?" he said.

"I'm really not sure," I said. "A couple of days."

"I don't know that I can do this," he said. "But if I can free up the Elvis Presley Suite, would you be interested in moving your bags on over?"

"The Elvis Presley Suite?" Mary said.

"Elvis always performed at the Hilton when he was in town," Nat told her. "The Hilton was his home away from home. He spent more nights with us than at any place other than Graceland.

"We knew from the beginning that we couldn't put Elvis Presley in a hotel room. Not even in our best suite. I mean, think about it—Elvis in a regular suite? So we built him a house on top of the hotel. That's what it is, really. Four bedrooms, two huge living rooms, six bathrooms, a full kitchen, a dining room, a bar—the average good-sized family house in America is about two thousand square feet. The house we built for Elvis on top of the hotel is five thousand square feet."

I'd heard of the suite, but I couldn't quite comprehend what I thought Nat was telling me. "Wait a minute," I said. "You're offering to put us in the Elvis suite?"

"I can't promise until I make a few calls back at the hotel," Nat said. "But I think it's sitting empty until Smokey Robinson comes in to perform next week. So if it's empty for a couple of days, and my bosses don't have any objections, I don't see where it would be much of a problem."

"I'm not sure I understand," Mary said. "No one else wants to stay there tonight?"

"Oh, it's not for rent," Nat said. "It would be occupied every night if it was. You can't reserve it or ask for it. After Elvis passed away in 1977, we've just used it for our headliners in the main showroom. Cosby loves it. But when the showroom is dark, or when we're between headliners, no one uses it. About once a year we let Colonel Parker host a reception for some of his Las Vegas friends, but even he doesn't sleep there."

"Colonel Parker's still around?" I said.

"Oh, yeah," Nat said. "We see a lot of him."

"So you're actually saying . . . ," I began.

"Don't start packing yet," Nat said. "I'll call you at the Mirage in about an hour. Then I'll know."

He started to get into the back seat of the Hilton's limousine.

"Nat, if you can do this . . . ," I said.

"Hey," he said with a throwaway flourish he had learned over the years. "Maybe this will convince you not to leave us for every new hotel that opens its doors."

"I cannot believe this," Ronnie said.

Nat had taken us up the elevator to the thirtieth floor of the Hilton. Now all of us—Ronnie, Michael, Gail, Mary, me, along with Nat and two bellmen and their carts—were standing in the hotel corridor outside a set of double doors.

Two armed Hilton security guards played cards at a table. "We really don't have any alternative but to post the guards here," Nat said. "The thirtieth floor is accessible by the regular elevators, because we have some function rooms and conference areas up here. But people are always trying to break into the Elvis suite. Look at this."

Next to the double doors was a bare rectangle on the wallpaper, as if something had been ripped away, with two shaved bolts in the center.

"We keep trying to put up a commemorative plaque," Nat said. "Just a piece of brass with 'Elvis Presley Suite' on it. But even with the guards here, people figure out how to steal it. They wait until the guards are on break, or when they're called somewhere else. When did this last one go, officer?"

One of the guards at the table said, "Must have been a day or two ago. I was assigned up here night before last, and it was still there."

"This is Mr. Kroeger, by the way," Nat said to the guards. "He and his guests will be staying in the suite for the next couple of days."

"Enjoy it, sir," the guard said.

Too weird. Nat had called the Mirage with the news within half an hour of when Mary and I got back from the airport. I had hunted up Michael and Ronnie and Gail. I sensed in Ronnie just the slightest hint of petulance; he'd gotten us the good accommodations at the Mirage, and now I think he felt he was being one-upped. Still, how could you say no to this?

One of the bellmen opened the doors. Straight ahead of us was a marble landing. Across the landing there was a wide flight of steps leading down to an even larger entranceway. Then more steps, then yet another entranceway, this one still bigger. The enormous living room was directly in front of the triple landing. Off in the distance was a set of French doors, constructed to open onto the roof of the hotel.

"Come on," Nat said. "Let me show you the lay of the land." We followed him through the dining room, with its long mahogany-topped table, through the kitchen—much bigger than the kitchen in the house where I grew up—and down a back hallway.

"These are the three guest bedrooms," Nat said. "Take your pick."

"Who used to stay in the guest bedrooms?" Michael said.

"Elvis' best friends and bodyguards would sleep in this wing," Nat said. "Usually it'd be Joe Esposito, and the West boys—you know, the cousins, Sonny and Red." Each room was spacious, and was elegantly decorated; two of the rooms had two queen-sized beds, one a single king.

"Is this decorated the way it was when Elvis died?" Mary said.

"No, no," Nat said. "Elvis' taste was a little . . ." He paused. "A little flamboyant," he said. "We've completely redone the carpets and wallpaper. Actually, I think we've redecorated two or three times since 1977."

We circled back, and were in a large sitting area off the living room. "This we would never change, though," he said. A white baby grand piano was positioned by the far wall; a bench with a plush fabric seat was pushed beneath the keyboard.

"He would play on this all the time," Nat said. "The maids would say that they'd come in at seven o'clock in the morning, and the bodyguards would still be asleep in their rooms, and Elvis would be sitting at the piano in his blue pajamas, just playing. Usually gospel music, they said. He didn't stop when he saw them; he would wish them a good morning and keep right on playing. It's really something when you think about it. Those maids were probably the smallest audience Elvis Presley ever played for."

"And where did he sleep?" Gail said.

"That's usually everyone's first question," Nat said. "Come on."

He led us toward the trio of landings where we had entered the suite. There was a short hallway right off the bottom of the third landing. The other three bedrooms we'd seen were clear on the other side of the structure.

"Don't be nervous," Nat said. "Come in."

It's funny; he was right. We were skittish about walking in. It was only a hotel room, and Elvis had been dead all these years, but just knowing what it was made us involuntarily hesitate, as if we needed to ask special permission. What an eerie hold to have on people. You're not alive, and you never even knew the people existed, but they get silent and shy because during part of your time on earth this was your home.

Twelve steps down the hallway, Nat said: "The master bedroom."

How strange. The room was not all that immense. The color scheme was dark red and brown, and the drapes were drawn. The big bed faced a long, low chest of drawers that divided the room into two parts.

"Hit the button next to the bed," Nat said.

I did, and there was a whirring. A color television set rose slowly out of the top of the bureau. Powered by a hydraulic device, it ascended into sight. When it was fully risen, the whirring stopped.

Behind the bureau was a study, with a desk and a couch. The bathroom opened onto this area; a Jacuzzi whirlpool with folding doors was within view of the couch.

"He always liked to keep it dark in here," Nat said. "I'm told that he never opened the draperies."

Elvis' bedroom was in contrast to what we had seen in the rest of the suite, which had been drenched in sunlight. "When we built this suite, it was at the highest point in Las Vegas," Nat said. "You'd think he would have liked to look out his windows. But I don't know."

The bellmen were waiting for us to tell them where to put our stuff.

"I'm going to get out of your way," Nat said. "Have you decided who wants to take which rooms?"

None of us answered. All of us knew what the others were thinking.

After a few seconds, Ronnie said: "Ah, go ahead, Ben. You're the one who liked him so much, anyway."

And so it was that I unpacked my clothes in Elvis Presley's bedroom.

"Is this a dream, or what?" Mary said.

We were out on the roof. Sure enough, the French doors at the far end of the suite were built to open up onto the very top of the hotel. Elvis, or so Nat had told us before he left, liked to be tan onstage, but he could never go down to the Hilton's pool. Imagine the scene—Elvis Presley lying on a pool lounge, the sight of him in his swim trunks available to anyone who wished to wander by.

Thus, up here on the gravel-covered roof, a patio of sorts had been constructed. It really wasn't very fancy at all; just a fence, the kind you'd see in the yard of a suburban home, providing a perimeter so that the user of the patio would not be tempted to walk to the very edge of the roof itself. If you did that, and you tripped or kept walking by mistake, you would fall thirty stories to the parking lot below.

Without any windbreaks up here, the breeze was severe. Mary's short hair was blowing back off her forehead, like it had when I'd first met her on the beach.

"Do you feel funny being here?" I said.

"In Elvis' suite?" she said. "Is there anyone who wouldn't?"

"I don't mean that," I said. "I mean being here with me. Flying out here to meet me."

"Oh, yeah, I feel terrible," she said.

"Well, I didn't know whether to call or not," I said.

"Every time the phone rang since the day you left, I was hoping it was you," she said.

316 · *Bob Greene*

That surprised me. People aren't usually so straightforward when they're talking about something that has the potential to make them look exposed or imprudent. I'm not used to it.

"That's really the truth?" I said.

"Yeah," she said. "I guess there's no accounting for taste, is there?"

Michael, Ronnie, and Gail had gone out to explore the hotel. So when we went back inside, we had the whole suite to ourselves.

"Look at this," Mary said. There was an elevator door inside the suite; one of the bellmen had said that the private elevator went directly to the showroom on the main floor.

"I guess he had to have it," I said. "It would be sort of anticlimactic for a guest to come out of his room and see Elvis Presley waiting for the regular elevator."

"I know," Mary said. "Elvis in that white jumpsuit and wraparound sunglasses, tapping his feet in the hallway and looking at his watch and standing with all the other guests until the elevator comes."

In the living room I sat on a long, overupholstered couch that made me feel as if I was going to sink straight to the floor. Mary joined me and said, "I don't want to talk about Elvis."

"We have to," I said. "In this place? How could we not?"

"Not now," she said. "I want to talk about what you've been doing since I saw you."

"Not nearly as interesting a subject," I said.

"I kept thinking about whether I should call you," she said. "I didn't know what you'd think of me if I did."

"How were you going to find me?" I said.

"That was the problem," she said. "I couldn't. I called your office in Washington to see if you were checking in for messages, but they said you were on a leave of absence and didn't call in."

"You're kidding," I said. I had been routinely calling the office about once a week, just to ask the desk assistants what mail had arrived, and to see if anyone was looking for me. It seemed that no one ever was. Now it appeared that the office wasn't even keeping track of my calls.

"Did they offer to take your name?" I said.

"No, they just said you were expected back in September," she said. "They sounded real busy. They sounded like they didn't have time to deal with it."

I tried to envision the bureau, and what she was saying made sense. I knew how it always was when someone went away for a two- or three-week vacation—the person would come back, expecting everyone to ask about his or her trip, and almost no one in the bureau would even know that he or she had been gone. In that place, preoccupied with covering breaking news twenty-four hours a day, if you're not physically there you cease to exist.

"So you were going to leave word that you called?" I said.

"I probably would have chickened out," she said. "I think I probably would have hung up if they'd offered to take my message."

"Why?" I said.

"I told you," she said. "I was worried about what you'd think of me."

"What were you afraid of?" I said.

"Same thing I was afraid of in Florida," she said. "That you'd think I was a jerk because I was too easy."

I squinted my eyes at her.

"I'm serious," she said. "Look at me. You call, and I'm on a plane flying across the country. Pretty hard to get, huh?"

"Would you prefer being more evasive?" I said.

She looked up at the ceiling and pretended to be pondering. Then she kicked off her shoes and dropped them to the carpet, reached down and pulled mine off too, and said: "Nah."

I glanced down at my shoes on the floor.

"Wouldn't seem right to put our shoes up on Elvis' couch," she explained.

"I thought we weren't going to talk about that guy," I said.

You go through your whole life guarding yourself; you talk, full of apparent confidence and optimism, and all the time you're wondering whether what you say sounds ridiculous, and whether you're revealing too much of the secret, scared fool who's inside you, and whether the people you meet will see the performance that's the long-running, open-ended stage show of your existence, and will find that performance wanting.

You guard yourself every day, and after a while you don't even know it's happening. You wait for a sign that they haven't fallen for it and that they know just how breakable you are.

It doesn't help that you're aware everyone is like that; it doesn't help that everyone in the world is guarding himself every minute. You do your best not to let on that you have any self-doubt or any fear, and almost all of the time you get away with it. You get through the day undiscovered.

And it's so good when that rarest of things happens, and you find yourself with someone in whose presence none of that is necessary. There's no specific signal that tells you; at least if there is, I am not conscious of where to look for it. But you know, and it's almost as if you are breathing cleaner, lighter air. You don't have to worry, and you don't know why.

Mary and I talked for hours that afternoon; we talked about important things and we talked about meaningless things and I didn't think that I could ever tire of it. It wasn't as if we were checking off items on lists, not as if we had to cover the most substantial, eventful particularities of our two worlds; there was no itinerary that started with family, and then career, and then future. It was much easier than that. It was being somewhere I wanted to be, and not being careful and really believing I didn't have to, believing it so much that it didn't matter if I turned out to be wrong. We talked and I listened to her voice and we'd laugh and it felt like time was going slow, but it wasn't slow enough.

"I've never been to this town before," she said.

"Do you want to take in a show or something tonight?" I said.

"No," she said.

Ronnie said he wanted to go downstairs and gamble.

"Why?" I said.

"I don't understand the question," he said.

They'd all come back up after roaming through the hotel complex; Gail was carrying a bag from the women's clothing store in the concourse, and Michael had one of those packs of film that's really a disposable camera.

"I've got to get some pictures of the suite," he said. "Otherwise everyone will say I made it up."

He began walking around, aiming and shooting.

"I think that's the underwater model," I said as he snapped a picture of Elvis' living-room bar.

"The bar?" he said.

"The camera," I said.

He held it close to his face. It was, indeed, made for shooting underwater pictures—families use cameras like that for taking pictures of their kids swimming below the surface of pools.

"I think I liked the world better before," he said. "Not only can you buy a pack of film that's a camera now, but you have to make sure the thing works above ground."

"It does," Ronnie said. "I've made the same mistake. You can use it on dry land."

Michael took a picture of Elvis' wastebasket.

That's when Ronnie said that he wanted to go down and play some craps. There was no dissuading him; he and Gail went around the corner to the pal/bodyguard wing, changed clothes, and said they would be in the casino.

After they'd left, Michael and Mary and I went into the kitchen and popped open some Cokes from the icebox.

"You ever gamble these days?" Michael said to me.

"Never," I said.

"You?" he said to Mary.

She shook her head from side to side. I was very glad she was here; for a moment I found myself thinking about how less fun this whole Elvis suite experience would be without her. It's just nice to have someone to be wide-eyed with.

"I don't even play the Ohio Lottery," Michael said. "What's that, a buck a ticket? I just never gamble at all. I wonder why Ronnie does it."

It didn't make much sense, at that. There are a lot of people who might be excused for getting sucked into the gambling routine in Las Vegas—people who hope they might get a couple of lucky rolls of the dice, and improve their lives a little bit, at least for a few weeks. With Ronnie, though, it made absolutely no difference. Whatever money he might win wasn't going to affect him one way or another, and he'd have to lose enormously for the loss to hurt him. But Michael and I were up here, we weren't even going to sample the slot machines, and Ronnie was down at the tables. Never try to figure out the nature of hunger.

In the morning I thought I heard a chiming. It seemed to be coming from a great distance. I ignored it at first, but when it continued I stopped shaving, walked down the short hallway leading from the master bedroom, and went to the front door of the suite.

No one there.

The chimes continued. I followed them all around the suite. The others were still sleeping. I moved toward the sound of the bells, and finally located it off a rear corridor.

The suite, it turned out, had a back door, for service personnel. I looked out the peephole and saw three figures.

When I opened the door, three bellhops—two young men and a young woman, they could have been Las Vegas high school students on a summer job—were holding a small laundry box between them. Now I remembered—Ronnie had sent a few shirts down yesterday.

"Your shirts are ready, sir," one of the bellmen said.

I reached for the box, and the other bellman said, "May we put the shirts in your closet for you?"

They were wearing neat gray uniforms. All of a sudden I got it—the fact that it took three of them to bring up one little box of shirts, the way all three of them had been holding it as if to signify their proprietary interest in that box, their desire to bring it in personally—when was the last time a bellman didn't merely hand a guest a shirt box at the door?

Of course. They wanted to see the suite.

"Sure," I said. "Come on in."

They seemed edgy—the same way we had when we'd first walked in yesterday. They were peering around the suite as if it were a secret cave. Finally one of them remembered why they were purportedly here.

"Which closet would you like these shirts placed in, sir?" the first young man said.

"Forget it," I said. "I can take the shirts. If you want to look around, feel free."

"Really?" the bellwoman said.

"Take all the time you want," I said. "I'm surprised you don't come up here all the time."

"We can't," the first bellman said. "The bellmen's regular passkeys don't work in here. It's a firing offense if you're caught in the Elvis suite without authorization."

Which probably made sense. If the employees of the Hilton—the housekeepers, the bellmen, the room-service waiters—had access to the Elvis suite the way they had access to regular hotel rooms, the place would never be empty. They've got to be as curious as anyone else.

"So you've never been up here?" I said.

"No, sir," the second young man said. "When we saw that the shirts were for this room, we all three hustled to the service elevator before our supervisor could see us. He'd kill us if he knew all three of us came up."

"Don't worry about it," I said. "I won't tell on you."

The young woman had a camera in her hand. "Would you do us a big favor?" she said.

They stood underneath a crystal chandelier, arms around each other. The second bellman—he was a full-faced, red-haired fellow—struck an Elvis pose, or what passed for it: legs bent, finger pointing at the camera, sneer on his face. I shot three times.

After the third flash I gave the camera back to them.

"Are you staying up here by yourself, sir?" the first bellman said.

"No," I said. "I've been traveling with some friends."

I went out with Mary for most of the morning; we had breakfast in the first-floor coffee shop and watched the people in the casino for a while. Michael joined us; he had the car keys, and the three of us cruised around town for half an hour or so, taking in the neon scenery.

He said that he wanted to drive way out onto the desert, just to see what it looked like and felt like. I didn't want to do that; I asked him to drop me back at the Hilton.

"You're not feeling abandoned, are you?" I said as he let Mary and me out of the car.

"Nope," he said, and I could tell he meant it. I think, ever since stopping in to see Ellen and the girls in Bristol, he was feeling more fortunate in his life than either Ronnie or me. I couldn't argue with that. I think he was content to let our trip lazily wind down, and then to return without regrets to the place he was happiest.

He drove out toward the freeway, and Mary and I reentered the Hilton. She said she wanted to check with the health club to see if there was a running path nearby; as far as we'd been able to determine, there were only parking lots and city streets. She said she'd meet me in the room in a few minutes.

I rode up to the thirtieth floor. The guards were looking at the elevator door as soon as it opened. They saw it was me, nodded hello, and I let myself into the suite.

Down the three landings, all the way across the long living room, the French doors were open. I didn't know whether the housekeepers had done it, or what.

So I walked across the thick carpeting to close the doors, and when I got there I saw three people on the roof. Two were women, and they were undressed above the waist.

They were lying on lounges, their faces toward the sun, and Ronnie was on a lounge between them. He didn't see me yet. A fresh cigar was in his mouth, and on the arm of the lounge he had propped a miniaturized portable TV set, at which he was staring.

I could tell that one woman was Gail. I'd seen her in skimpy bathing suits many times by now, but on the roof of the Hilton she was naked save for a scant bottom, and she was covered with what must have been some kind of tanning oil. She was quite a sight.

The woman on the other side of Ronnie, though, was even more striking. Her long blond hair was pulled back, and the tan lines on her chest were dark, almost black, against the white skin of her breasts. She held a bottle of Evian water so that its base rested on her belly.

Ronnie, his eyes on the miniature TV screen, blurted out: "That fucking Canseco!"

Gail turned toward him. "What's wrong?" she said.

"Oh, he just hit a home run," Ronnie said. "The Indians are down by four."

I didn't know quite what to do. So I just said, "Hello."

Ronnie sat up. "Where've you been?" he said. "You were gone when we woke up."

"We were downstairs," I said, seeing that Gail had sat straight up, too, giving me a welcoming wave as if I'd been looking at her with no clothes on for her whole life.

"Hi, Ben," she said. "Want to join us?"

Then:

"This is Ruthanne. Ruthanne, Ben." Like we were at dancing school, and it was time to introduce everyone to the couple next to you.

The blond woman sat up, flashed a big smile at me, and then stood. Just like that. "Hi!" she said. She walked over and shook my hand. "This place is so great!"

Ronnie was still watching the ball game.

Gail and Ruthanne stood in front of me. "We met Ruthanne down in the casino last night," Gail said. "She's here with some friends from San Diego."

"Girls' weekend away from the families," Ruthanne said. "Our husbands get to come to Vegas with their buddies, so this weekend it's their turn to stay home and babysit."

They didn't seem to be self-conscious in the least. Maybe I'm the one who doesn't understand the way the world works.

"We told Ruthanne about the suite, and said she should call us this morning if she wanted to get some sun," Gail said.

"You should have seen how much trouble I had getting the hotel operator to ring this suite," Ruthanne said. "I had to talk to two supervisors before they'd put my call through."

"There's another chair," Gail said to me. "You're sure you don't want to lie out with us for a while?"

Like a gracious hostess, as if I were suddenly her guest here. "I don't think so," I said. "Too hot."

"Oh, but it's such a good feeling up here," Ruthanne said. "You feel so free. No one in the world can see you."

Well, I could. And Ronnie and Gail could. But I suppose that didn't count. After all, they were developing a fast friendship. And me? I came with the room, like the ice bucket.

So they went back and lay beneath the high desert sun, and Ronnie concentrated on the American League on TV. It was hard to take my eyes off the two women, but in a way the most instructive sight of all was that of my friend, those beautiful undressed bodies on both sides of him, watching his television set. I'm not sure how you get to be like that—how you become a person who isn't surprised even by something like this, who takes it as his due in a high-flying, money-talks, jaded-beyond-humor world. I looked at Ronnie and I wanted to somehow find him when he was fifteen years old in some suspended-animation childhood summer past, and yank him out of that past and into right now, and hold the fifteen-year-old by the shoulders here on the roof of the Hilton, point him at the three people in the sun, and say: Here. See that? That's you. That's what you're going to turn into. Thought you might want to know.

But there is no suspended-animation past, and Gail rolled over onto her stomach and Ruthanne moved the bottle over her belly and Ronnie put some white cream on his nose as he turned temporarily away from the TV. I went inside, where it was much cooler.

The man at the door of the Hilton showroom said he wasn't supposed to allow anyone in. I explained where I was staying, and he made a phone call, then unlocked the door.

"When you're finished, just come back out this way," he said.

I had seen Elvis Presley perform only once, almost twenty years before, and it was on this stage. Tonight, even though there was no entertainment scheduled and the showroom was closed, I'd wanted to come down.

Michael and Ronnie and Gail and Mary were upstairs; we'd had dinner in the suite, and I had told them I'd only be a minute. Now I was walking toward the front of the showroom, past the tables and booths, until I was close to the massive raised stage itself.

A couple of union stagehands, on duty getting some equipment ready for Smokey Robinson's upcoming stand, saw me and asked if I needed something.

"I'm just looking around," I said. "I'm staying up in Elvis' room."

One of them motioned me toward a door against the wall. "There's a little flight of stairs, then take a left," he said.

So I did, and off to the side of the big stage we talked for a bit. They hadn't been working here during the years Elvis was performing at the hotel regularly; I told them what it had been like to see him, walking across the stage in that white jumpsuit, it not even mattering very much at that point whether he was good or not. The people out in the seats had come to this room from all over the world not because they required him to be good, but because it was enough for them that he was Elvis.

"He never played to an empty seat here," one of the stagehands said.

"Not once?" I said.

"Never," he said. "You ask the maître d'. That's never happened before, with anyone, and it hasn't happened since."

"May I?" I said, nodding toward the stage.

"Be my guest," the stagehand said.

So from the wings I walked across the wood, and unexpectedly I heard a high-pitched mechanical sound.

The heavy, multi-layered showroom curtain had been in its lowered position; the second stagehand had turned a key, and now the curtain was rising. As I reached the center of the stage it was pulled all the way to the ceiling. I walked to the front edge.

It was just a room. A huge room, decorated to please its particular customers, but it wouldn't feel like anything at all had Elvis not spent all those nights on this stage. I saw all the empty tables. What must it do to a person, to know that every night he will look out and see every face at every table, stretching back beyond his field of vision, every face staring raptly at him, every man and every woman here only because they want to be able to say that once in their lives they set eyes on him?

There had been no shortage of Elvis jokes during our time in the hotel; indeed, it would be difficult to be staying in that suite and not give in to the impulse. In the years since his death he had become a grotesque cartoon to many people—in the living room of his suite after I'd come inside from the sun deck, I had been watching a game show on TV, just to kill time, and the host, out of nowhere, had made a crack about Elvis eating thirty pizzas. In the Hilton gift shop the weekly tabloids featured their standard garish Elvis headlines. He's a generic icon now, a totem, an easy gag.

I'm sure that he, too, could not turn on the television or pick up a newspaper without knowing he might see that name. "Elvis." I stood on the stage and tried to imagine.

There was a person here—a person who, by all the accounts I had read, was awkward and lonely as a child, and who turned into this thing called "Elvis." How, in one lifetime, do you go from a shack in Mississippi to a place like this, riding the elevator downstairs twice a night to let the thousands look at you, riding it back up to a magnificent house on the roof with armed guards posted to keep adoring strangers from your door? Maybe some people could handle that. As the entire world now knows, Elvis could not.

I walked off the stage. I left swiftly and thanked the man at the door. I stood at the main bank of elevators in the lobby and when a car arrived I punched the top floor. When I got to the suite the rest of them were sitting around the living room, having some drinks and talking.

We'd bought an Elvis tape in the gift shop; it had seemed like the appropriate thing to do. Now they had put it into the stereo, and a post-Army Elvis song called "I Need Your Love Tonight" was pounding through the room. It was funny, I suppose—Elvis' voice in Elvis' room.

I looked over at the white piano. What must it have been like to be alone in this room, to look out the windows and see that name, the name that defined you, in letters forty feet high on billboards in all directions? How do you sit in a room and know that you are Elvis Presley?

I walked past the piano and opened the French doors. I went onto the roof, past the lounges where Ronnie and the women had sunned themselves in the afternoon, up to the little fence that had circumscribed Elvis' cloistered patio. It wasn't hard to climb over the fence; just a short step and I was out where the huge air-conditioning shed and the hotel's auxiliary water pumps were housed.

I looked back at the suite; I could see my friends in the living room. Elvis' voice from the stereo bled through the walls so that I could just make it out in the wind. I saw the lights of Las Vegas below me on three sides; nothing in the vicinity was higher than where I stood. I tried to conceive of him out here on nights like this. A person on a rooftop.

There was a line written by the late poet William Carlos Williams: "The pure products of America go crazy." Mary came out and then she was right next to me and she asked me what I was doing, and I said nothing, and she looked at me for a second and she asked me if I'd been crying, and I said no, and we went back inside.

Later, in bed, I tried to tell her about what I'd been thinking.

"I believe that any person who has any kind of success has got to identify with the guy, at least a little bit," I said.

"You mean in show business?" Mary said.

"Any business," I said. "That's the thing—no matter how big you get in any business, you're never going to be as big as Elvis was. It's impossible. You can be chairman of the board of the Ford Motor Company, making millions of dollars a year, running this huge corporation, thinking there's all this pressure on you—and then you realize you can walk down most of the streets in the world and no one will know you. So your highest highs are never going to even approach what Elvis went through.

"And no matter how low you go, whatever your deepest fear of failure, it would be hard to go out in a worse way than Elvis did. With the whole world examining the misery of your life and reading the lists of the drugs in your blood and watching videotapes of you when you're a physical wreck. Over and over, on TV every year on the anniversary of your death, and it's never going to stop. The worst kind of public humiliation. And it doesn't even matter whether some baseball star or CEO or senator thinks that Elvis was a no-talent hick. Elvis was bigger than they'll ever be, and he fell further than they'll ever fall, and I think that on some level Elvis represents their greatest dreams and their most awful dread, all at the same time."

I had pulled open the drapes. One reason that Elvis always kept them shut became immediately apparent: the huge red Hilton sign atop the hotel, visible from all over the desert, ran right along the wall next to the window by his bed. The red glow lit the room. It was like in one of those old 1940s detective movies, where the private eye always woke up with the hotel sign flashing on and off outside the window of his fleabag room. Apparently it had been the same thing with Elvis, but, as always, on a much loftier plane.

"Do you think he slept with a lot of women in here?" she said. She was propped up on one elbow.

"Well, I suppose," I said. "But do you know what I once read about this room? I don't know why it sticks in my mind, but it does. I read it in one of those meanspirited biographies of him—apparently the author thought this made Elvis look pathetic, but I don't think so. Here he was, performing before all those screaming people every night, making all the money in the world, having strangers tell him that he was their idol. And do you know the one thing he always kept by his bed?"

I pointed at the night table.

"Right next to the bed," I said. "The national Jaycees had named him one of the Ten Outstanding Young Men in America, and they gave him a trophy for it. I guess it meant something to him. Because every night, when he went to sleep, that's what was by the bed. Even in his worst days, with the drugs and the illness and the obesity, when he was just about incoherent, he kept that trophy there. Outstanding young man. I guess that's what he wanted to be."

I had told her about Gail and the other woman out on the sun deck; Ruthanne had left to join her friends from San Diego after a few hours, but it was a hard visual image for me to shake.

"Maybe she was flirting with you," Mary said.

"That woman?" I said. "No. I can guarantee you she wasn't flirting with me. It was more like Elvis had taken her top off."

Mary started laughing. "Now you're really getting nuts," she said. "Elvis took her top off?"

"Not literally," I said, knowing she already knew that. "But I'm not sure if that woman would have done that with just any people she'd met, even on a private sun deck. She was up here because she wanted to see Elvis' room, and I think she took her top off because she felt that in Elvis' room anything was allowed."

"Come on," Mary said. "She was flirting."

"No," I said. "Really. Elvis always had the power to make people lose their inhibitions. The guy's been dead all these years, and it's like he's still taking women's clothes off."

She was still laughing.

"I mean it," I said, laughing now, too, but serious. "Look at all of us this week—he never knew we were alive, but we're here because of him, and we'll be telling people we stayed here for the rest of our lives. Listen, long after you've forgotten about me, you'll be telling people you slept in this bedroom."

"Quiet," she said.

"You will," I said. "Come to think of it, staying with you in Elvis' bedroom is probably the best way to make sure that you do remember me. Sort of a built-in guarantee."

She took a pillow and held it over my head for a second. We talked some more and I closed the drapes to get rid of that constant red wash from the rooftop sign. Later, when I was just drifting off to sleep, I thought I heard her say she loved me. But when I opened my eyes she was looking the other way, and I couldn't tell.

We were due to check out of the hotel the next day. In the morning we had breakfast sent up, and we ate at the suite's big dining-room table. The room-service waiter brought a stack of newspapers—the Las Vegas paper, *USA Today*, the New York *Times*, *The Wall Street Journal*—so we read as we ate, and we discussed where to go next.

Michael had had enough of Las Vegas. Ronnie liked it here; even though we had to give up the suite, he was trying to talk us into going back to the Mirage. It didn't particularly matter to me. Mary was going to have to fly back East, so I'd go wherever Michael and Ronnie agreed on.

We hadn't come to any conclusion. Even at eight o'clock in the morning the sun outside was fierce, searing the windows in the dining room and promising another day of relentless heat. Ronnie said that he had to make a few phone calls, and he went into the living room to do it, and that is when he found out he was fired.

Twenty-five

HE WAS GONE QUICKLY. At first we didn't know anything was amiss. He was making his calls somewhere in one suite, and when fifteen or twenty minutes had passed and he hadn't returned to the table I went out to look for him.

He was in his room, throwing things into a suitcase. His face was ashen.

"Ronnie?" I said. He kept packing.

"Did something happen at home?" I said.

He turned to me, his voice shaking.

"They moved on me," he said.

At first I thought he meant his family.

"I'm out," he said.

"Ronnie, what are you talking about?" I said.

"My job," he said. "I'm out."

He was going to head right for the airport. He handed me one of his credit cards.

"Make sure Michael and Gail get plane tickets," he said. It was something he could have gotten away with not thinking of.

"Listen, do you want to talk?" I said.

"I have to go," he said.

In those few minutes he seemed to have become a different person. The bluff, blustering hotshot on holiday had evaporated. The man in the room with me now, trying to get everything crammed into his bags, was someone I'd known a long time ago, he was Ronnie before the world had taught him anything. Strip a person suddenly of everything he has come to assume, and what you're left with is the boy who started out. The Ronnie who was scared and shaken was someone I sensed that I knew. All of a sudden he wasn't sure of a thing.

"Is there anything I can do?" I said.

"Just ask Gail to come in here," he said. "I don't want the others to see me right now."

As he was leaving, no one knew quite what to say. He hadn't told us much more than what he'd said to me in the room. He was in a big hurry. Michael and I offered to drive him out to the airport, but he said he'd rather go by himself.

Gail rode the elevator down to the lobby with him. Michael and Mary and I tried to figure out what might have happened.

"I thought he ran the whole company," Mary said.

"He had the title of chairman," I said. "There were a lot of other operating guys who worked with him." It was funny, how easily I fell into the past tense when talking about his job. And I didn't even know the details yet.

"But didn't you say that the job was guaranteed or something?" Mary said. "Because of his wife?"

"That's what doesn't make sense," Michael said. "The way I always understood it, he was chairman no matter what. Part of Sidney Steele's deal when the company went public. A person designated by the Steele family remained as chairman."

That's what I had always thought, too; that's the way Ronnie had explained it.

"So he said nothing to you at all?" Michael said.

"You know everything I know," I said.

This was already scheduled to be our checkout day at the Hilton; now there seemed to be an unspoken urgency to it. Ronnie had departed with such haste that none of us had thought about where we'd go next. We knew we were getting out of here, though, and we went to our rooms to pack.

I'd been thinking about what Mary had told me—about how she'd tried to phone me at the bureau in Washington, and how no one had offered to take a message. It was about time for me to call in and check on the mail, anyway, so from my room I did.

"How's it going?" I said to the editorial clerk who answered the phone.

"Busy," he said. "The Secretary of State left for Egypt this morning. No one knew he was going until an hour before the plane left Andrews. We had to scramble a crew to go with him, and they just made the plane."

It was like something out of another world. Before June, I had been used to dealing with that kind of discourse every day. Today, I imagined all of the frenzied phone calls and directives at the bureau, all the raised voices and instant decisions. All for a story I wasn't even aware of.

Apparently something significant was happening in Egypt. Back before Memorial Day, I probably could have at least filled in the bare outlines of the story. Not now. I had no idea.

"Listen, Mel wanted to talk to you when you called in," the clerk said.

Mel Rothman was the bureau chief—the man for whom I worked. He had granted me the leave of absence, and I'd been planning on calling him soon, to decide when exactly I should return to work.

"Is he in?" I said.

"Yeah, he's on the phone," the clerk said. "Hold on."

I knew I'd be holding awhile. I could envision Mel's phone console, with fifteen or twenty lines blinking. He was always very calm as he worked his way through the endless calls all day. And we all waited our turns; that was part of the rules of the game, and the essential paradox of it always amused me. Those lights on Mel's phone represented some of the most famous and powerful people in America—cabinet members, department heads, our own White House and congressional correspondents. A cabinet member would probably be able to jump to the head of the line. But the rest of us—including the very top political correspondents, men and women who, because of the network's cachet, virtually never had to wait for news sources to take their calls—waited patiently for Mel. Our White House guy might be impressive to the viewing public, and the announcement that he was on the line might cause government officials all over Washington to leap for their phones. But he, like all of us, was just another light on Mel's board when he called in. We'd learned to sit on hold and like it. Or at least understand it.

So I waited. Mary came into the room. I was sitting on the bed, and she climbed on and rested her head against my shoulder. I put my arm around her and waited for Mel.

"Ben!" he said after about five minutes.

"How are you doing?" I said.

"Where are you?" he said.

I glanced around Elvis' bedroom. I decided there would be no point in being specific.

"Las Vegas," I said.

"Oh," he said, making no attempt to pretend he found that interesting. I appreciated that. Most people, if you say you're in Las Vegas, probably would offer the obligatory questions about whether you were winning or losing at the tables, or ask about the stage shows. Mel didn't care. I wasn't a person in Las Vegas to him; I was a lighted button on his phone, to be dealt with and dimmed and thus made free for another call.

"Listen," he said. "We need to talk. When are you going to be in town?"

My stomach jumped a little. Maybe it was because of what had just happened to Ronnie.

"I don't know," I said. "You and I were going to discuss when I should start back to work."

"This is something else," he said. "Are you going to be anywhere near here so you can come in for a few hours?"

"Is something wrong?" I said.

"No, no," he said. "We just need to sit down."

"Is it something we can do on the phone?" I said. I wanted to know—now.

"I'd rather sit down with you," he said. "I want some other people in on the discussion."

"Hey, Mel, you know how I am," I said. "If this is some kind of bad news, don't make me wait. Is something going on?"

"Now why are you thinking about bad news?" he said. I could hear his incoming phone lines chirping, and in his voice I could hear his chronic desire to get off this call and start the next one.

"If there's something you want to tell me, just give me a general idea," I said.

"It's very good news for you, as a matter of fact," he said. "Listen, there's really no big hurry. But if you're going to be in Washington, call in and we'll set up a time. Where did you say you were? Los Angeles?"

"Yeah, I'm west," I said, knowing it wasn't worth the effort to correct him.

"Well, whenever you have time," he said. "Bye." And then he was gone.

"What was that?" Mary said.

When someone tells me that there's good news and that there's no rush about it, my immediate assumption is that I'll be the one to determine what news about my life is good, thank you. And I'd better hurry to find out.

"Nothing, really," I said.

Ten minutes later I called the bureau back and said I'd be in to see Mel in two days.

From the thirtieth-floor hallway, there was a knock on the door of the suite.

"Sorry," Gail said after I'd opened it to let her in. "I don't have a key."

She came inside. After a few seconds I said: "Well?"

"Well, he's gone," she said.

"What did he tell you?" I said.

"Not much," she said. "That he'd call me when he could."

"And he didn't explain about what happened with the job?"

"I didn't ask," she said.

"You didn't ask?"

"No, I did not ask," she said, moving past me to the room they'd shared. "If he'd wanted to tell me, he would have."

I followed her into the room. "And now what?" I said.

She looked at me, irritated. "What is the question, Ben?"

"What are you going to do now?" I said.

"As far as you all are concerned?" she said. "I suppose what I'm going to do now is say adios."

She walked over to a chair by the window and sat down. "I know you haven't approved of my traveling with Ronnie," she said. "I hope your feelings won't be hurt if I tell you I don't much care what you think."

"He told us that he was moving out of his house," I said.

"He told you that he was thinking about moving out of his house," she said.

"He sounded like he was pretty sure," I said.

" 'Was' is right," she said.

"You think that's not going to happen now?" I said.

"Oh, use your head," she said. "Everything just changed. Your friend's life just blew up."

"And so you're going to take off."

"He's got enough to deal with," she said.

"And he doesn't have a job," I said. "Is that what you really mean?"

She gave me a long look.

"How much are you guys paying for this suite?" she said.

"I don't know," I said. "I don't think anything. It's not a suite you can pay for. It was empty for a few days, and I think they're comping it."

"Yes, I think they are," she said. "And why are they comping it, would you say?"

"I just told you," I said. "Because there's no price on it, and it wasn't being used."

"No," she said. "I mean why are they comping it to you?"

"Because that guy you met the first day here knows me from some work I did out here," I said.

"Work for your TV network, right?"

"That's right," I said. "What are you getting at?"

"So the reason we're in this suite is because the hotel wants to suck up to your network," she said. "And all this money that Ronnie's been spending all summer—where did that money come from?"

"You know where it came from," I said.

"From his wife's father, who's dead," she said. "Ronnie's a wealthy man because he married a girl who had a wealthy father and the wealthy father dropped dead."

"What's your point, Gail?" I said.

"My point is that you seem to think I'm somehow a less than moral person because I chose to travel with your friend this summer," she said.

"I never said anything about morality . . . ," I started to say.

"Let's not quibble over words," she said. "You don't think very highly of me. But I don't work for some TV network, so no one's going to put me in a room like this for free. And I don't have a husband whose father died and made him rich. So there's a lot of things in the world that are beyond my means to see."

Her voice wasn't angry, just balanced and even. She was looking directly at me.

"I happen to think your friend is a very nice guy," she said. "And I was very happy to be able to see some of the things I've seen this summer with him, and to go to some of the places I've gone. Did I want to spend the rest of my life with him? No, although I would have been quite content to spend some more time with him. Did I think I was the cause of the problems in his marriage? No, I knew from the start that I wasn't.

"But that doesn't matter, because that's not your point. Your point is that you think it's wrong for me to be here. And maybe it is. I happen to be aware that men like to look at me. I'm told that I tend to make their dicks hard. Sorry to be so indelicate about it, but I think you can take it. I'm saying it because it's a fact. It has nothing to do with who I may be inside. The same way that your job has nothing to do with who you may be inside, and the same way that Ronnie's wife's money has nothing to do with who he may be inside. So if the fact that men like to look at me sometimes enables me to go certain places and see certain things, I will not apologize to you for it. You may not want to think about this, but I am very much like you. Certain things are made available to me for all the wrong reasons. That's something I'm sure you can understand."

We were still looking right at each other. "Why don't we just call this a difference of opinion," I said. "I have no desire to pass judgment on the way you live your life. I was just watching out for my friend."

"And I'm sure it will come as no surprise to you that I made the decisions about the way I choose to lead my life long before I met any of you," she said.

"All right," I said. "Why don't we stop this."

"The best person of the three of you is Michael, anyway," she said.

"You won't get any argument from me," I said.

"That man is one of the kindest and most decent people I've ever met," she said. "And while you're condemning me for the selfish way I lead my life, you might think about how he must feel on a night like last night. Here you are, taking off for this summer together. And last night he's all by himself. Ronnie's in one room with me, and you're in your room with your little college friend, and Michael's by himself."

I didn't have an answer to that one. It's not like I hadn't thought about it.

"I swear," Gail said, "Ronnie fell asleep last night, and I was lying awake, and I came within about one second of getting up and letting myself into Michael's room and just crawling into bed with him and holding him."

"Why didn't you?" I said.

"You know why I didn't," she said. "Because he would have asked me to leave. Not just out of loyalty to his wife and kids. Out of loyalty to Ronnie, too. He wouldn't have done that to his friend. And you and I both know it."

Outside the window the sun was so harsh, I would have bet the desert was already well over a hundred degrees. "So what are you going to do?" I said.

"Eventually?" she said. "I suppose by the fall I'll be in Atlanta, working in some dentist's office scraping stuff off strangers' teeth. Same place I was going to be before I met you three."

"What about right now?" I said. "I'm sort of the travel agent today. I'm supposed to take care of getting everybody's tickets."

"I'm not leaving town for a while," she said. "I'm going to stay in Las Vegas a couple of days before heading east."

"But where will you stay?" I said. There it was again: this unexplainable impulse to look out for people who haven't asked to be looked out for.

"I'll be fine, Ben," she said. "I was taking care of myself fine before I met you all, and I'll be taking care of myself fine long after you're gone. But thank you for asking. And I'm not being sarcastic."

I looked at her. The world's a lot more complicated than we often fool ourselves into presuming.

"Drop me a postcard sometime," I said.

"What'd you say your name was?" she said, smiling and giving me a wink that meant goodbye.

Out at McCarran Airport late that afternoon, we stood together in the main lobby.

"Here you go," I said to Michael. I handed him his TWA ticket. I'd picked up the tickets for both of us at the hotel. He had decided to go to Bristol, at least until we knew what the story was with Ronnie.

"You want to call me, or should I call you?" he said.

"Either way," I said. "I'll be at my house in Bethesda tonight."

"Okay," he said. "If I hear from Ronnie before you do, I'll let you know right away." He turned to Mary and shook her hand. "I hope I see you again soon," he said.

"Me too," she said, not just as a courtesy but as if she meant it.

He walked toward the security checkpoint and the gate. Watching him head off for a destination of his own seemed odd; that was one thing I hadn't seen since the summer had begun.

Mary had her Delta ticket to Florida.

"So," she said.

"So you're going to be late," I said.

We stood there, our eyes not leaving each other.

"Thank you very much for the lovely occasion," I said.

I saw her start to cry.

"I'm sorry," she said.

"I'll call you soon," I said.

She nodded her head and turned abruptly and strode rapidly in the direction of her gate. I wanted to follow, I wanted to say something else. But my own USAir flight to Washington was loading on the other side of the airport complex.

I made it with a few minutes to spare. The plane was crowded; I was lucky to get an aisle seat.

On the runway I saw Michael's plane take off for Ohio; I saw Mary's plane take off for Florida. Then I was in the air, and I looked out the window and saw that curious city in the desert fade from sight, and then we were speeding across the country and I was a lone traveler in a jet high above America, as I had been so many times before.

This was my life; this was the way I spent my days and nights. In a few weeks I'd be back to doing this—setting out in a cab for an airport alone, sitting in a cabin full of strangers as the pilots steered us toward a city where one of my bosses in Washington or New York had decided I should be, checking into a hotel after midnight, meeting my crew at dawn.

It was a good way to make a living; I had been very lucky to be allowed to do it for so long. So I wasn't sure why I was feeling suddenly hollow right at this moment. Maybe it was just that I had come to take the summer for granted: I had come to take for granted the company of my friends, and the sound of their laughter, and the knowledge that every day they were going to be there.

Or maybe it was that the plane ride was reminding me too vividly about other aspects of my life. About how being so untethered and transient, so willfully portable, had gradually become the defining condition of my existence. I think it must have seemed romantic at one time. Now I thought of people who went home to families and dinner tables every night, and I felt something very much like envy. It sounded awfully good.

Which, in the context of the summer, at first glance did not seem to make a lot of sense. The promise of the summer, as we had envisioned it, was for us to be always at liberty, unfettered and without anchor. So the idea that I, among the three of us, would soon be returning to a traveling job should not have felt subduing.

Yet it undeniably did. By choosing the kind of life I had led for so long, or by having allowed it to choose me, I had given up something very valuable, even precious. I lived somewhere, but I had no home. I had been moving so fast, for so many years, that the concept of home now had very little to do with me. For Michael and Ronnie, perhaps the summer had been in large measure a temporary respite from the routines of home. For me, it had been almost a substitute for home, a surrogate for something I had never quite understood I was missing.

But I guessed this was my home now—a seat in an airplane five miles up in the sky. It had been for some time. It was a trade-off I had made many years ago, without being fully apprised of the consequences.

How can anyone know that, though? It's not something you can understand in advance. You make that first trip and the next thing you know you're a thousand trips down the line.

A man in the aisle of the plane, returning to his seat from the rest room, stood staring at me. He was trying to place me.

When I looked up he said, "I'm sorry. Don't I know you?"

I said I didn't think so.

At the front door of my house I pulled out my key ring and it took me a moment or two to find the right one. It had been a while.

When I opened the door, everything was as I had left it. I'd asked a neighbor to look in on things every week or so, just to make sure nothing was wrong. So there were no surprises. It was the house I had departed from right after Memorial Day. It might as well have been preserved in some museum of suburbia.

For a lot of people, coming back to an empty house after all this time might feel strange. I'd grown accustomed to the feeling. I walked up the front stairs and tossed my bags into the bedroom. It had been a long day, but there was one thing I wanted to be sure to do before I fell asleep.

I dialed the number in Cleveland. Marilyn answered on the second ring.

"Is this a bad time to call?" I said when I heard her voice.

"Hello, Ben," she said.

"Is he there?" I said.

"Let me see," she said.

A full minute passed, maybe more. When she returned she said, "He really doesn't want to talk."

"Is he going to be all right?" I said.

"I think he will be," she said. "It's just very hard right now."

I left word for him to call me as soon as he felt he could. I undressed and went to bed. When the phone rang I woke with a start, wondering for a minute what hotel room I was in. I reached for the phone.

"I woke you, didn't I," Marilyn's voice said.

"No, it's okay," I said. "Just give me a minute."

I sat upright and tried to gather my senses. The clock said I'd been sleeping for less than an hour.

"He's up in our room," she said. "I'm downstairs. I just thought you'd want to know about everything."

And she told me. The board of directors of Steele International, in what they had termed an emergency meeting, had voted to remove Ronnie as chairman of the board. Their stated reason was that they had determined that his continued presence was detrimental to the shareholders of the company; they felt that a professional manager should be in charge of the corporation, and that under Ronnie's stewardship the profits of the company were well below what they should be.

"Did you know about this?" I said.

"Not until the vote was taken," Marilyn said. "They sent some lawyers out to the house to talk to me. The lawyers were here when Ronnie called from Las Vegas. That's when he found out. I was the one to tell him."

"I thought they couldn't do that," I said. "I thought the chairman had to be from your family, and that it was mostly ceremonial."

"That's the reason they gave for getting rid of him," Marilyn said. "They said that Ronnie was conducting business he had no right to conduct. They said that by making certain decisions and authorizing certain expenditures, he was in violation of his employment agreement."

"And I take it he's not holding up so well," I said.

"Not good at all," she said. "He's been . . . he's been sort of falling apart, Ben."

"They couldn't let him stay on and keep the title under the old rules?" I said. "If he promised not to go beyond what they want him to do?"

"They say no," she said. "It was all I could do to keep them from changing the lock on his office and removing all the files."

"You're kidding," I said.

"No," she said. "They wanted to examine every piece of correspondence. They're playing real hard. They claim that by making all these deals on his own, he broke the law."

"Do you believe that?" I said.

"No," she said. "I think they just want him to go quietly, and making threats is their way of being sure that he does."

"Would they even listen to you?"

"Me?" she said. "It's not a family business anymore. I think that's what's behind what they're doing. It's a public company, and my dad's dead, and the board is tired of pretending that they have to consult with my family on anything at all. It just made it easier on them that Ronnie's really not a Steele."

"So what does this mean for you?" I said.

"Financially, we're fine," she said. "That's not in question. My dad made sure of that. But Ronnie feels naked. He feels like the whole town's laughing at him."

I didn't know what to say. It had seemed that every bit of Ronnie's self-regard had been tied up in being chairman of that company, that he had all but forgotten who he'd been before he was given that office. All the honorary civic committees he was on in Cleveland, all the charity dinners where he was seated on the dais, all the pictures on the society pages . . . everything stemmed from his being chairman of the board of Steele International. It was as if the person he used to be had never existed.

Now I sensed that all along he must have feared this. We're never really the men the words on our office directories say we are; we're merely people who happened to end up sitting behind certain doors.

"Is there anything I can do?" I said.

"I'm going to try to get him to call you," she said. "This isn't good, him just sitting around in our room. He won't see anyone."

"I'm here," I said.

"He really needs to talk to someone," she said.

Then: "I guess you know that things haven't been all that great between us for a long time."

I didn't want to say more than I should. So I said, "How's that going to affect what happens with him next?"

"I'm afraid he thinks I want him to leave," she said. "He's thinking that without his job he's nothing. I'm afraid he thinks I think that, too."

I didn't even try to respond.

"But I want him here with us," she said. "It's a little late in our lives to just give up. That's why I want him to call you. He needs someone he trusts to calm him down and tell him that he'll get past this."

"Is there any chance at all that the board will compromise?" I said. "From what I can tell, Ronnie's gotten to be pretty good at what he does."

"They would disagree with you," she said. "I don't know how much is because they think he's not qualified and how much is because they just want to run everything by themselves. But no, they're not going to compromise. The lawyers let me know that if we chose to take it to the shareholders, they'd be forced to bring up this summer."

"What about this summer?" I said.

"They just don't think it would go over too well at an annual meeting," she said. "The chairman of the company running away with his friends for an entire summer. For no good reason."

"We had our reasons," I said.

"I know," she said. "Think about explaining your trip to an auditorium full of Steele International stockholders."

I told her that I'd wait to hear from Ronnie. She said she knew it wouldn't be tonight. She'd do her best to get him to call just as soon as she could.

"If you want to call again, please don't be shy about it," I said.

"Thank you, Ben," she said. "And thank you for being his friend."

We hung up. I was hungry all of a sudden, but I knew there would be nothing in the refrigerator downstairs. I had cleaned it out at the beginning of the summer. I went back to sleep, or tried to.

"Hey, Ben," Carla, the morning desk assistant, called to me as I walked into the fourth-floor newsroom at the bureau. "How was your vacation?"

My vacation. My summer-long leave might have carried great symbolic weight on my own continuum of priorities, but in the scheme of the bureau's newsgathering mechanics, I was just a correspondent Carla hadn't seen in a while. It would have served no purpose to explain to her; telling her about my leave would have been no different from telling her that I'd been on assignment in, say, Ecuador. She would just have said, "Oh, I guess I knew that," and continued to check the Associated Press wires.

So I said, "The vacation's fine. Actually, it's not over yet."

"I'm taking mine next week," she said. "Going up to Maine."

"Well, enjoy it," I said. "Good to see you." I wandered through the office, saying hello to the few staff members who were in this early in the day, checking the new memos on the bulletin board, looking at the bureau's troop movement schedule for this day to see what correspondents and what camera crews and producers had been dispatched to what parts of the world.

Mel Rothman had said he'd see me at 10 A.M. The door to his office was closed. Part of me felt like I'd never left. I had the impulse to start making calls and get working on a story. I picked up the morning's edition of the Washington *Post*. Immediately the events of the world began to mean something more to me than they had when I'd read newspapers on the road all summer. I'd see a story on the front page of the *Post*, then check it against our crew list to see who was there for us.

In about fifteen minutes Mel was ready for me. "Looking good," he said, and motioned me into his office. It took only a fraction of a second to realize something was up.

Whitney Sherman, the news division's Washington-based vice president for business affairs, was in one chair. In another was Mark Kushner, the senior producer in charge of correspondents, who had flown down from New York.

"Thanks for coming in, Ben," Mel said. "I know your leave isn't over yet. We appreciate it."

For several minutes we made purposeless conversation. It was a patently artificial exercise: They didn't really care about how my trip with my friends was going, and I didn't really have the enthusiasm to tell them sanitized anecdotes about it. But that's the way something like this is played; they asked where I'd been and what I'd done, and I told them stories. We laughed dutifully, waiting to get down to business. Mark Kushner hadn't gotten on an airplane from New York so that I could tell him the name of a good rib place in Kansas City. He wrote the name of the restaurant down, though, saying he'd have to keep it in mind next time he was out that way. He was never going to be out that way. Each of us waited for someone else to start the real discussion.

"So, Ben," Mel said, taking some unseen signal from the others. "You're back at work when?"

"I thought that's what you and I should decide on," I said. "We always said September, but we didn't set a date."

"Have you given any thought to what you want to be doing this fall?" he said. Right then I knew that he and his management colleagues had already decided what I would be doing in the fall.

"I don't know," I said. "I'd like to do more of the stories I used to do. Just going out and finding stuff. Not so much on top of breaking news. I know you've needed me for basic news lately, but I think I serve you better by coming up with stuff that every other network isn't doing. Show closers—pieces you can end the broadcast with."

They didn't say anything for a moment. Then Mark Kushner said:

"What would you think about London?"

Since leaving Las Vegas, I had been trying to come up with every possibility in my mind; I knew they were going to do something with me, and I wanted to be prepared for whatever they said. But I hadn't given a moment's thought to the idea they might want to send me overseas.

"You mean the bureau there?" I said.

"Congratulations," Whitney Sherman said.

Congratulations were a little premature. "You want me to live in England?" I said to Mel.

"It's quite a tribute to you," he said. "We'll miss you here, but you'll do great work."

On the walls of his office were about a dozen monitors. Some carried satellite feeds from all over the world, coming live into the bureau. The others were tuned to network game shows and syndicated talk programs.

"You'll have to excuse me if I'm a little shocked," I said.

"You were our unanimous choice," Mark Kushner said.

There was an invisible alarm going off in my head telling me: This is not what it seems.

"Are you going to want me to find the kind of stories I used to find here in the United States?" I said.

"Of course," Mark said, and I knew he didn't mean it and he knew I knew he didn't mean it. This was all a little dance to get a necessary piece of business done.

"We're going to make our European operation the centerpiece of the news division," Whitney said.

As I asked questions and began to figure out what was happening, it all started to make sense. Like all the other networks, ours was trying to devise ways to save money in the newsgathering process. Instead of concentrating on producing individual pieces for the evening news, our bureaus would be directed to send back to the United States massive amounts of generic stories and raw tape for use on our break-of-dawn show, our morning show, our noon feed, our newsbreaks throughout the day and night, the evening news itself, our overnight service, and— most important—as a sort of video wire service for all our affiliates around the country. Our crews in Europe would chase stories all day so that local anchors at each of our stations across America could read their own words over the videotape.

This was the only way the news division could justify the staggering expenses of maintaining a full-time worldwide operation. And to do this, they needed experienced correspondents and crews who could turn out large numbers of workmanlike, broadcast-quality pieces in a big hurry. To that extent, I qualified—and to that extent I felt complimented. I can put a story together fast and I can deliver it to a broadcast on virtually any deadline.

But when, a few minutes later, they started throwing around the Murrow-in-London lines, I understood they weren't even pretending to be genuine about it. Every correspondent from every network who has ever been stationed in London has had his bosses remind him of Edward R. Murrow's legendary World War II radio dispatches. London was long the prestige post for a broadcast journalist, and Murrow's having been there was the primary reason why.

We are entering a different broadcast universe, though. In the age of CNN, there is nothing particularly breathtaking about the sight of television reports being delivered to American audiences from all over the globe. Today the Murrow turns are done by the New York– and Washington-based anchors; if war breaks out or a summit meeting is held, the famous anchors, the human logos, are sent to the site in a matter of hours. That is how the viewers at home know a story is important: if a Brokaw or a Jennings or a Rather or a Shaw shows up in person on the scene of a big European or Far Eastern or Russian event.

The rest of the year Europe is mostly the province of guys like me—journeyman correspondents who can be counted on to get the job done consistently and on time. It is honorable, important work. And by the offer of the London job I was being told two things:

First, the network trusted me to report the stories quickly and accurately, to get them on the satellite when they were supposed to be on the satellite.

The second message I was getting was that my years as any kind of a special correspondent were over. What had brought me to the attention of the network in the first place—their feeling that I had the ability to tell a quirky, human story in an unusual way—was no longer of value to them. I was forty-three now, and the news business was changing, and this was the final confirmation of what I guess I had already known for the past few years: that in the constellation of television news, this was as far as I was ever going to go. I was considered consistent but ultimately ordinary. I was competent on screen but not magical. People would watch my reports but not watch out for them. I was that correspondent in the rain, in front of the government building.

"The plan is not to keep you sitting around London, of course," Mel said. "You'll be based there, but part of our new operation will be to cover all of Europe from a London office."

Meaning that because of tight money, we'd be closing our bureaus in Bonn and Rome and maybe Paris.

"So you'll be flying into European cities the same way you've always flown into American cities," he said.

That I was sure of. I'd be standing in front of government buildings all over the world. This is Ben Kroeger, reporting from . . . I'm sorry guys, let's start that take over. I lost track of where we are.

"Do I have a choice here?" I said.

My bosses pretended to be surprised. I knew they weren't. They'd been anticipating this.

"We thought you'd be thrilled," Whitney said.

"It's just that I never thought of myself living in Europe," I said.

"It's a real vote of confidence in you," Mark said.

"I'm very flattered by that," I said. "It's just . . . is this a firm decision?"

"We think you'll shine over there," Mel said.

I asked if I could have a little time to think about it.

"Of course," Mark said. "But we want to have you in place in London by the first of October at the latest. We can talk about housing and logistics next time we get together."

Mark and Whitney shook my hand and they left. Mel and I remained in his office. I've always liked him.

"What do you think?" I said when the others were out of earshot.

"I think you shouldn't even question it," he said. "With the layoffs we've had here, and the layoffs that are probably coming, I think you ought to be ecstatic that you're so highly thought of."

I knew he was being straight; I knew that if, twenty-five years ago, someone had told me that one of the major television networks would someday want me to report for them from London, I would have done backflips.

The lights on Mel's telephone console were blinking, each light a correspondent or producer or newsmaker somewhere in the world. I looked at the lights and I saw myself, calling Mel from London or Prague or Madrid, trying to persuade him that he should push for my story to be included on the evening news. One light among many, begging to be singled out.

On the monitors above his desk, there were feeds coming in off the satellites. A correspondent I used to work with was standing in a public square somewhere. I couldn't tell exactly where, and there was no audio. In a moment the satellite feed was over, and the correspondent and the public square were gone, replaced on the screen in Mel's office by vertical bars representing each color of the television spectrum.

"Daddy!" Hannah said. "Come here! I want to show you something!"

She was in the living room of Nancy's house. They'd returned to Bethesda from the beach two or three days ago. I had called Nancy to say I'd be over just as soon as I was finished at the bureau.

"How did it go?" Nancy said to me.

"You wouldn't even believe it," I said. "I'll talk to you about it later."

"Dad!" Hannah said. "Now!"

I followed her up the stairs. She led me into her room; on top of her little desk there was a pink piece of paper.

"This was waiting for us in the mail when we got home," she said. "From school. These are the supplies we have to bring the first day. Listen."

I sat on the edge of her bed as she stood and read aloud from the sheet of paper.

"One large three-ring hard-cover notebook binder," she read. Her voice was just the slightest bit more formal than usual; reading out loud was like a recital for her, still something out of the ordinary.

"Two sets of notebook dividers," she said. "One spiral notebook, eight and a half by eleven."

Her feet were at attention, one ankle touching the other.

"One three-hole plastic case for binder to hold pencils, pens, et cetera." She didn't pause before the "et cetera"; I assumed that on the sheet it was "etc.," and that she had worked on the proper pronunciation with Nancy before I'd gotten here. There was a little punch to her enunciation of that word, a quick burst of emphasis, and it revealed that she was proud of knowing it.

She looked up from the paper. "Can you believe how much stuff we have to bring?" she said.

"Go ahead," I said. "I want to hear it all."

"Five number two pencils," she said. "One eraser. One supply box for desk for storage of pens, pencils, et cetera."

You talk about miracles—space travel, computer technology, laser science. I don't think there's any miracle that will ever match the triumph of a child learning to read. How does it happen? One day she's crawling and dependent on being fed and changed; so soon she is standing with a piece of paper in her hands, almost confident, knowing the words.

"One twelve-inch ruler," she read. "Two blue or black erasable pens. One red pen. One small scissors. One glue stick."

"One glue stick?" I said.

"Yes, Dad," she said, in a tone of voice she had discovered was the proper way to express exasperation. "A glue stick. Can I keep reading?"

"I just don't know what a glue stick is," I said.

"A glue stick, Dad," she said. Then, as if repeating it a little louder and a little slower would make me comprehend: "A glue stick."

"Like a jar of paste when we were in school," Nancy said. She had come to the doorway of Hannah's room without my seeing her. Now she was in the audience, too. "Remember? Those little jars of paste with the black dippers in them."

"Oh," I said. "They don't have them now, huh?"

"Can I go on?" Hannah said.

"I'm sorry," I said. "Go ahead."

"One package of one hundred index cards," she said. "One small stapler. One package of standard notebook paper . . ."

There was excitement in her voice. For her, September was going to represent the beginning of something. When you're eight each new school year is a fresh adventure, and such matters as who your teacher is and what your schoolroom looks like and which of your friends are in your class—such matters as what supplies you are asked to bring—represent something momentous. This isn't just another September; you haven't had all that many Septembers yet. This is a step into somewhere you still don't know about. This is the third grade, and you've never been there before.

"I'm nervous, Dad," she said after we went downstairs to eat lunch.

"About what?" I said. For a second I had the irrational thought that somehow she knew I was being sent to live in London.

"About division," she said. "I hear we have to do long division this year."

"Well, if you do, I'm sure you'll do fine," I said.

"No no no," she said. "This boy who was in my class last year? Arthur Ross? He already could do long division. He already learned."

"Has there ever been anything you were supposed to learn that you didn't end up learning?" I said.

"But not division," she said.

At the table I wanted to tell Nancy about the meeting with my bosses. This was not the time, though—I didn't want to take the focus away from Hannah's breathless preview of the school year. And besides, what was I looking for from Nancy? Advice? I was on my own here. Nancy doubtless had enough on her mind deciding when exactly to pick up and move to Boston to be with the man who was going to be her husband in her own new life.

New life in Boston, new assignment in Europe . . . awfully glamorous stuff. The enthralling antithesis of settling in and making do and staying put. Awfully thrilling. At least there was a time when I might have thought so.

"What year did you learn division, Dad?" Hannah said.

"I'm not sure," I said. "I never really did learn how to do it so well."

Ronnie's call came late that evening.

"Tell Michael I'm officially withdrawing the job offer," he said. His voice sounded hoarse but at least he was able to joke.

"Ronnie, I'm real sorry," I said.

"Fuck," he said.

There was stillness on the phone. I decided not to tell him that he should look at this as a potential blessing, as an opportunity to do something better. I decided not to tell him that the board of directors didn't know what they were talking about. I decided not to tell him that his future might turn out to be wonderful.

What I did was sit there and listen to the silence coming from the other end of the line, and wait until he was ready to unburden himself of his hurt. He wouldn't have called if he hadn't needed to talk. I saw no cause to hurry him into it.

The strange thing was, as I sat there waiting I was absolutely unable to think of what had happened as the story of a major executive being forced from the chairmanship of a global corporation. I was sure that's what the business pages were saying in Cleveland. And objectively the business pages were right.

But to me it was much more important than that. Ronnie was my friend who had been treated badly and who felt ashamed. Everything disagreeable I had sensed about him all summer—the flashes of mean-ness, the willingness to bully, the lofty attitude I sometimes couldn't understand—all of that had gone away for me now. He was this boy I had known all my life who had had something taken from him when he wasn't looking. Who had somehow gotten caught up in some things he could never have predicted and who had often handled them terribly. I was certain that there were businessmen in various parts of the country who were smirking with soundless delight at the news that Ronnie Hepps had finally crapped out. But he was my friend, had been forever, and I waited on the line.

"Ben . . . ," he said, and his voice cracked.

He knew I'd still be there when he was able to say something. It took a few more seconds.

"Ben, I'm just so embarrassed," he said.

For the next twenty minutes he talked with hardly a pause. He would stop only long enough to compose himself; I knew I wasn't supposed to interrupt and I didn't.

"I never thought I could get a job," he said at one point. At first I thought he meant that he would have great difficulty finding anyone to hire him in the wake of his humiliation. But that wasn't it; as we spoke more it became clear that on a level real to him he had been convinced, all during his adult years, that if he had not married into the Steele family he never would have been hired to do anything of significance anywhere.

"I would never sit in on job interviews," he said, the voice still verging on inaudible. He said that at Steele International everyone knew that he did not wish to be present when applicants were being considered for high-level employment. The other management people thought he was exercising a privilege of his office; why go through the drudgery of interviewing candidates when he could have the executives who worked for him do it instead? On this night he told me it was for a different reason.

"I used to go to the interviews when I first got the chairman's job," he said. "I would look at the people across the table, the people wanting my approval so they could be hired, and I would feel like my skin was transparent. I would feel that they could look right inside me, and that they would know I didn't belong there. I was afraid they could see."

No matter that he was wrong—no matter that he was no better or no worse at his livelihood than a million other men and women. What mattered was that he believed it. What mattered was that he had gone through his adult life waiting to be caught at being lacking.

I knew he was tired; I knew a lot of this came from exhaustion. There was truth there, though, the kind of truth that comes at moments when you have decided you have no defenses. "I will never forgive myself for what I did to Michael," he said. "I think I wanted him to say no to me. I think that's why I was treating him the way I was. I was so afraid of what would happen if he came to work. He'd know. He'd see what I was. He'd know and not say anything."

"Michael knows you already," I said.

"I didn't want him to feel contempt for me," Ronnie said. "I didn't want him to feel sorry for me."

I was almost sure that Ronnie would not have been able to say all this to me if we were sitting face to face. But in his darkened room at home he could talk into the receiver and not be afraid that I would think him foolish.

"I haven't left the house yet," he said. He meant since flying back after getting the news.

And: "I have to go to the office to clear out my things, and I don't think I can do it."

And: "No one has called. The people I work with—none of them have called."

I foresaw that he would never say any of these things to me again. Once this private poison was dislodged from him, whatever need he had to expel it would be fulfilled. That was all right. He might have been exhausted, but not so exhausted as to be unaware of what he was laying open about himself. He trusted me to honor his secrets.

When his hurts did start to mend—when he started to realize that this was something he was going to get through—I hoped he would not forget this night. Maybe right now he was fearful that he was showing himself at his most frail and brittle; maybe he thought that people would disdain him if they saw this. But Ronnie tonight was a person I valued knowing; Ronnie tonight, stripped of all his swagger, was a person I did not want to relinquish.

"I don't know what to do now, Ben," he said.

"Right now maybe you should try to sleep," I said. "Is Marilyn there?"

"She's downstairs," he said.

"Go get her," I said. "She's waiting for you."

"How do you know that?" he said.

"She's been waiting for you for years," I said. "Go get her."

Michael called the next night; he had just spoken to Ronnie.

"Is he any better?" I said.

"Actually, yes," Michael said. "He's going to have to deal with a lot of things, but he sounds like he's thinking about how to do it. My guess is he's going to be okay eventually."

"Did he say anything specific to you?" I said.

"Not really," Michael said. "I just thought there was a little bit of life in his voice. He didn't sound as bad as I had expected he might."

We were in three different cities. Maybe that's what was bothering me. Maybe that's what I wasn't ready for.

"I talked to Marilyn, too, when I called Ronnie," Michael said. "She asked me what we were going to do next."

"What did you tell her?" I said.

"I said I didn't know," he said. "And she said she hoped that we'd finish the summer off together. She said she thought it would be the best thing Ronnie could do for himself right now."

"I'm for it," I said. "What about you? Are you settled in at home?"

"Well, just about," he said. And a second or two later: "My first day of teaching isn't until after Labor Day. Where do you want to meet?"

I laughed and I realized it might have been the first time I'd heard myslf do that since leaving Las Vegas.

"Where do we want to meet?" I said, knowing that as soon as he thought about it for even a moment he'd know the answer. "It's almost the end of August, isn't it?"

Twenty-six

"ARE YOU SURE it's this way?" Michael said.

"Of course I'm sure," Ronnie said. "Right across from the main entrance."

He steered the car onto Eleventh Avenue. The huge red "O" that marked the gate of the Ohio State Fair was ahead and to our right.

"It costs a little more to park this close, but it saves you a long walk," Ronnie said.

I had flown to Port Columbus from Washington; Michael and Ronnie had been waiting at my arrival gate. Now, early on a bright and steamy afternoon, Ronnie was behind the wheel, looking for a place to park near the fairgrounds.

The car could barely move through the mass of pedestrians on Eleventh Avenue. "I don't know, Ronnie," Michael said. "I don't remember there being a lot on this block."

Ronnie took a left onto a little dirt road. In an open field, cars had been parked bumper-to-bumper.

"We've got to find someone who's in charge," Ronnie said.

He spotted a young guy in cutoff jeans and a bare chest.

"He looks official," Ronnie said, throwing the car into park and getting out to talk to the guy.

"That guy looks official?" Michael said to me.

But Ronnie was talking to the shirtless guy, and the guy was motioning toward a rear area of the field.

He jumped back in and got behind the wheel. "Five bucks," he said. "Not so bad."

He drove up to the shirtless guy, who said in a slow, rural Ohio drawl: "Pull it right to the very end there, and put it next to the red Blazer."

"The cars are really packed in there," Ronnie said to the guy. "Do you think our car's going to get dented?"

"Probably," the guy said.

Ronnie laughed. "It will?" he said. "You're telling me that my car's going to get dented?"

"Yeah, most likely," the guy said.

"Okay," Ronnie said, reaching into his back pocket, handing the guy a five-dollar bill, and steering onto the field.

He edged between the other cars that were parked there.

"Excuse me, Ronnie," I said. "But why did you ask the guy if the car was going to get dented if you were going to park here no matter what he said?"

Ronnie shrugged. "At least he was being honest," he said.

"Why don't you make him give you a written guarantee that someone will dent the car while we're at the fair?" Michael said. "Just in case he's wrong?"

"Can you get out that door?" Ronnie said, pulling flush with the Blazer. We already were; we were out the passenger-side door and heading to join the throngs of people on Eleventh.

If, when we were growing up, the symbolic beginning of autumn was the first day of school, then the symbolic end of summer was the Ohio State Fair. I hadn't been there in years. There was a time when to miss the fair would have been unimaginable.

The biggest annual event in Ohio, the fair was held on a massive plot of land on the north side of Columbus, near the Ohio State University. Millions of men, women, and children from all over the state descended on the fairgrounds for two and a half weeks each August; the fair mixed every element of Ohio—indeed, every element of society.

There were city kids and their parents from Columbus and Cleveland and Cincinnati and Dayton and Toledo; there were farm families from each agricultural pocket of the state. There were people from small towns and suburbs—kids like us, kids who would come in for the day from places like Bristol, and then go home to their moms and dads late in the evening. The fair opened its gates just after dawn each morning, and ran until almost midnight. There were midway games and farm-animal competitions and motorcycle races on a track in front of the grandstand, and there were singing groups in concert after dusk; there were boys and girls eying each other on the pathways between the carnival rides and the ball-toss booths, and elderly men and women gathering at the crafts exhibits and pie-baking contests, and people from everywhere checking out the prize pumpkins and championship corn. There was cheap food of every description and the governor in a golf cart and benches where you could rest your feet.

Beyond all that, though, beyond the specifics of the fair, was the ever-present understanding that one more summer was ending, never to come back. It was a fair, yes, but it was also a dusty, sunbaked secular ceremony; it was our last desperate endeavor to keep the summer alive, and at the same time our irrevocable goodbye to something we knew we could not detain. At least it used to be; at least that's what I think it was when we were growing up.

I don't know when the last time was that I'd been to the fair. Maybe twenty years ago; maybe more. We walked across Eleventh Avenue toward the big red "O," hearing already the discordant mix of overamplified music and overlapping voices and midway come-ons that make up the cacophonous annual melody. I wasn't even inside yet and I felt I'd never left.

That particular feeling went away quickly enough.

"What is this?" I said, looking at the back of my hand after we had each paid our six-dollar admission charge. A woman at the main gate had marked each of our hands with a rubber stamp.

"It's a logo," Ronnie said. "Taco Bell."

"What's going on here?" I said.

"Every day a different corporation is official sponsor of the fair," Ronnie said. "I have a friend who's in charge of lining up sponsorships. It costs seventy thousand dollars to be a full sponsor for a day. You get continual announcements made throughout the fairgrounds, you get your signs displayed all day long, and you get to have your logo stamped on the hands of the people who come in."

Amazing. It had come to this. Official corporate sponsors of the Ohio State Fair. As we walked into the heart of the fair itself, I immediately noticed there had been a certain change in the texture of the place. The way I remembered it, most of the vendors had always been of the come-as-you-are variety—the food stands had always looked as if they had been nailed up the night before by some hot dog cooker's nephew, and all the no-name lemon-shake and corn-dog booths were run by itinerant carnies.

Now, though, there were elaborately designed freestanding buildings along all the main pedestrian thoroughfares. A place called Cox's Food Corral was still there, and it had the look of the fair I'd grown up on— picnic tables and an outdoor grill and a hand-painted sign to show hungry patrons where to line up. But right next to it was a pagoda—I don't know what else you'd call it—constructed by the Wendy's hamburger chain. It was like going to a real Wendy's on the grounds of the fair.

"Now why would anyone want to do that?" Michael said. "That's like what you hear about people who go to Paris and look for a place to buy Kentucky Fried Chicken. If you want a Wendy's, you don't need to go to the fair. There are probably a dozen Wendy's between downtown Columbus and the fairgrounds."

But people were pressing toward the pagoda; apparently they now preferred the franchised food.

There was a towering slide off to our left. The idea was to climb a ladder to the top, sit on a cushion, and then skid down to ground level. At first glance it looked like any of a hundred different attractions from state fairs past.

"Check out the sign," Michael said.

The slide was sponsored, too—by White Castle.

"Not a bad tie-in," Ronnie said. "Sliders."

Suddenly the voice of a professional announcer boomed out of loudspeakers that were mounted high on wooden poles. This was not the nasal, singsong, taunting voice of some sideshow barker; this was a voice you would hear on a television commercial, or in an airline terminal advising you to step back because the tram was about to arrive. The voice was male and deep, impersonally friendly and perfectly modulated; it seemed totally out of place on the fairgrounds.

"Welcome to the Ohio State Fair from Nissan—Nissan, built for the human race," the voice said.

"Oh, no," I said.

"You pay for that, too," Ronnie said. "The deal you get is that you pre-tape your announcement, and it's broadcast simultaneously over the whole fairgrounds. So everyone at the fair hears it at the same time."

I momentarily wondered why it was so loud—the volume was high enough as to be disagreeable. But it wasn't hard to figure out.

The various hawkers and barkers selling doodads along the midway were completely drowned out by the Nissan tape. Some of the hawkers looked as if they'd been selling their inexpensive dolls and ceramic plates and metal trays since the last time I'd been here. But as soon as the car-company announcement was blasted from the speakers, there was no way anyone could hear the individual hawkers. That had to be part of the planning—the corporations were guaranteed that no one would hear anything else during their sponsored on-site commercials.

I looked at my hand again. How much more indelible can an advertising message get? Stamped right into human skin.

"Did we look like that when we were coming here?" Michael said.

Half the boys on the midway, it seemed, were wearing black heavy-metal T-shirts proclaiming their loyalty to Megadeth or Anthrax or Skid Row. Sullen-faced and pale and slouching, they traveled in groups past the Troy Amish Pie stand and the Maynard Avenue United Methodist Church baked-goods display.

"We hung together just like they are," I said.

"Yeah," Ronnie said, starting to laugh. "But as I recall, we were wearing Bermuda shorts and madras shirts."

In front of us two women, both in short shorts and halters, both barefoot, pushed strollers. One baby cried. One baby slept.

"I can't believe they came to the fair barefoot," Michael said. The women's feet were caked to the ankles with dirt and midway grime.

"Can you imagine the stuff they're stepping in all day?" Ronnie said.

The women were in their twenties; maybe when we were teenagers at the fair they had been here, too, babies then themselves, being pushed in strollers by their own mothers. I looked at the babies in the strollers. Twenty-five years from now would they be barefoot here, pushing babies in the sun?

The announcement started again:

"Welcome to the Ohio State Fair from Nissan . . ."

The noise buried everything. A child off to the side of us looked as if she was feeling miserable. Her face had been marked with bright yellow paint; someone at one of the booths had painted "Li'l Audrey" across her forehead. She was about two, and she appeared overheated and uncomfortable and exhausted. The personalized slogan on her face must have made her mother happy, though; the mom held Li'l Audrey's hand and pulled her toward a Coke stand.

Four of the heavy-metal kids—these had Ratt and Metallica T-shirts —shoved past us, talking "shit" this and "motherfucker" that. A fifteen-year-old girl in a bathing suit, splashed by the remnants of a Sno-Kone that one of the metal kids had tossed to the ground, yelled at him, "Prick!" Apparently they hadn't met.

"We'd better find the butter cow," I said. "It's our only hope."

"Is it over here?" Michael said.

"It's got to be in that building there," I said.

We walked through an arched entryway into the Dairy Building. A sign on the wall bore the words: "Ohio Dairy Industry. Your Faithful Servant."

"Look," I said. "It's right there."

Inside a refrigerated glass case was the butter cow. It was huge, sculpted from pure Ohio butter: a big pale yellow butter cow. The butter cow was bigger than a real cow.

The glass case was surrounded by spectators. They seemed to be different from the people we'd seen on the midway. These were families who looked as if they might have come straight from church services, or at least from an ice-cream social. PTA moms and Kiwanis dads.

The butter cow didn't have an audio track—no tape recording to explain what it was, no spokesman with a microphone to talk about it. It was just the butter cow, looking silently out at the people with its butter eyes, as it had at every Ohio State Fair. Each year a new cow was sculpted; it was probably the ultimate symbol of the fair. It wasn't advertised or promoted, but everyone who went to the fair knew to look for it.

Some years the butter sculptors got fancy and built companions for the butter cow. The year that Ohio resident James "Buster" Douglas won the heavyweight boxing championship of the world, or so I had been told, there was a butter Buster inside the case next to the cow. Douglas lost the title soon after, and did not reappear in the display. One year, in honor of Ohio's most well-known race car driver, there was a butter Bobby Rahal. People didn't come for the novelties, though. They came for the cow.

This year the cow was by itself. No one seemed disappointed. They filed into the Dairy Building, spent a few minutes with the butter cow, then returned to the sunlight.

"Didn't the butter cow used to be outside?" I said.

"Are you nuts?" Ronnie said. "Use your head. It gets to be a hundred degrees out there. How's the butter cow going to be out in the open? It would melt in a minute."

"Maybe they stood it in ice," I said.

"The butter cow has always been right in here, right on this spot," Ronnie said.

I love that butter cow. We paid our respects and then departed. Ohio dairy industry, your faithful servant.

Bobo was an oddly welcome sight.

"Hey, you, chrome dome!" Bobo yelled at a man who stood directly in front of him.

The man stared Bobo down.

"What are you looking at?" Bobo screamed. "Why don't you go through a car wash and get your head waxed!"

"Come on," Michael said. "We've got to check Bobo out."

Bobo was up in his cage, behind a wire wall. His voice, as always, was purposefully grating; his face was covered with a layer of greasepaint.

"Don't show off for the kid!" Bobo commanded the man, who had been talking to his son. "The kid knows you're a loser!"

The man reared back, fired a ball at the small circular target in front of Bobo, and missed.

"Nice shot, klutz," Bobo screamed.

The man fired again.

"Go home, you stink!" Bobo screamed.

The man paused for a second, took careful aim, then threw as fast as he could. The ball bounced harmlessly off the cage.

"You throw like a girl," Bobo screamed. "Who's next? You, four-eyes? Dump Bobo in the water! If you can throw the ball this far."

Bobo had been at the fair as long as I could remember. He sat in his cage all day and all night, taunting the midway crowd, daring them to hit his target and dunk him. There was nothing physically unusual about Bobo, except for his foghorn voice. I had no idea how old he was; the thick makeup always hid him.

There was something basically unthreatening about Bobo. He was making a living, that's all; you never sensed that he hated anyone. His vitriol was a late-summer tradition—if he didn't infuriate the people, they wouldn't pay to throw the balls at him.

The man with the glasses had taken Bobo's challenge.

"You're sweating, four-eyes!" Bobo screamed. "Better get some windshield wipers or you won't be able to see me!"

"You think the guy minds Bobo saying that?" Ronnie said.

"Nah," Michael said. "What Bobo says doesn't count. People know it's only Bobo."

"I wonder if that's the exact same Bobo from when we were kids?" Ronnie said.

"I doubt it," I said. "It's been twenty-five years."

"I think it is," Ronnie said. "Listen to him."

"Next!" Bobo screamed. "That's right—you, tomato face!"

"That's very interesting," Michael said.

The kid had a sunburn and his face was indeed florid and red. But he was also severely overweight. Bobo hadn't said a thing about that.

"I think Bobo kind of senses what he shouldn't say," Michael said. "I think he knows that this is a kid you don't call fat. I don't know how he knows that."

"What," Ronnie said, "you think Bobo can read minds?"

"No," Michael said. "But there's got to be a reason. The easiest thing in the world would be to call that kid fat. Bobo didn't."

"Go home, tomato face!" Bobo screamed.

"It's the same Bobo," Ronnie said. "I'm sure of it."

The overweight kid threw and the ball hit the dented old metal disc in front of Bobo and Bobo went tumbling into the filthy water in the tank below. The crowd cheered, and the kid raised his arms in triumph.

Bobo, using the cage and the base of his seat for support, pulled himself out of the tank. I could see that he was moving slowly and with some difficulty, stiff and halting and unlimber, but it was impossible to tell anything else from behind the greasepaint.

"You're next, stupid," Bobo yelled. He must have been running out of energy; the "stupid" came out of his mouth before he had really looked at the customer. A generic affront.

We walked away. Past the rides, past the back of the grandstand, past a cotton-candy counter, we rejoined the ever-moving multitude.

"Try me, short stuff!" a voice hollered.

We looked.

"It can't be," Ronnie said.

It was another Bobo in another cage.

"Dump Bobo in the water, shrimp!" this second Bobo screamed at the young man before him.

"Case closed," I said to Ronnie.

"I guess Bobo's more popular than we thought," Ronnie said. "They're franchising him."

The customer's ball just missed the disc that would have dropped the second Bobo into the water.

"One more, runt!" the second Bobo screamed.

We walked on, and I tried to remember a long-ago world in which the meanest thing you could ever imagine was Bobo making fun.

That sweaty, dried-out-inside, baked-in-dust feeling had started to set in. I didn't know where else but at the fair I'd had this precise sensation; probably nowhere. It was as much a part of the place as the sugar-covered elephant ears, and the big caramel apples that looked as if they'd been trucked in from the fields down in Jackson County, and the doilies for sale at rickety card tables. You probably wouldn't expect or want to experience this overcooked feeling in any other setting, but here it was somehow okay. Hard as it is to explain, here it felt pretty good.

The Ohio voices on all sides of me sounded like my own voice, and Ronnie and Michael were looking around at the booths and exhibits as if to miss something here would be to deprive themselves of a portion of the joy. By a corner of the WBNS radio tent a lady was drawing caricatures of teenagers and next to her another lady was cutting out lace-paper silhouettes of children who were posing in austere profile while their parents evaluated the emerging artwork, to be mounted on black paper and hung in family living rooms all over the state, and we stood and watched. A man at a sewing machine stitched names in red thread on the felt brims of black hats with feathers jutting from the top; a father with three children next to him told the man to make hats for

Timothy, Jeb, and Jackie. Someone sold fudge brownies. A girl wore a photo button featuring a picture of her face on top of a cardboard cutout of a weight lifter's body.

Ronnie said he was hungry and that he had seen a rib-supper stand run as a fund-raiser by a local Baptist congregation. It was too hot for ribs, at least I thought it was, but Michael and I went with him, cutting across the fairgrounds, and it occurred to me that in a little over a month I was supposed to be in London, a permanent alien resident with an apartment and a car and documents that said Great Britain was my current official address. Ronnie saw the big tent where the ribs were being cooked and we found a wooden table in the shade. I thought of myself waking up every morning in London and the picture would not form in my mind.

Inside the Bricker Building, the man with the kitchen knives had a microphone on a cord around his neck and a sheen of perspiration on his forehead.

"It's vegetables you want to dice?" he said with great urgency. "This polished steel blade will cut them into vegetables for your salad, vegetables for your dinner, vegetables for your kids to take to school." He had fourteen people watching him—seventeen after we walked up.

Down the aisle from him was a man selling electric blenders. On the other side of a pole was a man demonstrating a multifunction electric iron. Not only did the man with the kitchen knives have to contend with his audience's reluctance to hand over their money; he had to contend with the blender man and the electric-iron man. Every member of the crowd he lost was a customer he would never have.

"You say you never have enough steak knives?" he said.

I was never sure why, when I was a boy, the sight of the men selling products at the fair seemed so riveting compared to the other attractions, so compelling and hard to turn away from. Now I understood. This drama was real. This man needed to sell to survive. This was food and shelter for his family.

When you're little you think the man is there to put on a show. You're fascinated by the intensity of the pitch. But on some level you must know, no matter how young you are, that the dampness on the man's face, the dampness coloring his collar, is not strictly from the heat.

"But wait," the man said, searching for eye contact. "There's even more." A woman walked away.

As hard as it must have been for these men back when we were first coming to the fair, it must be so much harder now. Not only are the same products seen on late-night TV; not only is this man in competition with telemarketers with toll-free numbers, and catalogues offering overnight delivery anywhere in the United States. But the man's job, which perhaps was on the fringes of conventional commerce years ago, has long since evolved into a public joke. People cannot see these men selling their wares without envisioning Dan Aykroyd dropping a fish into a blending machine on the old *Saturday Night Live*.

Two more women had replaced the one who left; the man was ahead. Fifteen people now, eighteen counting us.

"Who'll come forward?" the man said. "Who'll be the lucky first customer to walk away with this luxurious leather cutlery storage case? Only our first customer this afternoon will walk away with this beautiful case."

I have no idea what it must be like to perform in front of thousands of people in Madison Square Garden or Carnegie Hall; it cannot be any more difficult than this. He must have sensed that another woman was about to depart, for he fastened his eyes on her as if trying to hypnotize her. Or beg her not to go.

"But wait," he said. "You have not heard the best thing." Pretending that he was talking to the world at large, wanting to persuade the woman to stay without scaring her into leaving.

"But wait . . ."

I do not know what series of decisions a man makes in his life that ultimately brings him to the Bricker Building, where even if the people stop to pause there is no assurance that they will buy, or even think about it. Where the children who watch him, if they are young enough, will go home believing that he was just one more part of the amusement.

And when this man goes home at night? When he leaves the Bricker Building with his box of knives?

I looked over at Ronnie. He was staring so hard at the man, staring as if he was trying to make out some words on a page very far away. "You say you already have knives?" the man said. "I know you already have knives. But wait. Wait one moment." Ronnie watched, and he listened, and the man scrambled because all of a sudden four people left him and walked down the row and out of the Bricker Building. "You've come here on a very special day," the man said, but the four kept walking, leaving eleven people behind, fourteen counting us.

The sheep barn might as well have been on another planet. Cool and dark and free from blaring radios, it did not seem to be at the same fair.

The massive barn was apportioned into open-topped metal pens, each bearing a sign identifying the owners of the animals within. Many of the signs were hand burned wood. We could differentiate the handwriting of the wood-burners. Some signs were in elegant script: "Columbia Sheep—All-American Breed—David Sherrick Family—Lima,

Ohio." Some were in fancy Old English: "Schubert Farms—Metamora, Ohio." Some looked like they had been a farm child's school project: "The Kraft Family—Lewisburg, Ohio."

"We're early for the contest," Ronnie said.

Right in the center of the big barn was the competition area. Aluminum risers were constructed to the side of the dirt floor; some families were already beginning to file in, staking out the best seats.

A lamb wearing a little cloth coat lay in its pen. We stood and smiled down at it. The lamb looked back, curious and friendly.

In an empty pen next to the lamb, four farm children sat on a low, orange-painted railing, dealing each other hands of slapjack. They giggled and slapped at the cards. These boys and girls had brighter eyes than the people we'd seen on the midway all afternoon.

"Excuse me," I heard a high-pitched, polite voice say.

I turned around. It was a boy who wanted to pass by so that he could join the slapjack game. He gave me a smile. "Excuse me"—it was the first time I'd heard those words at the crowded fair all day.

"A lot of the farm kids sleep in here, you know," I said to Michael and Ronnie. "They stay with the animals all night to make sure they're okay."

"I swear, if I was one of these kids the fair might scare me," Michael said.

Maybe so—maybe the clash of lives between the farm kids in here and the city kids out on the midway might be enough to frighten some of them. They sure didn't look scared, though. They sat with their brothers and sisters, with their moms and dads and friends, and everything was placid.

The same catalysts must be available on the farm—cable TV is everywhere in this country, and the same bands, the same MTV dancers, the same slash-and-sex movies were being delivered into these kids' farmhouses as into city apartments in Los Angeles and New York and Atlanta. The cultural stimuli were the same. Yet these kids were different, no doubt about it.

"Can I shuffle?" a teenage boy playing cards in the pen said.

"Yeah, you got that professional shuffle," a girl said. "We can't beat you when you shuffle."

All the kids laughed.

"Well," the boy said, "I'm a riverboat gambler."

After a while we headed out. Directly next to the barn, a fellow in his thirties, wearing jeans and a plain red T-shirt, was giving one of his sheep a bath. He held a garden hose and massaged the water into the sheep's wool.

"What kind of sheep is that?" Ronnie asked.

"Suffolk," the man said. "She's in the show later this afternoon."

"Why's she baaing like that?" Ronnie asked.

"She doesn't like to be away from the others," the man said. "She misses her friends."

I could understand that, I wanted to say to him. The day was getting late and the summer was almost over and I could understand that very well.

As the man cleaned the wool the sheep baaed even louder.

Ronnie, joking, said, "I think you're torturing that sheep."

The man stuck his thumb over the end of the hose and, kidding around, spritzed us with water. He hit each of us with a quick spray.

Anywhere else this wouldn't be done. On any street in any city in America, in any service station or parking lot—out there a few yards away on the midway—this would be asking for a problem. You didn't just turn a hose on strangers, no matter what your intention.

But here, right outside the sheep barn at the Ohio State Fair, was one of the few places in the world where it seemed like the natural thing to do, no questions asked. He spritzed us and we laughed and jumped away, and then he said to his sheep, "They were saying bad things about us."

Our shirts were soaked, but they'd be dry after a minute back in the sun. "Good luck in the show," Ronnie called to the man.

"Good luck to you guys too, wherever you're going," the man called back.

Ronnie was surprising me. I'd been afraid that the trip to the fair, so soon after what had happened, might not be the greatest idea. When a person is down, sometimes the worst thing you can do is put him in a place where the voices are loud and the music is happy.

All day, though, he'd been relaxed and seemingly content in a way noticeably different than I'd seen him all summer. Since we'd left on our journey in June it had been as if even his good times were driven by adrenaline; there had been days when I almost thought he felt a competitive need to show he was having a better time than Michael and I were. It was some kind of a contest, and he seemed determined to win it.

Today he was enjoying the fair, as simple as that. We'd be walking along the midway and all of a sudden he'd veer off to look at the cookies for sale in a booth, or to talk to the guy taking tickets at the house of mirrors. Clearly, in the months ahead, he had some somber decisions to make about his life. Today, though, he seemed unencumbered, and I wouldn't have expected it.

Up in front of us on the midway was a game I didn't remember from the fairs of our growing up. A large area had been penned in; mounted on the fence were tubular guns, designed to fire hard rubber balls. Inside the pen, big tanklike devices rambled back and forth across the ground in a random pattern; you put fifty cents into a slot atop the guns, and you shot the balls at the tanks.

All of the guns were in use, but when one opened up Ronnie appropriated it and fed his coins into the slot.

Next to him, in command of the adjacent gun, was a kid of ten in dirty cutoffs. The kid was plunking tank after tank.

"Are you aiming high so the ball comes down on the tank?" Ronnie said. "Or do you aim right at the tank?"

"Depends," the kid said. "Depends on how fast the tank's moving."

Ronnie watched.

"How'd you do that?" he said to the kid. "It looked like you did it backhand."

"Not backhand," the kid said. "You just do a reverse sweep. You bring your gun across so it catches the tank coming the other way."

"Like this?" Ronnie said. He swiveled the gun.

"No," the kid said. "Look." He smashed a ball into a distant tank. "Like that."

"But how do you know that the tank's going to turn in that direction?" Ronnie said.

"Here," the kid said. "Watch."

Ronnie wasn't putting the kid on; what he was doing was just about as far from making fun as you could get. He was playing the game, that's all; he was learning to play the game. "Like this, right?" Ronnie said, and the kid said, "Right. That's better. You're getting it."

The afternoon was growing short, but there were a few more things we wanted to see.

"Where's the pigs?" Ronnie said.

"I thought they were over here," Michael said. We had consulted a fair map; the swine pavilion was supposed to be right where we were standing, but it wasn't. We were surrounded by swarms of people chomping on cotton candy, trying to lick their ice-cream bars before the sun disintegrated them, slurping down lime freezes. Directly in front of us a woman dropped her banana-on-a-stick and seemed to be debating whether to pick it up, dust it off, and start back in on it.

In the middle of all this Ronnie said, "There really should be better directions to the pigs."

"Why don't you ask the concierge, Ronnie?" I said.

He broke into a grin and turned his head from side to side, looking. "There!" he said.

At the Ohio Pork Producers tent they were dispensing barbecue sandwiches and guidance on how to get to the pig barn. It seemed like less than an ideal combination—just as you're about to bite down on your pork sandwich you don't necessarily want to be told where the future pork sandwiches are living and breathing—but the people were very helpful.

The sign outside the barn said "O'Neill Building—Swine." Along aisle HH, an enormous pig snored, sound asleep. I was glad that Ronnie was so interested in these animals, but I looked at this particular pig and I couldn't help thinking that pig watching was better in concept than in reality.

Ronnie gravitated to a pen holding a pig from the Larry Price Swine Farm in LaPine, Ohio. A woman with two children was checking out this particular pig at the same time. Ronnie rested one leg on the bottom rail of the pen; he looked like a rancher in *Giant*, surveying his spread, but it was just the Larry Price pig he was looking at.

I came up behind him as he was making an observation to the woman.

"They say pigs are very intelligent," Ronnie said.

"They do?" the woman said.

"Yes, they really do," Ronnie said. I didn't know where he'd gotten that; certainly it was a piece of knowledge he hadn't shared with us during the summer.

The woman gave one last glance at the pig.

"Put some soy sauce and garlic on him," she said, leading her kids away.

"I hope she was being funny," Ronnie said.

We saw Michael over against the far wall, next to a window. He was motioning for us to join him.

"Look inside," he said. "They're just a few weeks old."

Behind the glass, a sow was lying on her side. Six tiny baby pigs were nursing. A hand-lettered sign on a piece of cardboard said: "Born August 3."

When we got closer to the mother pig we could see that there were not six babies, but ten. The other four couldn't get near enough to the mother to suckle.

"Not a very auspicious beginning," Michael said. "The battle of life begins."

"They'll get there," I said, having no basis at all for my assuredness. "Their mother won't let them go hungry."

We watched, and sure enough some of the first six had their fill and clambered away, making room for the others. We left the swine building and crossed over to the barn that housed the horses. Whatever small doubt there had been in my mind about whether asking Ronnie to join us back on the road was a wise thing to do, that doubt was gone now. Ronnie, I could tell, was loving this; for some reason it was making him feel peaceful. In the horse barn he wandered from stall to stall, talking with the owners, looking at each horse and not hurrying, seeing things he was not accustomed to seeing.

He crossed over to an area where a cow was being milked behind a glass window, and he watched, and then he wandered on and fifteen minutes later we found him standing by a pen that, according to its sign, was registered to Lou-Ida Farm, Holstein Cows, Mount Ridge, Ohio.

Michael and I approached him. Without looking over at us he said, "Hey, Ben?"

I had no idea what cosmic query or universal observation he was going to make. But when he did turn to me and speak, what he said was:

"What do you like better? Cows or sheep?"

I guess I'd never thought about it. "I don't know," I said. "Cows, I suppose."

"I think I like sheep," Ronnie said. "But these are very pretty cows."

Out in the sun the grandstand and the midway must have been full of people, but in the dim, cool, and cavernous barn we were the only visitors, the only visitors as far as the eye could see.

We left the fair before sundown. We all felt wrung out and agreeably blank, but that was to be expected; that's what the fair does to you. The midway noises fill your ears for hours after you've departed, and there's a dull fair headache that seems to be the inescapable consequence of the sun and the heat and the food, of the tens of thousands of people and things you've seen pass before you. When you're a kid you go home and you collapse into your bed and by the next morning you're already thinking about going back.

You think about going back because, for a few hours, the fair had made you forget that summer is ending. As long as you're at the fair— as long as you can wake up to a sunny morning and weigh the possibilities of returning to that main gate on Eleventh Avenue—then summer is still with you.

We drove west on I-70. We wouldn't be back, at least not this summer. August was ending and Labor Day was on its way. The fair would come to a close soon, and so would the summer, and we drove faster than we should have, toward the setting sun.

Twenty-seven

AFTER THAT we stayed on the road for about a week, but we knew it was just a prelude to the ending of the journey. From the fair we drove to Springfield, Ohio, and it didn't feel like we were on our way somewhere. We found a hotel downtown and turned in early, and in the morning there was not that impulse to decide where to go next. Wherever we might go, we felt like the clock was ticking; soon enough we'd be turning around and starting back.

Near Cambridge City, Indiana, there was a wooded area with a hiking path. We stopped at a hamburger stand and got takeout lunch and walked through the woods until we found a clearing with tables and a water fountain. We sat and ate and it was a splendid day, but the sun was beginning to feel cooler than it had, and did not seem to be as high in the sky.

In the Indiana city of Pendleton we parked our car on the main street and Ronnie asked a man outside a drugstore if he'd take some pictures of us. Michael still had that film-that's-a-camera he'd bought in Las Vegas, the one designed for underwater use. We stood by the car, smiling for the camera with our arms draped over each other's shoulders, and the man shot until the roll was finished. That night at dinner was the first time any of us said it out loud. It was Michael: "We'd probably ought to be thinking about when we should head on home." Just as simple as that, and of course we knew he was right.

We agreed to aim for Labor Day. By that Monday we'd end the trip.

"I hope neither of you are offended by this, but I'm really looking forward to getting home," Michael said.

"Well, that's the way we planned it," Ronnie said. "September and out."

"Do you remember what it would feel like when you came home

from summer camp?" Michael said. "The first time you went away to camp, and you were gone from home for six straight weeks?"

"I remember your mom and dad put that sign up," I said.

"That's just what I was thinking," Michael said. "It was the first time in my life I hadn't seen my house for that long. My dad had picked me up at camp, and as we turned onto our block I could see that there was something different in our front yard. They'd put that sign up on the tree."

" 'Welcome home, Michael,' " I said.

"Yep," he said. "I'd been homesick when I'd first gotten to camp, and then I had really ended up liking the place. But when I saw that sign nailed to the tree, it was one of the best feelings I'd ever had. I couldn't wait to run inside, and look at my room, and go through the icebox, and I remember when I got myself a glass of water in the kitchen, even the way the faucet worked made me feel good because it was so familiar."

He didn't have to explain. For Michael, this summer of ours had only made him cherish more that which was waiting for him. "Those couple of times I stopped in Bristol during the summer, I almost didn't want to leave," he said. "I think if Ellen had told me to stay, I wouldn't have argued for a second."

"You're not wishing you hadn't come?" Ronnie said.

"Of course not," Michael said. "I love this. But it's time."

He said he had gone by the school on his last quick visit home and picked up some materials for the first day of class. He had the papers with him in his suitcase now; he was going to be working on his course schedule while we were on the road.

"There's something about that building in the summertime," he said. "I can't walk into the school without feeling that I'm not supposed to be there."

"There were other people there, right?" I said.

"Just faculty people," he said. "Teachers in shorts. They all had all kinds of questions about our summer. I said I'd tell them all about it when I got back. I grabbed my stuff and got out of there."

The place where we were having dinner was emptying out; the waitress said they did most of their business at lunch and didn't get many customers in the evening, but that she had to stay anyway, so we shouldn't feel like we had to rush.

"Have you talked to Debby since she came to see you in Texas?" Ronnie said.

"A couple of times," Michael said. "I've called from the road. She and her family may be coming to Bristol at Christmas. If they do, we're all going to get together."

"You're kidding," Ronnie said.

"I'm not going to hide that she's my friend," Michael said. "Ellen said she'd be much more comfortable if we all got together with Debby's family than if I pretended I didn't want to see her. I think it's going to be good. I'll get to see her, and there's no pressure, and there's no weirdness. It's the ideal way, when you think about it."

"Don't say that until it happens," Ronnie said. "You never know."

"I'm pretty sure," Michael said.

But that was for later. There had been a jukebox playing over in the corner, and I'd punched up an old Skeeter Davis song I seldom heard anymore—"I Can't Stay Mad at You." Now the jukebox had gone dead, and I wanted to hear that song again and some others. I asked the waitress if she was sure we weren't keeping her, and she said she was certain, in fact she was glad to have the company.

I put a dollar into the jukebox bill-feeder and Ronnie came over and handed me another dollar and said he wanted to pick some, too.

"I never do get used to putting paper money in jukeboxes," the waitress said, and I said I didn't, either. We invited her to pick some songs out herself, and she joined us as we stood over the lighted panel. She didn't even have to look, she went straight for Mountain's "Mississippi Queen," which surprised me, she seemed like such a quiet person.

Two days later we were staying in an economy motel off the highway near Summitville, and I called my office to check on phone calls and mail.

"Mel's looking for you," the desk assistant said. "I'm supposed to ring you in to him."

I settled back to wait, but he picked up immediately. By his unaccustomed promptness I knew he must have something he needed to talk about.

"Greetings," he said. "Where are you now?"

"Summitville, Indiana," I said, realizing it would register with him for maybe a thousandth of a second, if that.

"Lucky you," he said. "Listen. Did you decide when you're coming back to work?"

"Well, we're kind of committed to ending our trip on Labor Day," I said.

"That's fine," he said. "What I wanted to run by you is this. The network wants to put out a release in early September, announcing all the changes. The expanded service to the affiliates, the new assignments in Europe, some bureau chief shifts—a lot of stuff. You'll be in the release, but you're not here to check it."

This was the first Mel and I had spoken on the phone since our meeting in Washington. I could tell that, in his mind, I was already bound for London.

"Were we going to talk some more?" I said.

"About what?" he said.

"You know," I said. "About whether I go or stay."

"It's been decided in New York at levels above mine," he said. "As far as they're concerned, you're in England. Are you having problems with that?"

"Well, you and I just haven't talked," I said. "I don't know what my options are."

"I don't know, Ben," he said. "What did you have in mind?"

"I just hadn't realized we'd come to a final decision," I said. "For example, if I don't go to London, do I stay based in the bureau?"

"Here?" he said. "In Washington?" He sounded puzzled. "We're moving Bill Rentzman in from Los Angeles to take your spot. We're not budgeted for any more correspondents. The assumption in New York, Ben, is that you'll be in London. That's the plan. The reason I wanted to talk to you really wasn't to discuss that."

"Then what was it, Mel?" I said. Outside my window a big semi-trailer truck roared by in the direction of Indianapolis.

"As I told you, they're going to be putting out a news release," he said. "The public relations department wants you to approve the wording and the biographical stuff concerning you. I need to fax you a copy of their rough draft, so you can call them with any changes or corrections."

I didn't know if this motel even had a fax machine.

"They're in kind of a hurry, Ben, and I'm tired of taking their phone calls," Mel said. "Can you get this done?"

"Give me a few minutes," I said. "I'll call you back with a fax number."

"The assignment desk will have the release," he said. "Give them the number. And be sure to call the publicity department as soon as you've approved it." I could tell he'd spent as much time on this matter as he intended to.

The motel did not, indeed, have a fax machine. But the front-desk clerk told me the little real estate office in a shopping strip down the highway had one. He made a call, and the real estate agent said I was welcome to use it.

So I gave Washington the fax number, and I left the motel and walked by the side of the highway, following the directions the desk clerk had given me. It was a windy morning, and the speeding cars threw up squalls of gritty air as they barreled past me going the opposite way.

The real estate office was a one-room operation. "Mr. Kroeger?" the fellow behind the desk said. "It's just coming in for you now."

"I appreciate this very much," I said.

"That's all right," the man said. "I bought this machine six months ago, so I might as well get some use out of it."

As soon as the real estate man saw the network logo on the cover sheet that was coming in, he looked more carefully at me. "Do I owe you for this?" I said, not wanting to explain.

"On the house," the man said, and I thanked him again and carried the sheets of paper outside.

I sat on the edge of an elongated tree planter in the parking lot of the shopping strip, the throbbing, soft-then-loud-then-soft sound of the highway traffic still close, and read the press release.

The thrust of it was that the network was going to be providing more efficient video service to its affiliates, and to achieve that end was assigning more producers, crews, and correspondents to Europe and the Middle East, so that the network "can continue its tradition of comprehensive coverage around the world." Translation: We know you think we're getting beat by CNN, so we'll put some more bodies overseas.

I wasn't mentioned until the seventh paragraph:

"Veteran correspondent Ben Kroeger will be reassigned to London from the Washington bureau, where he has been based for more than a decade. Kroeger, 43, has distinguished himself with stories emphasizing the human side of the news, which he has reported from every region of the United States and several foreign nations. He has also served the network on presidential campaigns and at national political conventions. He will bring his seasoned perspective on the news to the London bureau, from which he will be assigned to stories in all of Europe and the surrounding region. Kroeger, a former newspaper reporter on the now-defunct Washington *Star*, was born in Bristol, Ohio, and has made his home in Bethesda, Maryland. He has one daughter."

Well, all of that was true enough, I thought.

I got up and walked toward the highway. "Veteran correspondent." That's the line that was getting to me. I knew it was intended as a note of distinction, but I hate that term. When I was breaking into the news business, as soon as I heard that someone was a "veteran reporter" I sensed that the reporter was being written off. Oh, yeah, him. He's a veteran reporter. Don't worry about him; he's no threat. Been here forever.

I realized I was reading too much into it; hey, there are many worse things than being a "veteran correspondent." Lots of people would probably kill to be a veteran correspondent. The fact was, though, that this was the first time I'd seen that phrase used in print to describe me. I always sort of considered myself an energetic young scrambler, trying my hardest to do well and make a name for myself with my bosses. I guess every working person considers himself that way at the start, no matter what his job, and I guess every working person must react with a jolt when he wakes up one day to have it officially confirmed that around the shop he is considered one of the steady, comfortable old hands.

I got to the motel and I could see the reflection of my face in the plate-glass window of the registration office.

Yep. Veteran correspondent, all right. I didn't know what corrections I could phone in to the publicity department. They were only being accurate, right on the button.

At least that's what it seemed like from my seasoned perspective.

We saw Ronnie make his own television debut that night.

We were sitting around his room, and the TV was tuned to a baseball game. Between innings they broke for a commercial.

The commercial started with an extreme close-up of a woman saying one word: "Hilarious!"

Then a teenage boy, also in close-up—these shots were filmed to purposely distort and give a fun-house-mirror effect—said: "The funniest movie of the summer!"

Then there was Ronnie. Because of the camera angle, his face looked rounder than in real life. He was wearing a big, toothy grin, and the camera seemed to catch him in mid-sentence, picking up only his final phrase: "I laughed so much my fillings fell out!"

We were sufficiently stunned that I'm not sure exactly what happened on-screen in the next few seconds. The movie in question was a teen comedy about a country club lifeguard who can make himself invisible; I surmised from the clips that the invisible lifeguard spent a lot of time in the women's locker room. It was, of course, the movie that had been previewed out in the California mall; now apparently it was in nationwide release. Ronnie had fallen off the bed in the motel room, he was howling so hard. Not hard enough, however, to drown out the last phrase in the commercial.

An announcer—he seemed to be that announcer you hear in a million movie previews and commercials, the guy with the peppy, neighborly, syrupy, always-on-the-verge-of-chuckling voice, the voice you used to hear in the previews for all those *Shaggy Dog* movies Dean Jones starred in for Walt Disney—said the movie was playing at theaters everywhere, and then he closed with the tag line:

"Like the man says, you'll laugh till your fillings fall out!"

I thought Ronnie was having cramps of some sort; he was bunching up on the floor, just about crying as he roared.

"You never even saw the movie!" I said.

He couldn't talk yet. The baseball game was well into the first batter of the next inning before he could compose himself enough to speak.

His first words, through an exhausted, happy gasp, were: "I wonder if I'm getting paid?"

"Did you sign something?" Michael said.

"Of course," Ronnie said. "You saw me. You were there." He looked at the screen again, and even though it was just the ball game, he began to break up anew.

"The funny thing is," he managed to say, "if I do get paid, being a movie critic is the only job I have now."

And he seemed to think that the irony truly was funny. From these last few days I was convinced that Ronnie was going to be all right.

Here is what I knew:

Outward appearances aside, he was still terribly hurt and humiliated about what had happened with his job. He was well aware that, at least for the next few months, everyone he saw would be talking behind his back.

He was also aware that the same people who would be talking behind his back probably had been doing it for years: "If they're going to bad-mouth me for having my job taken away, then they've obviously always said that the only reason I had the job in the first place was because of Marilyn."

He was going to try to prove people wrong about his lack of business skill. At first he had briefly considered suing the board of directors that had tossed him out. Then he concluded that if he did, the board would without question countersue, and he would spend the next six or eight years, minimum, in depositions or in court. And all he would be demonstrating was that what he feared people were saying about him was true: that he was a person of no real merit, only a person with tricks and advantages at his disposal.

He fully realized just how indisputably lucky he was. With all the awful ways that a person can experience a personal business disaster, he knew that his was one of the very few that left the person's family with more than ample money and property.

He recognized that because of this, sympathy for him was destined to be minimal: "In that way, the people who talk behind my back are right. My family's financial security has nothing to do with me. It has to do with Sidney Steele having been a hell of a good businessman."

He was going to try to get back in business on his own. Not on a large scale; not at first. He just wanted to prove that what he believed about himself was true: that he was good at what he did.

He wasn't laying all this out to us in long monologues. The information was coming piecemeal, one detail at a time. Michael and I didn't ask a lot of questions. Ronnie wanted us to know these things, and we understood he had to do it at his own speed.

Here is what I also knew:

I knew that I hoped Ronnie made it. Not because, in the grand scheme of the world's problems, his ranked even remotely near the objectively tragic ones. They didn't, not by a long, long shot. But he was my friend, and I did not want him to go through the rest of his life believing that every appearance of worthiness he had ever shown the world was fraudulent.

I knew that I hoped whatever optimistic things were going on between him and Marilyn would flourish. Ronnie had long ago blown whatever chance he had to make the short list for the husband-of-the-year finals, but I was not the best person to lecture him on that. I hoped that he and Marilyn succeeded because for them to fail would benefit no one. Not him, not her, especially not their children. Their marriage was never going to be perfect; I'm not aware of many that are. A lot of people would undoubtedly conclude that the way he had comported himself on the road constituted a powerful argument that he had no business being married. I thought it might be an overwhelming argument for precisely the opposite; I thought it might be an almost heartbreaking argument that whatever love there had once been in his life with Marilyn, he had better do everything he could to find it again.

I knew that all of us sometimes lose our way in life. The one thing we can hope for when we are the most lost, though, is for our friends to keep us in their thoughts. I knew that in the coming months Ronnie would be harshly judged by a lot of people in a lot of ways. He didn't need another detractor; he needed someone who fervently hoped that he would come out okay on the other side.

I didn't say any of this to him. I knew he would laugh it off and wave me away, and would tell me that I didn't know what I was talking about, that he was already okay now. But when the summer ended, if he took nothing else with him from it, I hoped he would take this knowledge:

That the people who love you understand things about you that perhaps even you don't understand. Or maybe, because they love you, they want to believe they understand those things. They have to believe that. It's the reason they love you and the reason they are your friends.

"How's my movie doing, Ben?" Ronnie said.

We were on the road the next day; Michael was driving, Ronnie was next to him, and I was in the back seat with a copy of *USA Today*.

I looked in the "Life" section. "Number three for the week," I said.

"Told you it was great," he said.

"You've never seen it," Michael reminded him.

"Didn't have to," Ronnie said. "I could tell just by looking at the outside of the movie theater."

We had zapped channels for about two hours the night before, hoping to see the commercial again. Finally we did; there was Ronnie again, there—even more amazingly—was the announcer picking up on his phrase.

Michael, behind the wheel, imitated the announcer's mellifluous voice: "Like the man says, you'll laugh till your fillings fall out."

"Like the man says," I said.

"I wonder if I can copyright that statement?" Ronnie—the man—said.

"Maybe you can sell it as a movie on its own," I said. "A sequel. The invisible lifeguard goes to another country club the next summer, but the women in the locker room keep catching him because the only part of him they can see is his fillings."

"And when the fillings fall out, the women hear them hit the floor," Michael said. "Sort of a tragicomedy. An invisible lifeguard betrayed by his own fillings."

We were one day away from heading home, and we were all aware of it.

"Anyone have any preference for where we stop tonight?" Michael said.

It didn't matter. Any place would do.

We came upon a lake about twenty minutes outside a city called Anderson, north of Indianapolis. It was an unexpected patch of beauty—this was a bonus, this was the kind of place we would have driven out of our way to discover. Michael found a motel with plenty of vacancies, and we checked in late in the afternoon.

I told them I'd meet them in a few hours. In the morning we would be starting for home, and right now I wanted to be by myself, just for a little.

It was a short walk from our place to the edge of the lake. A number of families were having picnics, tossing softballs; one jogger had his dog with him, and they were racing each other by the shore.

I walked onto a pier where about a dozen people were fishing. Through the spaces between the wooden planks I could look down into the clear dark blue lake water. Out at the end I sat down, letting my legs hang over the side.

I wanted to keep going. I'd been feeling that way for a couple of days now, and I hadn't said it to the others. But here it was, time to stop the trip, time to do what we had said from the very beginning we were going to do when August turned to September. Even when the idea of the trip had been a fantasy, this was part of the rules: come September, it would be over.

But ever since we'd left the fair, not more than a few hours had gone by when I hadn't tried to think of some way to extend this. For some reason it's an instinct I seem to have had all my life, and I really don't know why. Keep moving, look for something more, don't let anything reach completion. Don't admit that where you've been or what you've done is good enough. Never let it end; keep on going.

But going where? I didn't know. Michael would be home in Bristol with his family by dinnertime tomorrow. And after we dropped Michael off, Ronnie would head straight to Cleveland, where Marilyn and their children were waiting.

Both of them, in very different ways, seemed to have come out of the summer with something good. That might not have been their intention back around Memorial Day—the only intention then was the trip itself. But, like an unanticipated glistening lake off an Indiana highway, they both seemed to have found something extra in the summer, something to value.

With Michael it was the knowledge that what he had was abundantly worth preserving. I knew there might be times in the future when he, like all of us, would ask himself again whether he had chosen the best path for himself and his family, or if he should pursue some vague, beguiling prospect for a better existence. But then he'd remember the summer when he'd had to make that choice, and had decided that what he already had was as rich a reality as he could ever desire.

With Ronnie it was almost the converse. At the beginning of the summer he had appeared to have no doubts at all about himself and how he had chosen to lead his life. I had a feeling that from now on there would seldom be a day when he would not question himself, and endeavor to examine his assumptions. Even better, I sensed he would welcome this; no matter how difficult it would be for him, he knew he would come out the better for it.

Which left me, on the pier, trying to figure out a way to keep the summer's journey going. If you're always looking ahead, you can't be disappointed with what you have right here; if you focus your attention on something far up the road, then you don't have to deal with what's under your feet. Today can't let you down if all you care about is tomorrow.

For this one summer I had been able to put that impulse aside; I had treasured every day and every night and not given a thought to tomorrow until the morning arrived. I had learned anew that I could pause and enjoy and not feel that I had to run.

But the summer was ending. What waited for me was a life in Europe that promised to be even more frantic and disconnected than what I had known before. What waited for me was the little girl I cherished more than anything in the world packing up for Boston with her mother sometime soon, for a new house and a new school in a new city. The others would be going home tomorrow; I would merely be moving on.

So it was probably little wonder that I wanted to make the summer last. There aren't many things in your life that live up to what you had dreamed. This summer had, and I didn't want to let it go. I wished I could say to them: Come on. Three more months. I was wrong back there in May. Summer's not over in September after all.

The late Indiana afternoon was gorgeous from out on the pier, and I took one more lingering look, and then I walked back toward the shore, past the fishermen, the clear water motionless beneath me.

That night we talked about finding a restaurant with a private dining room and buying ourselves a farewell banquet. But the more we thought about it, the dumber it sounded: a banquet for three. It would be destined for failure; we'd sit around the table looking at each other and trying to make an occasion out of it.

So we walked to a Burger King down the block and had a quick dinner. The last light of day was still hanging on as we got back to the motel.

"What, should we buy a bottle of champagne or something?" Ronnie said.

"Yeah, right, and corsages for each of us," Michael said.

"Well, I just thought we ought to do something," Ronnie said.

We didn't want to go inside. The motel parking lot was pretty much deserted; we leaned against our rental car and looked across the blacktop, past the customary satellite dish and over some hedges at the video rental place next door.

"I'll be back," Ronnie said, and walked off in the direction of the Burger King again.

Michael said he wanted to call home to tell Ellen he'd definitely be arriving in Bristol the next day. I didn't want to see the inside of my motel room right now, so I stayed by the car and watched the dusk come quickly in.

By the time Ronnie returned up the road, the outline of the moon was visible in the sky. Full darkness was about fifteen minutes away.

Ronnie was carrying a bag from a liquor store. I told him Michael was inside on the phone.

"Is that his room?" Ronnie said, pointing to a window.

"I think so," I said.

Ronnie went to the window and knocked on the glass. When there was no response he did it again. Michael pulled the drapes back. Ronnie gestured for him to come out.

Within a few minutes he did. "You didn't really get champagne?" he said, spotting the bag.

Ronnie put the bag on the hood of our car. "Go ahead," he said.

I reached inside. I could feel a cardboard container filled with bottles.

I pulled it out. It was a six-pack of Rolling Rock—the stubby little green bottles with the white lettering. Rolling Rock was the first beer we'd ever had. I think we'd been sixteen; some older guys were having a party in their parents' basement, and they'd given us our first beers. Made in Pennsylvania, as I recall. I hadn't seen a bottle of Rolling Rock for years.

"Drink slow," Ronnie said. "They just had this one six-pack."

So that is how we spent our last evening—sitting on the trunk of a car in a motel parking lot in the middle of Indiana, drinking a rationed two beers apiece, talking and laughing and not wanting to be any other place on the planet.

We must have talked for a couple of hours. We talked about things that had happened years ago; we talked about people we knew and we talked about hopes we had for our lives. Implicit in every sentence was the knowledge that the summer was over, but in those first hours that night we never said the words. It was sort of like when a baseball pitcher is working on a no-hitter. You know it but you don't mention it.

Michael was the first to say something. Ronnie had just told a story about an elderly woman who lives down the block from him and who claims to have once dated Clark Gable, and I was starting to tell them about a Clark Gable movie in which he plays a newspaper city editor— it defied credulity, Clark Gable as a city editor was like Fred Astaire as a thug, you can't hide the elegance and the audience won't buy it— and Michael said to Ronnie, "I feel like I ought to be in your den reading Cliff's Notes."

On the last night of summer every year in Bristol, we would find ourselves in the den of Ronnie's parents' house. It was just off the living room, where the World War II portrait of Mr. Hepps hung. The den contained their television set, and built-in cases filled with books; one of those books was a large volume of plot summaries. It wasn't actually Cliff's Notes, but it did contain brief condensations of hundreds of books, most of them literary classics. I don't know what it was doing there.

And on the last night of summer each year—the night before the first morning of school—we'd be poring over that book, trying to cover ourselves for the required vacation reading we hadn't done. The night wouldn't seem quite as warm as nights had all summer, and even though it wasn't very late we'd be going back home and to bed soon because we had to be up so early the next morning, and it just felt like all the air had been let out of something. Like someone had just put away the fun. We were looking up abridgments of works by Shakespeare and Faulkner and Poe, but it felt like pages were being turned in our own lives, too, like someone was taking a page we weren't finished with yet and turning it and commanding us to go on.

In the parking lot Ronnie said, "I thought this was going to be impossible."

"The summer?" Michael said. "Getting away?"

"Not just the getting away," Ronnie said. "But that it would work at all. It just seemed like this impossible thing."

"You know what's even more impossible, except it's true," I said. "From now on, when we look back on the best summer of our lives, this is probably going to be it."

"I know," Michael said. "I've thought of that. It really is the truth, isn't it? All these years of looking back on the summers when we were kids, and now this beats them all."

A lone car pulled into the parking lot. A family—mother, father, two young sons, daughter—climbed out as if they'd been on the road for a long time. They unloaded their luggage, nodded amiably as they passed us, and went into the registration lobby.

"We may be the only three guys hanging around drinking beer in a darkened parking lot who don't scare anyone," Michael said.

"Well, it's not that intimidating a sight," I said. "Three middle-aged guys who look like they ought to be running an insurance actuarial seminar."

"That guy who just went in with his family," Michael said. "Do you think if he knew what we were doing he'd think we were nuts?"

"That's the funny thing," Ronnie said. "Think about it. This whole summer, not one person we told about what we were doing said that it was stupid. Not one. Every single person understood it right away. Most of them said they would love to have this kind of a summer with their best friends."

"Maybe they were just being polite," I said.

"I don't think so," Ronnie said. "That guy who just went inside? He grew up somewhere. He had best friends. That's not to say that he'd ever do it, but would he understand? You bet he would."

The six stubby green bottles had been drained by now. "We ought to toss these," Ronnie said. "Unless one of you wants one for a souvenir."

The bottles were upright on the trunk. Michael reached over and took one. "You don't see Rolling Rock bottles much anymore," he said, as if that was his reason for keeping it.

Ronnie put the others in the bag and walked across the lot to a big trash bin and tossed the bag in. It made a hollow sound as it hit the bottom of the bin, and Ronnie walked back and we knew it was time to go inside but no one did.

After a few minutes Michael said: "Something so good happens that you wish you could run it over and over again, like an old movie, whenever you wanted."

We looked at him, and we understood.

The Litany of Adult Experiences. These would be our last entries in the Litany.

Ronnie said: "You're glad you weren't too scared to give something a try."

We were all standing there. I could hardly see them in the dark.

"You're very proud of yourself," I said. "You're proud because it turns out that when you were a kid you chose exactly the right friends."

For a moment no one spoke. Then Michael said, quietly, "Well, I guess I'll turn in."

He headed inside. "Me, too," Ronnie said. "I'll see you guys in the morning."

Maybe that was the way to end it; maybe there was nothing more to say.

"Are you going in?" Ronnie said to me.

"In a couple of minutes," I said. "I'll see you tomorrow."

I sat there on the car for a while. On the ground there was one of the Rolling Rock bottle caps. I knelt and picked it up and held it in my hand, and then I put it in my pocket. It never hurts to carry a memory with you. You never know when you'll need it.

We drove straight through to Bristol. The Labor Day traffic was surprisingly light. Radio stations faded in and out as we traveled east through Indiana and then Ohio.

We were on Michael's street by midafternoon. He was looking out the passenger-side window, and from a block away we could see that there were people on his lawn. As we got closer we saw that it was Ellen and the girls. They'd been waiting. As Ronnie steered the car into the driveway they cheered. They really did—the girls were clapping and hopping up and down.

"I'd say that's even better than a sign on the tree," I said to Michael, but he was already out the door and onto the lawn. The girls jumped on him, and Ellen stood a foot or two away, and Ronnie and I were in the car.

"Well?" I said to him.

"Let's give them a few minutes," he said.

So we sat there listening to the radio, and it wasn't until Michael came back to get his bags from the trunk that we got out too.

"Hi, Ellen," I said.

"Big day, huh?" she said, giving me a hug.

She looked at Ronnie and said, "I keep seeing you all over the TV!"

He looked a little surprised. "The movie thing?" he said.

"Yes!" she said. "You look great!"

He didn't look great; he looked like they were shooting him through a fishbowl. But he was clearly recognizable to anyone who knew him, and the commercial must have been getting big national play.

She invited us inside. It was apparent that Michael was already back to his real life; Ronnie and I were there but we weren't there. We were guests in the house, nothing more, and we felt like it. I saw Ronnie looking at his watch.

Ellen brought us soft drinks and as she handed them to us she said, "Oh, Michael, good news. The mayor dropped this off this morning."

It was an envelope, which she had opened. Michael took the letter out, read for a few seconds, then smiled. He handed it to me.

The stationery was embossed with the official seal of Bristol. In the letter the mayor said that, after giving due consideration to Michael's arguments before the council, the city had decided not to construct the four-way stop signs. He said that Michael's "persuasive presentation" had contributed to the decision, and thanked him for taking the time to be at the meeting. The typed signature was "Paul Singer, Mayor," but he had signed it merely "Paul" and had added a PS: "Welcome home, stranger!"

"I felt bad," Ellen said to Michael. "I think he assumed that you were going to be here. That's why he brought it over himself. I'd told him you'd be back today."

"I should call him to say thanks," Michael said. "That really is great news."

"I told him you'd be here by dinnertime," she said. "He said he might stop by again just to say hello."

Now was the difficult part. I didn't know exactly what to do. Shake hands with Michael and Ronnie? Say that we'd have to do it again sometime? Nothing seemed right.

Ellen delayed the need for a decision by bringing out a tray of egg-salad sandwiches. "I wasn't sure whether you would have eaten," she said.

We went out to their front stoop. There was already a hint of fall in the afternoon sunlight; the day was far from chilly, but there was none of that unrelenting heat, and it didn't seem impossible that people out walking in Bristol would be wearing sweaters tonight. The girls played in the yard, happy to have Michael watching them. We must have been out there for an hour, and Ronnie said he guessed he'd be going.

The mayor came strolling up the block. He was in shorts and running shoes and a white-and-blue Bristol High School Golf Team shirt; I remembered that Paul's oldest son was a varsity golfer at Bristol. He was waving, and Michael went out to the sidewalk to greet him. The two men shook hands, and Ellen and Ronnie and I got up to join them.

"Hello, Ben," the mayor said. "Hi, Ronnie. So you're allowing our friend here to come back, huh?"

I didn't know why I was feeling a twinge of jealousy, but I was. Maybe it was just the warmth of Michael's greeting from his family; maybe it was the overall good feeling so apparent in this front-yard scene. In a month I was supposed to be covering the Prime Minister of Great Britain at No. 10 Downing Street; at this moment Michael's welcome home from Mayor Singer on Harding Road seemed like a better deal.

Ronnie asked me if I wanted to get my bags out of his car; the plan was for him to drive home to Cleveland, and for me to catch a flight to Washington either tonight or in the morning.

He opened the trunk for me. So many times this summer in so many cities I'd yanked my suitcases out, ready to check in somewhere new. I picked up the bags and Ronnie and I didn't have to say anything. He knew, he understood.

The mayor approached us and said, "Let me ask you something, Ronnie."

Ronnie waited. The mayor was looking at him with genuine interest.

"That movie," the mayor said. "Is it really that funny? I was thinking about going."

"It's wonderful, Paul," Ronnie said. "Great fun for the whole family."

I walked knowing that whatever direction I headed, whatever part of town I ended up in, it would be okay. Some parts of Bristol are fancier than others, but to me there are no bad parts. The streets and neighborhoods are so familiar, it's like a game board on which I've played a thousand times.

Ronnie was gone. He'd said so long to us and driven up the road. As he'd pulled away from the house I had called, "Shane, come back." Might as well try to make a joke out of it, I figured. Michael's daughters asked me who Shane was, and I asked them if they liked cowboy films; if they did, maybe their dad would rent *Shane* for them sometime. Leslie said there was a boy in her class named Shane Goodman. Different Shane, I said. Shane Goodman. What a great world.

Michael and Ellen and I had sat with the girls as they ate their dinner, and afterward I'd decided to take my walk. It was early evening, with the light beginning to fade but still there, and I told them I'd be back as soon as I was finished. At that point I still didn't know if I'd try to catch a late flight to Washington, or wait until morning.

Every person I passed on the sidewalks said hello; every house I saw seemed welcoming. I had this unexplainable feeling that I could go up and knock on any door and the people inside would come out and sit on their front steps with me and talk about what had been going on lately in town. There's no other place in the world where I feel like that.

A ball made of blue plastic came bouncing out of a driveway. I looked and saw that two boys were playing home-run derby. I don't know if they called it that, but it was home-run derby when Michael and I used to play it; one guy pitched and one guy batted and the only way to score a run was to knock the ball all the way over the hedges. It wasn't so hard; the ball came with holes cut in it to make it float through the air, it was constructed to make you feel like you were good. I picked up the ball and tossed it to the kid who was pitching. I kept walking and within seconds I heard the bat connect with the ball and the batter whooping as it took off for glory.

A couple of families on Drommond Avenue were out together walking their dogs; the men and women strolled along the sidewalk as a group of four, talking, and the two dogs, a foot or so in front, strolled together, also, as if accustomed to this nightly routine. Burton Larke, who with his brother had run the most popular hardware store in town when I was growing up, was out for a walk, too; he smiled a hello at me, and I realized that he must be in his eighties now.

On Main Street I made a point of going past Swendell's; the summer might be ending, but there was still a line at the screen window for ice cream, and almost every seat at the picnic tables in front was filled. Some people were waiting for seats, as a matter of fact, eating their ice-cream cones standing up. I could see that there were plenty of seats available in the addition inside. It's never going to catch on, I thought;

that new section is going to be here fifty years from now and people still aren't going to want to go in there, they're still going to refer to it as the new part. They like the picnic tables and that's that.

Up near Costner Avenue I heard some young voices, and I saw that they came from two girls across the street. They were about fifteen, and they were out together before the streetlights came on. Their voices carried and they were talking about some boys they were planning to run into by accident. Apparently that was the plan; they didn't want the boys to know they were looking for them, but they had it on good authority that the boys were going to be out tonight, and they thought that if they stayed on this street for a few more blocks, there was a pretty good chance that the accidental meeting would come to pass.

I couldn't think of a better way for them to spend their evening, and I hoped the boys in question, whoever they might be, would be smart enough to be out doing their part to bring about this accidental encounter. A summer night and two girls who maybe you like, and maybe they like you . . . there are few possibilities more enticing and more happy than that.

At the corner of Dodge and Jefferson the traffic-light box was still buzzing and clanking. You can travel all around the world and see things you'd never imagined you'd see, but the town waits for you, whenever you're ready to return.

On that corner I tried to think about why it was so important for me to go live in Europe. I knew I would try to do good work—I've always tried my hardest at any job I've been given, I'm proud of trying hard. And along with taking pride in the work, there would be a certain prestige to it. Prestige for an instant, the prestige that comes when people watching television see you standing momentarily before a camera in a foreign capital far away.

And who did I hope saw me doing my job from London or Berlin or Warsaw—who did I hope approved of me and thought I was good and felt I had done all right with my life? These people here, mostly— these people in Bristol. It had always been that way. Everything I'd done, everywhere I'd gone, I had done it with the wish that the people in this town would think well of me, and would be proud that I had come from among them.

Tonight I thought about the life that lay ahead of me, and I wondered: Why is it so important that you run from city to city all over the world, traveling in the company of strangers and sleeping in rented beds, just so you can be sent up to a satellite somewhere in space and come down into these houses on these streets in this town? You don't have to do that, I told myself; you love this place, and you're here right now, you're here for real.

The sky was darker than the time of evening would warrant, and I saw low clouds and I knew we were due for one of those quick-hitting storms you get in central Ohio late in the summer, the storms that thunder in and dump torrents of water into the streets and fill the air with lightning and then move on as abruptly as they had arrived.

I began to walk toward Michael's house, hoping to beat the rain. The first drops were already splashing on the sidewalk, though, and I knew I'd have to find a place to get cover.

The stadium was just ahead. The rain was coming harder, so I walked quickly toward the fence, and the gate by the main entrance was open as always. There was a jagged flash in the sky off in the distance, and I hurried across the parking lot and into the short tunnel in the stadium that leads to the general admission section.

The sky became black and the rain slammed down and the football field turned muddy and slick in the space of seconds. The only thing to do was wait out the storm in the safety of the tunnel. No airplane flight out for me tonight.

From behind me in the tunnel I heard a door open. I turned toward the sound.

Brian Griffin, the young assistant football coach who'd introduced himself to me the last time I was here, was coming out of the trainer's room. He saw me and he said, "Mr. Kroeger?"

"How are you, coach?" I said.

"I'm good," he said. "What's up?"

"I got caught in the rain," I said. "I just came in here until it passes."

"Do you need a ride somewhere?" he said.

"Actually, that would be nice," I said. "I'm staying with some friends over on Harding."

He walked up to where I was standing and he said, "I'll be glad to give you a lift. We might as well wait for it to let up a little bit first."

We stood together, and the rain in front of us stayed furious for a few more minutes, and then it moved across the sky and out of town and the night was dry.

"You've been around so much lately, you ought to just move here," he said, kidding.

I wanted to tell him that I already had. But we turned toward the other end of the tunnel and walked toward his car in the stadium lot.

"Are you still going to be here next Friday?" he said. "We have our opening home game against Lancaster."

"I might," I said. "I don't know for sure yet, but I think I just might."

Twenty-eight

IT'S LATE SEPTEMBER NOW. I look out the front window. I've been in the house for a little over a week; of all the houses in Bristol I might have moved into, this is one I had never set foot in before. The first time I walked through the front doorway I knew I wanted it to be my home.

Even if I live here for the next forty years, I'm aware that to a lot of people this will always be "the Jackson house." That's how it works in Bristol; a house becomes known by the name of the family who lived in it before, and sometimes it takes generations for people to get used to the idea there's been a change. It's kind of nice, really; it's part of the continuity of the town. I think I'm going to like living in the Jackson house.

Thomas Jackson was the minister at the First Presbyterian Church over on Riverwood Avenue; when he died two years ago his wife stayed on in the house, but during the past summer she decided it was too big for her now, and made arrangements to move to an apartment complex devoted to senior citizens. She allowed me to move in while the paperwork for the sale of my house in Bethesda is still being completed.

My parting from the network was friendly and virtually painless. My bosses weren't really surprised that I was ambivalent about Europe; the only thing that may have surprised them was that I didn't make it difficult for them by disputing their right to order the reassignment or by arguing that they were obliged to give me back my old job. Instead, we parted company the way people who have worked together for a long time should—with mutual gratitude and genuine affection.

Some of my colleagues in the bureau did let me know that they found my plans to be an awfully uncertain way to make a living. And they're right. With this new situation I'm covered for the next year or

384 · *Bob Greene*

so, but if it turns out I'm not any good, there are no guarantees after that.

Which is fine with me; when I think back on my life, I realize that the times I've done my best work have been the times when I've had to prove to someone—and to myself—that I can handle the job. I may have been a veteran correspondent at the network, but I'm not a veteran author, and I'll have to find out if there's any chance for me. The book contract I signed is not for anywhere near the salary I made at the network, but maybe it will be the start of something. For years I've been keeping notes about the people I met on assignment around America, and the places I visited. So many times I would do my story for the evening news, and would realize that some of the most memorable moments I'd found in reporting the piece—the little nuggets of life that struck me as the things I'd want to tell people about at dinner—never made it onto the air. Two minutes and thirty seconds is an eternity for a television story, but there are so many lovely details you can never fit in.

So the book I'm going to be working on is my own portrait of America as I've seen it over the past twenty years. Going over my notes, I'm as excited again as I was the first time I passed through the towns and met the people. The editor who agreed to let me give it a try has warned me not to expect to sell millions of copies—we don't even know what form the book will take, and both of us just hope that it provides a picture of the country and the times that lets people see and hear and think about some things they may not have known were out there. I can't wait to get started. No matter how it ends up doing in the bookstores, I'm being given the chance to try something new. And besides—if nothing else, after I'm gone from this earth there will be something of me left on the shelves of some libraries. The thought of that thrills me. Ever since I was a child I've been in love with libraries—the feel and the smell and the sound of them. You reach incomprehensibly huge numbers of people on network TV, but you're always afraid that nothing you have done will last.

Out the window I can see Mary walking up the block, a grocery sack resting in her arms. She's been here for almost a week now—when I called her to tell her what I was doing, she insisted on flying up to help me get settled. I must admit, having her here has made all of this even better; it's nice when you can share the best parts of your life. She went down to Fleer's Foods to get steaks and corn and salad for our dinner tonight. In the morning she has to fly back to Tennessee, but she's already making noises about switching to the master's program at Ohio State. She says that it's a good one, and it's just up the freeway in Columbus. I can't tell whether she's teasing or serious—but she swears she means it. I don't know. You probably shouldn't change too many things all at once. But I surely like her company, and I guess we'll find out what happens next. Here she comes, walking across the front lawn. All these years later and it's still a matchless feeling: Someone is coming to see you and you know she's doing it because she cares for you.

Michael and Ellen and the girls have been dropping by just about every day. Ellen kids me that at the very least, one benefit of my move will be that it's going to get Michael out of the house and out of her hair. When she's not kidding she says it's the first time she can remember that Michael has had a best friend in town. It's been a while for me, too. School has started and he's teaching every day, but there haven't been too many afternoons when he hasn't come to my house or I haven't gone to his. It's a good kind of symmetry to have in your life; it's a good thing to look forward to every day.

Ronnie has called from Cleveland several times. He's trying to get his one-man business going; he's looking for office space and making plans. He says his dad and mom are coming to Bristol in October. His father, Ronnie says, is feeling good enough to travel; Ronnie says his dad seems to feel it is very important to get back to Bristol, where he spent most of his life, and to talk to old friends and visit familiar places. Ronnie wants to be here to see the town with his dad, and to share the experience with him. We're all planning to get together briefly during that week, and Ronnie says there will be many times when he'll come down to see Michael and me. The week in October, though, is really for him and his father. He wants to help make it something special for his dad.

Hannah arrives this weekend.

She's flying from Washington Friday afternoon; it's her first plane trip by herself. She doesn't seem nervous at all—the idea seems to make her feel like she's going off on a bold expedition. She even told me she wants to bring her sleeping bag.

She'll be moving to Boston with Nancy sometime in November. She's excited about that, too, which amazes me. I didn't believe Hannah was enchanted with the idea of moving when Nancy first told me. But I've talked to Hannah on the phone enough times in the past two weeks to know that she really does see the move as some great new excursion in the life she's discovering for herself. If, at her age, my parents had told me I had to leave my school and my friends to go to a new town, I think I might have chained myself to our dinner table. Hannah, though, has already made several trips to Boston, and she can't quit telling me about all the great places she's seen there, and the house she's going to live in, and the children's museum she and Nancy always visit.

Hannah and I haven't talked in any depth about the man Nancy is going to marry; I know that she likes him a lot and I know she understands that such a momentous topic is not best broached during idle phone conversation. She and I will be talking about it this week-end, I am certain; before she and Nancy move I'm going to go over to Boston to meet the guy. Nancy says she thinks I'll like him, a phrase that I will be quite satisfied if I never have to hear again in my life.

I am brand-new to this—the notion that my daughter will soon be waking up in a house where the man who greets her at the breakfast table each morning is not the man who is her father. As much as that thought hurts, I pray that the man at her breakfast table is deserving of her love, and of Nancy's; a little girl should be able to have breakfast each morning with two people who adore each other. I will always know that I failed in that way. It is fashionable when a marriage breaks up to say that it was really the fault of neither party. That may or may not be true. But if I did not fail Nancy, I most assuredly failed Hannah; both Nancy and I did, and no one in the world will ever be able to convince me otherwise.

And the miracle of miracles is that Hannah does not seem to blame us. Maybe that is because so many children she knows are in similar situations. When I was growing up in Bristol, I did not have one friend whose parents were divorced; the world Hannah and her friends are growing up in is very different. So maybe the idea of a father and a mother who couldn't manage to get it right seems even close to customary for her, which I find to be a profoundly saddening thought. All I can do now is see her as much as she wants and whenever she wants, and try to be the best father who doesn't live with her she could ever imagine. That's not much, but I can try.

This afternoon I called Swendell's to make sure the outside part is still open this late in September. I want to take Hannah down there every day while she's here. I want to walk these streets with her and show her all the places I cherish so much and I want to sit on the picnic benches at Swendell's with her and eat ice-cream cones at night. I want her to know that you can grow up in a place like this, and I want her to know that, no matter what, this is her home, too. She's a very brave and remarkable person, and someday I hope I am worthy of her.

On the morning I went to the Washington bureau for the last time to tell them my decision, Mel made a not very resolute effort to convince me I owed it to myself to go to London. He said that I owed it to myself because I needed to take a chance with my career.

But that wouldn't have been taking a chance. This is taking a chance.

This—staying put right here and living a life and not moving on—this will be something I have to learn all over again.

This week my arrival back home is still a curiosity in town. A few months from now that will be over. Going away and being accepted long-distance as the guy on the TV screen was relatively easy. Proving that the guy is someone you might like even when you know he's nothing special—even when he's just the new resident of the old Jackson house—that is what I have to prove now. Not to anyone else in town. To me. I'm kind of looking forward to it.

This is not the time to think about what will be, though. I have the rest of my life to consider that. This is the time to give one last thought to what was.

In the kitchen, on the door of the refrigerator, there is a snapshot. It was taken on the street of a small Indiana town during the last week of summer. There are three men in the picture who by even the most generous stretch of the imagination no one would ever mistake for being young. But they are smiling with the carefree exuberance of young men; they are tan and there is joy in their faces and even if you didn't know them you would know that they are in the midst of having some of the happiest times of their lives. If you hadn't been there when the picture was taken, you would probably never guess that the camera was really supposed to be used underwater.

The picture will fade someday; it will fade, or it will become tattered with age, or it will lie lost and forgotten in the bottom of some dresser drawer. But that afternoon on the Indiana street, and all the summer nights and days that came before it—those will endure. There are so few times when after something is past, you know without question that you have done exactly the right thing. The men in the picture, no matter what else may happen to them, will forever know that they gave themselves this one more summer in the sun.

Late September now. By nightfall the air will be cool. But the warmth of the summer sun will be inside me. It will be with me all through the winter, and every winter to come.

ABOUT THE AUTHOR

BOB GREENE is a syndicated columnist for the *Chicago Tribune*. His columns appear in more than two hundred newspapers in the United States, Canada, and Japan. For nine years his "American Beat" was the lead column in *Esquire* magazine; as a broadcast journalist he has served as contributing correspondent for "ABC News Nightline." He is the author of thirteen previous books, including the national bestsellers *Hang Time, Be True to Your School*, and *Good Morning, Merry Sunshine*.